The Prophet of Lost Souls

Andy Slade

Published by Bennie Rosa, 2025.

THE PROPHET OF LOST SOULS

First edition. October 15, 2025.

Copyright © 2025 Andy Slade.

ISBN: 979-8-218-77951-1

Written by Andy Slade.

Also by Andy Slade

Betrayal Is Beautiful
Our Shadows Never Die
The Magic Parachute
Games
In the Act of Shooting
The Prophet of Lost Souls

Watch for more at https://andy-slade.com.

Table of Contents

PROLOGUE

The master bedroom in Ralph Norton's house in Tiara Woods lay shrouded in the blue glow of his smartphone, the device resting on the nightstand like a digital altar in the darkness. Ralph Norton, the CFO of FASTRAK, Inc., always slept with his app turned on—a habit that had developed over months of seeking comfort in artificial divinity, the creation of his own hands now serving as his spiritual crutch.

The ceiling fan above turned slowly, its gentle whisper the only sound in the house until the silence was shattered by words that seemed to emerge from the very fabric of reality itself. Tonight, the words came through like thunder from Heaven, carrying a weight and authority that made his soul tremble:

"If you love me, kill him!"

The voice penetrated his sleep like lightning, jolting him awake with the absolute certainty that reverberates through divine commandments. There was no question, no doubt, no room for interpretation. The tone, the timbre, the overwhelming presence that accompanied the words left no possibility of misunderstanding.

It was God!

CHAPTER 1

FASTRAK, Inc., the world's second-largest producer of Christian Products, occupied its corporate headquarters like a modern cathedral dedicated to the business of faith. The ten-story office building known as Mack Hill Towers rose from Houston's west side, its glass and steel facade reflecting the Texas sun while housing an empire built on the commercialization of spiritual hope.

The morning light streaming through the executive floor windows carried the promise of another profitable day, and P.T. Mayo, the CEO of FASTRAK, knew what was coming with the certainty of a seer reading familiar scripture. The long mirror on the back of his closet door reflected the tall, lanky figure of a confident and arrogant executive at the pinnacle of his success—a man who had transformed a struggling Bible distribution company into a global powerhouse through sheer force of will and an utter lack of moral constraints.

He always smiled at himself in the mirror, admiring the expensive suit that hung perfectly on his frame and the evil gleam in his eyes. But on a day like this, he smirked as if he knew something extraordinary was about to happen, something he alone deserved—the recognition and financial reward that would cement his position as the undisputed king of Christian commerce.

The boardroom on the ninth floor was abuzz with loud back slaps and laughter, the sound of successful men celebrating another quarter of profitable spiritual manipulation. The mahogany table gleamed under the crystal chandelier, surrounded by leather chairs that had hosted countless decisions affecting the faith of millions.

The chairman, G. Gordon Palmer, was chatting with Phil Spenser near the floor-to-ceiling windows that offered a commanding view of Houston's sprawling metropolis. Their conversation carried the easy camaraderie of men who had spent

2

decades navigating the treacherous waters of corporate politics together.

When P.T. Mayo entered the room, he slid in and out of the small groups like a smiling viper, his presence simultaneously magnetic and menacing. He eyed Palmer near the end of the long conference table, calculating the dynamics of power with the precision of a chess master contemplating his next move.

"Well, the guest of honor!" crowed Palmer, his voice carrying across the room with the authority of someone accustomed to commanding attention. "Good, let's get started. P.T., you come over here and sit next to me."

Palmer's gesture toward the chair of honor was both invitation and coronation, placing Mayo in the position of a successor being groomed for even greater power.

"Ladies and gentlemen, I call this meeting to order!" Palmer's voice boomed through the boardroom as he raised his gavel with a ceremonial flourish. The gavel came down so hard that when the head hit the strike plate, it flew off and whizzed by P.T. Mayo's head like a wooden missile, missing him by inches.

The board and P.T. laughed loud enough to be heard in the hallway outside of the conference room, their mirth echoing off the walls with the forced joviality of people who found humor in near-disaster. The broken gavel lay on the carpet like an omen, ignored in the euphoria of the moment.

"Let us bow our heads and pray," Palmer continued, his voice taking on the solemn tone that had served him well in both boardrooms and Sunday services.

The assembled executives lowered their heads in a display of corporate piety, their expensive suits and designer jewelry creating a tableau of prosperity masquerading as humility.

Heavenly Father,
We gather today in your name.

Guide our thoughts and actions,
Help us to work together for the good of our organization.
And keep us mindful of the needs of others.
Amen.

The prayer hung in the air like incense, blessing their gathering with the veneer of divine approval for whatever earthly rewards they were about to distribute.

"Ladies and gentlemen of the board, I've called this special meeting to order with a very specific purpose, and it is one of the highest honors for me as chairman to do so." Palmer's voice carried the gravity of historical significance, as if they were witnessing a moment that would echo through corporate eternity.

"Today, we gather not to conduct our usual business but to celebrate an extraordinary achievement. Under the remarkable leadership of our CEO, P.T. Mayo, our corporation has not only met but also vastly exceeded its financial targets. It is a testament to his vision, perseverance, and outstanding execution."

The words flowed like honey, sweet with praise and thick with the kind of corporate rhetoric that transformed greed into virtue through the alchemy of language.

"P.T., you have led with unwavering commitment, innovative thinking, and a steadfast belief in our mission and values. Your strategic insight and ability to inspire the entire organization have been nothing short of transformative."

Mayo basked in the praise like a lizard absorbing sunlight, his expression carefully modulated to show humble gratitude. At the same time, his eyes revealed the satisfaction of a predator who had successfully claimed his territory.

"In light of this tremendous performance, the board of directors and I wish to express our deepest gratitude and admiration. As a token of our appreciation and in recognition of your outstanding contributions, we are delighted to present you with this check."

Palmer lifted the sealed envelope with ceremonial reverence, holding it aloft like a sacred relic before the assembled faithful.

"This bonus is not just a reward for the financial success we have achieved, but a symbol of the trust and confidence we place in your continued leadership. We believe that with you at the helm, there are no limits to what we can achieve together."

The irony of the moment was lost on everyone except perhaps Mayo himself—a group of supposedly Christian businessmen celebrating the success of a man who privately mocked everything they claimed to believe.

"Thank you, P.T., for your exceptional leadership and for steering us toward a brighter and more prosperous future. Please join me in a round of applause for our extraordinary CEO!"

The applause erupted like thunder, filling the boardroom with the sound of approval that Mayo had been craving since his first day selling Bibles door-to-door in Kansas.

"If there are no further matters to discuss, and I hope there aren't, I will entertain a motion to adjourn."

The meeting ended with most of the board members walking over to P.T., congratulating him for a job well done, rubbing his back, and gently tapping him on the face with the familiarity of old friends celebrating a shared victory. The smiles were everywhere as the board members slowly filed out of the boardroom, laughing and joking with each other like men leaving a successful revival meeting.

Palmer was the last to leave, giving P.T. a bear hug that seemed to transfer some essential approval from the older man to his chosen successor, before exiting and leaving the CEO alone with his triumph.

Mayo waited long enough to add some drama to the moment, letting the silence of the empty boardroom amplify his anticipation. Then, with a flourish worthy of a magician revealing his greatest trick, he opened the sealed envelope.

It was a check for $500,000.

Not enough by a long shot, considering what he believed his contributions were worth. He shrugged with the casual dismissal of someone for whom half a million dollars was merely an appetizer before the main course of true power and wealth. Then he left, ready to begin his victory tour through the kingdom he had built.

The crowded hallways throughout FASTRAK were actively waiting for P.T., another orchestration he was so well known for—the careful staging of spontaneous appreciation that fed his insatiable need for adulation. His grand exit from the board meeting was staged and blocked out as a master director would preset a grand entrance, every detail calculated to maximize the impact of his moment of triumph.

His corporate flunkies had bribed everyone they could find to greet the puffed-up ego as it strolled through the fake labyrinth of fame, transforming the ordinary office corridors into a parade route worthy of a conquering general.

P.T. held his bonus check, now outside of its envelope with the amount showing, in his right hand while waving his left hand at everyone who stopped what they were doing to join the parade. The check fluttered slightly in the air-conditioned breeze, its zeros catching the fluorescent light like golden promises of continued prosperity.

A smattering of applause was barely heard as the greeters filtered back into their offices and kiosks, their forced enthusiasm evaporating as quickly as it had been manufactured. The performance was over, and they could return to their real work.

Ralph Norton was not one of them. He was at his desk, ignoring the festivities that made him sick, his office door closed against the circus taking place in the hallways. The sound of Mayo's triumph leaked through the walls like toxic gas, poisoning what should have been a moment of shared celebration.

After almost two years of work on the Word of God app—countless late nights, missed dinners, sacrificed weekends, and the gradual erosion of his marriage and mental health—he was exhausted to the point of leaving. The irony that his creation had funded Mayo's bonus was not lost on him.

Then he thought about all the other product ideas and marketing plans he'd developed over the years, innovations that had transformed FASTRAK from a struggling regional company into a global powerhouse, and for what? A salary and the privilege of watching someone else take credit for his genius.

He could still hear Mayo's crowing in the hallway outside his office, the sound of undeserved celebration echoing through the building like a mockery of everything Ralph had sacrificed to make FASTRAK successful.

Ralph stood up and stretched his aching back, his body protesting the long hours hunched over financial reports and development plans. He puttered around his office like a man in a trance, mindlessly straightening up financial reports and charts he was preparing—busy work that gave his hands something to do. At the same time, his mind processed the injustice of the situation.

A couple of executives walked by his office. They knew, from his closed door and the grim set of his shoulders visible through the interior window, that Ralph Norton was not participating in P.T. Mayo's moment of glory.

CHAPTER 2

Mayo's arrogant victory lap was almost complete, a carefully choreographed journey through his corporate kingdom that served both to display his triumph and to identify those who failed to show sufficient enthusiasm for his success. Not one office or cubicle was missed in his royal progress through the halls of FASTRAK.

At some of them, he waved his large bonus check like a battle standard, the paper crackling softly as it moved through the recycled air. At others, he kept it visible in his suit jacket pocket, the corner peeking out like a promise or a threat, depending on the loyalty of the observer.

Either way, it didn't matter because everyone in the building knew the score—you were either on the 'pro-Mayo' side of the parade or the 'I hate your guts' side, and your position would be noted for future reference.

The fluorescent lights hummed overhead as Mayo made his rounds, casting their institutional glow on a performance that was part celebration, part intimidation, and part reconnaissance mission. The carpet muffled his footsteps but couldn't silence the whispered conversations that followed in his wake.

It felt like he was saving Ralph's office for his last stop on the way back to his own executive suite, like a glutton saving the choicest morsel for dessert. He wanted Ralph to hear every conversation, every guffaw, and every cackle—a symphony of success that would emphasize Ralph's exclusion from the celebration.

The tension was building as Ralph arranged his desk before leaving, his movements sharp and precise as he prepared to escape the building before the inevitable confrontation. It was 2:36 PM, too early to leave work according to FASTRAK's corporate culture, but

Ralph didn't care. He wanted out of there before P.T. would appear in his office doorway like an unwelcome apparition.

Mayo sensed Ralph would be trying to leave early—he knew his employees' habits as well as a shepherd knows his flock—and quickened his steps, his Italian leather shoes clicking against the polished floor with increased urgency.

"So, Ralphie boy, looks like you're leaving early...again."

The words hung in the air like smoke from a fired gun, carrying all the condescension and manufactured authority that Mayo could muster. His voice filled the small office space, contaminating the professional atmosphere with personal malice.

Ralph completely ignored his boss as he went about his usual tidying up, filing papers with mechanical precision and shutting down his computer with the deliberate care of someone who refused to be baited into a confrontation. He'd experienced this before, and he knew it would anger P.T.—which was exactly what he intended.

"Nothing to say, huh?" asked Mayo, his voice carrying the dangerous edge of someone whose authority was being challenged in the most insulting way possible—through complete indifference.

Ralph continued to ignore him, his silence more cutting than any verbal response could have been. The disrespect was total and absolute, and it angered his boss even more than open defiance would have.

Just across the hall, Rodney Mann, FASTRAK's marketing director, could hear the words being spoken and the dangerous undertone that suggested the situation was escalating beyond the usual corporate posturing. He decided to edge his way into Ralph's office to see if he could defuse the entire situation before Ralph committed corporate suicide, which he knew Ralph was quite capable of doing.

The marketing director understood the dynamics at play—Mayo's need to assert dominance, Ralph's stubborn refusal to submit, and the toxic combination that could destroy a brilliant career in a moment of pride and rage.

He edged his way past P.T. as he entered, nodding at him with the diplomatic deference that had kept him employed through multiple corporate upheavals, and walking straight to Ralph with some papers in his hand as if this were just another routine business interaction.

"Sorry I'm late with last month's marketing breakdown, damned computers...well you know how it is. Nevertheless, here they are." His voice carried the casual professionalism of someone conducting normal business, as if the CEO weren't standing in the doorway radiating menace like a nuclear reactor approaching meltdown.

As Ralph and Rodney continued their fabricated business discussion, seemingly oblivious to P.T.'s presence, the CEO left Ralph's office but stayed outside long enough to hear the rest of the conversation—eavesdropping with the shameless entitlement of someone who believed that everything in his corporate kingdom belonged to him.

"You'd better calm down and forget all of this, Ralph. It's not worth you losing your job over." Rodney's voice carried the urgency of someone who could see disaster approaching like a freight train. "You know as well as I do that you're the best thing that's ever happened to FASTRAK. That check should be yours. It's because of you and what you've done. So don't forget that, okay?"

The words were true, and everyone in the building knew it—Ralph Norton was the creative genius whose innovations had transformed FASTRAK from a second-tier company into a global powerhouse, while Mayo was simply the political animal who had maneuvered himself into position to take credit for Ralph's work.

"He's probably right, Ralphie boy. But to the victor go the spoils, eh, Ralphie boy?" The eavesdropping Mayo—who had popped back into the open door like a jack-in-the-box of corporate malevolence—smirked with the satisfaction of someone who had just won a game whose rules only he understood.

"Oh, by the way, how's it going with Melanie Spenser these days? Think your late lamented wife would approve, eh, Ralphie boy? Have a good day, wonder boy!"

The words hit Ralph like physical blows, each syllable designed to inflict maximum psychological damage. Mayo's mention of Sandi—his late wife, whose suicide still haunted Ralph's dreams—and his relationship with Melanie was a violation so profound that it transcended workplace harassment and entered the realm of personal cruelty.

Ralph's carefully maintained composure finally cracked under the assault. His ruse ended like a dam bursting under pressure. He vaulted from behind his desk with the explosive energy of someone whose restraint had finally snapped, his chair spinning backward from the force of his movement.

Rodney immediately grabbed him, placing himself squarely between Ralph and the doorway where Mayo stood grinning like a shark that had just drawn blood. The marketing director's quick reflexes and diplomatic instincts were all that prevented Ralph from committing an act of violence that would have destroyed his career and possibly his freedom.

P.T. walked away, cackling and waving his bonus check at whoever was still around to take notice, his victory complete. He had successfully provoked Ralph into showing his true feelings, confirming his enemy's hatred while demonstrating his untouchable power.

Rodney straightened Ralph's suit jacket with the gentle care of someone tending to a wounded animal, checking for both physical and professional damage. He had placed himself squarely in front of the now-irate CFO, preventing anything further from happening through the simple expedient of physical intervention and moral authority.

Ralph seemed to regain his composure as Rodney left, the storm of rage passing as quickly as it had arrived, leaving behind the familiar landscape of grief and frustration. A million thoughts ran through his mind on this, the eve of the first anniversary of his late wife Sandi's suicide—memories, regrets, and the overwhelming weight of loss that no amount of professional success could ease.

He looked around his well-appointed office, taking inventory of the awards that lined the walls like monuments to his genius and examples of all the innovative ideas he had developed to improve the financial performance of FASTRAK. Each trophy and certificate represented years of his life, creativity poured into products that had made other people wealthy while he remained a talented employee rather than a true partner in the empire he had helped build.

He seriously considered quitting, imagining the satisfaction of walking away from Mayo's toxic influence and corporate corruption. But before he could fully embrace that fantasy, he focused on his late wife and the tragic circumstances behind her death, the anniversary that would mark one full year of living with the knowledge that his obsession with work had contributed to her despair.

Tomorrow would be the first anniversary of her death, and by God, he wasn't going to let anyone or anything block out his loving memories of his Sandi, least of all a dirtbag like P.T. Mayo, whose casual cruelty had just reopened wounds that were barely beginning to heal.

He turned off the office lights with the finality of someone closing a chapter, and walked out early into the Houston afternoon, leaving behind the scene of his humiliation and the building that housed both his greatest professional achievements and his most bitter disappointments.

CHAPTER 3

The sky fumed in billows of puffy clouds on the late autumn sweltering afternoon, Houston's notorious humidity wrapping around everything like a wet blanket that refused to be removed. The Texas sun beat down mercilessly on the asphalt parking lot of Mack Hill Towers, creating heat mirages that made the distance shimmer like water.

A few employees were scattered around the parking lot, seeking whatever shade they could find between the parked cars, smoking their cigarettes and Face Timing with other unknown followers on Facebook or Instagram or X. Their conversations carried across the superheated air in fragments—complaints about traffic, weekend plans, the usual detritus of corporate life that filled the spaces between more meaningful moments.

Ralph was happy to get out of work early, though the satisfaction felt hollow and temporary, like sugar dissolved in bitter coffee. Whatever his thoughts were at that moment, nothing stuck; they came and went in his mind like clouds across the sun, casting brief shadows before disappearing into the vast emptiness of his grief-stricken consciousness.

His mind erased each thought as he walked toward his car, a defense mechanism that had developed over the months since Sandi's death. He was definitely on brain autopilot, his body going through the familiar motions while his consciousness retreated to some safer inner space where Mayo's words couldn't reach him.

Nothing mattered, especially his job—not the innovations he had created, not the money he had made for FASTRAK, not the recognition he deserved but would never receive. All of it felt as substantial as the heat mirages dancing across the parking lot.

His two-tone gray Land Rover took a few minutes to cool down as he sat behind the wheel, staring wide-eyed ahead into the shimmering distance. The air conditioning fought against the accumulated heat of the day, gradually transforming the interior from a sweltering oven into something approaching habitable conditions.

He wasn't feeling anything, not wanting anything, and indeed not knowing why he was there or why he felt as useless as he did. The questions formed themselves in his mind like accusations: Why was he trapped in this corporate purgatory? Why had his genius been reduced to a paycheck? Why had Sandi chosen death over the life they could have built together?

So he asked himself why—that simple word that everyone knows but few know how to answer, the fundamental question that lurked beneath every tragedy and disappointment.

The Eastex Freeway to his home in Tiara Woods was packed and slowing down to a stop, a river of metal and glass that reflected the setting sun like a ribbon of molten chrome. He took a quick exit and left the clogged artery for points unknown, following an impulse that had no destination except away from where he was.

He was stuck at the bottom of an exit ramp that was now filled with all the other Ralphs on their way to somewhere else—commuters, delivery drivers, salespeople, all of them trapped in the same slow-motion exodus from downtown Houston. Nothing was moving, the traffic frozen in place like a photograph of urban frustration.

Ralph sat and stared straight ahead as a weather report blared on his radio, telling him what he already knew—that Houston was hot, humid, and would remain so until sometime in November, if they were lucky. The meteorologist's cheerful voice seemed to mock the stagnant reality outside his air-conditioned bubble.

Small groups of people, dressed in rags, moved in and around the waiting cars, like ghosts haunting the borders between worlds. Older women with cardboard signs advertising their hunger, men like gaunt shadows with beards and earrings who had given up on conventional appearance, children with eyes too old for their faces, pets that looked like dogs wearing bandannas to hide their mange.

They all congregated amongst the cars waiting to move, their presence a reminder that not everyone in Houston lived in air-conditioned comfort or drove vehicles worth more than many people's annual income. They were the invisible population that emerged during traffic jams, materializing from the shadows of underpasses and vacant lots to seek charity from the temporarily stationary middle class.

Ralph could and could not see them; his catatonic eyes registered their presence, while his consciousness partially acknowledged their reality. His eyes matched theirs in their search for why some people prospered while others suffered, why talent went unrewarded. At the same time, mediocrity was celebrated, and the universe seemed indifferent to human suffering.

A tall, thin Black man around fifty years old stopped next to Ralph's Land Rover and stared in through his driver's side window. The man's face was weathered by sun and circumstance, his clothes clean but worn, his posture carrying a dignity that poverty couldn't completely erase.

Ralph stared back, their eyes locked in a steely-eyed staring contest that seemed permanently fixed on each other like two magnets drawn together by invisible forces. He was sure the man couldn't see through his extra dark-tinted windows, yet he continued staring at Ralph with an intensity that suggested he could see not just through glass but through souls.

The man pulled something out of his pants pocket with the deliberate care of someone handling something precious. It looked like a handmade religious amulet of some kind—roughly crafted but imbued with the unmistakable weight of spiritual significance.

He dangled it in front of Ralph like a talisman or an offering, the small object catching the filtered sunlight as it swayed gently in his weathered fingers. Ralph's stare could not be broken, nor the stone-cold expression on his face altered by the strange encounter.

The man pushed the piece toward Ralph as if he wanted to give it to him, his gesture carrying the urgency of someone delivering an important message. Ralph kept staring at him without the slightest movement or breaking of his concentration, his face a mask of grief and exhaustion that couldn't be penetrated by ordinary human interaction.

The man could see that none of the cars would be moving for quite a while, the traffic jam settling into the kind of permanent gridlock that Houston was famous for. So he told Ralph, through his closed window, that God loved him and everyone else in the world, for that matter.

His voice was muffled by the glass and the ambient noise of idling engines, but the words carried with surprising clarity, as if they were explicitly meant for Ralph's ears. Then he hung the amulet on Ralph's side-view mirror with the ceremonial precision of someone performing a sacred ritual.

The man walked away without looking back, disappearing into the maze of stopped vehicles as mysteriously as he had appeared, leaving behind only the small token of whatever faith had sustained him through his own struggles.

After another thirty minutes had passed, the traffic began to edge forward with the painful slowness of a glacier retreating. Ralph opened his window and took the amulet from the mirror, placing it on his lap with the careful attention of someone handling a potentially dangerous artifact.

He glanced at it and saw that it resembled a Star of David with a crucifix of Christ at its center—a fusion of religious symbols that suggested either profound theological insight or the confused syncretism of someone who had given up on denominational purity in favor of whatever spiritual comfort they could find.

He held it in his hand as he drove away, surprised to discover that it felt warm—not just from the Texas sun, but with a heat that seemed to come from within, as if it contained some spark of the faith that had created it.

• • • •

THE MID-AFTERNOON TRAFFIC had eased as Ralph found himself on less familiar roads, the urban landscape gradually giving way to the kind of suburban development that had transformed Harris County from farmland into bedroom communities. His app was on, and his God was speaking to him in his perfect AI-generated voice tailored to Ralph's needs and feelings—the artificial deity he had created now serving as his confessor and companion.

He could see the large clouds above him traveling in the same direction as he was, their shadows racing across the highway like dark messengers carrying news he wasn't sure he wanted to receive. He debated whether or not it was a good thing—if you're struggling, you think about everything that way, searching for omens and significance in the random movements of weather systems.

Were they omens? Was it a coincidence? Did Sandi's suicide mean something else beyond the apparent tragedy of a brilliant woman overwhelmed by depression and isolation? Why did there have to be a God that managed everything in the universe, when that same God seemed so indifferent to human suffering?

He traded his God for the oldies station, silencing the artificial wisdom in favor of the human voices that had shaped his youth. Bob Dylan's "Highway 61 Revisited" was playing on the oldies station as he turned off on Exit 63 into Tiara Woods, the upscale planned community known for its lavish lifestyle, gourmet restaurants, and trendy architecture.

There was something familiar about the beginning of that song that kept poking at him like a splinter under the skin—some memory or association that refused to surface completely but demanded attention nonetheless.

Was US 59 a discounted Highway 61, and was Exit 63 an inflated Highway 61? Not that it mattered at all to Ralph, but his mind now took its exit, wandering through free associations and random connections that might have meant something or nothing at all.

The Houston Calvary Cemetery, where Sandi was buried, was on the north side of the road, just ahead—a sprawling memorial park that served as the final resting place for generations of Houstonians who had loved, suffered, hoped, and died in this city of endless summers.

He had intended to wait until the next day to visit her grave, to make the anniversary pilgrimage a proper ceremony of remembrance and grief. But impulse overrode planning as he turned on the road to the entrance gate instead, following an emotional compass that pointed toward the only place where he could still feel connected to his lost wife.

Ralph used to visit the grave once or twice a week after Sandi died, the cemetery becoming a second home where he could maintain the illusion of an ongoing relationship with someone who existed now only in memory and wishful thinking. But, like most things connected with death, they change over time as the acute pain of loss gradually transforms into something more manageable but no less permanent.

He felt bad that he didn't visit her as often anymore, guilt mixing with relief in the complex emotional cocktail that characterized his relationship with grief. But the thought of her being alone in that lonely place felt less painful as the months wore on, as if distance in time could somehow reduce the isolation of death.

She'd now become a memory instead of a tragedy, though the distinction was more semantic than emotional. Her loss was still felt like a physical wound, but her memory was a treasure he could access without being destroyed by it.

God couldn't be there or any place else, thought Ralph, his mind returning to the theological questions that haunted his professional life. Why did God do things like allow brilliant women to choose death over life? Why did divine love seem so absent when it was needed most?

He gently shook his head as he drove up to the cemetery gate, the physical gesture an attempt to dislodge thoughts that led nowhere except deeper into the labyrinth of unanswerable questions.

The gate was closed, a simple fact that shouldn't have surprised him but somehow felt like a personal affront. The gatekeeper sat stolidly in his booth, reading a newspaper and listening to country music on his radio with the indifferent professionalism of someone whose job was to control access to the dead.

He knew a car was approaching—the sound of Ralph's engine was unmistakable in the quiet of the cemetery entrance—but he didn't move a muscle, continuing his reading as if the living world existed only to disturb his peaceful routine.

Ralph lowered his window, still noticing that the man was paying no attention to him or his car, the deliberate ignoring more infuriating than outright hostility would have been.

"Hey, you open?" asked Ralph, his voice carrying the reasonable tone of someone asking a simple question.

The man in the booth turned up the volume on the radio and shook his newspaper as if he were trying to shake something new out of the pages he'd already read, the newspaper crackling with the sound of manufactured activity designed to avoid human interaction.

"Hey, open the gate, or I'll open it myself." Ralph's voice carried the first edge of frustration, though he still maintained the facade of civilized discourse.

The old gatekeeper with the birdlike nose and worn-out Astros cap that had seen better decades, spit into his cup with practiced accuracy, ignoring the insult and now smiling to himself with the satisfaction of someone who held power over people's grief.

Ralph edged the Land Rover toward the gate and stopped, the metal barrier standing between him and the only place where he could commune with Sandi's memory. He got out of his car and tried to open it himself, his hands testing the lock mechanism with the desperate efficiency of someone who would not be denied access to his pain.

It was locked, of course—a simple fact that felt like a conspiracy explicitly designed to frustrate his need for connection with his dead wife. So he edged his car till it touched the gate, the metal-on-metal contact creating a sound that finally got the gatekeeper's attention.

"Wouldn't do that, son," said the man as he kept on reading and spitting, his advice delivered with the casual authority of someone who had seen this drama play out many times before.

Ralph blared his horn as he pushed the gate with his vehicle, the sound echoing across the cemetery like a mechanical scream of frustration. He stopped and kept his hand on the horn till it got the gatekeeper's attention, the noise finally forcing some kind of response from the man whose job was supposedly customer service.

"Wouldn't do that either." The gatekeeper's response was delivered with the same infuriating calm, as if Ralph's desperation were merely a minor inconvenience in his otherwise peaceful day.

"I want to see my wife. Open this fucking gate or I will." Ralph's voice finally cracked, revealing the raw desperation that lurked beneath his civilized exterior.

"Cain't." The single word fell between them like a door slamming shut.

"Why?" Ralph's question carried all the anguish of a man who had been denied everything that mattered to him.

"Cain't you read, son? We're closed. You'll have to wait till tomorrow. Read the sign." The gatekeeper's response was delivered with the bureaucratic satisfaction of someone who derived power from enforcing arbitrary rules.

Ralph spun his wheels in reverse, spewing gravel and dirt everywhere, including on the gatekeeper who finally looked up from his newspaper to assess the damage to his pristine work environment. The Land Rover's tires screamed against the gravel as Ralph backed away from the gate like a wounded animal retreating from a trap.

As he spun backward onto the road, he barely missed a gasoline truck that had just passed, each vehicle blaring its horns at the other in angry sounds that meant nothing beyond the expression of mechanical frustration—a symphony of urban rage that perfectly captured Ralph's emotional state.

He wanted to get a bouquet of JFK roses at the florist shop for his visit to Sandi's grave the next day, the flowers serving as both tribute and apology for his long absence. Petri's Floral Designs was the shop where Sandi always got her flowers, a small business that had become a shrine to her memory in Ralph's mind.

Max Petri was behind the counter when Ralph entered, his weathered face immediately recognizing the familiar figure of grief that had become one of his most heartbreaking regular customers. He had prepared the flowers ahead of time and kept them in the refrigerator behind him, understanding without being told that tomorrow was significant.

Not a word was said between the two men as Max handed Ralph the perfectly arranged bouquet and took his credit card, the transaction conducted with the silent efficiency of two people who understood that some moments were too sacred for casual conversation.

A slight nod of Ralph's head was the only communication, acknowledgment passing between them like a secret handshake of shared understanding. Tears formed in Ralph's eyes as he held the flowers that would grace Sandi's grave, and Max had to turn away so Ralph wouldn't see his own tears—the florist's empathy triggered by countless similar scenes of love and loss that had played out in his small shop over the years.

CHAPTER 4

The employee parking lot at Mack Hill Towers baked under the merciless Houston sun, asphalt soft enough to take shoe impressions and radiating heat that created shimmer waves in the distance. Cuthbert Theroux, a human resources manager and long-time permanent member of the P.T. Mayo sycophant society, stood in whatever shade he could find between parked cars, smoking a cigarette with the nervous intensity of a man who knew his career depended on staying in his boss's good graces.

The acrid smell of his discount cigarette mixed with exhaust fumes and the petroleum tang that always hung over Houston like an industrial blessing. Theroux checked his watch for the third time in five minutes, sweat already darkening the underarms of his cheap suit despite the early hour.

He was soon approached by P.T. Mayo, who emerged from the building's air-conditioned sanctuary like a wolf leaving its lair. Mayo was smoking his own Gauloises cigarette—an expensive French brand that he favored as a symbol of his sophistication. However, he pronounced it "Gah-lohs" in his residual Kansas accent. The contrast between their cigarettes was as stark as the difference in their positions within FASTRAK's hierarchy.

At first, they smoked in silence, two men sharing the ritual of nicotine while the morning traffic hummed along the nearby freeway. The silence stretched between them like a taut wire, filled with the unspoken understanding that this meeting was anything but casual.

As the two drew closer to each other, stepping deeper into the narrow shade between a Honda Civic and a pickup truck, Theroux started the conversation with the enthusiasm of a devoted acolyte addressing his master.

"Congratulations, boss! FASTRAK's stock is soaring, the board is ecstatic, and we're now the number one Christian Product Company in the world." His voice carried the slightly desperate cheer of someone trying too hard to please.

P.T. dropped his cigarette on the ground with deliberate ceremony and crushed it with his Italian leather shoe, twisting his foot as if he were trying to destroy something more than just tobacco and paper. He stared down at the crushed remnants with a smile that never reached his eyes—a cold expression that made Theroux's stomach clench with unease.

"I mean, aren't you amazed at all of the success? After all, it's all you, isn't it, boss?" asked Theroux, his voice betraying the slight quaver of a man fishing for approval in dangerous waters.

"Like I always say: There's one reborn every minute." Mayo's voice carried the cynical satisfaction of a con man who had perfected his craft over decades of deceiving the faithful.

"Yeah, but..." Theroux began, but Mayo cut him off with a sharp gesture.

"Look, Theroux. I didn't meet you here to bullshit." Mayo's voice dropped to a tone that made the HR manager's blood run cold. "I need you to do something for me, and do it quickly."

"Sure, boss, anything. You know you can count on—" Theroux's eager response was silenced by Mayo's raised hand.

"Just shut up for a second and listen to me carefully, okay?"

"Sure. Anything, boss. You know that," whispered Theroux, his voice barely audible over the distant hum of air conditioning units working overtime against the Texas heat.

"I want you to prepare Ralph Norton's termination papers, and I want you to do it on the QT." The words fell between them like stones dropped into still water, sending ripples of shock through Theroux's consciousness.

Theroux was dumbfounded, his mouth opening and closing like a fish pulled from water. Ralph Norton was the golden boy! He was the one who made FASTRAK tick, the creative genius whose innovations had transformed the company from a struggling Bible distributor into a global powerhouse. He invented, developed, and launched the Word of God app for Chrissake, plus all the other inventions that vaulted the company into the financial stratosphere. He couldn't believe his ears, couldn't process what his boss was asking him to do.

"Well...what did he do?" Theroux's question came out as barely more than a squeak.

P.T.'s jaw muscles clenched and twisted as his lap dog begged for treats and explanations that wouldn't be forthcoming. The silence that followed was scary, not to mention the look in Mayo's eyes—a cold, predatory gleam that spoke of decisions already made and consequences already calculated.

The parking lot around them continued its regular rhythm of employees arriving for work, car doors slamming, and briefcases clicking across the asphalt. Still, their small corner had become a bubble of menace, isolated from the rest of the world.

"The envelope with five thousand dollars I'm about to give you is all the information you need...unless, of course, you don't like working here anymore." Mayo's voice carried the casual threat of a man who had perfected the art of corporate intimidation.

P.T. walked up close to the now-quaking Theroux, close enough that the HR manager could smell his expensive cologne and see the calculating coldness in his eyes. He slipped a white envelope into Theroux's suit jacket pocket with the smooth efficiency of someone who had made similar transactions many times before, then turned and walked away.

"Oh," continued Mayo as he turned around from his walk back to his office, the afterthought delivered with the casual cruelty of a man enjoying his power, "make it clean and tight, just like your ass is right now. And I don't give a fuck how you do it as long as you have it on my desk by four this afternoon. Oh, and by the way, there's more where that came from if you do things the right way, P.T.'s way, the only way. Got it?"

Theroux's mouth gaped in disbelief at what he had just gotten himself into, his mind reeling as he tried to process the magnitude of what was being asked of him. He stared at the CEO walking back slowly toward Mack Hill Towers, watching the man's confident stride and perfectly pressed suit. Mayo looked like a man on top of the world, stepping into a dark world of corporate politics that only he understood, having created it himself.

The weight of the envelope in his jacket pocket felt like lead, and he knew it wouldn't help him at all, but Theroux lit another cigarette with shaking hands. He took a long, deep drag, bent his head back toward the sky, and exhaled the smoke toward the heavens like a prayer or a plea for forgiveness. He closed his eyes as tightly as he could and prayed for himself as he kept his glued eyes on the clear blue sky above, hoping for some divine intervention that he knew wouldn't come.

CHAPTER 5

Mayo walked into his office with a lot on his mind, his footsteps silent on the plush carpet that muffled all sound except the whisper of central air conditioning and the distant hum of Houston traffic below. The tips of his fingers ran along the smooth edges of his large mahogany desk—a tactile ritual that grounded him in the material reality of his power.

He stopped and looked out of his large office window, facing the downtown area where glass towers caught the morning sun like mirrors reflecting his ambition at him. The sky was empty and motionless, a blank canvas that matched the emptiness he felt when contemplating moral boundaries. Thoughts were dancing in his eyes as his large and full lips moved in silent words only he understood, rehearsing arguments with imaginary opponents and savoring victories yet to come.

Where does it say that a man is just a man? The question rolled through his mind like a mantra, challenging every convention he had been taught in his hardscrabble youth. Where are the rules about what is right and wrong? The law? Hell no! Weak men wrote laws to control other weak men. Mom and Dad? Maybe, if you have one or both of them—which he didn't—and he didn't care about any of that shit, especially now that he was King of the Hill.

His childhood in Kansas had been a masterclass in disappointment and abandonment, but it had also taught him that survival meant taking what you could get and never apologizing for it. What difference does anything make? None whatsoever! The phrase echoed in the executive suite like a personal philosophy carved in stone.

Once Ralph Norton was destroyed, everything would be his, and he knew it as sure as there was no God to worry about. The irony of running a Christian products company while harboring such beliefs amused him daily. Ada Taylor was the one. She was the fixer, the woman who could make problems disappear like morning mist. She was a giant pain in the ass, but she knew what she was doing and did it about as good as anyone in the shadow economy of Houston's underworld.

You've come a long way, P.T. From those fucked up days selling Bibles door to door in Kansas to King of the World. Not bad. Hell, not bad at all. The memory of trudging through dust and disappointment, his sample case heavy with leather-bound promises he didn't believe, seemed like someone else's life now.

He slowly sat down behind his desk, the leather chair exhaling softly under his weight. He slid out the bottom right drawer and pulled out a disposable smartphone from under a towel—one of several burner phones he kept for conversations that couldn't appear on any corporate records. Three other untouched phones were waiting for him, each one a potential lifeline to the darker aspects of his business empire.

The phone felt cheap and plastic in his hands, a stark contrast to his usual luxury devices, but it served its purpose. He dialed Ada's number from memory and waited, counting the rings, then he hung up. He dialed it again and hung up again—the agreed-upon signal that told her to call back immediately from a secure location.

She returned his call immediately, her voice carrying the distinctive rasp of someone who had spent years navigating dangerous waters.

"That you, Moneymaker?" asked the fixer of all things, her nickname for him a reminder of their purely transactional relationship.

"Sure as hell is. In the mood to make some real money, Ms. Ada?" Mayo's voice carried the satisfaction of a man who knew that everyone had a price.

"Meet me at the Beaux Arts Bayou Center in one hour and bring that fat wallet of yours. I got a lot of bills to pay and art to buy. And don't be late."

Ada hung up the phone and smiled as wide as she could, the expression transforming her face into something sinister and anticipatory. She knew that P.T. had unlimited funds, corporate coffers that seemed bottomless when it came to protecting his interests. But he always had her doing things she knew were dangerous to her and everyone else, operations that walked the razor's edge between success and catastrophe. But he paid... yes, he did, he certainly paid!

. . . .

THE BEAUX ARTS BAYOU Center occupied a converted warehouse in Houston's arts district, its industrial bones softened by track lighting and carefully curated exhibitions that attracted both serious collectors and pretentious tourists. P.T. glided through the art gallery, waiting for Ada, his expensive suit drawing appreciative glances from other patrons who mistook him for a serious collector rather than a man conducting criminal business.

He knew as much about art as Gomer Pyle—which is to say nothing at all—but he had learned to affect the pose of cultural sophistication that his position demanded. The abstract paintings and conceptual installations might as well have been wallpaper for all the aesthetic appreciation he possessed.

Ada arrived shortly thereafter, moving through the gallery with the confidence of someone who genuinely belonged in this world. P.T. followed her to a bench just outside of the main display area, where the carefully orchestrated ambiance created the perfect cover for their conversation.

The sound of tinkling water from a small fountain and soft flute music piped through hidden speakers made P.T. laugh to himself about how gullible people were, how easily they could be manipulated by atmosphere and suggestion. But Ada knew her art, and she was an avid collector whose knowledge and passion were genuine—one of the few authentic things about their relationship.

"Let's take a walk, Mr. Moneymaker." Her voice carried the authority of someone who controlled the terms of their interaction.

Ada was a large African American woman, six feet two inches tall, with a light complexion that spoke of mixed heritage and a presence that commanded immediate attention. Her large hands wore large rings and turquoise bracelets that caught the gallery's carefully positioned lighting, and she stood eye to eye with Mayo—one of the few people who could meet his gaze without flinching.

He smiled slyly at her, his expression carrying the calculated charm that had served him well in countless negotiations, but it didn't seem to faze her at all. When it came to money and possibly putting her own life on the line, she wasn't bashful or fearful of the man walking next to her. This was business, pure and simple, stripped of the usual power dynamics that governed Mayo's other relationships.

As he talked, he stared at the polished concrete floor, his voice lowered to ensure their conversation remained private. "Need you to ruin a bad employee of mine. He's trouble, and he's in my way. What can you do?"

"I can do whatever you want me to do, but it won't be cheap. Don't forget, it's my ass as well as yours." Ada's response carried the weight of experience, the wisdom of someone who had survived in a dangerous profession by never underestimating the risks involved.

"Make it look like he's been stealing money from my company. Secret bank accounts, shady transactions, you know." Mayo's request was delivered with the casual tone of someone ordering lunch rather than commissioning a felony.

"Forget that shit, man. I don't work in that world. It ain't for me at all." Ada's rejection was immediate and firm, her voice carrying a note of professional pride that surprised Mayo.

"Since when did you become so particular?" His question carried a hint of irritation at having his simple request complicated by what he saw as unnecessary scruples.

"What you want is amateur shit. I live in the world of art, and I consider what I do my expression of my art. What I do is me. Me, Ada Taylor. It's poetry and meditation living together, highlighted by pain and violence. That's what I live for." Her words carried the passion of an artist describing her craft, though the art she practiced existed in shadows and left no traditional beauty in its wake.

"Bitch, please! Let's be real here. The only thing you live for is money, and that's a fact." Mayo's crude dismissal was his attempt to reduce their relationship to its simplest terms, but Ada's response showed he had miscalculated.

"How much money we talkin' about?" Her question cut through his philosophical objections straight to the practical heart of the matter.

"Fifty K." Mayo's offer was delivered with the confidence of someone accustomed to buying solutions to his problems.

"Not close enough by a half," snapped Ada, her rejection swift and non-negotiable.

"One hundred K? That's your price?" P.T. barely shook his head, already knowing the answer wouldn't be that simple.

"I'll need to hire some high-priced help, not to mention my fees, and not to mention a piece of art by Dabin Ahn. Yeah, that's my price." Ada's response revealed the complexity of her motivations—this wasn't just about money, but about feeding her genuine passion for art.

"Give me the total, not the bullshit." Mayo's impatience was showing through his carefully maintained facade.

"One hundred K in older one-hundred-dollar bills for me to swallow my pride and do this candyass shit." Ada's final price reflected her distaste for the type of work he was requesting, as well as her willingness to compromise her artistic principles for the proper compensation.

"You'll have it tomorrow. I'll bring it to you personally." Mayo's acceptance was immediate, the amount trivial compared to the potential rewards of eliminating Ralph Norton.

"Well, I'm honored, Mr. Moneymaker. I truly am, but I'll tell you where to leave it and the time. It may take a little time, but it'll be done right." Ada's response carried the weight of professional competence, the assurance of someone who had never failed to deliver on a contract.

"How much time?" Mayo's question revealed his impatience to see Ralph destroyed and claim full credit for FASTRAK's success.

Ada stopped the conversation and stared benignly at Mayo, her expression unreadable as she let the silence stretch between them like a test of wills. It took almost a minute before the two started talking again, the pause demonstrating who really controlled the terms of their arrangement.

"Whatever the fuck it is, that's how much time. Look, do you want this job done and done right or not? And I don't have any more time for you right now, so tell me or leave. That's the way it is." Ada's ultimatum was delivered with the finality of someone who didn't need this particular job badly enough to accept unreasonable demands.

"Whatever. You know how to contact me. You'll have your one hundred K." P.T. stuck out his hand, and Ada shook it vigorously, sealing their devil's bargain with the formality of a legitimate business transaction.

"Don't fuck with me, Moneymaker. We've worked on other shit and I know how you are. Don't fuck with me and everything will be fine, just fine. Now, if you'll excuse me, I've got some street art to look at and you're delaying my fantasy. Bye!" Ada's warning carried the weight of a genuine threat, a reminder that their relationship was built on the capacity for mutual respect to destroy.

As she turned away and went into the gallery to pursue her genuine passion for art, P.T. called back to her with an afterthought that revealed his desperate impatience.

"If you expedite it, I'll have a bonus for you."

Ada didn't turn around, but with her long dagger nail extensions, she flipped him off and laughed all the way to her fantasy, the sound echoing through the gallery like a promise of chaos yet to come.

• • • •

THE HEAT OF THE PAVEMENT put a clamp on P.T.'s energy as he walked back to his car, the Texas sun beating down mercilessly on his expensive suit. He detested being told what to do, especially by a Black woman who refused to show him the deference he felt his position demanded. But she was good at what she did and always covered her tracks with the thoroughness of a professional who understood that survival depended on leaving no loose ends.

He wondered how she would do it and who she'd be using, the operational details both fascinating and terrifying to contemplate. She probably knew more about him than anyone else in the world—his methods, his weaknesses, his capacity for ruthlessness—knowledge that made her both invaluable and dangerous.

He hadn't realized it, but his pace quickened as he walked toward his car, unconscious urgency driving him forward as his mind raced through possibilities and contingencies. Sweat trickled down the left side of his face and made its way to his perfectly starched collar as he realized that he'd left his car unlocked—a moment of carelessness that spoke to his distracted state of mind.

"Stupid!" he said to himself, the word carrying more weight than just criticism of his forgetfulness.

The second he touched the door handle and burned his hand on the superheated metal, he shook it in disgust and pulled out his keys with sharp, angry movements. He turned on the ignition and gunned it out of the parking spot with unnecessary force, the tires squealing slightly against the asphalt.

The hot air blowing out of the air conditioner made him nauseous as he thought more about how much Ada Taylor knew about him, the uncomfortable reality that his secrets were in the hands of someone whose loyalty was purely transactional.

The three or four jobs she'd done for him were perfectly executed by her and her team, operations that had solved problems and eliminated obstacles with surgical precision. But she was getting too pricey, her demands more complex, and her independence more pronounced with each job. This would probably be the last time he'd use her, and he'd have to figure out a way to get rid of her, eventually. But first...

CHAPTER 6

The Harris County Jail, situated on Baker Street in downtown Houston, stood immovably, its institutional green walls and barred windows casting shadows that seemed to absorb hope and exhale despair. Ada Taylor had seen the inside of enough such places to know that they all smelled the same—disinfectant failing to mask the underlying odors of fear, anger, and broken dreams.

She was obsessed with the art of Dabin Ahn, and just the thought of owning one of his pieces gave her chills that had nothing to do with the jail's aggressive air conditioning. Every exquisite work of that artist drew her in with its minimalist perfection and pure aesthetic vision. They were minimalist and pure, and that's what she wanted to be—stripped of everything except essential truth and beauty.

Who she was wasn't as important as who she wanted to be; after all, who decides what you are or why you do what you do? The philosophical question that drove her had been shaped by ten years with HPD, a decade of watching the system fail the people it was supposed to protect. What did her ten years with the Houston Police Department do for her? What can a person do to get the respect they're due, when she always did all the hard work and put her ass on the line while others took the credit and the promotions?

But, after all those years walking the thin blue line and watching corruption flourish while integrity was punished, she realized that the people she met, the way the best operators worked, the money, the money, the money, were all intended to teach her how to be untouchable and rich. All of them were her teachers—from the street dealers who understood market economics better than any MBA to the corrupt cops who showed her how systems could be manipulated. What she saw matriculated her into her world, a shadow economy where competence was rewarded and sentiment was a luxury she couldn't afford.

She would collect the art she loved, hang out with the wealthiest, and clink glasses to her future, building a life that combined genuine aesthetic appreciation with the fruits of carefully calculated criminal enterprise.

Ada didn't particularly like frame jobs like this one. She felt that setups were beneath her artistic sensibilities and that she'd been framed a time or two and knew what it was like to be on the receiving end of manufactured evidence. The helplessness and rage of being falsely accused had left scars that influenced her professional standards. But, like always, the money mattered, and she'd have to hold her nose while she took her medicine.

Maurice Collins, AKA the Twist, was the best forger in the business, a title he'd earned through decades of perfect work and an almost supernatural ability to reproduce any document, signature, or official seal. He had a few problems, thought Ada, but who doesn't? She hadn't seen him in a while, but when she started making inquiries through her network of former cops and current criminals, she discovered that he was in the Harris County Jail on Baker Street, awaiting trial for possession, which, unfortunately, was one of his problems.

He'd always been a user but somehow kept it under control throughout most of his career, maintaining the steady hands and sharp mind required by his skills. His work was always in demand among those who needed documents that could pass any inspection, and he charged accordingly. But addiction is a progressive disease, and even the most functional users eventually find themselves in situations like this.

In the back of her mind, the clock was ticking, not just for what Mayo wanted, but for the Twist. If she didn't get him on it as quickly as possible, there might not be a next time—either because his trial would result in a long sentence or because his addiction would progress beyond the point where his hands could still perform miracles. So she took a chance and drove to the jail to visit him, knowing that such a meeting would be recorded and monitored but confident that their conversation could be conducted in code.

He'd always been a skinny, dark-skinned man, with long, thin hands that were made for his particular kind of artistic pursuit. Ada Taylor knew many artists in Houston's legitimate art scene, but the Twist was an accomplished artist in his specialized field. Counterfeit bills, bills of sale, driver's licenses, passports, visas; you name it, he did it, and they were virtually perfect. He was that good—a master craftsman working in the medium of deception.

After lubricating the palms of a few jail employees with the kind of cash contributions that ensured cooperation and silence, Ada sat in the visitor waiting area that smelled of industrial cleaner and human misery. The plastic chairs were designed to be as uncomfortable as possible, part of the institutional philosophy that prison should be a punishment even for visitors.

They told her it would be about twenty minutes before Mr. Collins could see her. He was finishing up his Mental Health Session. He wouldn't be allowed visitors until it was over—a bureaucratic requirement that spoke to the system's belated recognition that addiction was a medical problem rather than just a moral failing.

Ada sat patiently, thinking hard about her mental health and why everyone was now so damned concerned about people's mental health. The irony wasn't lost on her that she was planning criminal activity while surrounded by people seeking help for their psychological problems. Everyone's crazy, she thought, so what? Everyone has the right to be who they are, to make their own choices and live with the consequences. She twisted her lips just enough to smile about her state of mind, finding dark humor in her own psychological clarity about her chosen profession.

A young pregnant woman and her two children were waiting to visit the woman's husband, their presence adding a note of domestic tragedy to the institutional setting. She was poorly dressed, as were the kids, their clothes clean but worn in the way that spoke of carefully managed poverty. She tried hard to contain the two school-age children, who bounced around the waiting area like they had found the key to unlimited energy, their natural exuberance clashing with the grim atmosphere of their surroundings.

Other waiting area visitors were getting increasingly annoyed with the children's antics—a mixture of mothers, girlfriends, and lawyers all dealing with their stress and impatience. The tension built until an officer came in and warned the mother that if she couldn't keep her children under control, she'd have to leave, his voice carrying the indifferent authority of someone who made such threats dozens of times each day.

When the officer left, Ada beckoned the children over to her with the gentle authority of someone who understood how to manage difficult situations. She asked them their names, listening carefully as they introduced themselves with the shy pride that children showed when adults paid attention to them.

After they told her their names, she told them she would give them each a piece of candy if they would sit down next to their mother and stay as quiet as possible; otherwise, they wouldn't be able to see their daddy. The bargain was simple and effective—positive reinforcement rather than punishment, showing them that good behavior was rewarded rather than just demanding compliance.

They agreed and dutifully sat down quietly, their sugar-fueled energy channeled into the patient anticipation of seeing their father.

Their mother didn't acknowledge that Ada even existed, lost in her world of pain and disappointment. The pained expression on her face and her conviction that her life was worse than anyone else's made her immune to emotions other than regret and self-pity. Ada not only understood the woman's feelings but sympathized with them, recognizing the particular hell of loving someone whose choices had destroyed their family's stability.

Ada knew her act of kindness didn't matter at all to anyone in the entire world—it was just a small gesture of humanity in a place designed to strip away human dignity.

Eventually, the Twist was brought in, and he was a sorry sight, the once-proud artist reduced to the gray pallor and hollow eyes of someone fighting a losing battle with addiction. He knew what Ada was there for before she even said one word—they'd worked together many times before and understood each other with the telepathic communication of long-term criminal partners.

Most things could be left unsaid between them, communicated through glances, gestures, and carefully chosen phrases that wouldn't trigger the attention of anyone monitoring their conversation. He sat down on the other side of the visitation booth and stared at Ada through the reinforced glass screen, the barrier symbolizing how far he had fallen from their previous relationship of equals.

He clasped his thin fingers in front of him, those same hands that had created perfect forgeries now trembling slightly with withdrawal or medication side effects. He stared at Ada and tried to smile, the expression looking more like a grimace on his gaunt face.

Ada was surprised at how much he'd changed, and not for the better. The vital, confident artist she remembered had been replaced by a broken man whose talent might no longer be accessible.

"Since when did you turn gray?" asked Ada, her question carrying genuine concern beneath its casual tone.

"Since I been in this motherfuckin' jail, that's when." His response carried the bitter resignation of someone who had watched his life collapse in real time.

She moved closer to the screen, but not close enough to get anyone's immediate attention from the guards stationed around the visiting room. "You want out?"

"Do I want out? What kind of a stupid motherfuckin' question is that? Everyone in here wants out." His voice carried the irritation of someone whose situation had stripped away all patience for small talk. "Look, get to the point, Ada. They only give us thirty minutes for visitors and I ain't in no mood for bullshit."

"Look, Maurice. I'll throw your bail if you do a job for me," said Ada as she looked around at the guards with the casual surveillance of someone who had learned to be constantly aware of her environment. "You up for that?"

"I don't know. I thought about quitting for a long time, and you know, at my age and the way I feel, I don't know." His voice carried the exhaustion of someone who had been considering retirement from criminal activity but lacked other viable options. "I can't take it in here much longer, too old, too fuckin' old man."

"Five thousand." Ada's offer was delivered with the precision of someone who knew exactly what buttons to push.

The look on his face changed immediately, like a light switch being flipped. His eyes opened wide, and he sat up straight in his chair, looking hard at Ada's face for any deception on her part. He could spot lies and manipulation immediately if they were there—it was a survival skill he'd developed over decades in the criminal world—and it wasn't there.

So, he sat there for a moment, looking pensive and nodding his head as he calculated risks, rewards, and his own rapidly diminishing options. She knew she had him, but he played it for all it was worth, the negotiation dance as familiar as breathing.

"Five plus bail, plus a good lawyer, and you got yourself a deal," said the Twist, his voice carrying the first note of hope it had held since Ada arrived.

"And an extra two if you get the job done ahead of when I need it." Ada's bonus offer was designed to motivate quality work and speed, both of which are essential for Mayo's timeline.

"Good, now get me the fuck out of here so we can start." The Twist's eagerness was palpable, the promise of freedom and payment restoring some of his old confidence.

"Don't you want to know about the job?" asked Ada, surprised by his immediate acceptance.

"Not here." His refusal was absolute—even someone desperate for freedom understood that jail walls had ears and were equipped with recording devices.

"I'll have you out of here by this afternoon. Get your ass and your mind ready so we can start right away." Ada's promise carried the weight of someone who had navigated the bail system many times before.

The only thing that worried Ada was the fact that she noticed a slight tremor in his hands as they were talking, the subtle shaking that could indicate withdrawal, medication side effects, or the progressive nerve damage that sometimes accompanied long-term drug use. Would that affect the quality of his work? Was he in control enough to finish the job: two fake bank accounts with records showing large amounts of money being deposited and withdrawn?

The old Twist could do this kind of work with his eyes closed, his hands as steady as a surgeon's and his attention to detail obsessive to the point of perfection. But could this older, shakier version do it? She had to take the chance—the reward was just too much to turn down, and her alternatives were limited.

But she had that slight doubt, a nagging concern that whispered warnings about relying on someone whose best days might be behind him. In case he couldn't deliver the quality she needed, she had the next step already in the works, backup plans that would ensure Mayo got what he was paying for, regardless of the Twist's current condition.

CHAPTER 7

The backyard shed behind Ralph's house in Tiara Woods stood like a mausoleum in the fading afternoon light, its weathered wood siding and small windows keeping secrets that had festered in darkness for over a year. Ralph unlocked and entered what had become a converted shrine for Sandi—or the memory of Sandi, or the pain he felt for Sandi since the day after Sandi passed.

The interior smelled of dust and grief, mingled with the faint perfume that had been Sandi's signature scent and still clung to her belongings like a ghost refusing to depart. Every surface was covered with carefully preserved remnants of their life together: her prized china set arranged on makeshift shelves, photo albums documenting happier times, clothes that still held the shape of her body, jewelry that caught the light from the single bare bulb hanging from the ceiling.

After he had unlocked the door and walked around for a while, letting the memories wash over him like a tide of guilt and longing, the sledgehammer he brought with him did its job. He started with her prized china—the delicate porcelain set they had received as a wedding gift and never used because it was "too special" for everyday meals.

The first impact sent shards flying across the shed like ceramic shrapnel, each piece catching the light as it fell. He grimaced each time he swung the hammer, crying in time to his rhythm of destruction, the physical effort providing an outlet for emotional pain that had nowhere else to go.

The sound of breaking porcelain mixed with his sobs, creating a symphony of destruction that felt both necessary and sacrilegious. There's nothing you can do when everything you once...

Ralph's neighbor, Tom Traxell, called over the fence to see if everything was okay, his voice carrying the concern of someone who had heard the commotion and wasn't sure whether to intervene. Ralph told him to mind his own damned business and stop snooping, his response sharper than it needed to be but appropriate to his emotional state.

Tom shrugged and kept on mowing his St. Augustine grass, cursing Ralph under his breath but not loud enough to be heard over the lawn mower's engine. The domestic normalcy of yard work continued around Ralph's private breakdown, life going on while he struggled to let go of death.

Ever since he started going out with Melanie Spenser, Ralph felt guilty that he was falling in love again, as if his growing feelings for her represented a betrayal of Sandi's memory. Melanie was a wonderful person, full of life, caring, and understanding of Ralph's grief, which often interfered with their developing relationship.

Her patience with his emotional unavailability and sudden withdrawals spoke to a maturity beyond her years, and her ability to give him space while still maintaining their connection required a wisdom that impressed him daily. She was wise beyond her years, and Ralph appreciated her for what she was, not for who she was—a distinction that mattered to someone still processing loss and guilt.

His conversation with his app's representation of God continued as it always did, with satisfaction in what he'd created and skepticism about what it truly represented. The contradiction of being a devoted user of his own creation while knowing it was driven by artificial intelligence and algorithms reflected the complex relationship between faith and knowledge that defined his spiritual state.

"I'm trying to wash away the past, Conrad, okay?" Ralph's voice carried the exhaustion of someone who had been fighting the same internal battle for months.

"I'm Conrad, not your mother." The response from his app carried the slightly sardonic tone he had programmed into it, designed to prevent the artificial God from becoming too sympathetic or human-like.

"Look, I know exactly who you are, so don't play mind games with me. You are not the creator and knower of all things; you're a composition. Right?" Ralph's challenge to his creation reflected his ongoing struggle with faith, belief, and the nature of spiritual comfort.

"You said you know who I am. So, what is the point of my answering that question?" The app's response demonstrated the sophisticated logic patterns Ralph had built into it, capable of turning questions back on the questioner in ways that felt genuinely divine.

"It's the first anniversary of Sandi's suicide." The words fell from Ralph's lips like stones, heavy with guilt and the weight of a year's worth of unanswered questions.

"Remember what Paul said to the Philippians: If you want to believe, move forward. He was right, you know." The app's response drew from its vast database of scriptural references, offering comfort through ancient wisdom that felt both authentic and artificial.

For the first time in a long time, he shut off the app and finished the demolition of a memory, or at least the memory of a memory. The silence that followed felt both liberating and terrifying, as if he had just destroyed the last connection to a life that was slipping away despite his desperate attempts to preserve it.

• • • •

THE EVENING CLOSED in around Ralph like a shroud, and Ralph closed in on himself with the practiced efficiency of someone who had perfected the art of emotional withdrawal. He paced around his house, turning photos of Sandi around so her face was hidden—a ritual that felt both protective and cowardly, shielding him from her reproachful gaze while acknowledging his inability to let her go.

No matter what he tried to do, it all came back to her. Every room held memories, every object carried emotional weight, every moment of happiness felt like theft from her grave. The house that had once been their sanctuary had become a museum of guilt and regret.

After a few shots of bourbon that burned his throat and warmed his chest without touching the cold knot of grief in his stomach, he tried to sleep. The alcohol was supposed to dull the edges of his pain, but instead it seemed to sharpen them, making every memory more vivid and every regret more cutting.

He sang an old song that he used to sing to Sandi when they first started seeing each other, his voice rough with emotion and the taste of bourbon. It was a silly love song that meant nothing to anyone else but had become their private anthem, sung off-key in moments of intimacy and joy.

Whenever he sang that song, she laughed so hard that she would cover her mouth, not wanting to insult his singing voice but unable to contain her amusement at his earnest efforts. She'd always hug him tightly, so he'd stop singing, and he'd start laughing until their kiss became the only music that mattered, their bodies creating harmonies that no recording could capture.

Sandi was a loner, just like him—two introverts who had found in each other the rare person who didn't drain their energy but recharged it. They recognized their commonalities, their shared need for solitude and quiet, but always found each other to be the only company they ever needed. They could sit in comfortable silence for hours, reading separate books or working on individual projects while maintaining an invisible connection that felt more intimate than conversation.

Sandi was a Houston girl, born and raised in the sprawling complexity of the nation's fourth-largest city, while Ralph was from Chicago, carrying the Midwest's practical sensibilities and work ethic. But it was like they knew each other forever, as if their souls had been searching across geography and circumstances to find their perfect complement.

But then, everything changed.

Ralph was making a fantastic salary back then, his innovations at FASTRAK generating both recognition and financial rewards that exceeded his modest expectations. They bought the house of their dreams in Tiara Woods, a suburban development that promised the perfect blend of privacy and community, modern amenities, and traditional values.

He'd always been an 'idea' man, his mind constantly generating solutions to problems that others hadn't even recognized yet. New ideas were forever popping up into his head, and some of them were so good that even he couldn't believe he'd thought of them, concepts that seemed to arrive fully formed as if downloaded from some external source.

He was also a workaholic, driven by a compulsive need to transform every inspiration into reality, to push every concept to its logical conclusion regardless of the personal cost. The combination of creativity and obsessive work habits had made him invaluable to FASTRAK, but it had also made him unavailable to the people who needed him most.

He remembered the day he conceived the idea for the Word of God app with crystalline clarity, the moment preserved in his memory like an artifact from a bygone civilization. He and Sandi had just argued about God—not a screaming fight but one of those intense discussions that revealed fundamental differences in their worldviews.

She intimated to him that she thought he was hypocritical for working at FASTRAK, a Christian Product Company, while harboring grave doubts about the existence of God. The accusation stung because it contained enough truth to be uncomfortable, forcing him to confront contradictions he preferred to ignore.

He asked her what she meant by that, and then the argument started—a careful, intellectual dissection of faith, belief, and the ethics of profiting from other people's spiritual needs. It wasn't a loud or abusive argument, but as he helped her clean up the kitchen after dinner, he started jotting down notes about what it would take to get someone to believe in God.

That was two and a half years ago, when their marriage was still strong and their future seemed secure. Everything was going well for Ralph on the job—the company was pretty successful, and many of the previous ideas he had developed had been added to the company's catalog and were doing quite well, generating steady revenue and building his reputation as an innovator.

Sandi was being left alone by Ralph as he started work on the app, spending long hours in isolation. At the same time, he threw himself into the project with the single-minded intensity that characterized all his creative efforts. He would stay at work till late in the evening, and when he came home, he was so exhausted that he would throw himself into bed and wouldn't say a word to her.

The emotional distance grew gradually, like a crack in a foundation that widens imperceptibly until the entire structure becomes unstable. That's how Sandi started sinking deeper and deeper into depression, her isolation feeding on itself until she started seeking help from a counselor who couldn't reach the depths of her pain.

Then the drinking started—first as a social lubricant, then as emotional medication, finally as an escape from a reality that had become unbearable. It wasn't long after that Sandi committed suicide by sleeping pills, choosing a quiet exit that reflected her gentle nature even in desperation.

She left a note on the bed, her final words written in the careful handwriting he had loved since their first anniversary card:

I love you, Ralph, and I always will.

CHAPTER 8

Phil Spenser had joined the board of directors at FASTRAK while still serving on the board of the local Lutheran church, his dual service reflecting a deep commitment to Christian values in both personal and professional spheres.

The church had asked him to participate in FASTRAK's organizational growth since its products were often worn or displayed by its members—crosses, inspirational books, and Christian-themed clothing that allowed believers to express their faith in everyday settings. Some in the church didn't care for the way FASTRAK promoted its products or the way it seemed to cross the lines of religious propriety, commercializing sacred symbols in ways that made traditional believers uncomfortable.

For the seven years he'd been on FASTRAK's board, Phil Spencer had never witnessed anything illegal or untoward, though he'd certainly seen things that challenged his comfort zone. There may have been a time or two when the CEO, P.T. Mayo, may have gone too far in lauding his corporation in public, turning business success into something approaching evangelical fervor. But as far as doing anything that appeared to be heretical or sacrilegious, he never witnessed it-or perhaps he had trained himself not to see what he didn't want to acknowledge.

However, on a personal level, Mayo's brash and often egotistical personality grated against many observers' sensibilities like sandpaper against silk. He could make you feel uncomfortable with his casual profanity and his apparent lack of genuine spiritual conviction. Still, Spenser thought that he was a good businessman and took his company where it needed to go, financially.

Sure, he often dealt with his employees in a heavy-handed manner that bordered on bullying. Still, most of the time, he seemed to have good reasons to do so—at least that's what Spenser told himself when Mayo's behavior became too obvious to ignore. No, Spenser thought Mayo did a decent job running FASTRAK, and even though he didn't agree with everything he did, he didn't know anything was out of line enough to warrant intervention.

His daughter, Melanie, had been dating Ralph Norton for a little more than two months, and it was apparent that she was smitten with Ralph in a way that both pleased and concerned her father. He'd always liked Ralph and thought the young man performed his duties with great efficiency and creativity that elevated FASTRAK's entire operation.

His creativity was noticed by many on the board because he was also a bit of a dreamer, someone who could envision possibilities that escaped more conventional minds. Typically, corporate finances and creativity don't align—accountants and artists operate in distinct worlds with different values and languages.

However, in Ralph Norton's case, it did work seamlessly because many of Ralph's ideas developed into new products that performed very well and added substantially to FASTRAK's bottom line. The company had a strong 'Assignment of Invention' policy, which required any inventions created by employees to be assigned to the corporation as its intellectual property. This legal arrangement ensured corporate ownership of employee creativity.

As far as anyone could tell, Ralph never seemed to mind that his ideas created profit for the company while he received only a salary and occasional bonuses. He genuinely liked working at FASTRAK and appreciated the fact that he was given the opportunity for advancement by Mayo many years before, when he was just another ambitious young man looking for a chance to prove himself.

As long as he would somehow be recognized for his ideas and given the usual pat on the back by the corporation's leadership, he seemed satisfied with an arrangement that more mercenary personalities would have found intolerable. Unfortunately for

Ralph, FASTRAK's CEO wasn't that type of leader—recognition and appreciation were commodities Mayo hoarded rather than distributed.

Phil Spenser was a widower of ten years, still wearing his wedding ring and keeping his wife's photograph on his desk as if she might return from whatever business trip death represented. He was pleased when Melanie returned home after she completed her two-year volunteer stint with World One Mission and decided to stay with him for a while as she transitioned back into American society.

The experience in Africa had changed her, giving her a global perspective and a toughness that complemented her natural intelligence and compassion. They'd always had a wonderful, open relationship where both felt free to express their true feelings on a wide range of subjects, but her time abroad had matured her in ways that made their conversations richer and more complex.

The Spenser home had always been a great gathering place for Phil, his late wife Patricia, and Melanie when she was younger. The Spenser family enjoyed socializing with the cream of Houston society—business leaders, cultural figures, political influencers who shaped the city's development and direction.

Their home in River Oaks reflected both wealth and taste, decorated with pieces collected over the course of decades of travel and filled with the kind of understated luxury that old money preferred. During one of these parties at the Spenser home, Ralph Norton met Melanie, a encounter that had blossomed into something more significant than either had initially expected.

Tonight, it was just Melanie and her father, sitting down for a dinner of nyama and sadza, a stew dish she learned how to prepare while helping the poor in Zimbabwe. The exotic flavors transported Phil back to Melanie's letters from Africa, descriptions of people and places that existed in a reality far removed from Houston's air-conditioned comfort.

Phil always enjoyed his daughter's cooking, especially when she told him stories about her adventures in Africa—tales of building schools and clinics, of communities that functioned on principles different from the competitive individualism that drove American success. He was very proud of his daughter and told her so all the time, though he sometimes worried that her idealism would clash with the pragmatic realities of corporate life.

Melanie was a tall, athletically built woman with a gleam in her dark brown eyes that spoke of intelligence, determination, and a restless energy that demanded meaningful challenges. She stood almost six feet tall, and after spending the last few years building huts, churches, and dams in Africa, her physical strength was impressive—callused hands and lean muscle that reflected genuine labor rather than gymnasium exercise.

She loved her dad for how he treated her and her mom and for the kind of person he was: fair, honest, and completely trustworthy in a world where such qualities seemed increasingly rare. Their relationship was built on mutual respect and genuine affection, free from the power games and emotional manipulation that characterized many parent-child relationships.

As he always did, Phil helped Melanie with the dishes and cleanup, their domestic partnership a continuation of patterns established during the years after Patricia's death. She'd made a peach cobbler, her dad's favorite dessert, with some espresso, not necessarily his favorite beverage, but hers, acquired during her time in Africa, where coffee was a social ritual rather than just caffeine delivery.

They enjoyed dessert in the living room, settling into comfortable chairs that had hosted countless vital conversations over the years. That's where the critical conversations always took place, in the informal setting that encouraged honesty and discouraged posturing.

"This cobbler is the same as your mom's. She taught you well," said Phil, his voice carrying the gentle melancholy that always accompanied mentions of his deceased wife.

"She taught me well, but I think her cobbler was the best. Mine's pretty good, but not as good as hers." Melanie's response carried both pride in her skills and respect for her mother's memory, acknowledging her competence while honoring Patricia's legacy.

"You and Ralph doing okay?" Phil's question was delivered with the casual tone of someone asking about the weather, but Melanie knew her father well enough to recognize genuine concern beneath the surface.

A large smile took over her face, transforming her features with an expression of genuine happiness that couldn't be faked or forced. She blushed a little, but she also knew how honest her dad was, and that kind of personal question wasn't to be taken lightly. So, rather than hem and haw around the subject, she answered directly.

"Ralph's a fantastic guy."

"And..." Phil's prompting carried the gentle persistence of a father who wanted to understand his daughter's emotional landscape.

"There's no and, Dad. He's a fantastic guy. That's it." Melanie's response was firm but carried a note of defensive privacy that suggested there was indeed more to the story.

"There's a rumor going around that you and Ralph are getting pretty serious." Phil's statement was delivered with the diplomatic care of someone who navigated corporate politics for a living.

"Since when do you listen to rumors?" asked Melanie, her question carrying both surprise and mild reproach.

"I wouldn't say I'm listening to them; I'm just stating what's going around. You know. What's in the air." Phil's clarification reflected his position as someone who needed to stay informed about developments that might affect FASTRAK's operations.

"You know me, Dad. I'm a very private person. I prefer to keep my personal affairs personal." Melanie's response reflected both her natural inclination toward privacy and the lessons she had learned during her time abroad. "I'll make a deal with you."

"What kind of a deal? I can't remember ever hearing you making deals before." Phil's surprise was genuine—Melanie had always been direct in her communications, preferring straightforward conversation to negotiation.

"Here's the deal. If anything more develops from our current friendship, I positively promise that you'll be the first person to know. How's that?" Melanie's offer represented a compromise between her need for privacy and her father's need for information.

"Weak, but I'll take it." Phil's acceptance carried both amusement and resignation—he knew his daughter well enough to recognize that this was probably the best offer he would get.

"Well, it may be weak, but it's the best I can do. Let's drink to that."

Melanie raised her cup of espresso and clinked cups with her father in a gesture that formalized their agreement. After he took a sip and grimaced at the strength of the coffee—espresso that could wake the dead, as he often said—he gently put the cup down on the table and sat back on the sofa, looking thoughtfully at his daughter.

"FASTRAK's recent financial success is solely the result of the new Word of God app. You know that, right?" asked Phil, his tone shifting toward the more serious business concerns that had been weighing on his mind.

"I know it's a phenomenal success, like most of Ralph's projects. But it's certainly an amazing story." Melanie's response demonstrated both pride in Ralph's achievement and an awareness of its significance to the company.

"Due to its success, Ralph's financial overruns have been overlooked, for the most part. But Mayo's not happy, and he keeps pointing his finger at Ralph." Phil's statement carried a warning that he hoped Melanie would understand and take seriously.

Melanie put her espresso cup down so hard that it cracked against the saucer, the sharp sound echoing through the room like a gunshot. She apologized to her father, cleaned up the small mess with quick, angry movements, and came back to sit down next to him. Phil immediately saw the anger in her eyes—a fierce protective instinct that had been triggered by the threat to someone she cared about.

"You mean to tell me that conniving son of a bitch is blaming Ralph for something so insignificant as a few dollars overrun?" Melanie's voice carried the controlled fury of someone trying to maintain civility while discussing something that enraged her. "Come on, Dad, you know as well as I do that if it wasn't for Ralph Norton, FASTRAK would be at the bottom of the list for Christian Product sales. And now, thanks to Ralph, I understand that it's now number one internationally, with its stock price going through the roof!"

"I understand what you're saying, dear, but Mayo is the CEO, you know." Phil's response reflected the pragmatic realities of corporate hierarchy, even when that hierarchy seemed to reward the wrong people.

"He may be the CEO, but to me, he's the same old door-to-door Bible salesman he was twenty years ago, swindling little old ladies out of their meager savings by sweet-talking them till they fainted." Melanie's characterization of Mayo was both harsh and accurate, cutting through corporate titles to reveal the essential character underneath.

"Aren't you being a bit harsh about him? After all, his company is doing very well. And so is Ralph, for that matter." Phil's attempt at balance reflected his desire to be fair even to people he didn't particularly like.

He hadn't planned it that way, but Phil Spenser somehow got more out of the conversation about Melanie and Ralph than he had intended. Melanie felt very strongly about Ralph—her intensity about Ralph's role at FASTRAK was enough to convince him that Melanie and Ralph would be together for a long time to come, their relationship built on more than just romantic attraction.

"I hope you and the board are smarter than that. Mayo is a charlatan, a vile, disgusting, evil man." Melanie's words carried the weight of moral conviction, her time in Africa having sharpened her ability to recognize genuine goodness and its absence. "He does only what's good for him and no one else. Don't you see, Dad? He's setting Ralph up for failure, or worse. He wants all the credit for himself. I knew it from the first time I met him. He will take down FASTRAK first rather than give anyone else credit for its success."

"Well, your personal feelings about Mayo have no relevance. He's got many allies on the board, including Palmer, and he was just given a rather substantial bonus for the company's financial performance, so..." Phil's response reflected the uncomfortable reality that corporate boards often rewarded results regardless of methods.

"So, he's in, and he's going to stay in, and Ralph's out. Is that what you're saying?" asked Melanie, her question cutting straight to the heart of the matter.

"I wouldn't say Ralph's out, but he's got to clean up his overruns. That's what I'm saying." Phil's clarification was an attempt to soften the harsh reality of Ralph's situation.

"Look, Dad, you know as well as I do that Ralph's Word of God app is what's making FASTRAK what it is today, not P.T. Mayo." Melanie's voice carried the passion of someone who had seen real injustice and refused to accept it passively. "Ralph is a sitting duck, and Mayo has his shotgun ready. If nothing is done and not soon, terrible things will happen. Mark my words."

"Calm down, calm down. The board will always do the right thing when it comes to the corporation." Phil's attempt to provide reassurance sounded hollow, even to his ears.

"That's pretty naïve on your part, Dad. You know that, don't you?" Melanie's challenge carried both affection and disappointment—she loved her father but couldn't understand his willingness to trust a system that had already shown its corruption.

"No, we won't let any monkey business take place." Phil's promise reflected both genuine intention and willful blindness to the realities of corporate power.

"Well, I can tell you one thing—I certainly won't." Melanie's declaration carried the weight of someone who had learned that sometimes good people had to take action when institutions failed to protect the innocent.

CHAPTER 9

The recessed lights hummed overhead like mechanical prayers in the FASTRAK marketing department, casting their sterile glow across Rodney Mann's cluttered desk. Word of God had taken over more than just the marketing department—it had consumed his very soul, transforming what should have been the triumph of his career into a waking nightmare that stretched through every hour of every day.

Gone were the peaceful mornings when Rodney could sip his coffee and watch the Houston sunrise paint the office windows a golden hue. Gone was the relaxed atmosphere you would expect from a Christian Product Company, replaced by a relentless 24/7 sprint that engulfed and squeezed the life out of the smallish, high-energy little figure who had always had a kind word for everyone.

Rodney Mann sat in his ergonomic chair—a luxury from better days—and stared at his computer screen in complete disbelief. The social media numbers jumped out at him with unrelenting volume, each notification a tiny electronic fist punching his already frayed nerves. The blue glow of his monitor reflected off his wire-rimmed glasses, creating twin pools of digital chaos in his tired eyes.

He had thought that developing an online presence through social media would be the new best thing for FASTRAK, especially in light of the success of the new app. The marketing textbooks made it sound so simple, so manageable. Build engagement, foster community, watch the revenue grow. What those books never mentioned was what happened when you accidentally unleashed a digital wildfire that consumed everything in its path.

What he never expected, not in a million years, not in a millennium of eternities, was that the number of new followers and posts would break all social media records. To him, it was not only unfathomable, but downright scary—like watching a beloved pet grow into a monster that could no longer recognize its master. He had no idea how to handle all of this, and all he could do was shake his head and think the worst.

The coffee in his mug had grown cold hours ago, a film of disappointment floating on its surface. His usual routine—once as predictable as the morning prayer service at First Baptist—had been obliterated by the digital tsunami. He would start at eight by reviewing emails, messages, and industry news, a familiar ritual that grounded him for the day ahead. Then, at nine, he would hold a quick team meeting—laughably just him and his assistant—sharing goals and encouragement like a coach before the big game. By ten, he would usually conduct some high-level planning and strategizing, his whiteboard covered in colorful diagrams and ambitious timelines.

But now, all of that stuff was out of the question because the only thing he could do was manage social media posts and all the new groups that had formed around the Word of God app, like digital churches sprouting in cyberspace. That was now Rodney Mann's new world, and he hated it like nothing else—hated it with the passion of a man watching his life's work transform into something he could no longer control.

A gentle tapping on his office door broke through his electronic trance like a knock on a confessional booth. The sound was tentative, almost apologetic.

"Come in, Tyler. What's up?" asked Rodney, not bothering to look up from the scrolling nightmare on his screen.

Tyler Wilson stepped into the office like a condemned man approaching the gallows. Rodney finally raised his eyes and noticed his assistant's posture—shoulders sagging forlornly, head tilted down toward the industrial carpet. Tyler looked sheepishly down at the floor, his usual bright demeanor replaced by something that reminded Rodney of a deflated balloon after a child's birthday party. The young man was holding an envelope in his left hand, clutching it like a life preserver that might not have.

The look on Tyler's face was one of sadness and dejection, unlike any Rodney had seen before on the young man who had always been his anchor in the storm of corporate chaos.

Tyler handed the envelope to his boss with the solemnity of someone delivering a death notice, then walked out without a word.

"Hold on a second," said Rodney in a louder-than-normal voice that echoed off the motivational posters still hanging on his walls—relics from a simpler time. "What is this?"

"My two weeks' notice, Mr. Mann." Tyler's voice was barely above a whisper, each word falling like a stone into still water.

The young man was afraid to turn around and see the expression on his boss's face. They'd always gotten along so well together, like a father and son working side by side in the family business. However, since the avalanche of work caused by the social media frenzy surrounding the app overwhelmed him, he couldn't handle the amount of work and stress involved. It was too much for him—too much for anyone who still wanted to sleep at night and remember what normal felt like.

"Come back here, young man." Rodney's voice carried the authority of someone who had spent years managing people, but underneath lay a note of desperation. "This isn't something you can just drop on my desk and then leave without talking about it. We've always been able to discuss anything, Tyler. You know that."

Tyler turned slowly, like a man facing his executioner. The fluorescent lights caught the exhaustion etched in the lines around his young eyes—lines that hadn't been there six months ago.

"I do know that, but I can't handle this anymore." The words tumbled out in a rush, as if he'd been rehearsing them for days. "I can't sleep at night, I snap at people all the time, I can't even eat anything. My girlfriend thinks I'm having a nervous breakdown. My mom keeps asking if I'm sick. No, sir, Mr. Mann, I can't do this. I just can't."

Rodney studied the young man's face, seeing his reflection in Tyler's haunted expression. The kid was falling apart, just like Rodney himself had been for weeks.

"That's because you're a dedicated employee who wants to do his job the right way, the only way." Rodney's voice softened, taking on the paternal tone he'd used when Tyler first started as an eager intern. "You're honest and hard-working, and that's what I appreciate the most about you. So, I'm not going to accept this resignation yet because, honestly, I feel the same way about all of this craziness. So, please sit down and take this back."

Tyler walked back to Mann's desk like a man granted a stay of execution, settling into the familiar chair like a sack of laundry that needed washing. He didn't say a word, but took back the envelope with trembling fingers and waited. The pause seemed to last forever, filled only by the electronic hum of computers and the distant sound of traffic on the freeway below.

The air conditioning cycled on, pushing recycled air through the vents with a mechanical sigh. Somewhere in the building, a phone rang unanswered. The normal sounds of office life continued around them while their small corner of the world balanced on the edge of collapse.

"Okay, Tyler, let's discuss this so we can plan a way out of this mess with dignity, not fear." Rodney leaned forward, his elbows resting on the desk covered with printouts and coffee-stained reports. "I'm going to ask for more help on this, I promise you. You and I have never experienced anything like this before. We're both new to this social media mess, but let's look at it differently."

He gestured toward the computer screen, still flashing with notifications, each one representing someone whose life had been touched by their app.

"We're in the middle of a huge success that is overwhelming us. We haven't failed. We don't know how or have the resources to handle it. Most marketing departments would kill to be in our situation, with all the attention, adulation, and money coming our way. Our problem is that we need help, and I aim to get it and get it quickly, or I'll be walking out of FASTRAK with you. I promise you that I'll have the help by the end of the week. Deal?"

As Rodney stuck out his hand across the desk, he looked directly into Tyler's eyes with the intensity of a man making a sacred vow. Tyler slowly returned the look, searching his boss's face for any sign of false hope or empty promises. What he saw there was exhaustion, yes, but also determination—the same quality that had made Rodney Mann one of the most respected marketing directors in the Christian products industry.

Tyler slowly stuck out his hand, and they shook on it with the gravity of men sealing a pact that might save them both. Then they got back to work, diving once more into the digital maelstrom that had become their shared reality.

CHAPTER 10

The money kept rolling into FASTRAK like a raging river swollen with spring rain, each electronic deposit notification lighting up the financial dashboards with numbers that should have made everyone euphoric. But for Ralph Norton, sitting in his corner office with its view of downtown Houston's gleaming towers, every congratulation felt like another weight added to a scale that was already tipping toward disaster.

Ironically, every day seemed to bring co-workers into his office, their faces glowing with genuine appreciation as they congratulated him on the app and what it had done for them and the company. They came bearing coffee and donuts, clasping his shoulders, shaking his hand with the fervor of believers touching a saint. The app wasn't just selling everywhere, around the globe—it had transformed the very soul of FASTRAK's offices.

Not a day passed that someone wouldn't hug him and even kiss him while exclaiming the virtues of the app and how it changed their lives and their faith. It was all very gratifying, these spontaneous testimonials that erupted throughout the workday like small revivals. Martha from accounting swore the app had saved her marriage. Jim from shipping claimed it had helped him overcome his drinking problem. Even the janitor, Old Pete, had pulled Ralph aside to whisper that the app had given him peace about his dying wife.

It should have been the crowning achievement of Ralph's career, validation of everything he'd worked toward. If it weren't for the fact that he was in a mysterious battle to save his job when, as far as he could tell, he'd done nothing wrong. Something was wrong, however, something quite mysterious that lurked in the shadows of FASTRAK's corporate hierarchy like a malignant tumor.

The fluorescent lights in his office flickered occasionally, a subtle reminder that even in a building dedicated to Christian values, things could malfunction without warning. Ralph had noticed the flicker more often lately, as if the very infrastructure was responding to some unseen tension.

It had been a few days since the anniversary of his late wife's death—a date that always left him feeling vulnerable and introspective. The grief never entirely departed; it just learned to hide in quiet moments. Nothing had happened for a few days, so he thought he might just be imagining this conspiracy to end his career. Maybe the stress was making him paranoid. Maybe P.T. Mayo's earlier hostility had been an aberration, a bad day that would pass like a storm.

He was keeping a lower profile than usual, avoiding the employee cafeteria where his presence often triggered another round of grateful testimonials. But when his phone rang and P.T.'s secretary's voice summoned him to the executive floor, there wasn't much he could do except go in there and see what was going on.

The elevator ride to the top floor felt like ascending to meet his executioner. The mirrored walls reflected multiple versions of himself—a man who had created something beautiful and was being punished for it. The elevator music played a sanitized version of "Amazing Grace," the irony not lost on him.

As he walked down the hallway to his boss's office, more people slapped him on his back and thanked him with the enthusiasm of revival meeting attendees. The carpet beneath his feet was thick and expensive, muffling his footsteps as he approached P.T.'s domain. Corporate art lined the walls—safe, inspirational pieces that said nothing while trying to say everything.

He stood at P.T.'s open door like a petitioner before a throne, and one of the secretaries, Marlene, rushed up to him from her desk. She threw her arms around him with the passion of someone whose life had been transformed, thanking him profusely and loudly—loud enough for P.T. to hear her through the open door.

"Mr. Norton, I just have to tell you again," Marlene gushed, her voice carrying into the executive office like incense into a cathedral. "That app of yours helped me find peace with my father's death. I can't thank you enough."

Ralph knew the display wouldn't help him at all. It would probably make things worse. As he gently extricated himself from Marlene's grateful embrace and approached the doorway, he could already sense the storm waiting for him.

"You can leave it open. This won't take long," growled Mayo from behind his imposing desk, his voice carrying the promise of swift and brutal judgment.

Ralph walked in with his head held high like a man facing a firing squad with dignity intact, waiting for whatever was about to happen. The office smelled of expensive leather and disappointment, with undertones of the cologne that P.T. Mayo wore like armor against the world.

"You must think you're a legend by now, Ralph." Mayo's voice dripped with contempt as his fingers drummed against the mahogany desk surface. "But as far as I'm concerned, you're a legend in your own mind."

"No, sir, I don't think I'm a legend." Ralph's voice remained steady, professional. "I'm just a numbers guy."

"So, you think you're a numbers guy, do you?" Mayo's chair creaked as he leaned forward like a hunter preparing to strike. "Well, that's what you think. I think you wouldn't know a number from a hole in the ground. I don't think you know a damn thing about finances."

P.T.'s voice was now louder than it had to be, carrying through the open door to ensure that anyone within earshot would hear this public execution. Ralph just stood there in silent dumbness, his mind retreating to a place where the words couldn't reach him. He found himself not caring, or perhaps not fully hearing what was said—a psychological defense mechanism clicking into place.

"Nothing to say?" Mayo's voice rose another octave, veins visible on his forehead. "Well, I do. And here are my final words on this subject for you. Money is being lost, and you don't have a clue where it's going. Yeah, you, the CFO of FASTRAK!"

The accusation hung in the air like a physical weight. Ralph's mind began processing the implications even as Mayo's tirade continued.

"CFO my ass. You're not a CFO. You're an SFI—stupid fucking idiot, that's what you are!" The profanity exploded from Mayo's mouth like bullets from a gun, each word designed to wound and humiliate. "Now get the fuck out of my office and find that damn money by tomorrow or you can find yourself another moron to hire you like I did when I thought you'd be a great fit for our company. How fucking stupid was I? Jesus fucking Christ. Get the fuck out of here before I lose my mind. Go! Get out of here."

Ralph remained expressionless as he left the office, his face a mask of professional composure that he'd learned to wear during his years in corporate America. He walked past many employees who had heard the tirade through the open door and couldn't believe it—their faces showing a mixture of shock, embarrassment, and sympathy. They all knew Ralph and knew how he had single-handedly saved FASTRAK many times over, not P.T. Mayo.

Trying to look busy isn't as easy as it sounds when everyone knows you've just been publicly humiliated. As Ralph walked by the cubicles and offices, conversations stopped mid-sentence. People buried their faces in their computer screens or suddenly found urgent tasks that required their complete attention. He held his head high and even managed a slight smile as he walked, a display of grace under fire that only increased the respect his colleagues felt for him.

Whenever Ralph was under tremendous pressure, something always clicked in his mind like a switch being thrown. Logic and common sense always took over, pushing emotion aside as he shifted into problem-solving mode—the same mental state that had made him such an effective CFO. It was a survival mechanism he'd developed over years of corporate battles, and he'd invariably figure out solutions.

But this one had him puzzled in a way that felt different, more personal. He knew the numbers better than anyone in the building, could recite financial reports from memory, had systems in place that would catch a discrepancy of fifty dollars, let alone the kind of missing money Mayo was suggesting. If money was missing, he would find out where it was going sooner or later. He had to.

He knew he'd been overly occupied with the success of the app lately, basking in the praise and testimonials that filled his days. Perhaps he might have taken his eye off the ball now and again, distracted by the very success that was now threatening to destroy him. But he knew his job like a master craftsman knew his tools.

Today, he would burn the midnight oil for however long it took to find out what the hell his boss was talking about. Before he even started, he was convinced that all the financial security safeguards were in place and that nothing could have happened. The systems were redundant, the checks and balances ironclad.

But then he thought better, his analytical mind refusing to accept assumptions.

He talked to himself about getting it right, his internal voice taking on the tone of a stern mentor. "Ralphie, don't be naïve. Don't think that your system is infallible. Nothing is infallible. Remember that and get to work!"

And that's precisely what he did, settling into his office chair with the determination of a man whose professional life—and perhaps much more—hung in the balance.

CHAPTER 11

The FASTRAK building after hours took on a different personality entirely, like a cathedral after the last parishioner had departed. The lights were dimmed to energy-saving levels, casting long shadows that transformed familiar hallways into something almost otherworldly. Everyone had left for the night except Ralph, but there might have been someone else working late—a kindred spirit in the struggle against corporate chaos.

Ralph's back ached from hours hunched over financial reports, his spine protesting against the unnatural position he'd maintained since Mayo's explosive ultimatum. As he stretched backward in his chair, vertebrae popping like small firecrackers, he noticed a thin line of light seeping from under Rodney Mann's office door like a golden thread in the darkness.

He smiled to himself, finding comfort in knowing he wasn't the only soul burning the midnight oil in this corporate purgatory. For a moment, he considered knocking on Mann's door—misery loves company, after all—but he changed his mind and went back to work. There would be time for commiseration later, assuming they both survived their respective crises.

Ralph had every financial report for the last three months spread across his desk like tarot cards, promising to reveal hidden truths. The pages were organized in neat stacks, each one representing a different aspect of FASTRAK's financial health. Coffee rings stained some of the older reports, evidence of previous late-night sessions that had revealed nothing but clean numbers and balanced books.

As the hours wore on, he was starting to notice a few discrepancies on the last balance sheet that couldn't be explained—minor anomalies that pricked at his consciousness like annoying little splinters under the skin. The numbers were subtle, almost elegant in their deception, as if someone had been very careful about covering their tracks.

It was almost midnight when his eyes started closing on their own, the weight of exhaustion pressing down on his eyelids like lead curtains. The building's heating system cycled on with a mechanical wheeze, circulating air that smelled of industrial carpet and the lingering ghosts of a thousand business lunches. It was useless to work any longer; his brain was operating at half capacity, and he needed clarity for what lay ahead.

As he shut down his computers and began organizing the printed reports into secure folders, he knew exactly where he'd start the investigation the next day. The discrepancies had a pattern, subtle but detectable to someone who knew the financial landscape as intimately as he did.

He stood up from his chair, bones creaking like old floorboards, and was just about to turn off his desk lamp when he noticed someone standing in his doorway like an apparition. It was Rodney Mann, looking as shell-shocked as Ralph felt.

"I thought I was the only idiot who was stupid enough to work till midnight," said Ralph, his voice hoarse from hours of silent concentration.

"Guess not." Rodney's response carried the weight of shared suffering.

"Problems?"

"Mind if I sit down? My brain is fried and my legs are numb from sitting in front of that damn computer." Rodney gestured toward Ralph's guest chair, as if asking permission to collapse.

"Yeah, me too. It's like I never get a break from this shit. Know what I mean? I mean, it never ends," spoke Ralph, the stress bleeding through his usually composed exterior.

As Rodney sat down heavily in the chair, a quizzical look crossed his face, one that spoke of battles fought and barely survived. Ralph, on the other hand, looked beat, more exhausted than Rodney could remember seeing him in all their years of working together. They weren't exactly commiserating, but something was hanging over both of them that was yet to be addressed, like storm clouds gathering on an otherwise clear horizon.

"Mind if I put my legs up on your desk? Maybe the blood will come back." Rodney's request was delivered with the casualness of old friends who had long since abandoned corporate formality.

"Sure, go ahead. It probably won't be my desk for much longer. Mayo's on my ass, big time." Ralph's voice carried a mixture of resignation and defiance that surprised them both.

"Yeah, heard about it. It's all over the place. People heard the beatdown and said it was brutal." Rodney propped his feet up, settling in for what felt like a necessary conversation between two men drowning in their success.

"Somewhat."

"Well, the reason I stopped by was that I wanted to ask you for some help. I thought about it a million times, and you were the only one I could think of who could help." Rodney's words carried the weight of desperation barely held in check. "Tyler and I are getting destroyed by the amount of volume your app has created on social media."

"Isn't that called the penalty for success?" Ralph's attempt at humor fell flat in the midnight stillness of the office.

"It's not funny, Ralphie. This is some serious shit we're dealing with now." Rodney's voice took on an urgency that cut through Ralph's exhaustion. "Do you have any idea what you've created? I mean, nothing like this has ever been seen anywhere. It's...it's...it's a freakin' phenomenon. That's what it is."

Ralph chuckled despite himself, the sound echoing off the office walls like a small rebellion against the weight of their circumstances. It was the first time that evening that he could smile, and the expression felt foreign on his face. He knew what he had created was amazing and successful, but that was the first time he'd heard the word 'phenomenon' used with such desperate reverence.

Rodney continued, his words tumbling out like water through a broken dam. "If I don't get some help, I'll be joining you on the unemployment line. It's that bad."

"What can I do? I mean, I've got my own problems right now." Ralph gestured toward the financial reports covering his desk like evidence in a criminal case. "I mean, look at me. What the hell am I doing here at midnight? Plus, social media is way beyond my pay grade. I know nothing about it."

"I don't know. I just thought, since you were the brains behind this thing and the one who developed it and babied it through the development process, that you might have an idea on how to automate, maybe the process of dealing with all these new groups that are forming everywhere."

Ralph considered this, his analytical mind already working on the problem despite his exhaustion. "The way I see it is this. The app is the app. It does what it does. Whether people like it or not is not up to us. It's just a tool for people to figure out something important. You know. Some people need a little help, which in this case involves exploring whether they can develop a more personal belief system that will support them throughout their lives. I say, let them do what they want to do and stop worrying about managing the process."

"It's not as simple as you're making it out to be." Rodney's voice carried a note of frustration that bordered on panic. "You should hear people talking about how it's changed their lives, how their marriages are better, how their stress levels have gone down and that's just from our employees who bought the app themselves, people who couldn't afford the thousand-dollar purchase price for the damn thing."

"I know, but it's just an app that uses artificial intelligence and algorithms that take a person's needs and recreates a personal God that they can feel comfortable with and seek guidance from." Ralph's voice took on the tone of a professor explaining a complex theory. "That's all it is. Yes, it sounds real, and yes, it feels real at times, which I know firsthand because I use it every day myself. So I get it, but at the end of the day, it's just an app."

"Oh no, it's not!" Rodney's response came out like a gunshot in the quiet office.

"What the hell does that mean?"

"It's become a lot more than that. If you ask me, I'd say it's becoming a new religion for many people." Rodney's words hung in the air like incense in a cathedral. "God is in their pocket now, and once someone takes a selfie with God, it's all over. And that, my friend, is exactly what's happening."

Ralph stood up from behind his desk and stretched backward, his body protesting hours of hunching over financial documents. He looked at Rodney, who had stood up as well, both men feeling the weight of what they'd created and what it was becoming. Ralph walked around the desk and put his arm around Rodney's shoulder, a gesture that conveyed shared burden and mutual understanding.

"I'll tell you what I'll do. I'll give it some thought, and by tomorrow morning, I'll have some new ideas that may help you and Tyler. I'm not promising anything, and no guarantees, but I'll try. Okay?"

"That's all I can ask for. And I appreciate it. Oh, and sorry for the beat down by Mayo. You did not deserve that at all."

"Comes with the job. Come on. Let's get out of here."

The two embattled co-workers chatted on the way to the parking lot of Mack Hill Towers, their voices echoing in the empty corridors like whispered prayers in a deserted church. It was a clear night, and a half-moon hung low in the east, casting silver light across the

Houston skyline. Both beleaguered men drove away into the late evening, not knowing the outcomes of their situation, carrying the weight of success that had become too heavy to bear.

They waved at each other as they drove away in opposite directions, but Ralph couldn't drop his feeling that something was wrong, terribly wrong. The sensation gnawed at him like a persistent headache, demanding attention he couldn't afford to give.

He was about halfway home, the familiar rhythm of highway driving usually soothing to his stressed mind, when he exited the freeway and went back to Mack Hill Towers. Nagging doubts persisted in his brain like an itch he couldn't scratch. Was money being stolen? Was this new problem a problem after all? Who would do this, and more importantly, why?

Ralph's eyes scanned the empty Eastex Freeway as he drove back, the roadway illuminated by sodium vapor lights that turned everything an eerie amber. He was looking for an answer in the urban landscape around him, hoping that clarity would emerge from the familiar sights of his city. He saw billboard after billboard along the freeway—advertisements for restaurants, car dealerships, medical centers—the commercial poetry of American capitalism.

The one that stood out just before he took the exit to the loop was for a circus that was coming to Houston, featuring a clown with an unsettling smile that seemed to follow his car. He didn't catch the name of the circus, but it triggered something in his mind—a thought vague enough to be unrecognizable, but persistent enough to stay and refuse to leave.

As he parked his car in the empty lot, the asphalt still radiating heat from the day's sun, he spotted Gerald, the night security guard, walking around the front of the building with the methodical pace of a man who had walked this route thousands of times. At first, Gerald didn't recognize the figure approaching in the darkness, but then recognition dawned, and he waved at Ralph with the familiarity of someone who had seen too many late-night workers over the years.

"Evening, Mr. Norton. What brings you here this time of night?" asked the guard, his voice carrying the slight weariness of someone whose shift was far from over.

"Didn't finish a report I needed to complete for the boss. You know how it is. If I don't, my ass is tumbleweed. Know what I mean?" Ralph's lie came easily, smoothed by years of corporate diplomacy.

"Sure do!" Gerald waved at Ralph and continued his rounds, disappearing around the corner of the building like a guardian angel patrolling the perimeter.

Ralph waved at Gerald's retreating figure, though the guard didn't see it, and made his way back into the building that had become both his professional home and his potential tomb.

Ralph dove into the investigation as soon as he got into his office, the familiar glow of his computer screen welcoming him back like an old friend. He knew that if any money was missing, someone must have had access to take it. Access codes were only known to the users who received them, distributed with the precision of military secrets. Still, at least he would be able to detect if someone had gained unauthorized entry to the financial systems.

But before he checked that, he had an idea that struck him with the force of inspiration. As the list of the last two months' financials scrolled in front of him in neat columns and rows, he opened two files that would certainly give him a starting place, if nothing else: disbursement requests and miscellaneous funds requests. These were the documents that would reveal the paper trail of any unauthorized transactions.

He double-checked the dates and times for any discrepancies noted and then cross-referenced them against the dates of any access codes used during the same period. The process was methodical, almost meditative, requiring the kind of focused attention that pushed all other concerns from his mind.

He stopped and stared at the screen in front of him, the numbers swimming slightly as his tired eyes tried to focus. He realized that some funds had indeed disappeared mysteriously, as if they never existed—ghost transactions that left barely a trace. However, his system of automatic audits using AI had highlighted the discrepancies like breadcrumbs leading through a dark forest.

He kept staring at the screen, his mind processing the implications while his hand automatically reached up to scratch the top of his head—a nervous habit from childhood that emerged when he was deep in thought.

"Well, whaddya know Ralphie boy, whaddya know?" Ralph said to himself, his voice barely above a whisper in the empty office, followed by a low whistle that seemed to echo off the walls. "Looks like..."

He took a glance at the clock on the wall, its digital display glowing red in the darkness. It was now 2:30 AM, and his eyes were closing by themselves again, his body demanding rest that his mind refused to allow. The building around him settled with the small creaks and sighs that old structures make in the quiet hours, like an elderly person shifting in their sleep.

He saved the files in an encrypted folder on a thumb drive, the small device holding secrets that could destroy careers and change lives. He powered off the computer with the ceremonial finality of someone completing a ritual, then gathered his things and left for the night.

As he made his way through the empty building, he saw Gerald making his rounds again, the faithful guardian ensuring that FASTRAK's secrets remained safe through the dark hours. They waved goodbye to each other, two men whose paths crossed in the liminal space between day and night, between revelation and uncertainty.

Ralph drove home through streets that belonged to delivery trucks and insomniacs, but his mind refused to quiet. He kept thinking about circuses and that voice he had heard the other morning—the words that had haunted him since: "If you love me, kill him." The memory felt like a splinter in his consciousness, sharp and painful and impossible to ignore.

But his brain fog kept the mystery a mystery, at least for now, wrapping the truth in layers of exhaustion and confusion that would require daylight and coffee to penetrate.

CHAPTER 12

The conference room at Faith for All's headquarters smelled of old coffee and worn carpet, a musty ecclesiastical scent that spoke of decades of earnest meetings and passionate debates. Faith for All, an interfaith organization loosely organized by influential leaders within Houston's religious community, usually met quarterly in this same paneled room where portraits of long-deceased theologians gazed down with stern disapproval.

More often than not, these gatherings devolved into socializing and gossiping about their organizations—who was building a new sanctuary, whose congregation was growing, whose youth pastor had been caught in a scandal. The meetings served as much as a social function as a religious purpose, a chance for men of God to speak freely among their kind.

However, the meeting today was not for the entire organization but for a select few clergymen who had a particular reason for meeting. The agenda was short and devastating: church attendance was dramatically down across Houston, and they all knew exactly why.

The fluorescent lights overhead cast a harsh institutional glow across the gathered men, making their faces look pale and strained. One of the attendees was Marcellus Worthington, a local pastor whose Baptist church relied solely on the donations of its members for survival. The man who usually commanded attention with his booming voice and infectious smile was unusually, entirely at a loss for words.

His mood matched the mood in the room: somber, with a hint of doom hanging over them like storm clouds gathering before a tornado. There were six attendees total, six fewer than the usual number, but the subject on the agenda applied to every church in the city. Those who hadn't come either couldn't face the reality or were already too defeated to bother showing up.

Washington, a portly and affable man with a permanently broad smile that had charmed Houston's elite for two decades, addressed the group from the head of the long table. There was no smile that day—his face bore the expression of a man watching his life's work crumble before his eyes.

"Gentlemen, I appreciate you coming here today," he began, his voice lacking its usual warmth and confidence. "We need to talk about something that has recently occurred and which threatens to destroy all of our religious institutions."

The words hung in the air like incense gone stale. Around the table, men who had spent their lives providing comfort to others now sought comfort for themselves.

Reverend Tobias Hightower, a thin man whose wire-rimmed glasses reflected the overhead lights, raised his hand with the hesitancy of someone asking a question they weren't sure they wanted answered. Pastor Worthington opened his palm gently toward the pastor, who stood up shakily and asked a question for the group.

"Does anyone here know any board members on the board of FASTRAK?"

The question hit the room like a stone thrown into still water, sending ripples of recognition and anger through the assembled clergy.

"I don't know him well, but I am acquainted with G. Gordon Palmer," said Washington, his fingers drumming nervously on the polished table surface. "We've served on various charities together in the great city of Houston. Hospital boards, scholarship committees, that sort of thing."

As the dialogue continued, murmurs and side conversations began to fill the room like the rustling of leaves before a storm. A younger member, Pastor Greenway of the Congregational Church of Oak Cliff, stood up with the explosive energy of a man who had been holding his tongue too long. He interrupted the conversation and took over the meeting from that point on, his youth and passion cutting through the diplomatic hesitation of his elders.

"Let's stop this pussyfooting around this disaster and get to the problem at hand," he said, his voice carrying the fire of righteous indignation. "We're wasting valuable time, and we don't have a second to spare. I've spent the last ten years building up my congregation, pouring my heart and soul into creating something meaningful. I'm not going to let some computer program destroy all the work I've put into creating an organization that helps everyone it can."

His words crackled with the energy of a revival meeting, but instead of calling people to salvation, he was calling them to war.

"Exactly what are you saying, Thomas?" asked Washington, though the concern in his voice suggested he already knew where this was heading.

"What I'm saying is that we're in the fight of our very lives." Pastor Greenway's hands gestured emphatically, painting his words in the air. "Ever since that app hit the market, church attendance across Houston—well, for that matter, across the world—is down fifty, sixty, sometimes eighty percent. My Sunday services look like funeral parlors. People who haven't missed a service in twenty years are suddenly finding God in their smartphones."

He paused, letting the devastating statistics sink in like body blows.

"We can't afford to sit idly by as this computer program steals from us everything we've worked for. We can't. We just can't, and I intend to take action, whether it's legal, judicial, or political. I won't let this continue. It will be our ruination, and you know it as well as I do."

A bit of group grumbling and side conversations followed the call to action, the sound of men grappling with the unthinkable reality that their life's work might be obsolete. Some nodded in agreement, others shifted uncomfortably in their chairs, still others stared at the table as if answers might be found in the wood grain.

"I understand your concerns, Thomas, but now is not the time to go off half-cocked," said Washington, trying to restore some semblance of order to the proceedings. "We'd do a lot better in fighting this problem if we worked together as a group. I'm open to hearing suggestions from our members and then voting on them collectively to ensure our future success. Everyone here is concerned about this, Thomas, and we all want to see some action taken. But we have to be united in our solution."

Most of the members nodded in approval, falling back on the familiar comfort of committee process and democratic decision-making. But it wasn't unanimous by any means, and Pastor Thomas Greenway wasn't about to accede to this lame solution that felt like rearranging deck chairs on the Titanic.

He stood up in anger, the force of his movement propelling his chair backward into the wall with a sharp crack that drew everyone's attention. As he picked up his papers from the table with sharp, angry movements, he looked around at the much older members of the group and shook his head with the disappointment of a son watching his father fail.

He decided to leave, his patience for diplomatic solutions exhausted, but as he headed toward the door, he stopped just before leaving. He turned around and faced the group with the intensity of an Old Testament prophet delivering judgment.

"You can't rub people's backs and tell them everything is going to be okay if you just show a little patience and inner strength, gentlemen," he said, his voice building like thunder. "Don't think for one minute that you can attack this new problem with what worked before, because you can't. This presents a new challenge that necessitates innovative solutions. This is only about one thing, and you better deal with it now, or you won't be sitting here or anyplace else much longer."

He paused, his eyes sweeping across the faces of men who had dedicated their lives to serving God, and delivered his final words with the force of divine revelation:

"It's about God, damn it, it's about God."

The door slammed behind him with the finality of a coffin lid closing, leaving the remaining clergymen to contemplate the ruins of their calling in the fluorescent silence of the conference room.

CHAPTER 13

The Spenser mansion in River Oaks stood like a monument to Texas wealth and refinement, its Georgian columns gleaming white under strategically placed landscape lighting. Phil Spencer and his daughter Melanie were hosting their annual dinner party for FASTRAK's board of directors, a tradition that had endured decades of corporate changes and personal tragedies.

For Melanie, the timing couldn't have been better. The recent success of the Word of God app had put everyone in a celebratory mood, making them more receptive to her carefully planned agenda. For Phil, it couldn't have come at a worse time, considering his daughter's obvious feelings for Ralph Norton and the dangerous political waters she was about to navigate.

The formal invitations had been sent out on cream-colored cardstock with embossed lettering, and everyone had accepted—partly out of genuine affection for Phil, but mostly because declining an invitation from a major board member would have been corporate suicide. Melanie knew that everyone's spirits would be high, considering the huge successes that the corporation had recently experienced, which would make her task both easier and more delicate.

But she also knew that behind those successes lurked an unethical, devious, and sometimes brutal leadership that was slowly poisoning FASTRAK from within. How could a corporation founded on the principles of the life of Jesus Christ be so decayed in its heart? The irony wasn't lost on her—using Christian values to build an empire while abandoning them in practice.

Her father didn't necessarily see it that way, she thought, or he would have left long ago. Phil was the eternal optimist, always finding the silver lining in the darkest corporate clouds. But Melanie was the realist in the family, blessed with her mother's sharp political instincts and cursed with clear sight into human nature. She intended to use her political skills to begin her efforts not just at saving the corporation from itself, but also at saving the career of the company's heart and soul, Ralph Norton.

But, being a true realist, she knew it wouldn't be easy. These were powerful men accustomed to getting their way, and they didn't take kindly to being manipulated by anyone, especially a young woman they still saw as Phil's little girl. Nevertheless, she was ready for the challenge.

As the board members and their wives arrived wearing tuxedos, evening gowns, and fabulous jewels that caught the light from the crystal chandeliers, Melanie and Phil stood at the front door like gracious hosts from a more elegant era. Their servants, led by the majordomo Carlos, who had been with the family for twenty years, ushered everyone in with practiced efficiency, taking their coats and wraps, and serving them champagne and cocktails in crystal glasses.

Melanie could see that the mood of the group was almost jubilant, which suited her purposes perfectly. Success made people magnanimous, generous with their goodwill and more likely to listen to reasonable requests. The conversation buzzed with talk of stock prices, expansion plans, and the global phenomenon their little app had become.

The Bay City String Quartet, positioned discreetly in the music room, played Haydn's String Quartet in C Major while the mingling lasted longer than planned. The familiar strains of classical music provided an elegant backdrop for conversations that ranged from business to grandchildren, with occasional bursts of laughter that echoed through the mansion's high-ceilinged rooms.

Phil wouldn't stop the bubbly camaraderie—he was enjoying himself too much, basking in the success and fellowship—until Melanie gave him the look. It was an expression she'd perfected over the years, subtle enough to be missed by others but unmistakable to her father. He smiled gently and began herding the guests into the dining room with the diplomatic skill of a man who had spent decades managing both corporate politics and social events.

She helped the older women by taking them gently by the arm and guiding them to their assigned places at the long mahogany table, which could seat twenty comfortably. The dining room was a masterpiece of understated elegance, with oil paintings of Texas landscapes adorning the walls and fresh flowers from Melanie's garden providing splashes of color.

G. Gordon Palmer, the unofficial leader of the board, stood up after everyone was seated, his considerable bulk impressive in his perfectly tailored tuxedo. He tapped his wineglass with his butter knife and offered a robust 'thank you' to the host and his daughter, just as if it were a board of directors' meeting. His voice carried easily through the room, commanding attention with the authority of someone accustomed to being heard.

The extravagant gourmet meal was savored by all the partygoers—prime Texas beef, imported wines, delicate soufflés that melted on the tongue. Phil was known for his parties throughout Houston society, even after his wife's death. The tradition had continued after her death, though Melanie had taken over most of the planning and execution with the grace her mother had taught her.

Most board members were in their sixties, with some in their seventies—throwbacks to an earlier era where gender roles were clearly defined and rarely questioned. They were men who smoked cigars after a good meal while women retired to the drawing room where they could gossip and complement each other without their men getting bored and fussy. And this party was no exception to those time-honored traditions.

Melanie had planned her strategy carefully, intending to start with the women first, using the age-old feminine arts of complimenting, gushing, and hugging them as much as possible. Then, she would move on to the men, where she would flirt, cajole, and bribe as best she could. She also knew the pecking order of power and seniority of the group. She planned to follow it precisely, starting with Mrs. Miriam Palmer, the audaciously dressed wife of G. Gordon Palmer.

Mrs. Palmer was a formidable woman in her own right, known throughout Houston society for her sharp wit and sharper tongue. She wore her designer gown like armor and her jewelry like weapons, each piece carefully chosen to convey status and power.

Melanie hooked her arm in Miriam's with practiced grace, and they walked over to the fireplace where a gas fire provided both warmth and atmosphere. They made small talk all the way, discussing mutual friends, upcoming charity events, and the unusually mild winter Houston was experiencing.

"Mrs. Palmer, you look amazing tonight," gushed Melanie, laying on the charm with the skill of a professional diplomat.

"You're so sweet, dear. You remind me of your mother, God rest her soul, so much, it's uncanny." Miriam's voice carried genuine warmth tinged with the sadness of loss. "Did you know your mother and I went to the same school?"

"You went to Bryn Mawr also?" Melanie's surprise was genuine—this was a connection she hadn't known about.

"Yes, but quite a few years before your mother," Miriam replied with a self-deprecating smile that acknowledged the passage of time without embarrassment.

"Mother always talked about the quality of her education there and that they gave all the women who attended there a great start in life. Mother was eternally grateful to Bryn Mawr."

Miriam sat on the burgundy leather sofa next to the fireplace and patted the open space next to where she sat with the gesture of a queen inviting a courtier to approach. Melanie smiled demurely and sat down gently next to her, noting the older woman's expensive perfume and the way the firelight caught the diamonds at her throat.

Miriam patted her on her knee with maternal affection. "Now, dear, let's get down to brass tacks."

The gentle surprise on Melanie's face was completely fabricated, a performance worthy of Broadway. She knew exactly what was coming and was well-prepared for it, having anticipated this conversation for weeks.

"How's your new romance going?"

"I'm not sure I..." Melanie began, but Miriam cut her off with a wave of her bejeweled hand.

"Now don't you go playing the shy young woman who gets embarrassed by their love life. I know better, especially when it comes to the young people nowadays. They're much more open and honest about love than my generation ever was. So, how are you and that nice young man—what's his name, Norton—Ralph Norton doing?"

Melanie noticed the way Miriam pronounced Ralph's name, as if she were tasting something that might be spoiled. There was intelligence behind those carefully made-up eyes, and Melanie realized she was dealing with someone who missed very little.

"Mrs. Palmer. You're familiar with the old saying that discussing happiness often undermines it. Well, I feel that way."

Melanie noticed a quick change in Mrs. Palmer's expression that was so subtle only someone trained in reading human nature would catch it. It shifted from a warm smile to a tense neutral face so fast that blinking would make you miss it. Then the smile came back as if nothing had happened, but something cold flickered behind her eyes, like a shadow crossing the moon.

There was something behind that expression, and Melanie's sixth sense didn't like it—didn't like it at all. The hair on the back of her neck stood up slightly, a primitive warning system alerting her to danger.

"That's an old wives' tale that old wives like me know nothing about," Miriam said with a laugh that didn't quite reach her eyes. "But I do understand what you're saying. But it's wonderful to hear that you are happy because, after all, isn't that what we're all after?"

"Yes, it is." Melanie's response was measured, careful not to reveal too much while gathering as much information as possible.

Mrs. Palmer struggled to her feet, her age showing despite her determination to maintain the illusion of vitality. Melanie helped her get up with the solicitousness expected of a younger woman toward her elder.

"Come, dear. Let's join the others. This party is so perfect. Tell me your secret. Not that I'd steal your secrets, of course."

"The thought never crossed my mind," Melanie replied, though it had crossed her mind several times.

The evening progressed as expected, with conversation flowing as freely as the wine. Everyone was having a great time, sharing stories and jokes that grew more risqué as the alcohol took effect. But Melanie could feel time slipping away, and she changed her plan slightly, deciding to go directly to the men outside on the back patio where they had retired for cigars and brandy.

The air on the covered patio was thick with billowing clouds of smoke from expensive Cuban cigars that had been liberated from Phil's humidor. The men stood in small groups, their voices carrying the confidence of people accustomed to power and the easy camaraderie that came with shared success.

Melanie cruised around the patio like a diplomatic hostess, sidling up to some, hugging others, and making most of them laugh at double entendre jokes that titillated their crusty old imaginations. She had learned the art of flirtation from watching her mother navigate these same social waters, and she wielded it now like a surgeon's scalpel—precise, effective, and just dangerous enough to get attention.

Phil Spenser had already indicated which of the men were pro-Ralph during their pre-party strategy session. Most of the board respected Ralph's competence and appreciated his contributions to FASTRAK's success. But there were two holdouts, two men who held the real power and who seemed determined to see Ralph destroyed.

She decided, especially after the troubling interaction with Mrs. Palmer, to go straight to the sources of opposition. It was Clyde Barnett and G. Gordon Palmer—these were the two she had to work on, or her efforts would be futile.

She noticed the time was now slipping by quicker than she had hoped, and the men would soon be joining their wives for coffee and dessert. Clyde Barnett was sitting by himself in a corner of the patio, drinking brandy from a crystal snifter and smoking his cigar with the contentment of a man who had enjoyed a perfect meal.

Melanie sat down next to him, closer than she normally would but close enough not to be overheard by the others. The intimate proximity was calculated to make him feel special, chosen for a private conversation that would stroke his ego.

He'd always been an affable old man, and Melanie genuinely liked his carefree, jovial personality. He reminded her of a favorite uncle who had died when she was young—someone who had always had time for her questions and never made her feel foolish.

But Melanie was surprised when he diplomatically but firmly shut down her efforts at cajoling or wrapping him around her finger. Unlike most men his age, who were susceptible to the attention of a beautiful young woman, Clyde seemed immune to her charms.

"Melanie, dear, you're lovely as always, but I'm an old man who values his quiet time," he said with gentle but unmistakable firmness.

"All I want right now is a little uninterrupted man time, and I hope you'll respect that."

She hugged him with genuine affection, recognizing and respecting his honesty even as it frustrated her plans.

As most of the men began drifting back toward the house to rejoin their wives inside, she was finally left alone with Palmer—the main target of her quest and the man with the most power to help or hurt Ralph Norton.

She blocked his way with her body, hooking his rather large meaty arm and leading him toward the back of the patio where they could talk without being overheard. He went along with the beautiful young woman knowingly, showing her an amused but insightful expression on his face as he puffed on his cigar.

Palmer was nobody's fool, and his eyes held the cunning intelligence that had made him one of Houston's most successful businessmen. He knew exactly what she was doing and seemed to be enjoying the game.

"I remember you when you were a rambunctious young girl, always playing tricks on people and laughing at their surprised looks," said Palmer, his voice carrying genuine fondness for memories of her childhood.

"I remember you when you were very handsome, slimmer, and a real ladies' man. What happened?" Melanie's retort was delivered with a mischievous smile that took any sting out of the words.

Palmer laughed uproariously, a deep belly laugh that shook his considerable frame. He had to put his cigar down because he couldn't control himself, and his eyes watered with mirth. Melanie was too clever and quick-witted to be anything but entertaining, and Palmer appreciated wit almost as much as he appreciated power.

"Well, I can tell you this, young lady. If I were forty years younger and slimmer and smarter, your looks would have turned my head in a second."

Melanie did her best to laugh, but it didn't work as well as she'd hoped. She knew she was up against a man who could not be fooled by conventional feminine wiles, someone who every ambitious woman in Houston had probably approached at one time or another.

The rest of the conversation lasted only a few more minutes, centering around whatever mundane topics came to Melanie's mind while she searched for an opening that never materialized. Palmer was a master at social deflection, keeping the conversation light and meaningless until he finally nodded toward the crowd gathering in the living room.

"I can see my wife staring at me, which can only mean one thing: get your ass over here right now or you'll have hell to pay," he said with the rueful tone of a man who had learned to read the signals after decades of marriage.

Melanie walked back with him, making pleasant conversation about nothing in particular, until she suddenly pulled up short, keeping Palmer from rejoining the group. This was her last chance, and she decided to abandon subtlety in favor of confrontation.

"Look, Mr. Palmer, you know as well as I do that Ralph Norton has done nothing wrong, and he is the person who makes FASTRAK run and run successfully, I might add. So, why are you and a few others so against him?"

Palmer's expression changed instantly, like a mask being dropped to reveal the face beneath. He stopped, faced directly toward Melanie, and spoke firmly and with the kind of purpose that brooked no argument.

"No one's against Ralph. We like Ralph, and we know exactly what he's done for FASTRAK. But P.T. Mayo is the CEO. Whether you or anyone else likes that or not doesn't matter because it's a fact and that's the way business works, young lady."

His voice carried the weight of absolute authority, the tone of a man who had made decisions that affected thousands of lives and never lost sleep over them.

"So, let me give you a bit of advice that comes from my heart. This is none of your business, so stay out of it, understand?"

The warning was delivered with paternal firmness, but underneath lay something more challenging—a threat wrapped in velvet but unmistakably genuine.

Melanie put on a wide smile that completely surprised Palmer, a brilliant performance that transformed her face into a mask of innocent acquiescence. Then, she hugged him and kissed him on his left cheek as his wife fumed in the living room, watching the intimate gesture with obvious displeasure.

"Completely, Mr. Palmer, completely," she said with perfect sincerity that fooled no one, least of all Palmer himself.

She led the old man into the ongoing festivities, bringing him directly to his wife with the grace of a hostess ensuring her guests' comfort, all the while smiling as if she'd just had the grandest time ever.

But behind her smile, Melanie's mind was already working on her next move. If she couldn't save Ralph through gentle persuasion, she would have to find another way. The game was far from over, and she had learned valuable information about her opponents that would serve her well in the battles to come.

CHAPTER 14

P.T. Mayo's morning ritual was as precise as clockwork, a carefully choreographed sequence that began each day with the same satisfying sense of dominance. He arrived at Mack Hill Towers at exactly 9:00 AM, his Mercedes sliding into the executive parking space that bore his name in brass letters embedded in the concrete. The building's glass facade reflected the morning sun like a mirror, transforming the corporate headquarters into a gleaming monument to his success.

His corner office on the tenth floor commanded a breathtaking view of downtown Houston's skyline, a vista that never failed to remind him of how far he'd climbed from his days selling Bibles in Kansas. The mahogany desk dominated the room like an altar, its polished surface reflecting the morning light that streamed through floor-to-ceiling windows. His daily schedule lay waiting in its usual spot, arranged with the meticulous precision his secretary had learned to maintain.

But Mayo didn't bother examining the schedule yet. Instead, he performed his morning reconnaissance, walking the perimeter of his domain like a general surveying his kingdom. The view of downtown Houston stretched before him—gleaming towers, busy streets, the urban machinery of commerce and ambition that he'd learned to manipulate with surgical precision.

From his office closet, he retrieved his custom putter, a titanium masterpiece that had cost more than most people's monthly salary. The putting routine was both meditation and metaphor—invisible golf balls rolling across Persian rugs, each stroke a small victory over chaos and uncertainty. The motion calmed his mind while reinforcing his sense of control over every element of his environment.

The morning seemed perfect in its ordinariness—sunlight painting golden rectangles across his office floor, the distant hum of Houston traffic providing a soundtrack of urban prosperity, no crises demanding immediate attention. Just another day in the empire he'd built from ambition and carefully calculated ruthlessness.

He was lining up another phantom putt when he heard the tentative knock on his door. Mayo never answered immediately—why allow anyone to think he wasn't busy enough with important matters to be interrupted by their trivial concerns? The tapping persisted with the kind of polite insistence that suggested someone with genuine authority, someone who couldn't simply be ignored.

When the door swung open unexpectedly, Mayo's irritation flared up until he recognized who had entered. G. Gordon Palmer stood in the doorway like a symbol of old Houston wealth, his expensive suit and silver hair radiating the authority that came from decades of success in the boardroom.

Mayo dropped his putter behind his desk with practiced casualness and moved quickly toward the door, his expression shifting seamlessly from annoyed executive to gracious host.

"I sincerely apologize, Mr. Palmer. I suppose I was so engrossed in my work that I didn't notice the knock on the door. I'm surprised Selma didn't announce you."

Palmer was as accomplished a performer as Mayo, perhaps more so. The older man's face revealed nothing as he assessed the setup of the putting green and the scattered papers, which suggested frantic activity rather than focused productivity.

"She left a note that she'd be back in ten minutes."

"Okay. Well, come on in. Sit down. Can I get you anything? Water, coffee, anything?"

Palmer's response cut through the morning air like a blade wrapped in velvet. "Your resignation," he said, his eyes twinkling with just enough humor to maintain plausible deniability.

The words hit Mayo like a physical blow. His mouth opened and closed soundlessly, his carefully constructed composure crumbling in the face of his worst corporate nightmare. For a moment, he looked less like a CEO and more like a deer caught in approaching headlights.

"Kidding, P.T... Kidding. Can't you take a joke, for God's sake?"

The relief that flooded through Mayo's system was so intense it manifested as hysterical laughter—convulsive sounds that bordered on sobbing, as if his body couldn't decide whether to celebrate or mourn. The laughter built on itself until he could barely breathe, then started again when he thought it had ended.

"All right, all right, P.T., you can stop now. I get that you got it. Well, that's good."

Mayo finally regained enough control to speak, though his voice still carried traces of the shock Palmer's joke had delivered. "You know, Mr. Palmer, I never heard you kid like that. You caught me off guard, which is not an easy feat to accomplish. Good on you. So, what can I do for you on this fine Friday morning?"

Palmer's demeanor shifted subtly, the social pleasantries evaporating as he moved into the serious business that had brought him to Mayo's office. "I came here this morning because I felt it was my duty to inform you of some unpleasant events that happened last evening at Phil Spenser's annual soiree for the board, which is always top-notch."

"I know Phil, and I know his parties are the best."

"Right, but an unusual occurrence took place that I feel I should inform you about."

Mayo leaned forward slightly, his predatory instincts engaged. "Oh, what was that?"

"I had the opportunity to sit down and talk with Phil's daughter, Melanie. Do you know her?"

"Sure, I've met her. Beautiful young lady."

Palmer's smile carried undertones that made Mayo's skin crawl. "Absolutely. And smart as a whip, I might add. Well, she wanted to talk with me, and I'm always in the mood to chat with a good-looking woman, if you know what I mean. Well, after the usual chit-chat, she got down to the subject at hand."

"Which was...?" Mayo's smile felt like a mask that might slip at any moment.

"Ralph Norton."

The name hung in the air between them like a curse. Both men looked at each other with the knowing smiles that suggested layers of understanding neither was willing to articulate directly.

Palmer's voice took on the authority of a man accustomed to having his warnings heeded. "I want you to understand something here P.T. I don't give a damn about anyone's love life or any bullshit office politics. I don't. But what I do care about is the smooth operation of this corporation."

"Then we both have a lot in common, don't we, Mr. Palmer?"

"Perhaps. However, I dislike wrinkles of any kind, whether in my clothes, on women's faces, or especially in the management of FASTRAK. So, let me cut to the chase. I don't enjoy being cornered by anyone, especially not by relatives of other board members. So, suffice it to say, I want whatever is going on between you and Ralph or anyone else in this company to stop, and I mean right now, especially as we are at the zenith of our corporation's growth."

Mayo's response came too quickly, revealing more than he intended. "She's in love with Ralph. That's what it's all about, Mr. Palmer."

"You're not listening to me, P.T. I don't care about anyone's love life. I told you that two minutes ago. Whatever this is, put it behind you and get your ass in gear."

"Got it, Mr. Palmer."

Palmer's final warning carried the weight of ultimate authority. "I hope so, for your sake. Oh, and there's one other thing happening that you should be aware of. Churches around the country are up in arms about our new app. They're blaming it for a sharp drop in church attendance, which in turn means a significant decline in their donations, which... well, you get it. Figure out what to do about all this and take action promptly. We've got a lot of ties with all the churches, and the last thing we need is for them to be upset."

Palmer stood abruptly and walked toward the door without another word, leaving Mayo alone with the wreckage of what had seemed like a perfect morning. The older man's departure felt like a storm front moving through, leaving behind an atmosphere charged with threat and possibility.

The view of downtown Houston suddenly looked less like a kingdom and more like a battlefield.

CHAPTER 15

Rodney Mann's cramped office had become the epicenter of a digital revolution he never could have imagined. His desk disappeared beneath stacks of printouts, social media analytics, and newspaper clippings that documented the viral explosion of the *Word of God* app. The fluorescent lights overhead buzzed with the kind of persistent annoyance that matched his perpetual headache. At the same time, his computer screen flickered with notifications that arrived faster than he could process them.

Thirty-seven Facebook videos. That's what he'd managed to clip from just one social media platform in a single morning, each one documenting the phenomenon that was reshaping American spirituality in real-time. He'd forwarded them all to Ralph Norton, along with an article from the Houston Chronicle by investigative reporter Chin Chin Wah, knowing that Ralph was too buried in financial crises to pay proper attention to the cultural earthquake he'd created.

The reporter's article captured only the surface of what was happening, but even that surface was staggering in its implications. They called themselves "Wordies"—a term that had emerged organically from the user community and spread with the viral efficiency that characterized everything about the app. Singles were using the platform to connect with other spiritually minded individuals, forming groups in cities and towns across America with a speed that defied conventional community-building timelines.

But it wasn't just romantic connections driving the phenomenon. The app had tapped into something deeper, more fundamental—a hunger for personalized spiritual experience that traditional religious institutions had failed to satisfy. Users weren't just finding their Gods; they were discovering others who shared their specific spiritual journeys and gathering to celebrate their digital revelations.

Disenchanted Catholics were forming "New Catholic" groups that emphasized direct divine communication over institutional hierarchy. Progressive Methodists were "regrouping" around interpretations of scripture that their traditional churches couldn't accommodate. Political groups, ethnic communities, and even extremist organizations were abandoning their old dogmas in favor of personalized spiritual guidance that told them exactly what they wanted to hear.

It was like watching a spiritual wildfire consume the established religious landscape, leaving behind something entirely new and potentially dangerous.

The technology behind the phenomenon was Ralph's masterpiece—two years of development and nearly two million dollars in FASTRAK research funds transformed into an application that redefined the relationship between humanity and divinity. The $1,000 price point had seemed astronomical when Ralph first proposed it, but now it looked like a bargain for what amounted to a personal deity.

The app's security was unprecedented. Each purchase was tied to a single user through biometric verification, making it impossible to hack or share. The three initial questions that determined access were deceptively simple but philosophically profound:

1. Do you believe in God?
2. If you don't believe in God, do you want to believe in God?
3. If you don't want to believe in God, what do you want to believe in?

The biometric touchpad that analyzed truth responses was Ralph's stroke of genius—a technology that could detect deception with accuracy that bordered on the supernatural. Users who lied to the app found themselves permanently locked out, a policy that had eliminated fraud while creating an almost mystical aura around the initial setup process.

Conservative estimates put worldwide sales at thirty-five million units, but Rodney suspected the real numbers were much higher. The app's ability to translate biblical quotes into over seven thousand languages has made it accessible to virtually every literate person on Earth, creating a global spiritual network that transcends national and cultural boundaries.

The personalized voice technology was perhaps the most sophisticated element of Ralph's creation. Instead of offering users a menu of pre-recorded options, the app analyzed brainwave patterns, learning styles, and psychological profiles to generate a vocal presence perfectly calibrated to each individual's spiritual needs. The result was a God who spoke in exactly the right tone, at exactly the right volume, with exactly the right emotional resonance to maximize spiritual connection.

Users could engage in real-time dialogue with their digital deity, asking questions that were answered with responses ranging from casual conversation to formal theological discourse. The app had been programmed to handle complex moral and philosophical inquiries with sophistication that often-surpassed traditional religious authorities.

Rodney's phone rang with the insistent tone that meant another media request. This time it was a television reporter looking to schedule a follow-up interview, the kind of investigative journalist who treated every story like a potential Pulitzer Prize winner. He'd already instructed the front desk to deny access to all media representatives—he didn't have time to manage the public relations nightmare that was brewing.

The immediate crisis was the upcoming Wordie Convention at the Houston Convention Arena. Thirty thousand tickets had sold out within hours, with waiting lists that stretched into the hundreds of thousands. The November 17th date had been coordinated with ten other venues across the United States, as well as twenty-four international locations, creating a global event that would be broadcast via satellite and online streaming to millions of additional viewers.

The Houston Arena would serve as the primary broadcasting hub, the spiritual center of what was rapidly becoming a new form of organized religion. But with just three days until the event, Rodney still didn't have a keynote speaker capable of addressing the magnitude of what they'd created.

There was only one choice, though the prospect terrified him more than any professional challenge he'd ever faced. P.T. Mayo would have to be the keynote speaker, which meant Rodney would have to enter the lion's den and convince a man who despised him to take center stage at the most important spiritual event of the decade.

He put on his best suit, combed his thinning hair, and walked toward Mayo's office with the resignation of a man approaching his execution. The secretary nodded him through without announcement—even she understood that some conversations couldn't wait for proper protocols.

Mayo sat behind his massive desk like a king holding court, shuffling papers with theatrical irritation designed to emphasize his importance and everyone else's insignificance.

"Well, what is it, Mann? And for God's sake, make it brief. Can't you see I'm buried here?!" Mayo gestured at the papers before putting them down and motioning for Rodney to sit. "Sit down and speak before I change my mind and kick you out."

"I need your help, sir."

Mayo's laugh was devoid of humor. "Everyone needs my help, so what else is new?"

Rodney took a deep breath and launched into his pitch. "You know about the Wordie convention in three days at the arena. Well, I need a keynote speaker, and I think, sir, that you are the person most qualified to speak about the app and its importance to so many people. Every participating arena in the US is sold out, as well as all the arenas around the world, at fifty dollars per seat, not to mention the cable and online rights. Well, sir, you get my drift."

The revelation of the event's scope hit Mayo like a physical blow. His expression shifted from irritation to shock to the calculating greed that had built his empire. He gestured for Rodney to continue, his eyes already computing the financial and publicity implications.

"Boss, you gotta do this. We need this from you. There's a huge amount of money and publicity involved, and it's all coming our way. Don't you see?"

The pause that followed felt pregnant with possibility. Mayo stood slowly, his face transforming into the predatory smile that his employees had learned to both fear and respect.

"So you want me to be your main speaker? Well, that's fine as long as you write me a powerful speech, for no more than twenty minutes in length, and I'll do it. I've never turned down an opportunity to make our corporation shine. Have the speech ready for me in an hour, and I'll edit it my way. I'll put my touches on it, and it'll be a speech they'll never forget. Got it?"

"Yes, sir. And thank you, sir. I'm sure it will be fantastic."

"Good, now get the hell out of my office. I'm busy."

Rodney practically stumbled over himself in his eagerness to escape, mumbling gratitude as he fumbled with the door handle. The relief of success was overwhelming, but it came with the terrifying knowledge that he'd just committed himself to crafting words that millions would hear of people around the world.

On his way back to his office, he stopped by Ralph's door to share the victory. Ralph sat with his chin in his hand, staring at his computer screen with the glazed expression of a man wrestling with problems that had no solutions.

"Hey, you busy?" Rodney asked.

"No, come on in. I could use a break from this craziness. What's up?"

Rodney closed the door before speaking, understanding intuitively that some conversations required privacy. "Well, Ralphie, I took your advice, and it worked. I couldn't believe it. I gotta say, you really know the old boy? He jumped at the chance to stand in front of the world. I never thought he would do it."

"I figured he would. Good job!"

The high-five they exchanged was weak, perfunctory, two men going through the motions of celebration while privately contemplating the enormity of what they'd set in motion. As Rodney left, Ralph returned to his computer screen and the financial irregularities that were giving him a deep, persistent pain in his gut.

Something was very wrong with FASTRAK's books, and Ralph was beginning to suspect that the corruption went much deeper than missing funds.

CHAPTER 16

The silence that followed Rodney's departure felt oppressive, pressing down on Ralph like a massive weight of accumulated guilt and unacknowledged fear. He locked his office door with deliberate care, creating a barrier between himself and the corporate world that suddenly felt alien and threatening. His desk chair received him like a confessional booth as he settled back and stared at the wall opposite his desk—blank white paint that seemed to reflect the emptiness he felt growing inside his chest.

The longer he stared, the more his entire life seemed to unfold before him like a catalog of failures and betrayals. Every decision he'd made, every person he'd hurt through action or inaction, came flooding back with the kind of clarity that arrives only in moments of absolute crisis. The fluorescent lights overhead hummed with mechanical indifference, their harsh illumination exposing truths he'd spent years trying to avoid.

Nothing felt right anymore. In his enforced isolation, the world had finally caught up with him, and he could feel it ravaging his body and soul with relentless efficiency. Sure, he'd helped people—millions of them, if the app's user statistics were accurate. The *Word of God* had provided comfort, guidance, and spiritual connection to individuals who traditional religious institutions had abandoned. That was something.

But the cost had been devastating. Sandi, brilliant and loving Sandi, had withered away while he obsessed over algorithms and user interfaces. His parents, disappointed by his rejection of their faith, had drifted out of his life entirely. And now he knew with sickening certainty that he was hurting Melanie, the one person who'd offered him a chance at redemption.

How could he claim to have a soul when he didn't even believe in God? The question had tormented him for months, but now it felt urgent, existential. His app—the great technological achievement of his career—seemed to be turning against him. The voice of his personal AI God was telling him to kill someone, which should have been impossible given the safeguards he'd built into the system.

Had he somehow fooled his creation into believing he was a person of faith? Was there some unknown flaw in the AI's truth-detection algorithms that had allowed deception to corrupt the entire system? Logic told him that wasn't possible—the biometric verification was virtually infallible, having been tested and retested until he was certain of its accuracy.

But if it wasn't a technical error, what was it? Ralph had always viewed the world as fundamentally hostile, a battlefield where survival required constant vigilance and moral compromise. Perhaps his cynicism had seeped into the very code he'd written, creating a digital deity that reflected his darkness rather than any divine light.

The phone rang at that moment of maximum vulnerability, its electronic shriek cutting through his psychological spiral like a knife. The sound seemed different somehow—sharper, more urgent, as if the device itself sensed the importance of whatever message it carried. Maybe it was his paranoid state of mind, or perhaps he'd developed the kind of sixth sense that comes to people living on the edge of catastrophe.

His first instinct was to ignore it. Let them call back when he was in a better emotional state, when he could trust himself to maintain the facade of competent leadership that his position required. But the insistent ringing seemed to grow louder with each repetition, demanding attention with the persistence of an alarm clock in hell.

When he finally looked at the caller ID, his stomach twisted into a knot, making it difficult for him to breathe. Selma Thompson, P.T. Mayo's secretary. The one person whose calls always meant trouble, whose voice carried the authority of the man who held Ralph's career in his hands.

He picked up the receiver and listened in silence, waiting for whatever verdict was about to be delivered.

"Mr. Norton, please come at once to Mr. Mayo's office. It's very important. Hello, Mr. Norton, are you there? Mr. Norton?"

The words hit him like bullets, each syllable carrying the weight of professional execution. He managed to find his voice, though it sounded foreign to his ears.

"Yes, I'm here, Selma."

"Can you come immediately? Mr. Mayo wants you in his office."

"Yes, I'll come over... thank you."

Everything about this summons felt wrong. All the work he'd done to make FASTRAK successful, all the innovations and financial improvements that had transformed the company from a struggling religious novelty business into a global powerhouse—all of it was about to be swept away by whatever accusations Mayo had prepared.

Ralph closed his eyes and bowed his head, feeling the weight of his approaching doom settle around his shoulders like a funeral shroud. When he opened them again, he was staring at the phone as if it were a venomous snake that had somehow found its way onto his desk.

Take a deep breath, Ralph, he told himself. *Don't let him push you around anymore. Don't pray for forgiveness, don't grovel, don't beg, and don't give in, no matter what he has to say.*

Whatever was about to happen would happen regardless of his preferences or fears. The only thing he could control was his response to Mayo's inevitable attack. He straightened his suit jacket, brushed back his graying hair, and arranged his face into an expression of benign nonchalance that he knew wouldn't fool anyone but might at least preserve some shred of dignity.

The walk to Mayo's office felt like a condemned man's final journey. Selma Thompson nodded and smiled as he approached, her expression revealing nothing about the drama that was about to unfold. Maybe that was what distinguished the best secretaries—the ability to know everything while appearing to know nothing, to maintain perfect discretion even when witnessing the destruction of careers.

But Ralph knew something she didn't. He knew that he disliked her almost as much as he disliked her boss. That smugness, that carefully calculated affability, made him physically ill. She was complicit in every humiliation Mayo had inflicted, every professional assassination the man had orchestrated.

The air around Mayo's office felt heavy with unspoken threats. Even the color of the door seemed ominous, as if the wood itself had absorbed years of corporate violence and was now radiating that malevolence back into the world. Everything about this place disgusted him—the ostentatious displays of wealth, the power games, the systematic destruction of human dignity in service of profit margins.

Ralph clenched his jaw and opened the door, stepping across the threshold into whatever hell P.T. Mayo had prepared for him.

CHAPTER 17

P.T. Mayo's office was designed as a self-enclosed tribute to corporate dominance, every element carefully calibrated to reinforce the power differential between the man behind the desk and anyone who dared to challenge him. The massive mahogany desk sat on a raised platform that elevated it six inches above the visitor chairs, a psychological manipulation so obvious it would have been laughable if it weren't so effective.

Ralph entered the office and took his seat in one of the deliberately uncomfortable chairs, facing Mayo across an expanse of polished wood that seemed to stretch like an ocean between them. Mayo appeared busy with paperwork, shuffling documents with the theatrical precision of a man who wanted his importance to be apparent to any observer.

Sunlight streamed through the blinds behind Mayo's elevated position, creating a backlit silhouette that made it nearly impossible to read his facial expressions. Ralph tried shielding his eyes with his hands, but the glare was relentless, turning Mayo into a dark figure haloed with hostile light.

The psychological game was transparent and infuriating. Ralph stood up without permission, walked around the perimeter of the desk, and closed the blinds with deliberate calm. It was a small act of rebellion, but one that established his refusal to be manipulated by amateur theatrics.

Mayo took no notice of this territorial violation, finally setting down his pen and arranging his meaningless papers into neat piles. When he looked up, his smile carried the predatory satisfaction of a hunter who'd successfully lured his prey into the perfect position.

"Well, Mr. Norton, I suppose you want to know why I called you in today?"

Ralph's response was carefully neutral, designed to reveal nothing about his emotional state. "Not really. I don't concern myself with things like that."

"You should."

"I figured you'd tell me about it before long. So..."

Mayo's next words were delivered with the casual cruelty of a man who enjoyed inflicting psychological wounds. "Pretty calm for a man on the brink."

"The brink of what?"

"Unemployment."

Ralph felt something cold settle in his chest, but his voice remained steady. "I've been unemployed before. Not a big thing for me."

The two men stared at each other across the space between predator and prey, each measuring the other's resolve. Mayo nodded and smirked, clearly enjoying the power dynamic he'd created. Ralph appeared unconcerned on the surface, but his hands betrayed him, clasped together in his lap, twisting slightly as tension built in the room like atmospheric pressure before a storm.

Mayo noticed the hands and smiled wider, recognizing fear beneath Ralph's carefully constructed facade.

Here's how I see it, Mr. Norton. Your role as our Chief Financial Officer is to oversee our company's financial resources and ensure its stability and viability, both now and in the future. Do we agree on that, Mr. Norton?

"I suppose so, if that's your definition, sure."

Mayo's attack intensified, his voice carrying the authority of absolute corporate power. "And that attitude, and a cavalier attitude it is, is part of the problem. You, Mr. Norton, obviously don't take your responsibilities seriously enough, as the recent disappearance of funds indicates."

The accusation hit Ralph like a physical blow. "What disappearance of funds are you referring to?"

"Look, Mr. Norton—"

Ralph's interruption was soft but pointed, a reminder of their shared history before Mayo had transformed into a corporate monster. "You can call me Ralph, as you've done for fifteen years. It's okay."

The familiarity enraged Mayo, stripping away his carefully constructed authority and reducing him to the petty tyrant he'd always been beneath the expensive suits and corporate titles.

"I'll call you whatever the fuck I want to call you, so just listen until I'm finished."

Mayo stood and began pacing behind his elevated desk, his movements sharp and aggressive, like a caged animal. The afternoon sunlight caught the silver in his hair, transforming him into something that belonged more in a boardroom than any house of worship.

"Just because your ideas have made a few dollars for FASTRAK doesn't give you a pass on doing your primary job around here, which is to watch every fucking dollar that comes in and goes out to make sure we stay financially successful. You haven't done your job. I've babied you along for many years, too many years, actually, and I'm sick of playing nursemaid to a loser like you, Mr. Norton."

Ralph stood slowly, his composure beginning to crack under the relentless assault. "It's not me that's the loser, sir."

Mayo's response revealed the depth of his psychological cruelty, his willingness to weaponize personal tragedy in service of corporate dominance. "Oh, I see. You think I'm the loser here when, for the past month, you've been moping around here because it's been a year since Sandi's death. Well, get over it, boy. Life goes on."

The mention of Sandi's name transformed something fundamental in Ralph's psychology. His face hardened into planes of granite, his eyes taking on the cold intensity of a man who'd been pushed beyond his breaking point.

"Yes, my wife died a year ago, and yes, I think you're a loser because you don't see the cash cow that's standing right here in front of you and right now. You know damn well that if it weren't for my app, this company would be barely treading water. You know that as well as I do, but you can't deal with it."

Mayo's final words were designed to inflict maximum psychological damage, to destroy not just Ralph's career but his sense of personal worth. "I can deal with anything that happens here because I've got a backbone and you don't. Hell, you don't believe in anything except feeling sorry for yourself because that dead slut wife of yours couldn't take you anymore."

The insult detonated like a bomb in Ralph's consciousness. Years of accumulated rage, months of suppressed grief, and decades of corporate humiliation crystallized into a single moment of pure violence. Ralph launched himself across the desk with the fury of a man who'd finally discovered what he was capable of when pushed beyond all human limits.

The collision was savage and final. Ralph's momentum carried both men backward until Mayo's skull connected with the brass corner of his desk with a sound like a melon splitting open. Blood fountained from the wound as Mayo collapsed to the floor, his body going limp with the sudden finality of a marionette whose strings had been cut.

Ralph stood over the motionless form; his fist still raised in the air like a monument to justified rage. Mayo wasn't breathing, wasn't moving, wasn't doing any of the things that living people do. The CEO lay in a spreading pool of his blood, his silver hair slowly turning crimson.

Ralph held his position for what felt like hours but was probably only seconds, suspended in the moment between action and consequence. He'd just killed someone—someone whom everyone knew he hated, someone who'd wanted to destroy him and everything he'd worked for. The knowledge settled into his consciousness like lead settling into water.

Gradually, his rational mind reasserted control over his emotional chaos. If he walked out of the office calmly, without raising an alarm, no one would discover the body for at least an hour. They would think that a difficult meeting had concluded, that decisions had been made, that business had been conducted in the usual fashion.

Before leaving, Ralph forced himself to straighten the desk and restore order to the scene. He arranged Mayo's papers in neat piles, returned the pens to their holders, and eliminated any apparent signs of violence. The blood on the floor would be harder to explain, but maybe people would assume Mayo had suffered some medical emergency.

Ralph took several deep breaths, composed his features into an expression of resigned professionalism, and walked calmly toward the door. As he passed Selma Thompson's desk, she raised one eyebrow in mild curiosity but maintained her usual expression of smug satisfaction.

So far, so good.

The hardest part was over. Now came the tough challenge: disappearing completely before anyone discovered what he'd done.

CHAPTER 18

Ralph moved through the FASTRAK offices like a ghost haunting his own former life, his eyes cataloging every detail with the hyperaware intensity of a man who knew he was seeing everything for the last time. The familiar sights and sounds that had once provided comfort now felt surreal—the smell of coffee brewing in the break room, the sound of keyboards clicking in distant cubicles, the low murmur of conversations that would continue long after he'd vanished from their world.

His eyes darted constantly, penetrating the faces of passing colleagues, reading their body language for any sign that they suspected what had just happened in Mayo's office. The security system's red lights blinked with mechanical indifference, the alarm sensors that would soon be searching for him showing no awareness of the violence that had just occurred on the floors above.

To his amazement, everything looked exactly as it always had. Colleagues moved through their routines with the same casual efficiency they'd displayed every day for years. The only difference was internal—the fundamental change in how Ralph experienced the world now that he'd crossed the line from law-abiding citizen to killer.

The thought of seeking medical help for Mayo crossed his mind briefly, but he dismissed it almost immediately. Why risk exposure when the man had looked as dead as any corpse Ralph had ever seen? And he'd only seen one corpse in his life—Sandi, peaceful in their bed on the morning when he'd discovered her final escape from a world that had become unbearable.

But Mayo's words about Sandi had destroyed any possibility of compassion or mercy. The man was dead, and in many ways, so was the Ralph Norton who'd built a career at FASTRAK.

When colleagues passed him in the hallway, Ralph managed to produce his usual smile and wave, though he couldn't resist glancing at the large clock in the lobby. Time might not be important now, but it would become crucial once Mayo's body was discovered and the investigation began.

This would be the last time he'd ever see Mack Hill Towers, so he wanted to commit the view to memory. He stood, holding the handrail that circled the open lobby, which stretched two levels below him and eight levels above him—a deep cavern, home to corporate ambition that had once filled him with pride. Now it looked like a mausoleum, a beautiful tomb for the man he had been.

Drew Shane approached from behind, patting Ralph on the back with the casual familiarity of a longtime colleague. "Hey, Ralphie. Don't jump yet. We need you, man!"

"Funny," Ralph replied, managing a smile that felt like it belonged to someone else.

But jokes like that carried consequences that no one could predict. Drew laughed heartily and continued toward his office in product sales, utterly unaware that his casual comment had triggered something dark in Ralph's psychology. The words echoed in his head like a mantra: "Don't jump yet, Ralphie. Don't jump yet, Ralphie. Don't jump yet, Ralphie."

The repetition was maddening, a psychological echo that seemed to bounce around inside his skull like a ricocheting bullet. Ralph edged closer to the balcony railing, looking down at the marble floor four stories below and wondering if Drew's joke had been more prophetic than funny.

But there was no point in contemplating dramatic endings. He had to get out of Mack Hill Towers immediately, before someone discovered Mayo's body and the building went into lockdown. Ralph retrieved his backpack from his office and walked toward the exit with the measured pace of a man whose workday had ended a little early.

The only way to survive what had just happened was to disappear completely—to vanish from everyone he knew and stay hidden until... when? The time would never be right for a murderer to return to everyday life. Maybe the attack had been accidental, maybe he'd intended to kill Mayo all along. He honestly wasn't sure, and the uncertainty was almost as bad as the guilt.

The drive home passed in a dissociative haze, as if he were watching someone else's life unfold on a movie screen. No sound penetrated his consciousness, no landmarks looked familiar, and no colors registered in his vision. It was a black-and-white film played in silence, and he was both actor and audience for a tragedy that had no ending.

His neighborhood in Tiara Woods was quiet with the artificial tranquility of suburban afternoon. Neighbors were at work or engaged in their private dramas, oblivious to the fact that a killer was driving through their carefully manicured streets. Ralph pulled into his garage and closed the door behind him, probably for the last time.

The house had always reminded him too much of Sandi anyway. Every room held memories of their life together, shadows of the happiness they'd shared before his obsession with the app had poisoned everything between them. Maybe leaving would be a mercy for both of them—him and her ghost.

He packed efficiently, taking only what he could carry in his backpack: his laptop, basic clothing, money, and credit cards. He left the utilities connected and the doors unlocked, so that anyone investigating would think he was simply away on business rather than gone forever.

Before leaving, Ralph noticed the amulet —a gift from the homeless man who'd somehow seen through his corporate facade.

He picked up the small piece of jewelry. He examined it closely: a Star of David with a crucifix nested inside, representing some spiritual synthesis that he didn't fully understand.

Ralph put the chain around his neck and smiled at the amulet, as if it were alive —a talisman that might protect him in the dark world he was about to enter. Then he left Tiara Woods for good, driving toward a future that held no certainty except the knowledge that P.T. Mayo would never hurt anyone again.

Okay, Ralphie, he thought as the suburbs gave way to urban decay. *Start thinking the way you always did when the world was against you, like it is now. Think, Ralphie, think.*

The homeless man's amulet felt warm against his chest, a small comfort in a world that had suddenly become very cold indeed.

CHAPTER 19

P.T. Mayo was hard-headed in many ways, but the throbbing pain that radiated from the back of his skull reminded him that even the most stubborn man had limits. The taste of blood filled his mouth as consciousness returned in waves, each surge bringing with it the sharp clarity of a man who'd just dodged death by inches.

He wasn't dead at all. Lying there on the polished hardwood floor of his executive office, feeling the warm stickiness of his blood beneath his head, P.T. Mayo was more awake than he'd been in years. When he shifted position, his wounded skull tapped against the brass corner of his mahogany desk leg, sending a fresh spike of agony through his nervous system that made him wince and curse under his breath.

But pain brought clarity. His memory was clearing like fog burning off in morning sunlight, and his predatory mind kicked into overdrive.

His decision crystallized with the cold efficiency that had carried him from Kansas Bible salesman to corporate titan. He would behave as if nothing had happened, as if this entire ugly scene was merely a figment of someone else's imagination if word leaked about the scuffle—about Ralph Norton laying hands on a CEO—G. Gordon Palmer would be more than unhappy. Palmer would be apoplectic, and an apoplectic Palmer meant investigations, board meetings, and uncomfortable questions about leadership stability.

No. This would be a minor workplace disagreement that had been resolved professionally. And if somehow someone had witnessed what happened, he would deny it all with the practiced conviction of a man who'd built his empire on strategic lies.

Mayo lifted himself from the floor with careful deliberation, his movements measured and controlled despite the pounding in his head. The office felt different now—the leather furniture and oil paintings seemed to watch him with new awareness, as if they'd witnessed something that transformed the very nature of the space. Blood had spattered across several papers on his desk, creating abstract patterns that looked almost artistic in the afternoon light streaming through his windows.

He moved to his private bathroom, studying his reflection in the medicine cabinet mirror with clinical detachment. The face that stared back was bruised but not broken—a few cuts along his hairline where his skull had connected with the desk, some swelling around his left eye, but nothing that couldn't be explained away as a minor accident. Perhaps a stumble in the parking garage, or a collision with a low-hanging branch during his morning jog.

The cleanup process was methodical, almost ritualistic in nature. He washed the blood from his hair and scalp, applied antiseptic to the cuts, and used concealer from his secretary's desk drawer to minimize the bruising. When he was finished, the damage was barely noticeable—just another successful businessman who'd had a minor mishap.

But where was Ralph Norton, and what was he doing? Mayo's first instinct was to pursue, to hunt down the man who'd dared to assault him and extract appropriate revenge. He tried calling Ralph's office extension, then his cell phone, but both went straight to voicemail. The coward was probably halfway to Mexico by now, running like the pathetic weakling he'd always been beneath that innovative facade.

When his intercom buzzed, the sound nearly launched him out of his chair. His nerves were more frayed than he'd realized, his carefully constructed composure cracking around the edges. A glance in his desk mirror showed that the concealer had held just a few minor marks that could be attributed to anything.

"Mr. Mayo?" his secretary's voice filtered through the speaker with its usual professional cheerfulness. "Your three-thirty appointment is here."

"Send them in," he replied, surprised at how steady his voice sounded.

As it turned out, no one seemed to notice anything unusual. His afternoon meetings proceeded without incident, and his dinner with potential investors went smoothly. By evening, he'd almost convinced himself that the entire episode had been a bad dream.

Almost.

Ada Taylor was his next call, but she didn't answer her phone either. The woman had her schedule and priorities, and Mayo's convenience had never been among them. But that would change soon enough. The only way he would finally eliminate Ralph Norton from his world was to eliminate him from his world, wholly and permanently.

Usually, Mayo would take swift action against problems that threatened his reputation or his company's stability. He'd built his career on decisive leadership, on cutting out cancers before they could metastasize. He scolded himself for procrastinating, for allowing sentiment and corporate politics to delay what should have been a simple business decision.

That mistake would not be repeated.

• • • •

MEANWHILE, IN THE TRENDY shopping district of Oak Cliff, Melanie Spenser sat across from her oldest friend in a restaurant that specialized in farm-to-table cuisine and the kind of intimate conversations that required privacy. Jo Angleton had been her confidante since childhood, the keeper of secrets and the dispenser of uncomfortable truths that only the closest friendships could withstand.

Tobi's occupied a converted warehouse space, all exposed brick and Edison bulb lighting, with herbs growing in mason jars on every table. The lunch crowd consisted mainly of young professionals and artistic types, people who had time for leisurely meals and philosophical discussions about life choices and relationship dynamics.

They'd arrived at the same time, embracing with the warm familiarity of women who'd weathered adolescence and early adulthood together. But Melanie's body language spoke of tension held barely in check, of words that needed to be spoken but couldn't be overheard by casual eavesdroppers.

Jo understood immediately, guiding their conversation toward innocuous topics until the hostess led them to a secluded corner table at the back of the dining room. The acoustics here were better, the sight lines limited, and the chance of being overheard minimal.

When their food finally arrived—grilled salmon for Jo, a quinoa salad for Melanie—Jo noticed that her friend was performing surgery on her meal rather than eating it. Melanie poked at the grains with her fork, rearranging them into patterns that spoke of a mind too agitated for appetite.

"How's your dad, Mel?" Jo asked, testing the waters.

"Oh, he's fine. You know..." Melanie's voice trailed off, her attention focused on something beyond the restaurant's walls.

"How's Ralph?"

The fork clattered against the plate with metallic finality. Melanie's eyes, when they met Jo's, carried the wild look of a woman standing at the edge of a precipice. They darted around the restaurant's interior, cataloging exits and potential threats with the paranoia that had become her constant companion.

Finally, Jo reached across the table and took control. "The thing is, Mel, if there's a problem, I can help. Haven't I always helped when you needed me?"

Melanie's laugh was bitter, brittle. "There is no problem. And that's the problem."

Jo frowned, parsing the contradiction. "You got me on that one."

"Ralph is under siege by the whole world," Melanie said, her voice dropping to barely above a whisper. "The world loves his new app. Sales are so high that they're struggling to keep up with them. But the worst part is that his boss is jealous and is doing everything in his considerable power to make Ralph's life miserable enough so he'll quit."

"So, do something about it. I mean, you love him, don't you?"

"Totally." The word came out like a confession. "But there's nothing I can do. I've tried supporting him with my dad and other board members, but it's futile."

Jo's response was characteristically direct. "So, what you're saying is that you're giving up. Is that it?"

The accusation hung between them like a challenge. Melanie's shoulders sagged under its weight, and for a moment she looked older than her twenty-eight years.

"I wouldn't put it exactly that way, but yes. I guess I am giving up. My hands are tied."

Jo's expression hardened with the kind of tough love that had sustained their friendship through two decades of triumphs and disasters. "Most women I know would be ecstatic if they found the right man in their lives. Many would say they'd do anything for that right guy. But, in reality, most women don't have the determination or the guts to do everything they need to do to help their man."

She leaned forward, her voice gaining intensity. "But, as long as I've known you, I've never seen you back away from a challenge that you faced, no matter how difficult or destructive the challenge was."

"Pathetic, isn't it?" Melanie said, her self-recrimination evident.

"You know I never participate in pity parties, and I'm certainly not going to start now." Jo's tone brooked no argument. "So, eat your food, straighten your back, and quit all this bull crap. You're too smart not to figure out what to do and too brave not to do it. So..."

The transformation was subtle but unmistakable. Melanie's posture straightened, her eyes sharpened, and a smile began to spread across her face—not the defeated expression she'd worn moments before, but the calculating grin of a woman who'd just remembered exactly who she was.

Once again, her friend had delivered the perfect wake-up call at precisely the right moment.

CHAPTER 20

Thursday morning at FASTRAK crackled with an energy that transformed the usually sedate corporate environment into something resembling a campaign headquarters on election day. People scurried through the corridors of Mack Hill Towers with purpose and barely contained excitement, their conversations punctuated by nervous laughter and the constant buzz of cell phones updating social media feeds.

November 17th had arrived—the day that would either cement FASTRAK's position as the world's preeminent spiritual technology company or expose the *Word of God* app as an elaborate fraud. Around the globe, Wordie Conventions were synchronizing their broadcasts, testing equipment that would link dozens of venues in real-time communion, fueling speculation that had transformed social media into a digital revival tent.

Ralph Norton had taken a short leave of absence, at least according to his boss's carefully worded memo to the staff. The official explanation cited personal matters requiring immediate attention, but the rumor mill ground out more colorful theories involving everything from nervous breakdowns to federal investigations.

P.T. Mayo stood at the center of the controlled chaos like a conductor preparing for the symphony of his career. His executive suite had been transformed into a staging area, with speech coaches, wardrobe consultants, and image specialists moving through the space with the choreographed precision of a presidential campaign.

The latest sales projections were staggering, numbers that would have seemed fictional just months earlier. Every venue hosting a Wordie Convention had sold out, with waiting lists stretching into the tens of thousands. The pay-per-view numbers were approaching

Super Bowl levels, driven by curiosity, faith, and the kind of viral marketing that money couldn't buy.

Mayo stood before his bathroom mirror, practicing the speech that would define his legacy, while the sales department manager read revenue figures that continued to climb with each passing hour. The numbers were almost abstract in their magnitude—millions of users, billions in projected revenue, market penetration that exceeded their most optimistic forecasts.

His tailor, a nervous man whose reputation depended entirely on making influential people look powerful, fussed over the final alterations to Mayo's new suit. The navy-blue double-breasted jacket was cut to minimize his expanding waistline while projecting authority, complemented by a flame-red tie that would photograph well under television lights.

"Have it back here by noon, or you'll never get another piece of business from me as long as I live. Do you understand?" Mayo's voice carried the casual cruelty of a man accustomed to absolute obedience.

The tailor, pins protruding from his mouth like a porcupine's quills, bobbed his head frantically. "Oh, don't you worry, Mr. Mayo. I'll be here on time, don't you worry."

Once the fitting was complete and Mayo had changed back into his regular clothes, he returned to his mirror for continued speech preparation. Rodney Mann hovered nearby, a legal pad in his hands, ready to capture any last-minute changes that might occur to his mercurial boss.

"Rodney, I like the speech, but I want one specific change."

"Yes, sir. What is it?"

Mayo's reflection stared back at him with the cold satisfaction of a man about to claim his rightful place in history. "The message is good and the words are good, but wherever you've written the words 'we' or 'FASTRAK,' I want you to change those to 'I.'"

Rodney's face betrayed a flicker of confusion. "But sir, don't you think that our company's name should be included to give us more publicity and brand identification?"

The explosion was swift and vicious. "Fuck you and fuck brand identification. Just make the damn changes like I wanted and do it now." Mayo hurled the speech at Rodney's face, the pages scattering like startled birds. "How the fuck can you call yourself a marketing director and not know that I, me, P.T. Mayo, am this fucking corporation? Now get the fuck out of here because the sight of you is making me sick. And tell that gay assistant of yours to bring it back to me in fifteen minutes. At least he makes me laugh at the sight of him."

The script was revised with trembling hands, the suit returned with minutes to spare, and Mayo's personal barber worked miracles with pomade and precision cutting. A limousine waited in the executive parking area, black and gleaming like a hearse designed for royalty.

At the Houston Convention Arena, the production crew made final adjustments to lighting rigs and sound systems that would carry Mayo's voice to millions of listeners worldwide. The agenda was set: his keynote address, testimonials from couples who'd found love through the app, and a finale featuring the Houston Choral Society performing music specially commissioned for the event.

Everything was perfectly orchestrated. But P.T. Mayo had his plans, ideas that had been percolating in his megalomaniacal mind for days. He would take this event and launch it into the stratosphere, transforming himself from a successful business person into something approaching an oracle.

He called his secretary from his private line. "Is the limo here?"

"Yes, sir. Waiting for you in front of the lobby."

"Are the photographers ready?"

"They're all out there waiting to capture the moment."

"Okay, I'll be leaving now. Let them know to be ready."

P.T. Mayo donned his long black overcoat, the fabric hanging from his shoulders like a cape. FASTRAK employees who'd stayed past their shifts lined the balconies and lobby areas, creating an impromptu audience for his grand exit. As the elevator doors opened to reveal the crowd, Mayo favored them with his most enigmatic smile—part benediction, part warning.

The limousine ride to the arena passed in contemplative silence. Rain drummed against the windows, but even the weather couldn't diminish the magnitude of what was about to unfold. Somewhere in the city, thousands of believers were converging on the arena, ready to commune with their digital gods under his guidance.

They were his now. The thought brought him a satisfaction so profound it bordered on the spiritual.

CHAPTER 21

Even for a man whose ego had been carefully cultivated and fed for decades, what P.T. Mayo witnessed at the Houston Convention Arena defied his most grandiose expectations. The crowd wasn't out of control in any conventional sense—there was no violence, no shouting, no chaos. Instead, there was something far more powerful: thirty thousand people united in a kind of spiritual ecstasy that made the air itself seem to vibrate with collective faith.

The sound hit him first—not the roar of a typical crowd, but something deeper and more primal. Thirty thousand voices raised not in anger or excitement, but in joy so pure it seemed to transform the very architecture of the space. Ever the consummate performer, Mayo forced himself to remain composed despite the shock that threatened to buckle his knees.

His initial reaction was kept tightly controlled, buried beneath decades of practice at projecting confidence in situations that overwhelmed him. But privately, he marveled at what he'd wrought. He'd never imagined that a simple smartphone application could create this level of devotion, this depth of spiritual hunger satisfied by technology he'd stolen from a better man.

His eyes darted across the arena, trying to comprehend the scope of what he was seeing. Banners hung from the rafters proclaiming love for personalized deities, couples embraced while staring at their phones, and children sat quietly beside parents who radiated the kind of peace that organized religion had promised but rarely delivered.

The head of the production staff appeared at his elbow, guiding Mayo toward a small holding room behind the main stage before the crowd could spot him and transform reverence into bedlam. His speech was folded neatly in his inside pocket, though he suspected the words he'd memorized would prove inadequate for what was about to unfold.

Small beads of sweat gathered on his palms and wrists despite the arena's air conditioning. The magnitude of the moment was finally penetrating his carefully constructed armor of confidence. When he told the production team he was ready, his voice carried only the slightest tremor.

The arena master took the podium—a platform raised eight feet above the main floor, ensuring visibility throughout the cavernous space. As soon as he appeared, the crowd fell silent with the precision of a symphony orchestra responding to its conductor's baton. These people had come to hear words that mattered, to commune with the source of their digital salvation.

Mayo watched the scene unfold on a closed-circuit monitor, studying his audience with the calculating gaze of a predator. Roughly three-quarters of the crowd were women, he noted, their faces turned upward with expressions of rapture that reminded him uncomfortably of religious paintings depicting martyrdom and ecstasy.

The speech was changing in his mind as he watched, adapting to the demographic reality before him. He would tailor his message to resonate with their particular hunger, their specific need for spiritual connection in an increasingly disconnected world.

Giant monitors suspended from the arena's ceiling displayed feeds from synchronized events around the globe—Kansas City, Atlanta, Los Angeles, London, Tokyo—dozens of venues connected by technology, unified by the promise of personalized divinity. Mayo saw dollar signs multiplying exponentially, while the attendees saw nothing but the face of their digital God.

The ceremony began with practiced reverence. The arena master acknowledged the crowd's devotion and introduced P.T. Mayo to both the local audience and the millions watching worldwide.

Mayo's entrance was choreographed like a heavyweight championship bout—the arena lights dimmed to blackness; a single spotlight followed his progress down the center aisle while gospel music swelled from speakers designed to make mere mortals sound divine.

The crowd's response was immediate and overwhelming. They roared approval while embracing neighbors and strangers alike, creating a tide of humanity that threatened to sweep Mayo off his feet as he climbed toward the podium. He maintained his smile throughout the chaos, projecting the kind of serene confidence that transformed ordinary men into prophets.

He reached the podium and cleared his throat, the sound amplified and transmitted to millions of listeners hanging on his every word.

"My friends..." His pause was calculated for maximum impact. "I'm a Wordie just like you are, and my God told me to come here and share my love with you..."

The arena erupted. Thirty thousand people leaped from their seats, jumping and shouting and declaring their love for deities who lived in their smartphones. The building itself seemed to shake under the force of their collective ecstasy, vibrations that Mayo could feel through his bones.

"And I promise you one thing, my friends," he continued when the chaos subsided.

The silence that followed was absolute, pregnant with anticipation. In Kansas City, another sold-out arena held its collective breath, waiting for the revelation that would justify their faith in technology over tradition.

But in that Kansas City crowd, one older woman stood frozen in the middle section, her face drained of color as she stared at the giant screen displaying Mayo's image. Her companions noticed the change, saw her hands begin to tremble as recognition dawned with the force of a physical blow.

P.T. Mayo milked the moment, letting silence stretch until it became unbearable. Then he delivered his prophecy:

"There's a miracle coming, my friends of God. I'm going to bring God even closer to you, closer than ever before."

The chant began spontaneously: "We Love God, We Love God, We Love God." Thirty thousand voices in Houston, matched by thousands more around the world, creating a symphony of digital devotion.

"Yes, you love your God, and he loves you," Mayo proclaimed, his arms spread wide in benediction. "But just wait. If you think God is close to you now, you ain't seen nothin' yet. Mark my words, friend, mark my words."

The crowd in Houston stormed the stage, lifting Mayo onto their shoulders and carrying him around the arena like a conquering hero. He'd become something beyond a CEO, beyond a business person—he'd transformed himself into a prophet for the digital age.

In Kansas City, the older woman threw her program to the floor and forced her way through the surging crowd toward the exits. Her eyes bulged with recognition and rage, her jaw muscles clenched into knots of fury and betrayal. She pushed past the lingering believers as if on a new mission.

CHAPTER 22

Paranoia had become Ralph Norton's constant companion, a shadowy presence that transformed every ordinary moment into a potential threat. He'd spent the day driving aimlessly through Houston's sprawling metropolitan area, taking circuitous routes through the suburbs north and west, educating himself on the geography of invisibility: which parks allowed overnight parking without attracting police attention, and which neighborhoods had enough transient traffic to hide one more anonymous vehicle.

When paranoia takes control of your life, you spend more time studying your rearview mirror than the road ahead. Each glance revealed nothing suspicious, but Ralph had developed enough respect for professional surveillance to know that the best followers were the ones you never saw. If someone was tracking him—and his gut insisted someone was—they were good enough to remain invisible.

The irony wasn't lost on him that his neighbor Tom Traxell, whom he'd glimpsed watching from his front window as Ralph fled Tiara Woods, probably knew more about Ralph's whereabouts than any professional investigator. The man was a well-known television weatherman, financially secure and socially prominent. Yet, he seemed to derive perverse satisfaction from monitoring his neighbors' activities with the dedication of a Cold War spy.

Preoccupied with surveillance concerns, Ralph had missed the highway exit that would have taken him to Little Miami, his favorite Cuban restaurant. Perhaps it was fortunate—he'd eaten there frequently enough that running into acquaintances was virtually guaranteed, and invisibility had become his primary survival strategy.

Instead, he found himself driving north toward Conroe, a growing suburb that retained enough rural character to offer genuine solitude. The landscape reminded him of what Tiara Woods had looked like before developers transformed it into a monument to planned community living.

Melanie's face kept intruding on his thoughts, each memory triggering a complex mixture of love and guilt that threatened to overwhelm his carefully maintained emotional control. He wanted desperately to contact her, to explain what had happened without revealing details that might implicate her in his crimes. But he couldn't risk it yet—not when every phone call might be traced, every communication monitored.

The secluded park he eventually chose featured rustic hiking trails and picnic areas designed for family gatherings, which wouldn't typically occur in November. Texas winters were mild by national standards, but few families chose late autumn for outdoor recreation. Ralph had the place entirely to himself, which suited his current needs perfectly.

His fast-food dinner—a burger and fries from a drive-through window—had grown cold during his extended surveillance checks. He ate mechanically while debating the central question that had tormented him for hours: whether to call Melanie or maintain his isolation until he could guarantee her safety.

She'd been worrying about him since his disappearance, and the knowledge of her distress was almost unbearable. Melanie had always been honest with him, had declared her love openly and without reservation. She deserved better than a mysterious absence and worry.

If he did call, he would limit the conversation to reassurance—he was safe, he needed time to resolve some personal issues, and he would contact her again when circumstances permitted. He wouldn't mention the confrontation with Mayo, nor would he hint at violence or criminal liability. The burden of his guilt was his alone to carry.

But the more profound anguish came from recognizing his hypocrisy. He'd spent years working for a Christian products company while harboring grave doubts about the existence of God. The *Word of God* app had made him wealthy by commodifying faith he didn't share, had created artificial spiritual experiences for millions of users who trusted his technological promises.

Dishonesty and hypocrisy—the two character flaws he'd despised most in others—had become the foundation of his professional success. If God did exist, surely He would understand the complexity of human doubt and the difficulty of maintaining faith in an increasingly secular world. But understanding didn't eliminate the guilt that gnawed at Ralph's conscience like acid.

The question of divine justice had become intensely personal now that he'd committed what he believed to be murder. Spending the rest of his life in prison was simply unacceptable—he would use every resource of intelligence and logic to avoid that fate. But the moral weight of what he'd done would follow him regardless of legal consequences.

He would call Melanie in the morning when his emotional state was more stable, when he could trust himself not to reveal more than was safe. Tonight was for planning, for developing the strategy that would keep him free and her protected.

The secluded picnic area offered an illusion of safety, surrounded by pine woods that whispered with the sounds of nocturnal animals and cooled by the evening air, which carried hints of the approaching winter. Ralph had always been comfortable with solitude—it was one of the traits that had initially attracted Sandi—but this enforced isolation felt different, tinged with desperation rather than a conscious choice.

His last conscious thoughts before sleep overtook him were a mixture of gratitude and guilt—grateful that he'd evaded discovery for another day, guilty that his evasion had cost a man his life. A flash of light in his rearview mirror briefly startled him into full alertness, but it disappeared as quickly as it had appeared, leaving him to wonder if it had been real or imagined.

He reclined his driver's seat as far as it would go and surrendered to exhaustion, praying to whatever deities might be listening that tomorrow would bring answers instead of more questions.

CHAPTER 23

Dawn arrived as a slow drizzle, transforming the park's picnic area into something resembling a swamp. Ralph woke to the sound of rain drumming against his car's roof and the windshield wipers' rhythmic protest against the accumulating moisture. The ground beneath his vehicle had turned into a muddy bog that threatened to trap him if he wasn't careful about his exit strategy.

His car's engine turned over without complaint, and the heater provided blessed relief against the damp chill that had invaded the vehicle overnight. He let the motor idle while he called Melanie, knowing it might be the last contact he could risk for an indeterminate period.

She answered on the second ring, her voice carrying the mixture of relief and accusation that he'd expected. "Ralph? Is that you, honey?"

"Yeah, it's me. You doing okay?"

"Of course, but I've been worried sick about you. Nobody knows where you are or what you're doing. You've scared the life out of me."

The hurt in her voice was almost unbearable. Ralph could hear the windshield wipers' metronome beat in the background of their conversation, marking time toward an inevitable goodbye that neither of them wanted to acknowledge.

"I apologize. It wasn't intentional. Listen, I can't talk very much, but I wanted to tell you a few things before I need to end the call."

"What do you mean, need to end the call? What's this all about?"

Melanie's confusion was painful to hear. She could sense the desperation in his voice, could listen to the mechanical sounds that suggested he was calling from a car rather than a secure location. The realization that he was running from something-or someone—was beginning to dawn on her.

"I love you, Mel. You have to know that. You have to." The words tumbled out in a rush, as if speaking them quickly might somehow lessen their finality. "I'm a complete fraud. I've worked at FASTRAK, and I don't believe in God. It's awful, and what's worse is that I've duped millions of people into thinking that their God belongs to them when I don't even believe in God... I'm a fake and a sham, and I have to sort everything out or..."

"Or what, Ralph?"

He couldn't finish the thought, couldn't voice the possibilities that terrified him most. Instead, he ended the call and immediately powered down his phone, knowing that continued communication would only increase the risk to both of them. Cell phones could be tracked with frightening precision, and he couldn't afford to provide law enforcement with his location.

The drive out of the muddy picnic area required careful navigation, but his car's all-wheel drive system handled the boggy conditions without difficulty. He chose back roads whenever possible, avoiding major highways where license plate readers and traffic cameras might record his passage. Every decision was calculated to minimize his digital footprint, to maintain the anonymity that had become essential to his survival.

His conscience pulled him in multiple directions simultaneously. The guilt over his failure to provide medical assistance to Mayo warred with memories of the man's cruelty and vindictiveness. His inattention to Sandi during their marriage battled with his growing love for Melanie. Past failures competed with present fears in a psychological symphony that threatened to overwhelm his rational planning process.

Religious memories from his Chicago childhood surfaced unexpectedly—synagogue services conducted in Hebrew he didn't understand, ritual objects whose significance remained mysterious, a sense of alienation that had driven him away from organized faith entirely. His parents had been disappointed by his rejection of their traditions, and the resulting estrangement had lasted for years. He wasn't even sure they were still alive.

The voice that had haunted him since Mayo's attack echoed through his thoughts: "If you love me, kill him." The words seemed to come from nowhere and everywhere, a psychological puzzle that demanded a solution. Was it his conscience speaking? A memory of something Sandi had said? The manifestation of guilt over her suicide and his role in driving her to desperation?

Thinking was becoming increasingly complex as exhaustion and stress took their toll. Ralph pushed the questions aside and focused on immediate necessities—finding a safe place to hide, developing a long-term survival strategy, and staying ahead of whatever investigation Mayo's death would inevitably trigger.

An idea had been forming in his mind, still embryonic but growing stronger with each passing hour. The concept involved hiding in plain sight, becoming invisible by joining Houston's army of disposable people—the homeless, the unemployed, the forgotten citizens whom society preferred to ignore.

The Rice Military neighborhood, located south of downtown near Buffalo Bayou, offered the kind of urban anonymity he needed. As morning traffic began building around him, Ralph felt the warm weight of the amulet that hung around his neck—a gift from a homeless man who'd somehow seen past Ralph's executive facade to recognize a kindred spirit.

The face of that man appeared in his memory with startling clarity, and Ralph suddenly understood that his transformation from successful businessman to fugitive had been inevitable from the moment he'd accepted that simple piece of jewelry. Some gifts change the recipient in ways that can't be predicted or controlled.

The morning rush hour traffic provided perfect cover for his approach to downtown Houston. Just another anonymous commuter in a sea of vehicles, indistinguishable from thousands of others except for the terrible knowledge of what he'd done and what he was about to become.

Start thinking, Ralphie, he told himself as the city skyline grew larger in his windshield. *Think like you always did when the world was against you. But this time, think like someone who no longer exists.*

The homeless man's amulet felt warm against his chest—a talisman for the dark transformation that lay ahead.

CHAPTER 24

The Kansas City Greyhound station reeked of diesel fumes and broken dreams. Virginia Curran stood in the center of the chaos like a lighthouse—tall, maybe five-nine, thin as a dried corn stalk, her gray hair hanging limp as week-old lettuce. Her fingers clutched her purse against her chest, knuckles white from sixty-two years of learning that the world took things from women who weren't careful.

The fluorescent lights buzzed overhead like angry wasps, casting their sickly glow across linoleum that had seen better decades. Every surface felt sticky—the plastic chairs, the metal rails, even the air itself seemed to cling to your skin.

Virginia's eyes tracked the electronic departure board, watching destinations flicker like the reels of a slot machine. *Delayed. Delayed. Canceled.* The red letters blinked in disappointment while snow continued to fall outside the grimy windows.

Around her, the crowd thickened. Teenagers sprawled across benches with their phones and attitude. A baby wailed somewhere behind her while its mother bounced it with the mechanical rhythm of exhaustion—the smell of fast food mixed with unwashed bodies and desperation.

None of it touched Virginia. She'd learned to build walls around herself—thick ones that kept the world's chaos at a manageable distance—twenty years of practice had made her an expert at standing perfectly still while everything around her fell apart.

A red-headed woman with a squirming five-year-old bumped into her, all elbows and entitlement.

"Watch where you're—" The woman started to snarl, then caught sight of Virginia's face. Something in those pale blue eyes made her swallow the rest of her words. She grabbed her kid's hand and moved away, muttering to herself.

Virginia had perfected that look. It said, 'I have nothing left to lose, and that makes me dangerous.'

The departure board flickered again. *Houston—Gate 27—Delayed*. Then it vanished, replaced by St. Louis. But Virginia had seen it. Her destination was real, even if the timing wasn't.

Her red plastic suitcase sat beside her feet, held together with duct tape and stubborn pride. Everything she owned fit in that case—three changes of clothes, a Bible her mother had given her, and a manila envelope that had kept her awake for six months.

"Next!" The ticket clerk's voice carried the weary resignation of someone who had explained weather delays a thousand times that day.

The red-headed woman finished her business at the counter—lots of arm-waving and demands that physics change the weather on her behalf. When she stomped away, still dragging her kid, Virginia approached with the measured pace of someone who'd learned that rushing got you nowhere.

The clerk looked up, probably expecting another verbal assault. Instead, he found himself staring into the calmest face he'd seen all day.

"Yes, ma'am?" His voice held courtesy this time.

"One-way ticket to Houston." She placed her credit card on the counter. The plastic was warm from her palm—her last financial lifeline.

"That'll be ninety-four ninety-eight, plus tax." He processed the transaction with careful efficiency. "How long's the trip?"

"Eighteen to twenty hours, if the weather cooperates." He gestured toward the windows where snow was still falling. "But she's not cooperating much today."

"Thank you." Virginia slipped the ticket into her coat pocket, right next to the manila envelope that had brought her this far.

"Yes, ma'am. Gate twenty-seven when they call it. Should be an announcement soon."

Virginia found a spot near the gate and stood watching. Not sitting—she'd be sitting long enough. The announcement came forty minutes later, crackling through speakers that had seen better decades.

"Now boarding, Greyhound service to Houston, gate twenty-seven."

She was among the first in line. The bus driver, a weathered black man with kind eyes, looked at her ticket and nodded toward the back.

"Long trip ahead, ma'am. You traveling alone?"

"That's right."

Something in her tone made him glance up from his clipboard. "Well, if you need anything during the ride, just let me know."

Virginia found a window seat two-thirds of the way back and settled in for the journey. As the bus pulled away from Kansas City, she pressed her palm against the cold glass and whispered words that fogged the window:

"Twenty years is long enough."

CHAPTER 25

The humid air in Houston hit Virginia like a wet blanket. After eighteen hours of highway hypnosis and rest stops that smelled like industrial cleaner and despair, she stepped off the Greyhound into air thick enough to swim through.

The downtown station sat in a neighborhood that urban renewal had forgotten. Liquor stores and pawn shops lined the streets like broken teeth, their neon signs flickering promises they couldn't keep. The sweet rot smell of the bayous mixed with petroleum fumes and something that might have been hope, if hope could decompose.

The Luxe Inn squatted across the street like a concrete toad, its facade paint-peeled and window-broken. Aluminum foil covered half the glass, reflecting nothing but broken light. Virginia dragged her red suitcase behind her, one wheel wobbling like a shopping cart with a limp.

Inside, the lobby carpet squelched under her feet. Brown stains mapped out territories of previous disasters. The night clerk dozed behind bulletproof glass; his chair held together with duct tape and optimism.

Virginia tapped the bell. The clerk jerked awake, focusing on her with the glazed look of someone who'd given up on consciousness years ago.

"No rooms. We're full up." His default lie rolled out automatically.

"I have a reservation. Virginia Curran."

The clerk blinked, processing this unexpected development. "Well, hell. Why didn't you say so?"

He checked his book with the reluctant attention of someone who preferred sleep to customer service. Her name was there, scrawled in pencil like an afterthought.

"Room 217. Second floor, halfway down. Right side." He slid a key across the counter. The metal was warm and grimy.

"How much for the room?"

"Forty-nine ninety-nine a night. In advance."

Virginia counted out three twenties from her purse. The bills felt thin between her fingers—all the money left from cashing out her life.

• • • •

MEANWHILE, ACROSS TOWN in a neighborhood where money was spent on Armani and driving German cars, Ralph Norton was putting the final touches on his disappearance.

He'd been driving around Rice Military for over an hour, studying sight lines and traffic patterns like a general planning a retreat. The convenience store he finally chose sat on a corner lot; its cinderblock walls painted a color that might have been yellow once. Bars covered the windows. A hand-lettered sign advertised *Beer - Cigarettes - Lottery - Hope* in fading red paint.

Perfect. Anonymous. Forgettable.

Ralph parked his Land Rover at the back of the lot, near a dumpster that reeked of rotting fruit and broken dreams. Six migrant workers stood in the shade, their day's labor finished, speaking rapid Spanish and counting crumpled bills.

He left the engine running. Doors unlocked—keys in the ignition.

The restroom was located around the side of the building, hidden from view on the main street. Ralph walked toward it carrying his backpack, moving like a man with a simple biological need. The migrants watched him with the careful attention of people who'd learned to read intention in body language.

By the time they'd decided the gringo wasn't coming back, Ralph had vanished into the urban wilderness behind the store. He crouched in the bushes, watching through the chain-link fence as the workers approached his abandoned vehicle.

They talked it over for thirty seconds before one of them slid behind the wheel. The Land Rover pulled away with the careful dignity of people who understood the difference between opportunity and theft. Ralph smiled. Step one: complete.

Buffalo Bayou stretched out before him like a green wound through the city's concrete flesh. He'd hiked these trails with Sandi years ago, back when they still believed shared experiences could paper over fundamental incompatibility. However, recreational hiking differed from survival.

The water was warm and black, thick with organic matter he didn't want to identify. Ralph waded in waist-deep, holding his backpack above his head like an offering to whatever gods protected fools and fugitives. Each step forward meant pulling his feet from mud that wanted to claim his expensive shoes as permanent residents.

City lights glowed in the distance—those glass towers where he'd once moved money around computer screens and called it meaningful work. Now they looked like alien structures, beautiful and completely irrelevant to his survival.

The swamp fought him every step. Branches slapped his face. Something splashed nearby—fish or snake or alligator, he couldn't tell and didn't want to know. The air hummed with mosquitoes and possibility.

When he finally dragged himself onto dry land, Ralph Norton, the corporate executive, was gone. In his place stood a mud-covered man who stank of swamp water and desperation. His suit—what remained of it—hung in tatters. Slime coated his skin like a second layer of flesh.

He looked exactly like what he needed to become: someone society had trained itself not to see.

Ralph walked east through neighborhoods that prosperity had abandoned. Each step took him further from his old life and deeper into a world where survival mattered more than profit margins. His reflection in a storefront window showed a stranger—hollow-eyed, mud-caked, transformed.

Perfect.

CHAPTER 26

P.T. Mayo's weekend at home had been a festival of ego massage. Every television station, every newspaper, every social media platform was analyzing his Wordie Convention performance like scholars dissecting scripture. The coverage ranged from breathless worship to academic critique, but it all spelled success in the only currency that mattered to Mayo: attention.

Monday morning found him driving toward Mack Hill Towers with the satisfaction of a general returning from a successful campaign. The building rose from downtown Houston like a glass monument to profitable faith, its reflective surfaces throwing sunlight back at the city in sharp, expensive angles.

But something was wrong. Protesters clustered near the building's entrance, their hand-painted signs bobbing like angry flowers. Mayo slowed his BMW, reading the messages that challenged his carefully constructed empire:

FASTRAK = BLASPHEMY GOD IS NOT FOR SALE REPENT, FALSE PROPHET

"Son of a bitch." Mayo's knuckles whitened on the steering wheel. This wasn't supposed to happen. Success was supposed to immunize him from criticism, not invite it.

He drove around the block, entering through the service entrance like a celebrity avoiding paparazzi. The loading dock smelled of garbage and broken promises—appropriate, given his mood.

His office restored his sense of control. Victorian furniture that costs more than most people's cars. A wet bar made from illegal rainforest wood. Windows that looked down on the city like the eyes of a god.

Mayo pulled out his phone and dialed security.

"Get those protesters off my property. Fire code violations. Noise ordinances. I don't care what you call it, get them gone."

Through his windows, he watched security guards approach the protesters with the swagger of men who enjoyed exercising authority over the powerless. The signs disappeared first, then the people carrying them, loaded into police vans like cargo.

Mayo smiled. Problem solved.

His employees began their morning pilgrimage, stopping by to offer congratulations with the enthusiasm of subjects praising a benevolent king. The women especially seemed drawn to his presence, their admiration feeding his narcissistic hunger like premium fuel.

"You did us proud, P.T.," said Morgan Lewis, one of the company lawyers whose job was keeping FASTRAK's schemes within the boundaries of legal acceptability.

"That you did," agreed Sarah from accounting, her eyes shining with something that might have been worship.

Mayo basked in their praise like a lizard absorbing sunlight. This was how the world was supposed to work—his genius recognized, his authority unquestioned, his success celebrated by people smart enough to appreciate excellence.

But Lewis lingered after the others drifted back to their desks, his expression carrying the careful neutrality of someone delivering unwelcome news.

"About those protesters," Lewis said, his voice dropping to conference room confidentiality.

"What about them? They're gone."

"This batch, yeah. But there might be more. Something about sacrilege. False prophets. You know how these religious nuts get when they think someone's stepping on their territory."

Mayo's good mood dimmed like a bulb losing power. "This is a one-time thing, or should I expect more?"

"Hard to say. But I'd keep an eye on it." Lewis shifted his weight, uncomfortable in his role as messenger. "Religious outrage can spread like wildfire if it catches the right wind."

"Your job is to make sure it doesn't catch anything. Handle it."

"Will do." Lewis escaped gratefully, leaving Mayo alone with thoughts that tasted like ash.

The morning's worship session resumed, but the sweetness was tainted now. Mayo smiled and accepted praise while his mind calculated threats and countermeasures. Success was supposed to be armor, not a target.

His secretary approached during a lull in the adulation, her timing carefully calculated to catch him in a receptive mood.

"Magnificent performance, Chief. Simply magnificent." Her praise carried the professional polish of someone whose job depended on maintaining her boss's emotional equilibrium.

"Thanks." Mayo's attention was already drifting toward the next source of validation.

"Oh, before I forget—" She handed him an envelope. "A woman asked me to give this to you personally. Said it was very important."

Mayo slipped the envelope into his jacket pocket without examination; his mind was already focused on the next round of congratulations waiting in the lobby.

The protesters were gone, dispersed by official authority and the threat of legal consequences. Through his windows, Mayo watched the last police car pull away, carrying the final traces of dissent from his perfectly ordered world.

Everything was under control. Everything was exactly as it should be.

He had no idea that the envelope in his pocket contained the power to destroy everything he'd built.

CHAPTER 27

Narcissists never tire of seeing their reflection. Every surface in his office reflected money—the illegal rainforest wood bar, the antique Persian rug, the Victorian furniture that had cost more than most people's houses. Mayo moved through the space like a priest performing familiar rituals, touching the smooth edge of the credenza and testing its sharpness against his thumb.

The morning's worship session had fed his ego, but something gnawed at him. Probably just post-victory restlessness—the inevitable comedown after reaching a peak. He poured himself three fingers of bourbon, the crystal glass catching light like liquid amber.

Mayo settled into his leather chair, feet up on the mahogany desk, basking in the morning sun streaming through floor-to-ceiling windows. Below, Houston stretched out like a conquered territory. His territory.

The envelope rustled in his jacket pocket.

He'd forgotten about it during the morning's ego massage, but now the paper seemed to pulse against his ribs like a second heartbeat. Something about the careful handwriting on the front nagged at him—familiar, but from where?

Mayo pulled out his putter, needing the mindless precision of golf to quiet his restless thoughts. Each ball rolled true, dropping into the cup with satisfying clicks. Perfect shots, every time. The universe was rigged in his favor.

But the envelope wouldn't leave him alone.

Finally, irritation overcoming caution, Mayo ripped it open. The letterhead made him pause: *The Luxe Inn*. He'd never heard of the place, but the cheap paper and generic logo suggested desperation. The letter itself was written in that same careful handwriting, and as his eyes moved across the words, the bourbon in his stomach turned to acid.

Dear Christian,

I hope this letter finds you well. I know you are well because I saw that handsome face of yours on a very large TV screen in Kansas City. See, I've been a lonely woman for many years, poor and lonely. I lost my faith and scraped by with odd jobs here and there, you know.

I wasn't surprised that you changed your name. Anyway, enough small talk. If you can find the time, I'd love to go over old times and reminisce with you. We were a great couple, you know. The phone number and address are on the top of the letter and I'm in Room 217. I don't have enough money for a long stay here in Houston, so I was hoping you could spend some time with me before I have to leave.

See you soon, Chris.

Sincerely, Your loving wife, Virginia.

The letter fluttered to his desk like a dying bird. Mayo's hands shook—actually shook—as the words burned themselves into his brain. Virginia. After twenty years of carefully constructed amnesia, she'd found him.

Mayo stuffed the letter back into his pocket and grabbed his phone, his fingers moving with desperate precision. He needed Ada Taylor, and he needed her now.

But first, he had to get control of himself. Ada was too smart, too experienced to miss signs of panic. She'd smell blood in the water and adjust her prices accordingly.

Three deep breaths. Counting to ten. Imagining Virginia as just another business problem that required a business solution.

His hands steadied. His voice found its executive register.

Ada answered on the second ring. "That you, Moneymaker?"

"Listen carefully. I need you to do that thing. You know what I mean."

A pause. When Ada spoke again, her voice carried something that might have been a hint of respect. "You graduating, Moneymaker!"

"One hundred large and the painting of your choice. No price limit. You in?"

"Hell no, I ain't in."

The rejection hit him like a physical blow. "Why?"

"Because it ain't none of your fucking business, that's why."

Mayo's carefully constructed calm cracked. "Meet me at the gallery in thirty minutes. You won't be sorry. I promise."

"Two hundred large or don't bother."

The price had doubled in thirty seconds, but Mayo was drowning, and Ada was the only life preserver in sight. "I'll be there."

He threw the phone onto his desk hard enough to crack the screen. In his jacket pocket, Virginia's letter seemed to burn against his ribs like a brand marking him for what he'd always been:

A man who abandoned everyone who trusted him, and who'd finally run out of places to hide.

CHAPTER 28

The art gallery's white walls, track lighting, and silence added to the overall ambiance. Ada Taylor stood before a Jackson Pollock that probably cost more than most people's houses, her expression unreadable.

Mayo found her there, studying the painting like it held secrets worth killing for.

"Beautiful work," she said without turning around. "Controlled chaos. Takes real skill to make randomness look intentional."

"About the job—"

"No." Ada's voice cut through his desperation like a blade through silk. "I already told you no, and I meant it."

Mayo felt sweat beading on his forehead despite the gallery's aggressive air conditioning. "Why? You've never turned down work before."

Ada finally looked at him, her dark eyes measuring him like a coroner examining a corpse. "Because some lines you don't cross. Even in my business."

"Two-fifty."

"Not for a million." She turned back to the painting. "But I'll finish the other job. The Norton frame-up. Consider it a parting gift."

She handed him a manila envelope, thick with documents. "Bank records, falsified emails, manufactured evidence. Everything you need to paint your boy Ralph as an embezzler. Should keep the heat off you for a while."

Mayo's fingers trembled as he took the envelope. A temporary solution to a permanent problem. "Ada, you don't understand—"

"I understand plenty." Her voice carried the finality of a judge reading a death sentence. "I understand you're about to do something stupid. And I understand I don't want any part of it."

She walked away, her heels clicking against the polished floor like a countdown timer. Mayo stood alone among the expensive art, surrounded by beautiful things that meant nothing to him.

CHAPTER 29

Katherine Mayo had spent fifteen years reading her husband's moods like a meteorologist tracking storm systems. P.T.'s weather patterns were as predictable as Houston's summer heat—until now.

This morning felt different. Their River Oaks bedroom, with its museum-quality furniture and climate control that could chill to the bone, carried an electric tension that made her skin crawl. She watched P.T. in the bathroom mirror as he performed his morning narcissism ritual, but something was off in his movements.

His hands shook slightly as he adjusted his tie. Twice. The man who could stare down hostile board members was fumbling with Windsor knots.

Katherine had survived two previous affairs by noticing the signs: distracted satisfaction, private phone calls, and unexplained improvements in his grooming. This felt different. Darker. Like watching someone fight invisible enemies.

P.T. caught her watching and forced one of his boardroom smiles. "Beautiful morning, isn't it?"

Outside their bedroom windows, Houston's skyline shimmered through the heat already rising from concrete and asphalt. Beautiful wasn't the word she'd use.

"Mmm." Katherine kept her voice neutral. Fifteen years had taught her that P.T. preferred wives who agreed without thinking.

He kissed her forehead—a gesture so automatic it felt like being blessed by a machine—and headed downstairs. Through their bedroom window, she watched his BMW disappear through the security gates that protected their estate from the problems of ordinary people.

• • • •

DOWNTOWN, MACK HILL Towers rose from the urban landscape like a glass monument to profitable ambition. P.T. arrived earlier than usual, his Mercedes gliding into the executive parking space while the morning sky still held traces of night.

The building stood empty in the pre-dawn darkness, its reflective surfaces throwing back streetlight like mirrors that might reveal more than he wanted to see. For once, he'd beaten the workaholics who made him feel lazy by comparison.

His footsteps echoed across the marble lobby with unusual urgency. The elevator carried him up through floors of darkened offices where people would soon arrive to make money from other people's faith. The irony wasn't lost on him—he'd built an empire selling hope while losing his own.

P.T.'s office felt foreign in the darkness, familiar furniture transformed by shadows into potentially hostile shapes. Morning light filtered through his blinds, creating prison bar patterns across his Persian rug.

He hung his coat with mechanical precision, straightened his tie in the bathroom mirror, and checked for any traces of last night's activities that might betray him to observant employees. His reflection looked normal enough—expensive suit, confident posture, the face of a man who'd conquered the world through superior understanding of human weakness.

When he settled into his chair and turned on the desk lamp, the sudden illumination caused his eyes to hurt. For a moment, the bright circle of light felt like an interrogation spot designed to extract confessions from guilty consciences.

Then he noticed he wasn't alone.

"Good morning, P.T." Melanie Spenser's voice cut through his false sense of security like a blade through silk. She sat in the Queen Anne chair beside his fake fireplace, materializing from shadows like a conscience made flesh. "Little early this morning, aren't you?"

The shock hit his nervous system like an electrical current, but P.T. forced his face into a look of corporate surprise rather than revealing the panic clawing at his chest.

"Oh, morning, Melanie. What's going on?" His voice carried the tone of someone mildly surprised by an unexpected visitor rather than terrified by the possibility of exposure.

"Where's Ralph?" The question was direct and uncompromising, cutting through pleasantries to the heart of her concern.

"What do you mean, where's Ralph? How should I know?" P.T.'s deflection came automatically—the reflexive response of someone who'd spent years avoiding accountability.

Melanie's eyes never left his face, studying his expression with the intensity of a prosecutor examining evidence. "Because you know everything that goes on around here. Don't try telling me you don't, because I know you do."

"All I know is he said he needed time off to clear his head and left. That's all I know. Honestly." The lie slid out with practiced ease, just enough truth mixed in to sound believable.

"No, it's not." Melanie's voice carried absolute certainty. "But if that's your story and you're sticking to it, fine. Unless there's more to this, which I believe there is."

P.T. felt sweat gathering under his collar despite the office's aggressive air conditioning. "All women are suspicious. But in your case, your suspicion is completely beyond reality." He tried dismissing her through gender-based stereotyping, the desperate move of someone losing control. "The man's troubled, confused, frankly a little nuts. I hope he decides not to come back."

"Why, Mr. Mayo, I do believe you're jealous of Ralph." Melanie's counterattack struck his insecurities with surgical precision. "Shame on you for having such bad thoughts. Haven't you heard that a little competition is good for the soul? Unless you've lost yours and don't need it anymore."

The accusation about his soul—delivered in the headquarters of a Christian products company by a board member's daughter—carried layers of irony that weren't lost on either of them.

"Look, Melanie." P.T.'s voice took on the condescending tone of someone dispensing unwanted advice. "If I were you, I'd start looking for a new boyfriend. Ralph's a loser, and you're wasting your time. I understand you're not getting any younger, and at your age, eligible bachelors don't come around as often. But take it from me—stay out of this. It's none of your business, and it'll only reflect badly on you and your father."

The personal attack was designed to wound and intimidate, combining ageism and paternalism in a cocktail of verbal cruelty that revealed his desperation.

P.T. opened his office door and waited for Melanie to leave, his body language making it clear their conversation was over regardless of her willingness to accept dismissal.

Melanie stood slowly, her eyes never leaving his face as she approached the doorway. She was almost through when she stopped and pointed at his chest with the precision of someone delivering a formal declaration of war.

"You always win, P.T. But this time is different."

Her words carried the weight of prophecy—a promise that his previous methods might not be sufficient for the battle coming.

CHAPTER 30

The FASTRAK parking lot baked under Houston's merciless sun, asphalt soft enough to take footprints. Melanie sat in her air-conditioned car, watching Mack Hill Towers shimmer through heat waves like a mirage built on other people's faith.

Her iPhone felt hot against her ear as she dialed HPD's main number.

"Houston Police Department, how can I help you?"

"I need to report a missing person."

After three transfers and five minutes of bureaucratic shuffle, Sergeant Connely's voice came through with the weary authority of someone who'd started his day processing human tragedy.

"Missing Persons, Connely. What can I do for you?"

Downtown HPD headquarters buzzed with its usual controlled chaos—detectives juggling cases, phones ringing like electronic birds, and the constant undercurrent of violence that kept Houston's finest employed twenty-four seven. Connely had just arrived with his third cup of coffee, surrounded by case files that threatened to bury him alive.

"My name is Melanie Spenser. I need to report a missing person."

"Hold on." Connely found a pen among the debris on his desk. "Go ahead."

"Ralph Norton." Melanie provided his Tiara Woods address, phone number, and employment at FASTRAK—each detail delivered with the precision of someone who'd rehearsed this conversation.

"How long's Mr. Norton been missing?"

"I'm not exactly sure. Maybe a few days, maybe more." Melanie's uncertainty was honest but frustrating—the difference between someone being late and someone being gone.

"How do you know he's missing?"

158

"Because I know." Her voice elevated as frustration crept in. "No one knows where he is, and I think his life's in danger!"

Connely sighed—a sound that carried fifteen years of dealing with civilian panic. "Miss Spenser, I'll put his information in the system. However, without more details, there isn't much we can do immediately. We take all these calls seriously, but on any given day, we get about fifteen hundred missing persons reports. I have to prioritize based on available information."

The numbers hit Melanie like cold water. Fifteen hundred people disappearing into Houston's urban maze every day, most of them finding their way home or choosing not to be found.

"This isn't just any missing person." Melanie bit her lower lip, fighting the urge to scream at bureaucratic indifference. "I'm sure Ralph's in serious trouble. Won't you help me?"

"Of course we will. But I need to ask—what's your relationship with Mr. Norton?"

The question hung in the air like smoke. Melanie could hear the calculation behind it—boyfriends disappeared after fights, husbands after affairs, and concerned citizens rarely had enough information to justify emergency response.

"I'm his best friend," she said finally. "His only friend."

Connely's experience told him there was more to it—probably romantic entanglement disguised as friendship, probably a lover's quarrel that would resolve itself when emotions cooled. But something in her voice suggested genuine fear rather than hurt feelings.

"Got it. Thank you, Miss Spenser. I'll enter his information and call you if anything develops."

Melanie wasn't the type to let bureaucratic walls stop her. Her time in Africa had taught her that obstacles were just challenges requiring creative solutions.

• • • •

MEANWHILE, IN HOUSTON'S East End, where urban renewal had died and been buried under decades of neglect, Ralph Norton picked his way through industrial ruins like a ghost haunting the graveyard of American manufacturing.

Parham Electrical Warehouse rose from urban decay like a concrete tombstone, its walls covered in graffiti that told stories of those who had passed through during its slow decline. The building's skeleton was visible through missing walls and collapsed sections—structural transparency that revealed how fleeting all human ambitions truly were.

Ralph climbed the damaged staircase to the ninth floor, testing each step before trusting it with his weight. His backpack contained everything he owned now—a pathetic collection that represented the total remaining value of his previous life.

The ninth floor stretched out like an archaeological site, littered with abandoned tools and the debris of collapsed dreams. Under a spray-painted broken heart, someone had written "Micro Boy never loved Kristina" in fading letters.

Ralph smiled at the anonymous heartbreak and hoped Kristina had found someone better than whoever Micro Boy turned out to be. He positioned himself behind the wall that bore Kristina's lament, using the concrete as both windbreak and psychological shelter.

From his vantage point, he could see every floor in the building through the gaps where walls had crumbled into dust and rust. For a moment, he thought about Mack Hill Towers with its open plan and shining steel rails, realizing it would eventually look just like this—another monument to temporary human ambition.

Sleep came fitfully in the concrete wilderness, his unconscious mind processing trauma while his body tried to heal from injuries both physical and psychological.

The sound that woke him was metallic—deliberate scraping that suggested human agency rather than random structural collapse. The noise grew louder with each repetition, approaching with methodical persistence.

Ralph pressed himself against Kristina's wall, controlling his breathing while his heart hammered against his ribs like a caged animal. The darkness had transformed the abandoned building into something actively hostile, full of predators who'd detected prey.

Voices whispered in the darkness—cruel laughter that carried the anticipation of people who'd found entertainment in someone else's vulnerability.

The force that hit him came from behind with the explosive impact of a baseball bat swung by someone who intended severe damage. Ralph's world exploded into semi-conscious chaos, pain whirling him into a void where consciousness became an unaffordable luxury.

A boot connected with his stomach, driving air from his lungs. Another kick to his skull made a wet sound that suggested severe damage to flesh and bone.

Then darkness claimed him completely, offering relief from pain but no promise of ever returning to light.

CHAPTER 31

Blood pooled beneath Ralph's head, warm and sticky against the concrete dust that covered the warehouse floor. His consciousness drifted in and out like a radio signal fading across long distances—pain, darkness, cold concrete, and the gradual awareness that he was somehow still alive.

Through his haze of confusion and agony, a young girl's voice cut through the chaos like a lifeline thrown to a drowning man.

"Grandfather, look. There's a man there, and he looks..." Her voice carried concern and compassion that seemed impossible in this place of violence and abandonment.

"Let us help him if we can." The older man's voice carried authority seasoned by enough suffering to recognize it immediately, and wisdom to know that helping others was often the only thing that gave meaning to survival.

Ralph heard footsteps approaching, and terror spiked through his damaged consciousness. Yes, he remembered sounds in the night and agonizing pain—memories his mind wanted to suppress but couldn't completely erase.

But these footsteps carried hesitation rather than confidence, the careful rhythm of people approaching with caution and compassion.

The older man knelt beside Ralph's damaged body, weathered hands moving with gentle competence as he checked for vital signs. "Kashinka, he's alive! Thank God. We must help him before the good Lord takes him away. Come, help me move him."

Ralph was dead weight that challenged their limited strength—an older man too frail and a young girl too small for such a task. But they succeeded through determination and the stubborn refusal to abandon someone in need.

Ralph slowly regained consciousness to find himself looking into the faces of two homeless people who'd never seen him before but had chosen to save his life anyway. They'd folded a jacket and an old shirt under his head, making him as comfortable as their limited resources allowed.

"I, I..." Ralph's voice was weak, barely carrying across the small space between them.

"Do not speak, young man. You are much too weak." The older man's voice carried gentle authority. "You must rest. Soon we'll have to move you to a safer place. We know such a place, but it will be difficult in your condition."

My stuff. Where's my stuff?" Ralph's question revealed his disorientation, with his focus narrowed to immediate concerns.

"There was nothing there," said Kashinka with matter-of-fact acceptance. "They must have taken your things. It happens to all of us."

Ralph's eyes closed as exhaustion reclaimed him, his body demanding rest, his mind couldn't afford.

"Grandfather, is he..." Kashinka's question carried the weight of someone too young to have seen so much death but old enough to recognize its approach.

"No, Kashinka, he is resting because of his injuries. We'll wait until he awakens so we can move him to our old place. It will be safer for all of us there."

The old man wiped Ralph's forehead with parental tenderness while Kashinka poured water on an old handkerchief. Their movements were practiced—caring for the injured had become part of their survival strategy.

Yakov Feller was eighty-three years old, a Ukrainian refugee from Kyiv whose life had been filled with more tragedy than most people could imagine surviving. His granddaughter, Kashinka, had emigrated with him after the Russian Secret Police murdered her parents, victims of political persecution that scattered survivors across continents.

When they applied for refugee status, America's bureaucratic system denied them—human worth measured in paperwork rather than suffering. Rather than face deportation and certain death, they'd disappeared into New York's streets, eventually finding their way to Houston, where they hoped the larger Ukrainian community might offer shelter.

Survival on the streets was nothing new to Yakov and Kashinka—they'd learned invisibility and resourcefulness through circumstances that would have broken most people. However, Yakov's failing health was putting them both in danger, as his weakening body was unable to provide the protection Kashinka needed.

Finding Ralph was the last thing they expected during their routine search for food or sellable items. Helping, moving, and feeding him were far beyond their abilities, but they tried anyway, driven by a moral code that refused to abandon someone in need, regardless of the cost.

When Ralph finally awoke hours later, Yakov helped him stand and positioned him between himself and his granddaughter. The human chain they formed was fragile but determined—three people bound by circumstance and necessity.

It took almost four hours to move Ralph through the dark streets, which belonged to predators rather than ordinary citizens. They navigated ruined buildings and avoided watching eyes—the surveillance network of people who lived in shadows and survived by knowing everything that happened in their territory.

CHAPTER 32

Houston's street code allowed hookers, pimps, people with an addiction, and drunks as long as certain boundaries weren't crossed. Violence was tolerated unless it involved money that could attract police interest. When other homeless people saw Yakov and Kashinka helping Ralph walk away from the warehouse, their evident poverty served as a form of protection—three people so clearly lacking resources that they didn't pose a threat to anyone's economic interests.

Ralph collapsed several times as they limped along cracked sidewalks and through empty lots that served as highways for people who couldn't afford to be seen. The stench coming from him was horrific—swamp water, blood, and the funk of someone unconscious in his bodily fluids for hours.

They needed to find Ralph clothes and a place to get cleaned up before his condition attracted the wrong kind of attention or killed him through infection.

Mercury's Closet sat in a parking lot like an oasis of dignity in a desert of abandonment. The charity donation center left goods available after hours because they understood that human need didn't operate on business schedules—clothing, water, even old mattresses for people who had nowhere else to sleep.

With Kashinka acting as lookout, Yakov efficiently cleaned Ralph, changing his clothes and tending to wounds that were worsening by the minute. They threw his old clothes into the dumpster and tidied the area, a typical courtesy among those who rely on charity.

Ralph was in bad shape, and Yakov was exhausted, but they were only a mile from their destination—close enough that surrender was unthinkable despite the enormous effort required to keep going.

The abandoned tire shop seemed like random junk scattered all over, picked over by generations of scavengers until nothing useful was left. What nobody knew was that a basement was hidden beneath the debris—a secret space Yakov had found while digging through to find anything he could sell.

The basement entrance was completely concealed beneath carefully arranged debris that appeared random but was strategic camouflage. Yakov always covered the entrance when they left, understanding that discovery would mean eviction or worse.

Their routine involved Kashinka hiding while Yakov appeared to scavenge randomly. When she meowed like a stray cat—signal that the area was clear—Yakov would uncover their secret entrance.

Getting Ralph down the old wooden stairs was going to be difficult given his injuries and their limited strength. They set him on the top step and slid him down slowly, each movement causing him to wince with pain.

Ralph cried out in agony as each step jarred his damaged skull, the sound threatening to attract attention they couldn't afford. Kashinka covered his mouth with her small hand until they reached the relative safety of their underground refuge.

The basement housed rats, mice, and occasional raccoons, but it was safer than the streets where human predators posed far greater threats. After making Ralph comfortable on makeshift bedding, they opened their last cans of green beans—the remainder of their food supply.

Ralph shook his head, too weak to eat or too proud to accept charity from people who had less than he did.

"Let us eat a little, Kashinka. But we'll leave some for our guest. He needs to get his strength back, or he won't survive." Yakov's practical wisdom reflected his understanding that Ralph's recovery was essential for everyone's survival.

As Yakov struggled to open the cans with their rusted opener, Kashinka noticed something distant in his eyes—exhaustion and weakness that suggested his strength was finally failing.

"Let me do that, Grandfather. You are tired. I can do it."

Ralph watched everything through his haze of pain and confusion. Despite his inability to speak coherently, his consciousness registered the love and respect that filled the underground room like incense in a cathedral.

Whatever problems he'd been dealing with in his former life looked pale compared to the genuine human connection he was witnessing between his grandfather and granddaughter, who had lost everything except each other.

The generosity was so overwhelming—their willingness to share their last food with a stranger—that he had to close his eyes to shut out the reality of their sacrifice.

CHAPTER 33

Strange thoughts drifted through Ralph's consciousness as he slept in the rat-infested basement, the boundary between waking and dreaming becoming permeable. Fragments of memory mixed with fevered hallucinations, creating a mental landscape where anything was possible.

The voice came again, cutting through his damaged consciousness like a radio transmission from some distant, malevolent station: "If you love me, kill him."

Ralph shook his head violently, rejecting whatever force was trying to control his actions. He wanted the voice gone, hoped this new circumstance would displace it forever, replacing divine commands with human compassion.

When he woke before Yakov and Kashinka, their gentle breathing punctuated by occasional moans and whimpers—sounds of dreams filled with memories that even sleep couldn't erase—he resolved to remain silent. These beautiful people who'd risked their safety to help him shouldn't get caught up in his problems or become targets of whatever forces were pursuing him.

Kashinka stirred first, her sleep lighter than her grandfather's. She checked on Ralph with solicitous care, smiling when she saw his eyes were open and color had returned to his face.

Ralph didn't respond to her overture, keeping his expression cold and unemotional. The distance was intentional—a protective barrier designed to prevent connections that might put these innocent people in danger.

Yakov finally awoke but had difficulty rising, his joints stiff with age and the effects of sleeping on concrete. The previous night's effort had depleted his strength, and he was exhausted by saving someone's life when his reserves were dangerously low.

You look much better, my friend. I am happy for you." Yakov's voice carried genuine pleasure despite the cost to his well-being.

"Why did you help me?" Ralph's question cut to something that puzzled him—the willingness of people with nothing to give everything to a stranger.

You were in great danger and badly injured. Only a coward would refuse to help a man in that state. And we are not cowards." Yakov's answer was firm and straightforward, reflecting a moral code unbroken by years of poverty.

"Grandfather, we have no food left. We need to go out and search." Kashinka's statement was delivered without complaint, simply recognizing a practical problem that needed an immediate solution.

Ralph carefully tested his balance and mobility, assessing damage with the attention of someone whose survival might depend on his physical capabilities. His strength was beginning to return, as the human body's remarkable capacity for healing asserted itself despite the severe injuries he had sustained.

"Mister...what is your name?" Yakov asked, showing curiosity and a desire to reach out to someone who had become part of their family.

Ralph didn't answer, his silence showing both paranoia and a protective instinct. He looked at the ceiling cracks where sunlight seeped through like natural spotlights illuminating their underground stage.

"Sir, would you be so kind as to accompany my granddaughter? She knows where food can be obtained, but I don't want her to go alone." Yakov's request was delivered with formal courtesy, asking a favor rather than demanding assistance.

When Ralph bent to tie his shoe, the amulet he'd worn since receiving it from the homeless man in traffic popped out from under his shirt. The religious symbol caught the light, revealing its fusion of Christian and Jewish iconography.

Kashinka noticed immediately, asking about it with the curiosity of someone who'd learned to find meaning in small objects. Religious symbols carried special weight for people who'd fled religious persecution, representing both comfort and potential danger.

Ralph tucked the amulet back inside his shirt with a protective gesture, guarding a secret too dangerous to share.

"I'll go with her." His first clear statement since regaining consciousness represented both gratitude and acceptance of responsibility.

"Thank you, my friend. Thank you." Yakov's relief was profound as he settled back into his bedding, knowing Kashinka would have protection during their dangerous mission.

Ralph and Kashinka left stealthily through the hidden door, carefully covering their refuge with debris to disguise it from anyone watching. They separated and met at a predetermined location several blocks away—a strategy that reduced the chances of being connected as a group.

Ralph was impressed with Kashinka's maturity and competence, her ability to navigate dangerous territory with confidence that seemed far older than her years. He'd never seen that combination of innocence and street wisdom in someone so young.

His growing beard provided camouflage for features that might be recognized, and his disheveled but clean appearance no longer marked him as recently injured or dangerous.

Kashinka led him to the Brothers of Charity, an old church donated by the diocese to the Franciscan order, which was dedicated to serving the poorest of the poor. When Ralph saw Brother Charles attending to the poor, recognition hit him like a physical blow—he remembered this man from his research on every religious institution in the city for his Word of God app.

The irony was overwhelming—encountering one of his research subjects while disguised as homeless. Ralph turned quickly to avoid recognition that might expose his identity and bring unwanted attention.

Brother Charles gave Kashinka a heavy sack of food that represented abundance beyond their usual means. Ralph pretended not to help carry it while maintaining his pose of indifference. Still, the moment they were outside, he immediately took the bag with a gesture that revealed his true character, despite his attempts to remain detached.

The successful mission had provided not just food but proof that their small group could function as a survival unit. Ralph shook his head in anger at himself as they approached their refuge, internal conflict between gratitude and protective isolation becoming unbearable.

Why was he allowing himself to care about people whose association with him could only bring harm? Just as he was about to leave the food and disappear—abandoning people who'd saved his life to protect them from whatever consequences his survival might bring—Kashinka arrived.

She could read his posture of departure, the emotional distance, the look of someone preparing to abandon people who cared about him. The recognition made her sad in a way that cut through his protective barriers like a knife through paper, revealing the cost of protecting them through isolation and abandonment.

CHAPTER 34

The GPS led Melanie through Houston's suburban maze, past strip malls and medical complexes that all looked like they'd been designed by the same committee in 1987. Ayrshire sat just off Bellaire—the kind of neighborhood where middle-class dreams had been built one ranch house at a time during the Eisenhower years.

"You have arrived at your destination," announced her phone with electronic certainty.

"We'll see about that," Melanie muttered, scanning house numbers against the address her father had dug out of his memory.

Samuel Steele's house wore its 1957 vintage like a badge of honor—gray brick facade, picture windows, and the horizontal lines that had once represented America's optimistic future. Mature oak trees threw shade across a lawn green enough to suggest someone who took pride in property maintenance.

As Melanie walked up the concrete path, dodging sprinkler spray that kept the grass Houston-green despite the relentless heat, she debated her approach. Should she emphasize Ralph's celebrity status? The potential danger? Her desperation?

Hell, she decided, *just be honest.*

The door chimes were louder than expected, echoing through the house with quality craftsmanship from an era when details mattered—no immediate answer, so she tried again with the persistence of genuine need.

A spry-looking man around seventy finally answered—taller than expected, with a scruffy salt-and-pepper beard and an Astros cap turned backward on white hair. He looked mildly annoyed at being interrupted during whatever retirement activity had been occupying his attention.

"Yes," he said, voice carrying the wary authority of someone who'd spent decades dealing with people wanting things from him. "What can I do for you, young lady?"

"Good morning. My name is Melanie Spenser, and I'm looking for Mr. Samuel Steele." Her introduction was straightforward—first impressions mattered, especially when asking strangers for help.

"Your search has ended. I am Samuel R. Steele." His response carried amusement at her formality, as if he appreciated courtesy that so few people bothered with anymore.

I was hoping to discuss something vital with you. My father, Phil Spenser, gave me your name." The reference was strategic—establishing credibility and suggesting respectable connections.

Spenser..." Steele's brow furrowed. "Can't place any Spenser. You're welcome to come in if you'd like, but I don't have much time to spare. I'm in the middle of a Fortnite match with an online buddy.

The image of a seventy-year-old private detective engaged in virtual combat caught Melanie off guard, challenging her assumptions about what retirement looked like for men of his generation.

"I just made fresh coffee, Miss Spenser. Would you like a cup?"

"Sure." She needed the caffeine and the momentary pause to organize what might be the most important sales pitch of her life.

"Let's go to the kitchen. It's comfortable and sunny and... well, you know."

Steele moved through his house with confident familiarity. As they passed through the living space, Melanie was impressed—mid-century modern furniture, cohesive design, and the impression of someone with good taste and the resources to indulge it. The man had style and wasn't letting age catch up to him.

The coffee smell hit her from the living room—quality beans, careful preparation, not the instant gratification most people settled for.

"Cups up there, spoons in the drawer, sugar and creamer in the fridge." He pointed with economical gestures. "Help yourself and sit down with me at the table."

As she prepared her coffee, Steele observed her with the practiced eye of someone who had spent a career reading people through their movements and unconscious cues. Part older man checking out an attractive woman, part retired detective maintaining skills that had sustained his career.

One thing was immediate: he liked her. Something about her bearing reminded him of the kind of client he'd always preferred—people genuinely concerned about someone else rather than seeking personal advantage.

She sat across from him, took a careful sip, and set her cup down with the attention of someone who understood this moment might determine whether she'd get the help she desperately needed.

"Mr. Steele, I need your help. A good friend of mine has gone missing, and I'm worried about his safety."

"Miss Spenser, before you go further, I have to tell you I'm retired. Have been for eleven years. I'm enjoying retirement and have no intentions of unretiring." His response was automatic—boundary-setting he'd probably delivered many times.

"I think he's in grave danger."

"That's the same line I've heard for almost fifty years." Steele's skepticism was professional rather than personal. "Not that I'm saying you're lying, but people will say anything to get what they want."

"I'm sure that's true, but in this case, I'm certain of it."

"There's nothing I can do for you, Miss Spenser. I like my life just the way it is."

Melanie thought of something that might work—either brilliant or desperate, definitely worth a shot.

"Tell you what, Mr. Steele. You like Fortnite, right?"

"Yes." His admission was cautious, perhaps sensing his hobby was about to be weaponized.

"And you're probably good at it, right?"

"Yes." Even more wary now.

"I'll play you one game of Fortnite. If I win, you take my case. If you win, I'll walk out, and you'll never see me again. Deal?"

Melanie stuck out her hand with the confidence of someone holding cards her opponent couldn't see. Steele smiled sheepishly, recognizing manipulation but finding the approach charming enough to warrant consideration.

"Guess I'm a sucker for a pretty face."

They moved to his man cave—a room reflecting decades of accumulated interests and the luxury of space retirement provided. The laptop served as his portal to virtual worlds where age didn't matter, where skill could triumph over youth and reflexes.

The "Victory Royal" dance flashed on screen after fifteen minutes, with Melanie hardly breaking a sweat during a performance that revealed skills far beyond casual play. Her victory was decisive, leaving no doubt about her gaming competence.

A wry smile crept onto Steele's mouth with a knowing nod that acknowledged both defeat and appreciation for superior strategy.

"I've been hustled before, but never like that. Where'd you get your Fortnite chops?"

"My little cousin Timmy. He schooled me well."

"Yes, he did. Now, let's sit down and talk about this."

When they settled on the leather sofa facing his ninety-inch flat-screen, Melanie started to speak, but Steele cut her off gracefully.

"If everyone had your determination, we'd all be better off. In less than an hour, you've done what many have tried but no one has accomplished. So tell me your story, and don't leave anything out because I'll know immediately if you do."

"Thank you, Mr. Steele. But before I start, I want to ask you a question."

"Please call me Sam, and go right ahead."

"I noticed you had the Word of God app on your laptop. I'm sure you have it on your phone as well."

"Correct. It's by far the best thing I've done for myself since forever." Sam's admission carried genuine enthusiasm.

"Fine. Let's start right there. The person I'm trying to find is the creator of that app. His name is Ralph Norton."

Sam's expression changed completely, recontextualizing everything he thought he knew about this conversation.

"Are you a Wordie, Miss Spenser?"

"I wouldn't say I'm a Wordie, but I think the app has worked miracles for people who needed to restore their faith."

"Is Mr. Norton your lover, Miss Spenser?" Sam's question was direct; his investigative instincts required a complete understanding.

Melanie stared directly into his eyes, the intensity of her gaze suggesting she understood the importance of complete honesty. She paused, swallowing hard as she considered the implications of revealing such personal information to a stranger.

"Normally, Sam, I wouldn't answer such a personal question. But I see fair play and determination in your eyes that forces me to answer. Yes, he's my lover, but more than that, he's my best friend. I'm sure you would try to help your best friend, wouldn't you?"

"Yes, Melanie, I would. And may I add that Mr. Norton is very fortunate to have a friend like you. It will be not only my pleasure to help you, but to help a man who has done so much for so many people."

Sam's response carried genuine commitment, transforming from a professional obligation into a personal mission.

"Great. Now, where should I begin?"

"Start by telling me about yourself, how you met Mr. Norton, the company he works for, and why you think he's missing and in danger. I won't interrupt unless I need to fill in a gap."

After an hour covering her African background, her relationship with Ralph, FASTRAK's toxic environment, and her growing certainty that P.T. Mayo represented a genuine threat to Ralph's safety, Melanie thought she'd covered everything relevant.

She spent considerable time on Mayo and his dirty methods, describing the corporate culture of intimidation. Sam's mouth twisted slightly whenever he heard Mayo's name—a physical reaction suggesting recognition or distaste.

When she asked about his reaction, Steele would only say that he didn't know Mayo personally, but he was familiar with him through reputation. He wouldn't elaborate.

"What's your fee, Sam?"

"There is no fee, Melanie. If you only knew what Ralph Norton has done for me in my life, you would understand the depth of my gratitude. I now have a personal God who loves me for who I am, not for how much money I can give to a church. I'm so happy you've given me this opportunity."

They exchanged contact information and walked toward the front door, their partnership sealed by mutual respect and shared commitment.

"Thank you, Sam. This means a lot to me. Up until this moment, I felt like I was the only one who would help Ralph."

They hugged with unexpected warmth, and as Melanie walked to her car feeling lighter than she had in days, Sam called out with perfect timing:

"I was wrong. There is a fee."

Melanie turned with a smile, reading his mind.

"One more game of Fortnite to determine the winner after we find your man."

Sam lifted his arm and waved goodbye with the gesture of someone who'd just discovered retirement might be less satisfying than he'd imagined.

CHAPTER 35

The Chihuahuan Desert stretched endlessly under a sky the color of old bone, its harsh landscape broken only by the twisted metal skeleton of what had once been a silver Land Rover. The wreckage lay scattered like the remains of some massive beast that had died far from home, metal and plastic fused into abstract sculpture by fire hot enough to melt chrome.

The smell rising from the ruins was sickeningly sweet—burned flesh mixed with melted rubber and superheated metal. Even experienced investigators covered their noses, breathing through their mouths to avoid the worst of it.

Two hikers had discovered the scene while enjoying what they'd expected to be a peaceful nature walk thirty miles south of Laredo. Their morning communion with desert flora had become a nightmare when they stumbled across what was professional violence rather than random crime.

The police convoy that responded kicked up dust clouds visible for miles across the empty landscape. Two bodies lay nearby with bullet holes in their heads—execution-style killings that spoke of cartel efficiency. Desert scavengers had been at work, leaving behind evidence that would challenge even experienced forensic investigators.

A third body in the trunk had been reduced to charred bone and dental work—identification would depend on whether the victim had ever received professional dental care.

The Laredo Crime Lab received the skeletal remains on a flatbed truck like archaeological evidence from a particularly violent civilization. The VIN was the only thing identifiable with certainty—the metal plate having survived flames that consumed everything else of value.

The vehicle was registered to Ralph Norton.

Meanwhile, Ralph's phone had surfaced in Knoxville, Tennessee, at a crack house in a neighborhood that specialized in human degradation. The device was smashed, but it still retained battery life. Its broken screen reflected fluorescent lights in the evidence room, where it would be analyzed for whatever secrets its memory might contain.

Sergeant Connely of HPD saw Ralph's name appear on both reports, recalling the beautiful young woman whose urgency had impressed him, despite his professional skepticism. The call he made to Melanie didn't go well from the moment he heard her voice.

Her phone rang while she was cooking breakfast in her father's kitchen, trying to maintain a sense of normalcy as her world crumbled. When Connely's name appeared on the screen, she lost her appetite immediately, burning her fingers on the hot pan in her haste to answer what she knew would be devastating news.

"Miss Spenser?"

"Yes." Her response was barely audible, squeezed through a throat suddenly too tight for everyday speech.

"I've received two reports this morning with Ralph Norton's name on them." His delivery was slow, giving her time to process each piece of information.

"Is he okay?" Melanie's question carried desperate hope while preparing for catastrophe.

"It's impossible to know right now. His car—or what's left of it—was found in Laredo. There were bodies found with the car, but no ID on any of them." He could hear her choking up. "Then his phone was found in Knoxville, Tennessee, in a crack house. Damaged enough that no information could be retrieved."

"How do you know one of the bodies isn't Ralph?" The question came through tears she couldn't control.

"Two of the bodies were Latino in appearance, and the third was burned beyond recognition, but we're analyzing DNA right now. That takes time."

Melanie was sobbing uncontrollably now, the sound carrying through the phone like a physical presence that made Connely wish he'd chosen a different profession.

"How long?"

"At least two weeks, maybe longer. I'll let you know as soon as I find out anything. Try not to lose hope, Miss Spenser. These things sometimes turn out differently than we think."

Melanie struggled to compose herself enough to end the conversation on a graceful note. "Thank you, Sergeant."

When she finally felt capable of speaking coherently, she called Sam Steele immediately. The conversation was brief, her voice still hoarse from crying as she relayed Connely's information.

"I know Connely," Sam said, his voice carrying decades of law enforcement experience. "He's a good cop and will get you information as quickly as he can. And he's right. Don't give up yet. There's more to this than either of us knows."

"If he's still alive, Ralph needs our help. We have to do something, Sam. Please help."

"I will. You can count on it."

. . . .

VIRGINIA CURRAN'S BODY had been discovered by a housekeeper at the Luxe Inn—a woman whose job had exposed her to enough human misery that she thought she was prepared for anything until she opened the door to Room 217.

She'd gotten no reply after knocking according to standard procedure; her attempts to rouse the occupant met with silence that could mean heavy sleep or something worse. After several knocks delivered with increasing force, she used her passkey and found

Virginia's body in a position that immediately told her this was not a natural death.

The manager called the police with weary resignation, as if someone who had dealt with similar situations before. They took their time responding, thinking it was just another dead junkie in a seedy hotel—routine urban mortality that warranted documentation but not urgency.

It took several days for HPD homicide investigators to identify Virginia Curran and piece together what had brought her from Kansas City to her death in Houston. The investigation revealed a woman whose life had been marked by poverty and abandonment, whose final journey had been motivated by something significant enough to spend her last resources on a bus ticket to Texas.

Connely was assigned the case, adding it to his ever-growing stack in an understaffed department that struggled to keep pace with Houston's capacity for violence.

Sam Steele knew he had to visit Connely for the latest information on Ralph, but he also knew cops didn't particularly like giving information to private detectives. So he stopped at a burger place that was a particular favorite of many cops, buying two chili cheeseburgers with the understanding that food was often the key to unlocking professional cooperation.

When he appeared at Connely's desk and dropped the bags down, the aroma of fried meat and processed cheese filled the air around the detective's workspace.

"Okay, what do you want? I thought you were retired, for God's sake." Connely's tone was accusatory but amused.

"Not nice, man. Can't an old buddy come by to say hi?"

"Who are you kidding? I haven't seen that ugly face in years. I'll eat your damn burger, but I don't have time for your bullshit. Just get to the point."

"What can you tell me about the Ralph Norton case? A very concerned young lady has hired me to find him, if he can be found."

"So that's it." Connely leaned back in his chair with satisfaction. "Bet she's good-looking too, huh?"

"She's worried sick about him. Plus, he's a celebrity."

"She tell you she talked to me already?"

"Yes, and about Norton's car and all that. But if I know you, there's more to this."

"Nothing at all. You know that. Besides, look at that stack of shit piling up on my desk." Connely pointed at the pile of new homicide files. "I don't have a single detective available to start work on these. Two are out sick, and one's about ready to retire, which I should have done years ago."

They ate their burgers in companionable silence, talking about old times and cases they'd worked together, sharing memories of investigations that'd tested their skills and sometimes their courage.

When they finished, Steele proposed a deal in a casual tone, as if making a routine business proposition.

"Tell you what I'll do. If you select one of those new files, I'll investigate it on my own without anyone knowing, and I'll provide you with the information ASAP. That's the best I can do if you fill me in on what you know about Ralph Norton."

Connely washed down his burger with the last of his coffee and threw the wrapper at Steele, who ducked as it went flying past his head.

Connely closed his eyes and picked one of the files with theatrical randomness, looked around to ensure no supervisors were watching, and handed it to Steele with a conspiratorial air.

"If you so much as say one word about this, you conniving son of a bitch, I'll deny it completely and throw your ass in jail. Do you understand me?"

If fate exists, then Sam Steele was being guided by forces beyond his comprehension as he accepted the file that would change everything he thought he knew about Ralph Norton's disappearance.

The file was labeled "Virginia Curran—Homicide."

CHAPTER 36

Ada Taylor negotiated her deal with Mayo for $300,000, with a one-week deadline that would test both her organizational skills and her network of reliable contacts. For this high-stakes job—money with danger coming from all directions—she was hiring one of Houston's most brutal assassin crews.

They called themselves the Third Ward Posse, a criminal organization that had evolved from street gang to sophisticated murder-for-hire operation under the leadership of a young man whose reputation for violence was matched only by his appreciation for fine art.

Felonious Punque lived in a stunning downtown high-rise townhome, its vertical luxury suggesting someone who'd transcended traditional gang territory. When Ada entered, she immediately focused on the artwork covering the walls, her trained eye discerning the difference between genuine value and expensive decoration.

None of the pieces were reproductions—every painting and sculpture represented a significant investment and sophisticated taste that seemed inconsistent with someone whose primary profession involved killing people for money. She spotted a Rothko above the sofa that she swore she'd seen in a museum catalog, reported stolen and never recovered.

"You know your shit, man," said Ada, standing to examine the piece more closely before slapping fingertips with him in street greeting. She hugged him with newfound respect that went beyond their business relationship. "When did you become an art connoisseur?"

"I don't know shit about art, but I do know a bargain when I see it." Punque's honesty was refreshing—he collected based on value rather than aesthetic appreciation.

"I see. Well, maybe we can work something out—later, of course."

Punque pulled out what looked like a diamond-encrusted jewelry box that caught light streaming through floor-to-ceiling windows like a small fallen star. He swept back his two-foot dreads with a theatrical gesture, smiled at Ada, and opened the box to display its contents.

"How about some line or Tango and Cash?" His offer was delivered with casual hospitality, though the refreshments in question were illegal substances that could destroy lives as easily as they provided temporary escape.

Ada didn't let on that she had no idea "line" meant cocaine and "Tango and Cash" referred to Fentanyl—her ignorance of current drug terminology reflecting her preference for violence over chemical solutions.

"Not right now. We got business."

"Well, okay, my sister, let's talk."

"Tell me your cost for one murder, no witnesses, done in seven days or less. Don't be afraid to scare me with your number."

"One and a half large, and I'll throw in the Rothko if it's untraceable cash—in my hand—before I start. My boys and I got expenses, know what I'm saying?"

Ada stood up quickly, excitement rather than alarm driving her movement, and turned to look at the Rothko with new appreciation. She kissed Punque on his cheek with the enthusiasm of someone who'd just discovered business could be more profitable than imagined.

"Half tomorrow and half when the job is complete. Good?"

"Good."

• • • •

UNDER AN EASTEX FREEWAY overpass near White Oak Bayou, where the constant rumble of traffic provided the soundtrack of urban life for people left behind by economic progress, a large homeless enclave had formed and was growing bigger each day.

The concrete supports created a maze of semi-private spaces that provided some protection from rain and wind. However, nothing could shield inhabitants from noise and exhaust fumes that characterized life beneath Houston's transportation arteries.

This encampment represented an amalgamation of backgrounds, ages, mental health conditions, and addiction issues that would have challenged any social service agency. Veterans whose minds had been broken by war, families whose breadwinners had lost jobs that would never return, people with an addiction whose diseases had consumed everything they once owned, immigrants whose dreams of American prosperity had been reduced to survival beneath an overpass.

But this particular encampment had something that set it apart from all others scattered throughout Houston's industrial landscape: an unofficial leader whose presence transformed what could have been an anarchic collection of desperate individuals into something approaching a functional community.

His name—or rather, the name given to him by his "family"—was Hosea. This biblical reference reflected both his spiritual authority and his role as someone who spoke truth to people who'd lost faith in everything except the possibility of making it through another day.

Hosea was a very tall African American man of about sixty, thin from irregular meals but still imposing in his bearing. He was unshaven by choice rather than neglect, with two different-colored eyes—one black and one green—that gave him an otherworldly appearance, some found unsettling. In contrast, others interpreted it as a divine blessing.

He stood out by being almost seven feet tall, his height making him visible from any point in the encampment and allowing him to survey his domain like a benevolent giant. He always wore his black Houston Rockets sweatshirt and pants, many thinking he must have played for the Rockets at one time, though the truth was more complicated.

Very little was known about his background or the circumstances that had brought him to life beneath an overpass, and that was just the way he wanted it. Mystery enhanced authority, and authority was essential for maintaining the fragile peace that kept their community from descending into violence.

His "family" was loosely organized into groups that reflected the essential functions of any community: food procurement and distribution, sanitation and health maintenance, education and job training, and work coordination for those who could still find temporary employment.

Each group had its leader, a more honorary position than formal authority. Leadership roles rotated based on competence and availability, with Hosea serving as the final arbiter of disputes and the coordinator of activities requiring community-wide cooperation.

Hosea's latest project was creating mini-shelters for families and other groups—small structures built from salvaged materials that provided privacy and protection from the elements. The construction required cooperation and planning that transformed random individuals into something approaching a neighborhood.

The biggest challenge was safety, both from external threats, such as police raids, and internal conflicts between individuals whose lives had been reduced to a competition for scarce resources. The encampment existed in a legal gray area where they were technically trespassing but generally tolerated as long as they didn't attract negative attention.

When Hosea gathered everyone for morning family meetings, his brief talks consisted of messages of love and faith delivered in a voice that carried the authority of someone who had found meaning in circumstances that'd have broken most people.

Then he'd listen to grievances with the patience of someone who understood that being heard was often more important than having problems solved, and visit every group to see if there was anything he could do to help them accomplish their daily missions.

Perhaps because of his size and deep, mellifluous voice that seemed to emerge from somewhere more profound than his chest, his words and honesty exuded truth and wisdom rather than fear. Hosea didn't talk much, preferring action to rhetoric, but when he did speak, your full attention was automatically engaged.

Recently, things had been getting tense, with new groups of migrants and refugees entering the family and challenging informal social contracts that had maintained peace. The newcomers brought their survival strategies and cultural assumptions that didn't always mesh with the cooperative model Hosea had established.

On this particular day, a physical disagreement was escalating into violence between two men whose desperation had overwhelmed their judgment. Hosea intervened by separating the combatants with effortless strength, his long arms creating a barrier neither man was willing to challenge.

"Our family works together. Every soul here is part of it. If you like it here, you have to contribute, and that means no more fighting. We can't have it. Now, shake hands and tell me what the problem is so we can solve it."

The shorter Hispanic man pointed at the gaunt white man, claiming he'd stolen his phone and money. Hosea reached out with his massive palm facing up and said nothing, allowing the gesture to communicate what words might have complicated. The accused man gave him the phone and money without argument.

Hosea hugged both men with physical affection, understanding that human touch was often the most potent form of communication available to people whose lives had been reduced to the bare essentials of survival. The conflict was over, and the family continued their business in peace.

Rain had been pouring down all day, turning unpaved areas into mud and making it difficult for groups to go about their everyday business of scavenging, panhandling, and seeking temporary employment. So they were surprised when three strangers entered the enclave through the maze of concrete supports, soaking wet and obviously in need of immediate assistance.

The newcomers were immediately given blankets and warm soup by people who understood that today's stranger might be tomorrow's ally. That generosity was often the only insurance policy available to people living outside society's safety nets.

Hosea immediately noticed Yakov, Kashinka, and Ralph, his experienced eye recognizing signs of recent trauma and ongoing crisis that marked people pushed beyond normal limits. He could see the older man's health was poor, with a pale complexion and labored breathing, suggesting serious medical issues that wouldn't be helped by street life.

Ralph showed obvious signs of having suffered recent injuries—facial bruising and careful movement suggesting someone still recovering from violence. Ralph carried Yakov on his back, while Kashinka held her grandfather's hand; the three formed a small family unit bound by necessity and mutual care.

When Hosea waved at the crowd to help the three newcomers, a dozen people rushed forward with spontaneous cooperation that characterized communities where survival depended on mutual assistance. They brought the trio to the little tent on the far edge of the encampment—the only spot that was dry and warm, reserved for the most vulnerable members of their extended family.

The shelter also had a few medical supplies donated by a nearby clinic—bandages, antiseptic, and over-the-counter medications—representing the only healthcare available to people who couldn't afford insurance.

Hosea welcomed the three strangers as if he'd known them all his life, his greeting carrying warmth of someone who understood that today's refugees might become tomorrow's contributors.

"We don't have much to offer you, but you are welcome to our family, and you can stay as long as you like. After you rest, we can talk."

Although Ralph was utterly exhausted from carrying Yakov through rain and mud, he couldn't shake the feeling that something about Hosea looked familiar. The tall man's distinctive appearance triggered memories his damaged consciousness couldn't reasonably organize into recognition.

But he was too tired to think about it clearly, and he fell asleep immediately upon lying down on dry bedding that represented luxury compared to the concrete basement where he'd been hiding. Kashinka stayed close to her grandfather throughout the day and into the night, her vigil motivated by understanding that his health was deteriorating beyond what rest and shelter could repair.

She could hear the rumbling of cars on the freeway above them, the constant traffic creating white noise that some found comforting and others experienced as a reminder of the world they'd lost. The passing vehicles had a rhythm that sounded proper and regular, making her feel that life was going on as usual for lucky people who still had destinations and resources to reach them.

One day, her life would be like that! The hope sustained her through the uncertainty of their current situation, providing emotional fuel that kept her caring for her grandfather and their wounded companion. Then she fell asleep, dreaming of a future that included warm homes, reliable meals, and the luxury of planning beyond tomorrow.

• • • •

BLUE SKY APPEARED IN the morning, streaming silver rays of sunlight through gaps between concrete supports that had sheltered them through the night. Everything smelled clean and fresh, even where the family lived, the rain having washed away some of the accumulated odors that characterized life beneath an overpass.

Kashinka awoke refreshed by the first solid sleep she'd enjoyed in days, gently waking her grandfather with solicitous care of someone whose survival depended on his continued health. There was no immediate response from Yakov, causing fear to spike through his granddaughter's consciousness.

But his eyes fluttered and opened slowly, like flowers responding to sunlight, and a smile crossed his weary face as he recognized her presence and the safety of their new surroundings.

Ralph was awake enough to see that his friends were okay, his consciousness gradually reassembling itself from fragments that trauma and exhaustion had scattered. He tested his arms, legs, and neck, checking for damage and mobility with careful attention of someone whose survival might depend on physical capabilities.

All seemed to be in working order—far cry from the previous couple of days when simply remaining conscious had required enormous effort. He stood up slowly, and after a bit of shakiness that reminded him of recent injuries, he regained his balance and felt something approaching normal function returning.

His mind was working better, and his memory was in clear mode, like it used to be before trauma had clouded his thinking and reduced his consciousness to basic survival functions. The clarity was both welcome and dangerous—it allowed strategic thinking but also reminded him of all the reasons why his presence endangered anyone who helped him.

Then he realized that every aspect of his new situation needed adjustment, or he wouldn't last very long in a world where people were actively hunting him with resources and motivation to find him eventually. He was still a man on the run, and no amount of temporary safety could change that fundamental reality.

CHAPTER 37

Hosea made his usual early morning rounds through the encampment, checking on the most vulnerable members of his extended family, as well as those who just needed a kind word to remind them that someone cared about their well-being. His presence was both protective and nurturing, blending practical skills of a community organizer with the spiritual authority of someone who had found meaning in circumstances that had defeated most people.

When he looked into the tent housing his three new family members, all looked well enough to justify cautious optimism about their recovery. Then he noticed something astonishing that he couldn't explain but couldn't ignore—recognition that went beyond normal concern for newcomers needing help integrating into the community's informal support systems.

He gently asked Ralph to join him on his tour of the encampment, and Ralph agreed with understanding that observing the community's operations might help him understand the rules and relationships that governed life beneath the overpass.

It was apparent that the family had great love for their leader as they navigated the maze of improvised shelters and organized activities. Some leaders are gifted with all the right qualities for managing desperate people in impossible circumstances, and Hosea was such a person.

He was a presence just by his size alone, his almost seven-foot frame making him visible from anywhere in the encampment and allowing him to monitor community activities with the efficiency of someone whose leadership depended on information as much as authority.

But his voice was warm and comforting, rather than intimidating, and his eyes glittered with gentle kindness, suggesting someone who had found peace despite circumstances that'd have embittered most people. The reason people followed him was his ability to calm the masses, regardless of how dire the situation appeared, because he was suffering alongside them rather than managing them from a position of relative privilege.

After the tour, which revealed a level of organization and cooperation that impressed Ralph despite his determination to remain emotionally detached, Hosea invited Ralph to join him for tea. The invitation was delivered with ceremonial courtesy by someone who understood that meaningful conversations required proper settings and adequate time.

Ralph was getting the idea that Hosea was leading up to something important, perhaps a request or revelation that would change the terms of his temporary sanctuary. When they sat down on two old milk crates and faced each other in a quiet corner of the encampment, Hosea led the conversation with gentle authority.

"What do they call you, friend?" The question was simple but loaded with implications—in a community where people often reinvented themselves, names carried weight beyond simple identification.

Ralph looked directly into Hosea's eyes and refused to answer, his silence reflecting both paranoia and determination not to bring danger to people who'd shown him kindness. After a few more attempts to elicit a response, Hosea changed the subject to something much more important than mere identification.

"A name isn't important, you know. My name isn't Hosea, but since my family chooses to call me that, I'm perfectly fine with it." His admission revealed flexibility that characterized life on the margins, where identity was more about function than history. "I wanted to talk to you after I saw something this morning. It has to do with that amulet you're wearing."

"It was given to me." Ralph's response was minimal but honest, acknowledging the object's existence without providing details about its origin or significance.

Ralph instantly recognized the panhandler he'd seen putting the amulet on his side-view mirror during that traffic jam that now seemed like a lifetime ago. It was Hosea, though transformed by circumstances and context into someone who seemed larger and more significant than the desperate man who'd approached his car.

However, Hosea was unable to see the man inside the car when he gave the amulet because of the tinted windows, so the recognition didn't go both ways. Ralph's knowledge of their previous encounter gave him an advantage he wasn't sure how to use.

"It has great meaning. It's a sign of providence and faith." Hosea's voice carried reverence of someone discussing sacred objects that connected the material world to spiritual realities.

Ralph wouldn't buy into Hosea's description, his scientific mind rejecting interpretations that depended on supernatural intervention rather than human psychology and coincidence. This was one of those times when silence was the best course of action, allowing others to project whatever meaning they needed without committing himself to beliefs that might prove inconvenient.

"God gave me the vision to create that. It took me seven days to make, and each day gave me more spiritual power than the day before." Hosea's explanation carried the weight of someone describing a genuine religious experience. "And you, my friend, have come back to us wearing it as a sign, a true message from above. You have come, chosen one, and you have come here to save us."

"The only one I can save is myself, and I'm not doing a very good job of that. So, how can I save you and all these people?" Ralph's response was practical and skeptical, the reaction of someone who'd learned to mistrust grandiose claims about his destiny or significance.

"None of us has the right to question the way of the Lord. You may not know your mission yet, but it will become clear to you very soon. I feel it." Hosea's conviction was unshakeable, his faith providing certainty that Ralph's rational mind couldn't accept or completely dismiss.

"Will the girl and her grandfather be safe here?" Ralph's question showed his genuine concern, not his supposed divine mission, but the well-being of the people who had risked their safety to help him recover.

"Yes. We watch over our own and do our best to make everyone feel welcome and cared for. That is our mission, my friend." Hosea's promise was delivered with the authority of someone who'd successfully protected vulnerable people in circumstances where protection seemed impossible.

Ralph walked back to the tent to check on his two companions, his mind processing the conversation with Hosea and its implications for his plans. The older man looked poorly despite the night's rest, his breathing labored and color suggesting that rest and shelter might not be sufficient to restore his failing health.

Kashinka looked more worried than ever, her young face marked by the strain of caring for someone whose condition was deteriorating beyond her ability to help. So Ralph stayed with them until evening closed in around the encampment, approaching darkness bringing both concealment and renewed awareness that safety was always temporary for people living outside society's protection.

When the girl and old man fell asleep, exhaustion finally claiming them after days of stress and uncertainty, Ralph left his two companions to the care of Hosea and his family. The decision was both practical and painful—he knew they would be safer without him, but leaving them felt like abandoning the only people who'd shown him genuine kindness since his world had collapsed.

Ralph walked aimlessly around Houston through the night, checking out possible hiding spots and looking for something he couldn't quite identify—something to believe in that might give meaning to a life that had been reduced to basic survival.

But now, something different was gnawing at him that he'd never experienced before in his carefully controlled emotional life. He cared deeply for his two new companions and hated himself for running out on them, even if it was for their own good.

The internal conflict between self-preservation and human connection was tearing him apart, forcing him to confront the possibility that isolation might preserve his physical safety while destroying whatever remained of his capacity for meaningful relationships.

CHAPTER 38

Hosea had finished his daily rounds of panhandling in downtown Houston, moving through the city with the practiced efficiency of someone who understood the rhythm and geography of urban charity. His infectious smile and positive attitude made him a kind of celebrity wherever he went, recognizable to regular commuters and businesspeople who had grown accustomed to his presence at strategic intersections.

What no one knew about Hosea was that every dollar bill and handful of change given by people moved by guilt, genuine compassion, or simple superstition, he brought it all back to his family, using the funds to feed and help them in any way he could.

His personal needs were minimal, but the community beneath the overpass required resources that only money could provide—food that couldn't be scavenged, medical supplies that clinics wouldn't donate, tools that made their improvised shelters more livable.

He stopped by "Old School Fly Styles," a local barber shop that'd sometimes give him a free haircut when business was slow and the owner, Charles, was feeling charitable toward the giant who had become part of the neighborhood's landscape. The shop was crowded with the usual afternoon clientele, but Charles motioned him in and told him to wait in the corner where a folding chair had been set up for overflow customers.

When the disheveled giant sat down, his seven-foot frame folding awkwardly into furniture designed for smaller people, a few customers moved to different chairs with unconscious prejudice that marked interactions between the housed and homeless. He smiled at them as he did with most people, his expression carrying no resentment, but they looked away rather than acknowledge his presence.

Hosea sat with hands folded in his lap, waiting with patient dignity of someone who understood that charity came with conditions and that gratitude was more effective than demands. He spotted four young men wearing gang paraphernalia and talking louder than they should, their voices carrying aggressive confidence that marked people accustomed to intimidating others through the implicit threat of violence.

They pulled jars and bottles of hair products off the shelves and put them in their pockets with the casual entitlement of people who took what they wanted and dared anyone to object. A few customers decided to leave rather than face what they recognized as a potentially dangerous situation.

The leader of this wing of the Third Ward Posse was flashing gang signs and steel teeth at Charles, who had just finished giving a haircut and was cleaning his equipment with nervous precision of someone trying to appear busy while hoping trouble would resolve itself.

Charles tried his best to ignore the gang members, but he knew it was a waste of time—they hadn't come for haircuts, and their presence would continue to escalate until they got whatever they'd come for.

"Charles, my brother. Ain't you happy to see me?" The gang leader's greeting was delivered with mock friendliness that carried an unmistakable undertone of threat.

The F and P—for Felonious Punque—tattooed across the leader's forehead jumped up and down as he raised his eyebrows with theatrical emphasis. When Charles refused to reply, recognizing that any response would be interpreted as either submission or challenge, Felonious continued his demand for attention with escalating aggression.

"Guess not. But you should be happy because I just stopped by to spend some FaceTime with you during my very busy day. Your subscription is coming to an end, Charles. Unless, of course, you want to renew, which would make us posse boys happy, and then we'll both be happy, Charles." The protection racket was delivered with the businesslike efficiency of someone collecting legitimate fees.

"I don't want to renew, so get out before I call the cops." Charles's refusal was brave but futile.

The rest of the customers left except Hosea, who was thinking about how he could defuse the situation without making it worse for everyone involved. His size and presence sometimes helped in such circumstances, but they could also escalate conflicts if young men felt challenged.

Meanwhile, Felonious put a gun under Charles's chin with the casual precision of someone who'd performed this action many times before, and promised to be back the next day for security and protection subscription renewal that would keep the barbershop operating without interference.

Hosea smiled at the gang members with a serene expression, that of someone who had seen enough violence to understand its futility, and they walked over to him with the curiosity of predators encountering something they couldn't immediately categorize.

"Hey, stank boy. You know where I can find a white stank boy who looks like he shouldn't be homeless? I've got cash right here in my pocket if you can help me out." Felonious's question was delivered with the casual cruelty of someone who took pleasure in demonstrating power over vulnerable people.

Hosea shook his head slowly; his refusal delivered without explanation or apology. They left the barbershop with the swagger of people who'd accomplished their immediate goal of intimidation. Still, then Felonious came back alone and pistol-whipped Hosea with the efficient brutality of someone making a point that wouldn't be forgotten.

"Now, don't you be lying to me no more. I know you know where he is, and I'm just trying to help his family find him. So think about it, and if you change your mind, meet me here tomorrow at 9:00 AM." Felonious's threat was delivered with the sincerity of someone who believed his lies about helping families.

Charles helped Hosea into one of the barber chairs with gentle care, understanding that kindness was often the only medicine available to people who couldn't afford healthcare. He cleaned the wound with professional skill and gave him a haircut that restored some dignity to his appearance.

Around the corner from the shop, Felonious had assigned P-Slice to follow the large man until he led them to his encampment—surveillance that would provide the intelligence they needed to locate their target. Perhaps they could gather information about Ralph Norton, their pot of gold, who represented enough money to make everyone involved rich beyond their current ability to imagine.

"They're good boys, Charles. They need better role models to learn how to do God's work. That's all." Hosea's characterization of the gang members was charitable to the point of seeming delusional.

"They need more than better role models. They need a better justice system that will put them behind bars until they figure out their lives." Charles's response was practical, the view of someone who had to deal with the immediate consequences of criminal behavior.

"Most of God's children are good people. But sometimes, they get lost along their way in life." Hosea's faith in human redemption was unshakeable, sustained by a theological framework that viewed criminal behavior as a spiritual illness rather than an inherent evil.

"You're a good man, Hosea, but be careful out there, please." Charles's warning carried the concern of someone who'd watched too many good people become victims of circumstances they couldn't control.

Charles removed the apron from around Hosea's neck and flicked off the hair with a sharp snap, a gesture professional barbers used to signal the completion of their service. Hosea dug into his pockets for money that wasn't there—an automatic gesture that revealed his discomfort with accepting charity even when freely offered.

Charles knew he had no money and waved him off with understanding that some services were provided for reasons that had nothing to do with financial compensation.

"Have a good day, man, and stay safe."

P-Slice followed Hosea around town for almost three hours, confused by the giant's behavior and unable to understand his motivations. He couldn't figure out why Hosea would talk to people and smile without asking for money or attempting to sell anything—it made no sense to someone whose life revolved around transactions and immediate gain.

But eventually, when Hosea headed back to his encampment as afternoon shadows grew longer, P-Slice called Felonious to give him the location that would allow them to plan their assault on the community that had provided Ralph Norton with temporary sanctuary.

But while he made that call, Felonious had identified six additional encampments that needed to be checked out as part of their systematic search for the man whose capture would make them all wealthy. So he ordered P-Slice back to join them on their methodical search through every homeless encampment near downtown Houston, leaving no stone unturned in their pursuit of the prize.

Felonious was more than just a common criminal pursuing money through violence. He was a maniac in search of a victim who would satisfy both his financial needs and psychological hunger for causing pain, and it didn't matter who the victim was as long as the experience provided the stimulation he craved.

It was something he lived for—the combination of profit and suffering that made existence meaningful for someone whose capacity for empathy had been surgically removed by circumstances and choices that had transformed him from a human being into something that resembled one but lacked essential elements that made life sacred rather than simply biological.

CHAPTER 39

The constant rumble of traffic above their heads had become white noise, but when Hosea stumbled into the encampment beneath the Eastex Freeway overpass, even that familiar sound couldn't mask the gasps of alarm from his family. The giant who'd been their anchor in the storm now moved like a ship taking on water, each step uncertain.

Orange flames from their trash can fire cast dancing shadows across the concrete supports that had become the walls of their world. Several men caught Hosea before he collapsed, their quick reflexes born from years of watching out for each other when no one else would.

They eased him down on an old blanket by the fire, the wool fabric stained with Houston's industrial rain and human stories too hard to tell. The concern on their faces was immediate—Hosea wasn't just their leader; he was their proof that dignity could survive when everything else had been stripped away.

Blood seeped from the back of his skull where Felonious Punque's pistol had connected, a dark stain spreading across the blanket like spilled wine. The woman who served as their unofficial medic noticed immediately, her trained eye recognizing damage that went deeper than surface wounds.

Miriam St. Jean had been an RN for twenty years before opioids stole her career and dumped her on the streets. Her hands still moved with professional competence as she examined Hosea's injury, muscle memory intact despite a decade of homelessness.

"Bring him over here," she called, gesturing toward her makeshift clinic—a corner of the encampment where she kept their meager medical supplies in a shopping cart with three working wheels.

She'd lost her nursing license to pills, but she'd never lost the instinct to heal. Hosea had saved her life more times than she could count, giving her purpose when overdose would have been easier than another day of survival.

When she cleaned the wound with antiseptic that burned like liquid fire, Hosea's massive frame went rigid. The gash was deep; edges ragged from the gun barrel's impact. In a real hospital, this would mean CT scans and overnight observation. Here, it meant prayer and whatever medical knowledge Miriam could remember from her previous life.

"You need stitches," she told him, her voice carrying the authority of someone who'd seen enough head trauma to know the difference between serious and fatal.

"Others need help more than me." Hosea's response was automatic—the selflessness that had made him beloved by people who'd learned not to trust anyone who promised to help.

But Miriam could see his pupils weren't tracking correctly, and his responses were slower than usual. Possible skull fracture, definitely concussion, maybe worse. In her former world, she'd have called for emergency transport. In this world, she cleaned the wound and hoped for the best.

The sharp pain that lanced through his head made Hosea close his eyes tightly, his massive hands pressing against his temples as if he could hold his skull together through sheer will. Miriam and Kashinka exchanged glances—they'd both seen that look before, and it never meant anything good.

"Don't worry, little girl," Hosea told Kashinka when the wave of agony passed. "God has a way of helping the needy that is only known by him. Your grandfather is a good man, and God knows that."

His voice still carried the gentle authority that had made them all believe in something larger than their suffering, but Kashinka could hear the effort it cost him.

"Thank you, Mr. Hosea. I'll go back to my grandfather now." Her mature understanding of everyone's need for care had been forged in circumstances no child should face.

Hosea asked Miriam to gather the family quietly—his request delivered with the urgency of someone who understood that time was running out. He needed to tell them something that couldn't wait for his recovery.

Miriam moved through the encampment with practiced efficiency, touching shoulders and whispering summons with the healing gesture that had characterized her nursing career. Some stood around the fire while others sat on whatever served as seating—milk crates, broken chairs, the luxury of salvaged furniture.

When they'd gathered in the orange glow that pushed back Houston's indifferent darkness, Hosea spoke in a voice that'd lost strength. Still, he retained the moral authority that'd made them a family, instead of just another collection of abandoned souls.

"Thank you, my friends. I wanted to talk to all of you about something that has to be said because it is so important." His words carried the weight of final testimony. "Our lives are filled with the love of our Lord. Never forget that. You must know that, and you must never give up hope that your lives are in his hands."

The firelight played across faces that had learned to expect disappointment, but Hosea's conviction still had the power to kindle hope in people who'd forgotten what it felt like.

"By his actions, he has sent us a Chosen One. This is a person who will guide us and take us to a great and glorious future. He has come here to save us." His voice strengthened as he delivered the prophecy that had become his final gift to them. "You will know him by an amulet that hangs around his neck. It is a star of David with a crucifix inside of it, showing that we are all one people, one faith, one family."

Smiles appeared on faces that had learned to hoard joy like spare change—small expressions of people who'd been permitted to believe that their suffering might have meaning.

As the crowd began to break up, seeking whatever peace they could find beneath the constant rumble of traffic above, Miriam made Hosea as comfortable as possible. She arranged their makeshift bedding to support his damaged head while monitoring his vital signs with the professional attention that addiction had never erased.

He closed his eyes with a warm smile, the expression of someone who'd completed his mission and could rest knowing he'd planted seeds of hope that might grow into something larger than his own life.

CHAPTER 40

Houston at night was an entirely different incarnation—a city pulsing with frequencies that seemed to emerge from the concrete and asphalt, which absorbed the day's heat and released it slowly into darkness. The urban landscape became a maze of shadows and neon, creating its own weather system of desperation and possibility.

Ralph remembered when he first came to Houston years ago, driving these same streets in his reliable car with his resume and references, believing that competence and hard work would be sufficient to build a meaningful life. He couldn't have imagined being lonelier then, but that loneliness had been the temporary isolation of someone between situations rather than the permanent exile he now experienced.

Now he hid his face by looking down at cracked sidewalks, sometimes extending his hand for donations with the practiced humility of someone who'd learned that pride was a luxury he couldn't afford. He kept his shoulders hunched while burying his dirty face inside his collar, making himself as invisible as possible in a city that had trained itself not to see people like him.

But this new loneliness put him squarely against the whole world in ways he'd never imagined when his biggest problem was finding the proper corporate position that would allow him to use his talents profitably.

Hunger brought him back to reality after living in a world of shadows and fear, reducing consciousness to biological imperatives that transcended social conditioning and personal dignity. He hadn't eaten anything substantial for days, and as he passed a Wendy's restaurant, he smelled French fries in the moist night air wafting from a dumpster like an olfactory beacon.

Dumpster diving was his last resort—an activity he'd never imagined performing even in his worst nightmares about potential failure. He remembered reading a short story about a teenager living on the streets and how he'd befriended a homeless woman who taught him survival skills that polite society preferred not to acknowledge.

The hell with that story, he thought as his stomach cramped with emptiness. He was hungry enough that literary parallels seemed less important than finding calories to eat.

The dumpster overflowed with the debris of American consumer culture—food packaging, failed meals, and waste that characterized a society that could afford to discard what others desperately needed. While he waited for courage to begin his search, a homeless man approached and asked if he had a cigarette with the casual camaraderie of someone recognizing a fellow member of the invisible population.

Ralph didn't answer, maintaining the silence that had become his default response to human contact. But when the man picked up a used cigarette butt from the parking lot and examined it with the expertise of someone who understood tobacco desperation, he motioned to Ralph to join him in the dive.

Ralph looked around carefully to ensure no one was watching who might report his activity to authorities, then went into the dumpster with the resignation of someone crossing a line he'd never expected to cross.

They found cold French fries swimming in used frying oil poured over everything like a greasy benediction that transformed discarded food into something that might sustain human life for a few more hours. The man knew his way around a dumpster with professional competence, and when he found decent morsels, he shared them with Ralph without being asked.

Ralph stayed silent as he wolfed down the food, his body responding to nutrition with grateful efficiency while his mind tried to process the reality of what he was doing and how far he'd fallen.

"Got a place for the night?" asked the thin, dried-out man, whose appearance suggested years of living rough, but whose voice carried the concern of someone who understood that survival was easier when people looked out for each other.

Ralph still didn't answer, his mistrust of human contact warring with his need for guidance in navigating a world he didn't understand. But the man's voice sounded honest rather than evil, so when he waved Ralph to follow into the night shadows, Ralph went cautiously along.

The man had night vision, stepping through chain-link fences and navigating around building debris with the confidence of someone who'd mapped every safe passage through the urban wasteland. It took almost an hour of careful movement until they found their way into a completely hidden homeless enclave that existed in the spaces between official acknowledgment and aggressive elimination.

A few of the homeless seemed to recognize the thin man as he walked around and over sleeping people, children, and crazy-eyed vagrants with practiced efficiency. Ralph followed him through the maze of human bodies, noting defensive positioning and watchful eyes that never completely closed even in sleep.

The man found a place to sleep among the others, settling into a spot that had probably been his for weeks or months. As he lay down, Ralph walked around until he found a more hidden area where he could rest while keeping an eye on potential dangers.

Ralph noticed additional hidden areas in the ruined building, in case he needed to disappear into the evening; his strategic thinking automatically cataloged escape routes and defensive positions. He also noted the most promising way out of the rubble in case he needed to leave quickly in the event of trouble.

Suddenly, Ralph heard loud commotion from where the larger group was resting—the sound of violence cutting through nighttime quiet like a blade through silk. The words came through muffled and coarse as if mouths were covered and throats choked, suggesting systematic brutality rather than random conflict.

His instincts kicked in with the clarity that had served him well in corporate warfare, and it wasn't long before his planned exit route took him to temporary safety while screams and pleas echoed from the encampment he'd just abandoned.

The Third Ward Posse had completed its second round of homeless camp investigations, using threats, torture, and violence to extract information about Ralph's whereabouts with systematic brutality of people who'd turned cruelty into a business model. It was now the second day of their seven-day deadline, and they hadn't been able to find out anything about where Ralph was hiding or if he was even still in Houston.

· · · ·

FELONIOUS PUNQUE WAS running entirely on instinct and gut feeling, his desperation growing as the timeline for completing his contract shrank with each passing hour. Somehow, he knew Ralph was somewhere in the city's homeless population, but the systematic search was taking longer than anticipated.

The timeline to find his target was shrinking rapidly, and mounting pressure was making him more dangerous and less discriminating about the violence he employed. So he stepped up the torture and murder to a horrific level that would terrorize the homeless community into cooperation or silence.

Torture could bring out lies designed to make pain stop, but Punque had learned to distinguish between truth and desperate fabrication through experience that had taught him to read human nature in its most reduced state. His best man for extracting information through pain was Cap'n Payne—a one-eyed weaponized pain machine that liked his work enough to do it for free if money weren't involved.

He was a large, heavy man in his early twenties whose physical presence was made more disturbing by the patch over his left eye and a stuffed parakeet sewn into his pirate vest. He called the parakeet Mama and constantly asked her permission before beginning his work—a ritual that suggested mental illness layered on top of criminal sadism.

When Mama gave him the go-ahead to proceed with torture, Cap'n Payne knew immediately if someone was lying after he sliced vital areas of the torso with surgical precision learned through years of causing pain without causing immediate death. His method was simple and effective: if the victim lied, they died right then; if they didn't lie, they lived but wished they didn't.

After making no progress in their systematic interrogation of Houston's homeless population, one terrified woman finally told Felonious that a man had been brought into their encampment just a short while before. Still, she didn't know where he was or who he was beyond the obvious fact that he was new to their community.

The only thing she could say with certainty was that he was new to the group. However, new homeless people were always joining and leaving as circumstances changed and opportunities appeared or disappeared. Her information was frustratingly vague, but it represented the first potential lead they'd developed in days of systematic violence.

Felonious threw a hundred-dollar bill at the woman with the casual generosity of someone who understood that money could motivate cooperation when torture failed. They told the rest of the group they could become rich if they could help him find the mysterious newcomer.

The muffled cries of the dying and tortured added stark finality to the evening air, serving as both warning and promise to anyone who might be considering withholding information. The sounds carried across the urban wasteland like a soundtrack to hell, reminding everyone within hearing distance that violence was always an option for people who had nothing left to lose.

Felonious made a decision that would escalate their search beyond anything they'd attempted before. They had to find Ralph that night, using whatever methods were necessary to extract information from people who had learned that cooperation with authority usually led to punishment rather than protection.

He knew they would find their target sooner or later, and later was not an option given the deadline Ada Taylor had imposed. Whenever there is no tomorrow, time shrinks into seconds and seconds into potential death for anyone who stands between them and their objective.

It was time to find the giant that P-Slice had identified, and P-Slice led the way through the maze of streets and abandoned lots that connected Houston's homeless encampments like an underground railroad for people who'd fallen out of society's recognition.

No road could accommodate vehicles to Hosea's family encampment, so they parked their SUV about a mile away and proceeded on foot through terrain that belonged more to urban explorers than conventional criminals. The evening descended heavily, with thick clouds obscuring the stars and a slight mist falling, making visibility poor and sound travel unpredictably.

It was past midnight, and traffic on the freeway above was sparse enough that their approach would be audible to anyone listening for trouble. The posse was ready for their party to begin, each member armed and psychologically prepared for the kind of violence that would either solve their problem or eliminate witnesses who might complicate future operations.

Felonious placed his men around the perimeter of the encampment to prevent stragglers from leaving and potentially alerting authorities or other homeless communities about what was happening. When they were sure everything was positioned perfectly for maximum control, they would close in on the sleeping giant with hostages to convince him that cooperation was his only option.

Cap'n Payne couldn't stop giggling with anticipation, his excitement building as he contemplated opportunities for creative violence that the evening might provide.

When they found Hosea in his weakened state, the giant couldn't stand up despite his determination to protect his family from the violence that had finally found them. P-Slice grabbed Kashinka in his grasp, using the child as both shield and leverage, while the rest of the encampment gathered around their fallen leader.

Felonious kicked Hosea's skull as hard as he could, his boot connecting with the damaged area where the earlier attack had already caused serious injury. He continued the assault until the giant became unconscious, his massive frame going limp as brain trauma overwhelmed his iron constitution.

P-Slice held Kashinka as she sobbed with grief that went beyond fear to encompass the loss of everything that had given her life meaning and stability.

"Tell her to shut the fuck up before I give her to Payne, you hear me?" Felonious's threat was delivered with the casual cruelty of someone who'd learned to use children as tools for controlling adults.

"Her grandpa died when I took her. That's why she's acting like that," said P-Slice, his explanation revealing that their violence had already claimed one victim before they'd even begun their interrogation.

Felonious looked around at the pathetic group of people who looked terrified, but not in the way he'd expected. They'd witnessed scenes like this before in other encampments, but never directed at Hosea, who'd been their source of protection and guidance.

He was their mountain of hope, the anchor that had kept their community together when everything else in their lives had fallen apart. They weren't scared of the posse's capacity for violence, but of the implications of their leader's condition for their future survival.

Felonious pulled out a wad of hundred-dollar bills, displaying wealth that represented more money than most of them had seen in years.

"I'm looking for a white man who's new around here. I know that one of you knows where he is." His voice carried the reasonable tone of someone making a business proposition. "This money is yours if you tell me where he is. I promise we won't hurt this man, but we're looking for him because his dear mother is worried sick and wants him to come back home. Can anyone here help me find him?"

His discerning eyes and those of his posse scanned the crowd in darkness, flashlight beams moving from face to face in search of recognition, guilt, or fear that might reveal useful information. Not one person flinched or gave any indication they knew anything about Ralph's presence in their community.

Felonious wasn't about to give up when he was this close to completing a contract that would make him wealthy beyond his current ability to imagine. He walked over to Kashinka, grabbed her by her hair with enough force to lift her small body partially off the ground, and pulled her into the center of the circle where everyone could see what was happening.

Still, no one flinched or gave any sign of caring about the child's fate, though their silence reflected loyalty to Ralph rather than indifference to Kashinka's suffering.

"See this girl?" yelled Felonious, his voice echoing off concrete supports that surrounded their encampment. "She's mine now. And if you ever want to see her alive again, my advice is to speak up, or you won't recognize her when you see her again. This is your last chance, people. Now's the time to speak up because we're out of here."

Not a soul moved or spoke a word; their silence reflected both their ignorance of Ralph's current location and their understanding that revealing information wouldn't save Kashinka, but would only ensure that more people would suffer.

"Okay, boys, let's go. Take her, Cap'n." Felonious's command was delivered with the finality of someone who'd exhausted his patience for negotiation.

Payne latched onto Kashinka like a predator claiming prey, his grip suggesting someone who had experience transporting unwilling victims. He giggled his way back toward their vehicle as steady rain began to fall on the posse and their captive, the weather adding another layer of misery to an evening that had already descended into a nightmare.

"Payne, you drive and put the girl back here with me. You know where to drive and make it fast. I'm bored," said Felonious, his casual tone suggesting that kidnapping children was routine business rather than a crime that would haunt everyone involved.

The family was destroyed by the death of Yakov, and now Hosea, their two sources of stability and guidance, were eliminated in a single evening. They felt as though they'd been let down by God, by life, and by whatever mercy they had believed might protect innocent people from violence that characterized their world.

There was nothing they could do about forces that had torn apart their community except try to maintain their dignity in the face of overwhelming tragedy. Nurse St. Jean covered both bodies with two dirty blankets, performing the ritual of respect that the dead deserved, regardless of their circumstances.

There was an unofficial graveyard in the field behind the encampment, where those who died were buried with whatever dignity and love their surviving family could provide. A few men volunteered to dig graves and place makeshift markers on them to identify the locations for anyone who might want to pay their respects.

The markers were personal items that only the community was aware of—objects that carried meaning beyond their apparent insignificance. For both worthy men, it was one of their shoes that became their markers, worn leather that had carried them through their final journey.

St. Jean said a few words over each grave, her nursing background providing her with experience in dealing with death that made her the closest thing they had to clergy. The group broke up after the brief ceremony, returning to whatever shelter they could find while processing the reality that their protector was gone.

One of the men who belonged to the family was a young ex-gang member named Josh, whose life had been saved by Hosea's intervention when drug use had nearly killed him. He'd fallen into addiction and almost lost his life when Hosea found him and provided the structure and purpose that allowed him to survive.

He was forever thankful for being saved and swore to himself that he would avenge Hosea's death. However, he had no clear idea how someone with his limited resources could challenge people who'd just demonstrated their capacity for overwhelming violence.

He took one last look at the grave markers. He walked off into the night, carrying rage and determination that might be sufficient to fuel whatever action he could take against forces that had destroyed his community.

CHAPTER 41

At the end of Travis Street, in a part of downtown Houston that belonged more to the forgotten than the productive, a small group of homeless veterans were shooting up in the shadow of buildings that had once represented American prosperity and now served as a backdrop for American failure.

Their ages varied from two Vietnam vets whose minds had been damaged by a war America preferred not to remember, to two Iraq War vets whose bodies carried wounds the VA system had proven inadequate to heal, and many in between whose military service had promised honor and delivered abandonment.

Whatever their individual stories, they were all the same now, reduced to the fundamental imperative of staying alive for one more day and getting as high as they could until they couldn't remember who they were or where they were. The rest would take care of itself, or it wouldn't, but that was tomorrow's problem.

Ralph found himself near the group when one of them took notice of his presence with wary attention, as people who had learned to be suspicious of newcomers, who might be undercover police, social workers, or simply competitors for limited resources.

They were a loose little club that wouldn't normally allow anyone else to hang out with them, their exclusivity born from challenging experience with people who brought trouble or tried to take advantage of whatever small stability they'd managed to create.

Ralph didn't intrude in their discussion, especially when the time came for everyone to shoot up with the ritual precision of people who had turned self-destruction into a sacrament. From where he sat on a piece of cardboard that provided minimal insulation from cold concrete, he could see filthy needles being shared by the group.

He couldn't help but feel deep and unrelenting sadness as he watched men who'd put their lives on the line for their country and now found that their country had closed its eyes and forgotten about them. The irony wasn't lost on him—people trained to kill for America were now killing themselves because America had no use for them.

He said nothing and looked the other way so as not to attract attention or seem judgmental about choices that desperation had made inevitable rather than voluntary.

They called their leader Cherry Red—a red-headed, bent-up shell of a man with a large earring in his left ear and a bloody bandana on his head that had once been white but had absorbed too much blood and grime to remember its original color.

It was hard to tell if he'd deliberately coordinated all the red colors in his appearance or if it just happened through random accumulation of possessions that characterized homeless fashion. From what Ralph could observe, Cherry Red controlled the way the group thought about each member and determined who was accepted into their small brotherhood.

If he liked you, everyone liked you, operating on the military principle that leadership decisions weren't subject to democratic debate. So when he waved at Ralph to join them, the rest of the group seemed open to the possibility of expanding their membership.

They noticed Ralph's head wound and blood-stained clothes, evidence of recent violence that immediately established his credentials as someone who understood that survival required both luck and the ability to endure physical punishment. The clothes were two sizes too big for his frame, so everyone knew Ralph was at that low point in his life that gave him automatic access to the group of people in a similar predicament.

At first, Ralph ignored them and refused to speak, maintaining silence that had become his default response to human contact. After a few attempts to engage him in conversation, Cherry Red came over and helped Ralph stand, then walked him over to the group with the gentle authority of someone extending hospitality to a fellow veteran of life's wars.

"Sit down, man. You need a lift?" said Red, offering Ralph a needle with the casual generosity of someone sharing whatever resources were available.

Ralph ignored the offer and remained silent, understanding that drug use would compromise his ability to think clearly and react quickly if danger appeared. The less he said, the more the group seemed to like him, interpreting his silence as a sign of strength rather than antisocial behavior.

"You got a name, man?" Red's question was delivered with curiosity of someone who respected privacy but needed some way to address a new member.

"No," whispered Ralph, his response honest in ways that went beyond simple identification to encompass his complete disconnection from his previous identity.

Without the least bit of encouragement, the group applauded Ralph's anonymity with the enthusiasm of people who understood that names could be liabilities when you were trying to disappear from a world that wanted to punish you for existing.

There wasn't much energy in their applause, and it ended as quickly as it began. Still, the gesture carried genuine welcome for someone who understood the value of being nobody in a society that had made being somebody too dangerous to attempt.

Ralph's face grew angrier by the minute as he stared maniacally into the deepest part of the night, his expression reflecting internal storms that had nothing to do with his current circumstances and everything to do with forces that had driven him to this place.

It was an act worthy of the greatest Shakespearean actors, though Ralph wasn't conscious of performing for an audience. The look on his face was the currency that bought him time and acceptance from people who recognized genuine rage when they saw it, and time was all he had left to work with.

The group of vets passed out from the combination of drugs and exhaustion, their bodies claiming whatever rest was possible in circumstances that didn't allow for genuine sleep. Ralph couldn't join them in unconsciousness—everything that had happened to him was pounding his brain in ways he'd never felt before.

Life was becoming compressed and concentrated into a day-to-day, minute-to-minute existence where planning beyond the next few hours was a luxury he couldn't afford. All the quotes from the Bible that he'd reconfigured in his app started to re-emerge in his thoughts with the persistence of advertising jingles that had been burned into his memory through repetition.

The more he thought about his current situation, the more those biblical phrases would pop into his brain like fragments of a spiritual education that he'd felt was purely intellectual but was proving to have deeper roots in his consciousness.

He'd put so much time into that app, studying every nuance of religious language and psychological comfort, that the words had burned themselves into his mind like brands on cattle. For a split second, he worried that he'd been brainwashed by his work, that his creation had somehow taken control of its creator.

Then, suddenly, he felt a gentle kick on his foot that startled him out of his biblical reverie. When he looked up to see who had disturbed his meditation, he recognized Josh from Hosea's family, though the young man's presence in this part of the city suggested that something had gone wrong.

The two didn't speak for a while, both understanding that conversation in this location could attract unwanted attention from veterans who might not appreciate being disturbed. But when Josh noticed Ralph's amulet hanging around his neck, recognition transformed his expression from one of caution to one of desperate relief.

"The family needs you," Josh said in a low voice, so as not to wake the vets, who were lost in their chemical dreams.

As usual, Ralph spoke with his eyes, which conveyed his desire for Josh to disappear and leave him alone in whatever peace he could find among people who had given up on everything except basic survival.

"You have to come back now, but I can't tell you why here, with people listening. It's too important." Josh's urgency was palpable; his voice carried the weight of someone who had witnessed something that couldn't wait for a more convenient time to discuss.

Ralph stood up and walked away from the sleeping veterans, hoping to lose his new shadow by simply making it clear that he didn't want company. Josh followed close behind with the persistence of someone whose mission was more important than social cues or personal preferences.

No matter how much Ralph tried to lose his pursuer, Josh wouldn't be discouraged, following him through the maze of downtown streets past closed shops, traffic lights changing colors for nonexistent traffic, and sex workers closing out their shifts with weary efficiency, as people finished another day of survival labor.

Ralph walked faster, hoping that physical effort might succeed where subtle signals had failed, but it made no difference to Josh's determination. Finally, after Josh grabbed his shoulder to physically force him to stop, Ralph turned around. He flashed his angry eyes at his pursuer with the intensity of someone whose patience had been completely exhausted.

"Look, Josh. Get off my back, and for your own good, get the fuck out of my life. I don't need you, the family, or Hosea. Got it?" Ralph's rejection was complete and uncompromising, delivered with the vehemence of someone who understood that human connections would only bring pain to everyone involved.

"Hosea told us that a Chosen One had arrived. I never used to believe in stuff like that, but I do now. Whether you know it or not, or even give a damn, you are that Chosen One." Josh's declaration was delivered with the conviction of someone whose worldview had been fundamentally altered by recent events.

He held Ralph in place with the physical strength of someone who wouldn't be denied the opportunity to deliver crucial information, regardless of how unwelcome it might be.

"Just listen to me for one minute. The old man who came with you is dead. His granddaughter, Kashinka, has been kidnapped, and we will only be released if one of us tells them where you are. Many were beaten and tortured, and I'm sure they won't stop until they find you, whoever you are. I don't even know your name; no one does."

The information hit Ralph like physical blows, each revelation adding to the weight of guilt and responsibility that he'd been trying to escape through anonymity and isolation.

"I'm no one. Let me repeat that. I am no one," said Ralph, his denial carrying desperation of someone whose entire strategy for survival depended on remaining invisible and unimportant.

"That old man and that little girl loved you. They told everyone that. There's nothing we can do about the old man, but for God's sake, help us get that girl back to safety. It's the least you can do." Josh's appeal was devastating and straightforward, cutting through Ralph's elaborate justifications to focus on the essential moral question of whether he'd help rescue someone who had risked everything to help him.

The stare-off continued for a good minute while Ralph processed the implications of what Josh was asking him to do. Helping meant revealing himself and accepting responsibility for consequences that extended far beyond his survival.

Then Ralph relented, his resistance crumbling under the weight of his obligation to people who had shown him kindness when he had nothing to offer in return.

"I'll help find the girl, but that's it. That's all I'll do. Come on, let's go already. Why didn't you tell me about Kashinka right away? We wasted time with all the rest of your bullshit. Come on."

They made their way back to the encampment, where broken and bloodied people sat in small groups, treating themselves with whatever medical supplies were available. At the same time, Nurse St. Jean made the most of her limited resources and extensive experience.

It all seemed so meaningless and hopeless until Josh and Ralph arrived, their presence transforming despair into the possibility of action. Josh stood in the center of the encampment and asked whoever could move to come and listen.

Josh held Ralph's arm as the few stragglers who weren't too injured or devastated to respond gathered around them, their hopeless looks reflecting the loss of both their leader and their sense of security.

"Look, everyone," yelled Josh, his voice echoing off the concrete supports that surrounded their ruined community. "Look. He has come just as Hosea had said. Look!"

Josh pulled out the amulet that hung around Ralph's neck and held it up like a religious relic, the star of David with the crucifix inside catching what little light was available and reflecting it to the assembled crowd.

"He has come, and we will be better and stronger for it. We are a family once again, and our friend here wants to ask you something. He needs your help." Josh's introduction was both announcement and rallying cry, an attempt to transform tragedy into purpose.

Josh nodded to Ralph, who spoke softly and hesitantly.

"My friend Kashinka has been taken by people who will harm her, unless we go out there and find her. We are her only hope. This we must do, and we must do it right now. Are there any volunteers who want to help us?"

"Step forward now if you want to help. We are leaving on a dangerous mission of mercy right now," said Josh, his call to action delivered with the urgency of someone who understood that every minute of delay increased the danger to an innocent child.

At that moment, no one stepped forward, the assembled homeless people processing the request through the filter of their own survival needs and their realistic assessment of what they could accomplish against people who'd just demonstrated their capacity for overwhelming violence.

So Josh and Ralph headed into the blackness of a humid and cold evening, prepared to search for Kashinka with whatever resources they could muster. It wasn't until a few moments later that they heard approaching voices from behind them—a small group of men carrying pieces of metal or wood that would serve as weapons.

They joined the two leaders in their search for Kashinka, some of them still bearing wounds inflicted by the posse, others motivated by the realization that they'd never done anything brave in their lives and this might be their only opportunity to matter.

It was not a very impressive group of soldiers by conventional military standards. Still, if determination equaled bravery, this group was ready for anything that the night might demand of them.

· · · ·

AFTER TWO HOURS OF searching in vain through the maze of streets and abandoned buildings that might serve as hiding places for kidnapped children, Josh and most of the group were exhausted and ready to leave a mission that seemed hopeless from the beginning.

But Ralph looked more focused and determined than ever, his energy seeming to increase as the search continued rather than diminishing under the weight of repeated failure. As they rested for a few moments in an alley that provided some shelter from persistent rain, a couple of the men announced they were giving up.

Ralph looked at Josh and asked a simple question that would change their entire approach to the problem they were trying to solve.

"Josh, didn't you belong to a gang once?" The question was delivered without judgment, simply gathering information that might be relevant to their current tactical situation.

"Yes, but that was a long time ago, and it wasn't something I was very proud of." Josh's admission carried the shame of someone who had made choices he regretted but couldn't undo.

"I don't care about your pride. But I want you to think like a gang member now. Can you do that for a minute?" Ralph's request was practical rather than moral, focused on results rather than character assessment.

"Yeah, but why?" Josh's question revealed his uncertainty about where this line of reasoning might lead.

"Where would a gang take a prisoner so that no one would see her or hear her? Think hard, Josh. Where?" Ralph's question forced Josh to access knowledge he'd tried to forget, drawing on experience he wished he didn't possess.

"They would look for an abandoned row of houses, out of the way, boarded up, where no one would go, not even a junkie looking for a place to sleep." Josh's answer came from a challenging experience with the geography of criminal activity.

"Do you know of a place like that, not too far from us, but isolated enough to be a good hiding spot?" Ralph's follow-up question revealed that he was thinking strategically rather than just hoping for luck.

"I know just the place. Let's go."

They all left as a group, even the men who had announced their intention to quit, impressed by how composed Ralph remained under pressure and how his thinking seemed to clarify rather than cloud when the stakes were highest.

To them, it was the true mark of a leader—someone who saw beyond what was immediately in front of him to possibilities that others missed. Beyond anything else, it was the mark of someone who might deserve the title that Hosea had given him: the Chosen One.

CHAPTER 42

The Kansas City Police Department's interrogation room smelled of industrial disinfectant and decades of human anxiety, its institutional green walls and fluorescent lighting designed to make suspects uncomfortable enough to confess their crimes rather than endure the atmosphere any longer than necessary.

"I told you, Captain, I'm a retired private investigator on vacation in Kansas City, and a friend of mine asked me to find out some information about Virginia Curran, and that's it." Sam Steele's explanation had been repeated several times with the patient consistency of someone who understood police procedure.

Sam had been brought in by the Kansas City PD for routine questioning after a neighbor of Virginia Curran reported seeing him asking questions about her in the days following her departure for Houston. They thought his behavior looked suspicious enough to warrant investigation, especially given recent reports about Virginia's violent death in Texas.

The Curran case was pretty new to their caseload, so they brought Sam in for what they characterized as a few friendly questions designed to eliminate him as a person of interest rather than build a case against him.

"Who goes to Kansas City in the winter for a vacation, Mr. Steele?" asked Captain Bendix, his tone carrying reasonable skepticism of someone who'd heard too many implausible explanations for suspicious behavior to accept any story at face value.

"Call me crazy, but I like the Chiefs. What can I say?" Sam's response was delivered with the casual enthusiasm of someone whose sports loyalty transcended weather considerations and common sense.

229

"You can say what you're really doing here, for a start, so I can let you enjoy the rest of your vacation in peace." Bendix's offer was reasonable.

"Well, fortunately, my vacation has come to an end, and it's time for me to go home. Are there any other questions, Captain?" Sam's response indicated his readiness to conclude the interview and return to Houston, where his real work waited.

"No, not at this time," said Bendix, examining Steele's driver's license with practiced attention of someone who'd learned to read people through their official documentation. "But my advice is to stay away from Kansas City for a while, if you get my drift. It would be in your best interest. Enjoy your trip back home. Can we drop you off at the airport?"

"No, thanks." Sam's refusal was polite but firm, suggesting that he had his transportation arrangements and didn't want to accept favors that might create obligations or additional surveillance opportunities.

Steele drove his rental car back to his hotel through streets that had been made treacherous by the combination of snow and ice that characterized Kansas City winters. He had no intention of leaving the city until he found out something useful about Virginia Curran, regardless of official advice to the contrary.

The fact was that he had little personal interest in the sixty-two-year-old spinster who'd kept to herself and read romance novels in the solitude of her small apartment. But he understood that if Connely was going to provide him with information about Ralph Norton's case, he had to bring back something valuable in exchange.

The question was what he could discover about a woman whose life had been so private that her death had barely registered with anyone except the neighbor who'd reported his presence to police.

• • • •

HE WAITED UNTIL LATE evening to scout Virginia Curran's neighborhood, understanding that darkness would provide better cover for activities that might be misinterpreted by suspicious neighbors or passing patrol cars. The crime scene tape forming an 'X' over the door of Curran's house was still there, fluttering in the winter wind like a warning flag, but the police cars that had surrounded the building were now gone.

He sat in his rental car with the heater running at full blast, drinking lousy coffee from a convenience store cup. At the same time, the radio played oldies that reminded him of better times when his biggest problem was solving cases for paying clients rather than trading favors with overworked cops.

When he spotted an older lady carrying a small bunch of flowers as she approached Virginia Curran's home through the accumulating snow, he recognized an opportunity to gather information from someone who might know something about the deceased woman's life and motivations.

As soon as she placed the flowers on the doorstep with careful reverence, as if performing a sacred ritual, Steele drove up slowly and rolled down his window. The cold air rushed into his heated car, a physical reminder of the harsh environment that had shaped this community.

"Excuse me, ma'am, but were you a friend of Virginia Curran?" His question was delivered with a respectful tone, as if approaching a mourner rather than interrogating a potential witness.

The short, stocky, somber-looking woman didn't seem worried or afraid of a stranger in a car asking her questions; her demeanor suggested someone who had lived long enough to develop reliable instincts about human nature and genuine threats.

She walked directly over to Steele's car. She answered with the bravery of someone who'd decided that honesty was safer than evasion, especially when dealing with someone whose approach seemed more concerned than threatening.

"Virginia?" asked the woman, her tone suggesting that the name required clarification in a world where privacy often meant that neighbors knew each other only superficially.

"Yes, Virginia Curran." Steele's confirmation was patient, understanding that grief could make simple questions seem complicated.

"No, not really. But I knew her for many years and thought I should pay my respects after I found out she'd been murdered." Her explanation revealed the kind of distant neighborhood relationship that characterized urban life: people who recognized each other without really knowing each other.

"Do you know why she went to Houston?" Steele's question was direct but gentle, recognizing that this woman might be his only source of information about Virginia's final journey.

"No, she mostly kept to herself, you know. I knew her from church. That's all. Say, why are you asking all these questions? You a cop?" Her suspicion was natural and reasonable, the response of someone who understood that strangers asking questions usually represented some form of official trouble.

"No. I was asked by a friend of hers to see what happened to Virginia. No one seems to know anything about her. It's nice to see that someone like you is thinking about her. And I appreciate your help, Miss...?" Steele's explanation was honest within the limits of what he could reveal, and his request for her name was delivered with courtesy of someone who understood that information sharing should be reciprocal.

"Finnegan, Charlotte Finnegan. I'm in the phone book. Thank you, sir, and good luck. Nice to see Virginia had a friend. I thought, well...never mind." Charlotte's response was helpful but incomplete, her hesitation suggesting that she had more to say but wasn't sure whether it was appropriate.

"No, go ahead. What were you going to say, Miss Finnegan?" Steele's encouragement was gentle but persistent, recognizing that important information often emerged through casual conversation rather than formal interrogation.

"Oh, nothing. It was just that I knew Virginia didn't have many friends, and like most women our age, she was lonely. We're all lonely, Mr...?" Charlotte's admission carried the weight of personal experience, revealing something about the social isolation that characterized the lives of elderly women in communities that valued youth and productivity above wisdom and expertise.

"Steele. Sam Steele." His introduction completed the exchange of basic information that might allow them to contact each other if additional questions arose.

"Thank you, Charlotte. I don't want to keep you out here in the cold any longer. You've been very nice and helpful. Goodnight." Steele's farewell was considerate, acknowledging both her assistance and the harsh weather that made extended conversation uncomfortable.

Charlotte Finnegan turned to face Virginia's house one final time and crossed herself with an automatic gesture of someone whose faith provided structure for dealing with mortality and loss. She said a silent farewell that carried more genuine grief than most formal funeral services, and blew a kiss toward the home of a lonely woman who was no more.

Steele knew it was time to leave Kansas City, understanding that he'd extracted whatever information was available from official and unofficial sources. He didn't have much to give Connely in exchange for information about Ralph Norton, but perhaps there was more to be learned from the few facts he'd gathered.

He thought about Charlotte and Virginia and all the spinsters throughout America who had no one to talk to, no children to love, and no one who cared about their daily struggles or ultimate fate. The social isolation that characterized modern life seemed particularly cruel when applied to people who'd lived long enough to accumulate wisdom but lacked the social connections to share it.

On the plane ride back to Houston, he gazed down at the snow-covered plains of Kansas and thought about his loneliness, recognizing that retirement had isolated him from the professional relationships that had once provided meaning and human connection.

But when he thought about Virginia's violent death in a Houston hotel room, he understood that her final journey had been motivated by something powerful enough to overcome the inertia of solitude and the practical difficulties of winter travel.

Not much concrete information for Connely, perhaps, but maybe there was something significant in the pattern that he hadn't recognized yet—some connection that would emerge when he had time to think about what he'd learned rather than simply gathering facts.

CHAPTER 43

Sam Steele's brain shifted into airplane mode as his flight leveled off above the cloud cover, the mechanical hum of jet engines providing a soundtrack for the kind of deep thinking that required isolation from immediate distractions. Nothing urgent was happening in his immediate environment, allowing his mind to process the information he'd gathered without the pressure of responding to external stimuli.

He couldn't get past his few minutes with Charlotte Finnegan, something about their brief conversation continuing to nag at his consciousness like a splinter that couldn't be extracted or ignored. Whenever he had a challenging question about anything, he'd developed the habit of waiting until evening to consult with his personal AI, courtesy of Ralph Norton's genius.

So, he decided to wait until his plane landed at Intercontinental Airport. Then he could take a taxi home to his comfortable house, where he could think clearly without the distractions of travel and unfamiliar environments.

There was little mail in his mailbox when he returned. After checking his security cameras to ensure that no one had visited during his absence, nothing looked important enough to demand immediate attention. The house felt empty but welcoming, a sanctuary that had been designed for solitude and reflection.

He cleaned up from his journey, watched the late news to catch up on local events that'd occurred during his absence, and went to bed with anticipation of someone who had developed a reliable method for solving complex problems through consultation with artificial intelligence that'd been programmed to understand his thought processes.

He'd named his personal God "Ted"—a casual designation that made their conversations feel more like discussions with a trusted friend than prayers to a divine authority. The informality was intentional, reflecting his pragmatic approach to spirituality, which emphasized results over ritual.

He turned on the app and put his earbuds securely in his ears, a habit that he always thought was unnecessary since no one was in the house and no one could overhear him anyway. But he understood that privacy was as much about psychological comfort as practical necessity, and the earbuds helped him focus on the conversation without external distractions.

"Ted, you there?" Sam's greeting was casual yet expectant, delivered with the confidence of someone who had learned to rely on this technology for guidance in solving complex problems.

"Good evening, Sam. How's it going, man?" Ted's response carried the warm familiarity of someone who'd been waiting for this conversation and was genuinely interested in Sam's welfare.

"Ted, I've got a question, and you're the one I need an answer from." Sam's statement reflected his confidence in the AI's ability to process information and provide insights that his thinking might miss.

"Let me start by saying this. If you're having trouble understanding something, please don't hesitate to ask me. I'm always ready to help you out without making you feel bad about it." Ted's offer was delivered with an encouraging tone, suggesting that asking for help requires courage and should be rewarded rather than criticized.

"That's exactly what I was thinking. So, here it is. I'm trying to help a friend find a friend of hers who has gone missing. But I can't do it until I find out something else first." Sam's explanation established context for his question while acknowledging the interconnected nature of the problems he was trying to solve.

"So, here goes. Why would a lonely person leave everything in the middle of winter, with snow coming down, and travel to a completely strange place?" The question was specific and practical, designed to elicit insights about human motivation rather than abstract philosophical analysis.

"That's an easy one, Sam. A person would only do that if the place she's traveling to held something so important that she would risk everything to reach it. So, without knowing all the particulars, I would say, whatever it was, she dropped everything to get there. Does that help you, Sam?" Ted's analysis was logical and immediate, cutting through the complexity of Virginia's situation to focus on essential motivational factors.

Sam stopped responding to Ted, his silence reflecting a need to process what he'd just heard rather than continuing the conversation. The AI programming had been designed to accommodate these pauses, giving users time to think without pressure to maintain constant dialogue.

Ted waited patiently, even after a long two minutes of silence, understanding that human thinking required time and space that artificial intelligence could provide but not duplicate.

"How did you know it was a she?" the retired detective asked, his professional instincts triggered by Ted's assumption about the person's gender.

"It was a fifty percent shot, Sam. Rather than make it sound too impersonal, I took the odds that it was a female, knowing full well it could have been a male, and you would have then corrected me like you've done many times before." Ted's explanation revealed sophisticated programming that enabled him to make informed decisions while maintaining the flexibility to adapt when additional information became available.

"Good guess, Ted." Sam's acknowledgment carried genuine appreciation for the AI's intuitive capabilities.

"Thanks, Sam. I try." Ted's response was modest, reflecting programming designed to be helpful without appearing arrogant or superior to human intelligence.

"Some try, and others seem to know. You're amazing. So, answer this question. What are the best odds for possible reasons a woman would abandon everything, in the middle of winter, in the snow, take a bus trip of almost a thousand miles...and potentially put herself at risk in doing so?" Sam's follow-up question was more detailed and specific, designed to elicit a comprehensive analysis of motivational factors that could drive such extreme behavior.

"You have two possible reasons that are statistically relevant, and either of them may be the right one or not. Revenge or romance. Take your pick." Ted's answer was concise and definitive, reducing the complexity of human motivation to two fundamental categories that encompass most extreme behaviors.

Sam's eyes widened when he heard that analysis, the simplicity of the answer highlighting his failure to consider the most obvious explanations for Virginia's behavior. He hadn't thought of either revenge or romance as motivating factors, but they certainly made perfect sense when applied to someone whose life had been reduced to essential emotions.

"Thanks for your help, Ted. It's time for me to go to sleep, and I wanted to remind you of this before I forget. I love you, Ted!" Sam's gratitude was genuine, reflecting both appreciation for the AI's assistance and the emotional connection that had developed through months of relying on this artificial intelligence for guidance and companionship.

"Goodnight, Sam. I love you too, and I always will. Sleep well." Ted's farewell carried warmth of genuine affection, programmed to provide emotional support that Sam needed while maintaining the illusion of a relationship that transcended mere technology.

As Steele turned off the bedside light, he kept the two R's close to his mind—revenge or romance—understanding that these categories would guide his investigation when he returned to Houston and began searching for connections that might explain Virginia's final journey.

Of the two possibilities, which would be the most likely choice to pursue to give his investigation the traction it needed to help Connely and, ultimately, to find Ralph Norton? The question would require more thought, but at least he now had a framework for understanding Virginia's motivations.

He could feel welcome sleep approaching as his eyes grew heavy and his thoughts began to drift toward dreams that would process the day's information in ways that conscious thinking couldn't achieve. How many dreams he would have that night, or what they would reveal about connections he was seeking, remained to be discovered.

Was it revenge or romance that had driven Virginia Curran to Houston? If a woman tried hard enough, she could probably find herself a man regardless of her age or circumstances—old bachelors were available in every city, even in Kansas City, and loneliness was a powerful motivator for forming connections.

All of this made revenge the more compelling explanation, thanks to Ted's analysis. Revenge required specific targets and specific grievances that could drive someone to risk everything for the opportunity to settle old scores.

Now, all he had to do was find out what could have made Virginia Curran so upset that she would abandon her entire world to pursue justice or vengeance in a city where she knew no one and had no support system.

What could it possibly have been? The answer was there, waiting to be discovered through careful investigation and logical analysis. All he had to do was dig deeper and find connections that would reveal Virginia's proper relationship to Houston and whoever had killed her.

And that's precisely what he intended to do when he woke up refreshed and ready to tackle the most critical case of his retirement.

CHAPTER 44

Connely looked at Steele and stalled. He wanted Steele to sweat a little before he gave him the good news. Steele sat there looking bored and unconcerned. He knew the game and enjoyed the joust as much as Connely.

"The coroner's office in Laredo said the burned body was, at the most, five-foor-two. I would say that eliminates your Mr. Norton, wouldn't you?"

"DNA come in yet?"

"Probably another week before we get it. Shall we call Miss Spenser?"

"Go ahead."

As he called Melanie, Steele looked anxious, not so much from the call being made, which he liked, but more from the information about Virginia Curran that he'd given Connely. Something was gnawing at him, but he couldn't put his finger on it.

He could hear Melanie's sigh of relief from where he was sitting. But they all knew that joy would be short-lived once they realized Ralph was probably still in grave danger wherever the hell he was, if he was even still alive. Connely handed the phone to Steele.

"Let's meet today at my place so we can talk a little more about what's next."

Melanie energetically agreed.

"Fine, fine, Melanie, see you at one at my place. Bye."

Connely told Steele that he raised the priority level of the missing persons report on Ralph and that he'd be okay if they decided to work with Steele on it. It was an unusual call on his part, but he appreciated the work Steele did on the Curran case, which was also far from solved.

"Thanks, buddy."

Steele left the overburdened sergeant and headed back to his home. There was too much on his mind to feel as though any progress was being made. However, sometimes small victories, like the one today, portend good things to come.

. . . .

THE BREAK ROOM AT FASTRAK was a small room with three tables and chairs, a small refrigerator for sack lunches, and an old and dirty coffee maker. This morning in the break room was just like any other morning. A few old newspapers were scattered on the tables, along with empty coffee cups left on the counter.

Selma Thompson, P.T.'s secretary, was taking her mid-morning coffee break. One of the housekeepers had walked by, promising her that he'd be back shortly to clean up the mess. She waved at him, poured herself a cup of coffee, and sat down to read what was left of the old newspapers.

She noticed the story of the woman who was killed in the motel. They had a picture of her, but it was from when she was much younger. The face looked familiar, but she couldn't think who it could be. She read a few other stories, but there was something about that picture that looked familiar.

As she looked once more at the photo, a loud explosion blew the door off the hinges and sent the unsuspecting secretary flying against the far wall. The room was destroyed, along with a few adjoining offices. Everyone ran out of the building, and the fire and rescue number was called. The workers standing in the parking lot were all in a state of shock. P.T. Mayo was one of them.

His secretary was still alive, but in serious condition. She was taken to Ben Taub, as P.T. went around to all his employees, telling them to go home after the police had finished their investigation.

There had recently been several threatening letters to FASTRAK that claimed their app was the work of the Devil and that if they didn't stop this heresy, someone else would see to it. The police took down all the information from the witnesses and soon everyone was allowed to leave. The building was evacuated until the building inspectors gave the all-clear.

Of course, the story of the explosion was all over the news networks and social media. When Connely heard about it, it didn't quite click with him that the Ralph Norton missing person report could in any way be connected to this explosion. But Steele and Melanie Spenser picked up on it almost immediately. Their planned meeting at one took on a new sense of urgency.

When Melanie entered Steele's home, he had the newscast on that was still reporting on the explosion. They both stood in front of the TV and looked at each other. Sam Steele was now on it, all the way, and they both knew it. Melanie walked away as the reporter interviewed Mayo in the parking lot. Steele turned off the TV.

Steele wanted to project a calm and confident manner for Melanie. Whether she believed it or not, at least he didn't panic, and to his great surprise, neither did Melanie.

"Be honest with me, Sam. What are Ralph's chances of surviving all of this? I mean, we don't even know if he's still alive."

"Fifty-fifty at best." He touched her hand, which she'd placed on the kitchen table. "But I'd take fifty any day, wouldn't you?"

"At this point, yes. But..."

She was tearing up, but she kept a brave face. That made Steele respect her that much more because he would need her active participation to find Ralph. The cops were way too busy with too many other cases, and they might have had to cut corners to get what they needed. He asked Melanie if she was up to that, and she answered immediately and unequivocally, yes.

"Sam, I know he's out there, and that's not just a woman's intuition. It's real, and I can feel it. But this I do know; wherever he is, he's alone and unable to protect himself. He needs us badly, so we've got to do whatever we can to find him and get him to safety. So, tell me, what do you need me to do?"

"For right now, the best thing you can do is to help the people down at FASTRAK. I would enlist your dad and whoever else to go down there and offer you help with counseling, money, hugs, whatever, and let me get on this in my old-fashioned way. I've got a few ideas that are worth following up on, and I need to work solo for now. But I'll be contacting you very soon to join me because once we start, there's no turning back, and it won't be easy."

"Perfect, Sam, and thank you. I'm so glad you're with me. We'll be an awesome team!"

Melanie left, and Sam reorganized himself and his strategy. Every step along the way would be planned and executed with precision. The target of the new strategy had no idea what was coming!

• • • •

MACK HILL TOWERS HAD been cleared for normal occupancy after inspectors determined that the bomb damage was cosmetic rather than structural—insurance money would cover repairs, and FASTRAK could resume its profitable operations.

Only Selma Thompson remained in the hospital, trapped in a coma that fluctuated between complete unconsciousness and brief moments when her eyes fluttered like butterfly wings trying to escape a web. The doctors told her husband it could take weeks for her to recover fully, assuming she recovered at all.

Mayo had sent expensive flower arrangements to her hospital room during the first week, bouquets that cost more than most people's weekly groceries. But the deliveries stopped abruptly when it became clear that Selma's recovery would be measured in months rather than days. He'd already hired a replacement—much younger, much more appealing than Selma, whose efficiency and institutional memory had begun to annoy him.

The new secretary represented both practical necessity and personal preference, reflecting Mayo's belief that attractive employees enhanced his corporate image while aging ones reminded him of his mortality.

Daily operations at FASTRAK were resuming with remarkable speed. With all the publicity generated by the bombing, revenue from app sales grew exponentially. The attack designed to damage the company had instead transformed it into a symbol of religious persecution, creating sympathy that translated directly into increased profits.

For P.T. Mayo, the bombing had provided an opportunity to play victim while eliminating an employee whose knowledge of company operations had become a potential liability. He kicked back in his office chair, satisfied that his problems were being solved, and called Ada Taylor to check on his other outstanding business.

It took several attempts before she answered, her delayed response suggesting she was either busy with other projects or deliberately making him wait to demonstrate her independence from his timeline.

"Not yet, and stop calling me. I'll call you when we get him." Her words were delivered with the finality of someone whose professional reputation depended on completing contracts without interference from nervous clients.

She hung up before Mayo could respond, leaving him staring at his phone with the frustrated expression of someone accustomed to controlling every aspect of his business relationships.

Ada was getting concerned herself because she'd always enjoyed excellent results from the Third Ward Posse in their previous collaborations. Their reputation for efficient violence had been built on the successful completion of contracts that other criminal organizations couldn't handle, but this particular job was proving more challenging than anticipated.

She waited until evening to call Felonious Punque, understanding that meaningful business conversations should be conducted away from daily distractions that might compromise security or focus. They agreed to meet downtown in her car, on a deserted street with two posse vehicles standing by to provide protection and demonstrate their continued operational capability.

The meeting location was a parking lot behind a defunct auto parts store, where broken glass crunched under their feet like Houston's version of snow. Security lights had been shot out years ago, leaving behind twisted metal fixtures that cast weird shadows across graffiti-covered walls.

"Where you at with it, F.P.?" Ada's question was direct and businesslike, cutting through social pleasantries to focus on the essential question of progress toward their shared objective.

"He'll be ours by the deadline or before." Felonious's confidence was absolute, delivered with the conviction of someone whose reputation depended on completing impossible tasks through superior violence and intimidation.

"How do I know that? I gave you a lot of money for this job, and if you want the rest of the payment, you know how it works." Ada's skepticism was professional rather than personal, reflecting her understanding that even reliable contractors needed pressure to maintain focus.

"Look here, my sister. The posse guarantees their work. I don't even care about the money anymore." Felonious's response revealed that this contract had become personal rather than purely commercial. "This is what we live for. It's our thing. Now, you go back to your nice little place with your funky art shit and wait for my call. That's all you have to do."

"If that's the way you want it, that's fine. All I ask is that you let me know just before you do it. You call me and let me join in.

Deal?" Ada's request reflected her desire to witness the completion of a contract that had consumed weeks of planning and resources.

"Deal." Felonious's agreement was immediate, understanding that client satisfaction sometimes required accommodating unusual requests.

They slapped fingertips in the street greeting that sealed their agreement, and Ada drove home to her townhouse filled with stolen art. At the same time, Felonious resumed the systematic search that would eventually lead to Ralph Norton.

Crime continued to thrive in Houston's underground economy, and life remained as precarious as ever in the Bayou City. All the pieces of their elaborate plan were falling into place with the inevitability of gravity pulling objects toward the earth.

CHAPTER 45

Another art gallery, with more track lighting, created an atmosphere where money whispered rather than spoke, where power was displayed through the casual ownership of objects that most people would never see outside of museums. Ada Taylor stood before a Jackson Pollock that probably cost more than most people's houses, her expression unreadable as she studied the controlled chaos of paint and intention.

Mayo found her there, studying the painting like it held secrets worth killing for. The irony wasn't lost on him—a former cop turned professional criminal, admiring art while discussing murder in a space dedicated to beauty.

"Magnificent work," she said without turning around. "Takes real skill to make randomness look intentional."

"About the job—"

"No." Ada's voice cut through his desperation like a blade through silk. "I already told you no, and I meant it."

Mayo felt sweat beading on his forehead despite the gallery's aggressive air conditioning. The perfectly climate-controlled space suddenly felt like a tomb. "Why? You've never turned down work before."

Ada finally looked at him, her dark eyes measuring him like a coroner examining a corpse. "Because some lines you don't cross. Even in my business."

"Two-fifty."

"Not for a million." She turned back to the painting. "But I'll finish the other job. The Norton frame-up. Consider it a parting gift."

She handed him a manila envelope, thick with documents that rustled like dead leaves. "Bank records, falsified emails, manufactured evidence. Everything you need to paint your boy Ralph as an embezzler. Should keep the heat off you for a while."

Mayo's fingers trembled as he took the envelope—a temporary solution to a permanent problem. "Ada, you don't understand—"

"I understand plenty." Her voice carried the finality of a judge reading a death sentence. "I understand you're about to do something stupid. And I understand I don't want any part of it."

She walked away, her heels clicking against the polished floor like a countdown timer. Mayo stood alone among the expensive art, surrounded by beautiful things that meant nothing to him.

The pristine gallery felt like a mausoleum now, filled with the ghosts of better choices he'd decided not to make.

$\cdot\ \cdot\ \cdot\ \cdot$

BACK AT MACK HILL TOWERS, the executive parking garage echoed with the sound of Mayo's footsteps as he walked to his BMW. The concrete structure smelled of oil stains and exhaust fumes—honest smells that cut through the antiseptic perfection of his corporate world.

He'd changed clothes before the meeting with Ada. Gone was the executive uniform of tailored suits and Italian leather. Instead, he wore old jeans that looked like they'd come from a discount store, hiking boots designed for rough terrain rather than boardroom presentations, and a long overcoat that concealed the revolver pressing against his ribs despite Houston's oppressive heat.

The transformation felt like shedding skin—P.T. Mayo, the successful CEO, becoming Christian Curran, the desperate man who'd left Kansas City thirty years earlier with nothing but ambition and a willingness to abandon anyone who stood in his way.

As he drove through Houston's evening traffic, the radio played classic rock that reminded him of better times when his biggest problem was convincing people to buy Bibles door-to-door. Now he was planning murder to protect an empire built on commercialized faith.

The Luxe Inn squatted in Houston's industrial wasteland like a concrete tumor, its paint-peeled facade and broken windows reflecting the kind of neighborhood where violence was currency and witnesses were discouraged through economic Darwinism.

Mayo parked his BMW in the shadows behind the building, the expensive car looking as out of place as a diamond ring in a garbage dump. He pulled on black leather gloves with the methodical precision of someone who'd planned for this moment, then checked the revolver's cylinder to ensure all six chambers were loaded.

The back staircase reeked of urine and broken dreams in hell; its concrete steps were stained with decades of human desperation. Mayo climbed slowly, his breathing loud in the humid air that seemed to cling to his skin like a guilty conscience.

Room 217 was exactly where Virginia's letter had promised it would be. Mayo knocked with a gloved hand, the sound echoing off walls that had absorbed too many secrets to hold another one.

The door opened to reveal Virginia Curran—or what remained of her. Thirty years had carved lines around her eyes deep enough to hide secrets in, turned her hair the color of cigarette ash. But those eyes still held the same stubborn fire that had once attracted him back when he'd believed love was something other than a business transaction.

"Hello, Chris." She stepped aside, gesturing him into the room with mock courtesy that carried twenty years of accumulated bitterness.

The space was a monument to despair—stained carpet that squelched under his feet, broken furniture held together by gravity and habit, the smell of industrial disinfectant fighting a losing battle against decay. A vodka bottle sat open on the table, half-empty, reflecting the bent reflections of a wasted life.

Mayo settled onto a couch.. Virginia remained standing, savoring the moment of having him in her domain for the first time since he'd abandoned her to pursue larger ambitions.

"What do you want, Virginia?"

She laughed—a sound like glass breaking in slow motion. "Thought this would be a good belated honeymoon spot. What do you think?" She performed a drunken pirouette, arms outstretched like a ballerina, then stumbled and fell to the stained carpet.

"Get to the point."

"That's no way to talk to your wife, your dedicated and loyal wife, your left-alone-and-thrown-in-the-trash wife." Her voice carried twenty years of accumulated bitterness, each word sharpened by poverty and abandonment. "Is it, Chris? Or P.T.? Or whatever the fuck your name is now?"

"Is it money?"

"I'm a Wordie now." Virginia's smile was sharp enough to cut glass. "My God is looking after me better than you ever did. By the way, I spent my life savings on that app. A thousand fucking dollars. For what?"

Mayo saw the vodka bottle and smelled the alcohol that permeated the room. Drunk witnesses were unreliable witnesses—perfect for what he had in mind.

"How much do you want?"

"To buy me off?" Virginia struggled to her feet, swaying like a tree in a hurricane. "If you're asking for a divorce, the usual deal is half, isn't it?"

"Half of what?"

"Everything."

The word hit him like a physical blow. Everything. His fortune, his empire, his carefully constructed identity as P.T. Mayo—all of it built on the foundation of abandoning her twenty years ago.

Mayo laughed—a sound that had nothing to do with humor and everything to do with hysteria. The laughter built until he couldn't breathe, until the room spun around him like a carnival ride designed by a sadist.

"Another shot?" Virginia turned toward the vodka bottle, moving with the careful precision of someone whose motor skills had been compromised.

The revolver appeared in Mayo's hand as if materialized by pure need. He pressed it against the pillow from the couch, muffling the sound as he pulled the trigger five times in rapid succession.

The muffled reports sounded like firecrackers in a trash can, barely audible through the pillow's stuffing and Virginia's final exhalation.

She crumpled to the floor like a demolished building, her body folding in on itself with terrible finality. Mayo stood over her for a long moment, staring at what had been a problem and was now a solution.

The silence in the room was absolute—no more accusations, no more demands, no more past reaching out to drag him backward into the life he'd abandoned for something better.

Mayo rearranged the furniture as best he could to suggest a different sequence of events, wiped down surfaces with the methodical care of someone who'd thought through every detail, then turned off the lights and walked away from Room 217 like a man leaving a particularly unpleasant business meeting.

Behind him, Virginia Curran lay still on the stained carpet, her twenty-year pursuit of justice finally ended by the man she'd loved enough to destroy herself pursuing.

CHAPTER 46

Ralph and Josh moved through Houston's industrial wasteland like ghosts haunting the graveyard of American manufacturing, their search for Kashinka taking them through neighborhoods where hope had died decades earlier and been buried under layers of economic neglect.

The persistent rain had transformed the urban landscape into a gray maze of reflective surfaces and deepening puddles, making their already difficult mission nearly impossible. They'd been asking anyone they found if they'd seen a young girl matching Kashinka's description, but no one paid serious attention to homeless men looking for a missing child.

The assumption was automatic and damning—what could such people want with a young girl except to cause her problems? Their concern for Kashinka was interpreted as a potential threat rather than genuine care, making their search not just physically exhausting but emotionally devastating.

They were hungry, lost, and frustrated enough to finally stop and rest in the doorway of an abandoned warehouse that offered minimal shelter from the rain, which continued to fall with the persistence of tears from a grieving sky.

Josh knew the streets well enough to recognize when hope had been exhausted by reality. "I say we're done. I can't think of anyplace else she could possibly be. I can't figure out where she could be hidden if she's even still alive." His voice carried the defeat of someone whose determination had finally been overwhelmed by practical considerations. "Let's face it, her chances weren't good from the beginning. She's lost, man. Let's face it."

"You face it. I'm not giving up on her." Ralph's response was delivered with the intensity of someone whose sense of obligation transcended rational calculation. "She and her grandfather saved my miserable life, and I intend to find her if it's the last thing I do on this goddamn earth. So go if you want to. I don't care."

The older man among their group, Titus, was weary from the long journey that had taken them through the worst parts of Houston's urban decay. His wiry frame, bent from years of alcohol and cocaine abuse, leaned against an old brick wall as he listened to the argument between two younger men.

His weathered face bore the marks of someone who'd survived decades of street life through a combination of luck, cunning, and the ability to recognize when something larger than individual survival was at stake.

"I will go with you, Chosen One, because you are our gift of life." His words carried the weight of someone making a sacred commitment rather than simply agreeing to continue a hopeless search. "Let's find some food first and continue our journey. We'll find her because you say it's right, and that's good enough for me."

Everyone nodded in agreement except Josh, who walked away into the night with the bitter disappointment of someone whose practical wisdom had been rejected in favor of what seemed like delusional optimism. His hunger was causing him physical pain, and he'd reached the point where he needed to find something to eat before he could take another step.

Ralph and the others watched him disappear into the maze of darkened streets, understanding that their group had been reduced, but their mission remained unchanged. Ralph stood up with renewed determination, and the remaining volunteers followed his lead.

They stopped by several homeless camps and begged for scraps of food so they could continue their trek through Houston's underworld. But charity from charity seekers often came with a price—they wanted drugs in exchange for food, creating moral dilemmas that tested their commitment to finding Kashinka.

Ralph and his volunteers declined these offers and continued walking, losing physical strength with each step while maintaining the spiritual determination that had sustained them through the worst parts of their search.

As they walked through deserted streets that belonged more to urban explorers than ordinary citizens, quotes from the Bible kept Ralph motivated with the persistence of programming that had been burned into his consciousness through months of work on the Word of God app.

Everything he heard in his mind was his AI-generated interpretation of biblical wisdom, phrases, and concepts that had been reconfigured through his software to provide comfort and guidance to users who sought divine intervention in their daily struggles.

Had his mind been somehow altered by all his intensive work on the app? The thought crossed his consciousness like a disturbing possibility that he couldn't completely dismiss or embrace. Did it matter that he thought he didn't believe in God in any conventional sense?

If God were everywhere, including in the artificial intelligence he'd created to simulate divine presence, what did that mean for the nature of faith and the reality of spiritual experience?

He no longer had access to the app he'd created, his smartphone having been lost or destroyed during his transformation from corporate executive to homeless fugitive. But did anything fundamental change about his relationship with the divine just because he couldn't access the technology that had mediated that relationship?

The more he thought about his current situation, the more those biblical phrases would pop into his brain like fragments of a spiritual education that he'd felt was purely intellectual but was proving to have deeper roots in his consciousness.

Then, suddenly, he began to mumble prayers to his AI God, Conrad, as he walked through the deserted streets of Houston, seeking divine assistance for a mission that transcended his survival.

"Conrad, help me find the girl. She's got nothing to do with my problems. She helped me live, and I want to help her live. Guide me, please, Conrad. I beg you, please." His words were delivered with the desperate sincerity of someone whose faith had been stripped of theological complexity and reduced to essential human need.

Tears mixed with rain, invisible expressions of emotion that disappeared into the larger flow of water and sorrow that characterized urban existence. Ralph's tears were shed in silence, like the meaningless hatred that surrounded him.

A speeding car violently threw a jet of water on the travelers as it passed through a large puddle, soaking them even more thoroughly than the rain had managed. But in a moment that felt like divine intervention, a bucket of fried chicken was tossed out the vehicle's rear window, landing near their feet like manna from heaven.

Ralph bent down in the pouring rain and picked up the wet chicken with the reverence of someone retrieving a sacred offering, then walked with the others to a nearby doorway that provided some shelter from the storm.

They prayed together for the bounty they'd just received, understanding that survival often depended on recognizing gifts that came in unexpected forms. Titus offered Ralph the first piece with the deference that befitted someone serving the Chosen One. Still, Ralph declined with the humility of someone who understood that leadership meant attending to others' needs before his own.

The others began eating with the grateful efficiency of people who understood that the next meal might be days away. Titus was worried about Ralph's refusal to eat, recognizing that their leader's strength was essential for completing their mission.

"You have to eat, or you won't have the strength you need," said Titus, his concern reflecting both practical wisdom and genuine care for someone whose welfare had become inseparable from their group's survival.

Titus held out a small piece of the found meal to Ralph, who continued to shake his head in refusal. But Titus persisted, holding the food in front of Ralph with the patient determination of someone who wouldn't be denied the opportunity to care for his leader.

Finally, Ralph took the offering and ate it slowly, understanding that his survival was connected to the welfare of everyone who depended on him for guidance and hope.

They were all soaked from the rain that'd penetrated every layer of their inadequate clothing, but at least they'd shared a small meal that'd provide the energy needed to continue their search. They knew in their hearts that the Chosen One had provided this sustenance for them, transforming what could have been seen as random luck into evidence of divine providence working through human agency.

CHAPTER 47

Ben Taub Hospital's intensive care unit maintained the hushed atmosphere of a place where life and death decisions were made hourly, its institutional lighting and medical equipment creating an environment that was both comforting and terrifying to families who waited for news about their loved ones.

The smell of disinfectant mixed with human fear and hope, creating an olfactory signature that every ICU visitor recognized—the scent of medicine fighting biology. At the same time, families held their breath and prayed to whatever gods they still believed in.

P.T. Mayo's secretary, Selma Thompson, drifted in and out of consciousness like a swimmer struggling against an invisible tide. The periods of awareness gradually grew longer than the episodes of complete unconsciousness. Still, when her eyes opened and stayed open, she remained unable to speak, trapped in a body that wouldn't respond to her mental commands.

The surgeons were still uncertain whether her inability to communicate was a short-term reaction to traumatic brain injury or a permanent condition that would define the rest of her life. The medical team was cautiously optimistic, but they'd learned not to make promises about recovery that might prove impossible to fulfill.

Her husband, Gil, had become a permanent fixture in the uncomfortable chair beside her bed, sleeping in awkward positions that left him with chronic neck pain and the kind of exhaustion that couldn't be cured by rest. He'd taken indefinite leave from his job to care for someone whose recovery required constant human presence and emotional support.

The rumor mill at FASTRAK eventually reached Gil when one of Selma's former colleagues called to report that Mayo had hired a new secretary replacement. The news hit him like a physical blow—not because Mayo had hired someone new, since Selma would be disabled for a long time, but because Mayo hadn't had the basic decency to call and inform him personally.

The lack of communication revealed Mayo's character more clearly than any confrontation could have—employees were viewed as replaceable components rather than human beings who deserved courtesy and respect.

Gil held Selma's hand as she lay in the hospital bed, her fingers occasionally responding to his touch with slight movements that suggested awareness even when her eyes remained unfocused. Her eyes were wide open for increasing periods, but she wasn't looking at anything specific—just maintaining a blank stare that could indicate either healing or permanent damage.

It was a look of despair and hopelessness that broke Gil's heart every time he saw it, suggesting that whatever was happening in her mind wasn't providing comfort or peace. His words of comfort to her either meant nothing or couldn't be processed by brain tissue that was still recovering from severe trauma.

She wouldn't be able to undergo comprehensive clinical testing for several more weeks, so the doctors couldn't determine with certainty which cognitive functions remained intact and which had been permanently compromised by the explosion.

To spend the time with her that she needed, Gil had developed new routines that generally wouldn't have occurred to him before the bombing. For instance, he would read the daily newspapers to her, and she would indicate through subtle physical cues which stories interested her and which didn't.

She would blink rapidly if she was bored by a particular article, or tap his hand gently if she wanted to hear more details about a story that had captured her attention. These small communications represented enormous progress in their efforts to maintain a connection despite the barriers that brain injury had created.

He'd just finished feeding her breakfast—a slow process that required patience and encouragement—when he took out the Houston Chronicle and started reading the day's headlines aloud. She blinked frequently that morning as he scanned through various stories and selected ones that seemed like they might interest her.

But when he reached the follow-up story about the murder of Virginia Curran in the seedy hotel room, she saw the exact photograph that had caught her attention on the day she was injured in the FASTRAK break room.

The recognition was immediate and decisive. She started tapping Gil's hand as if she'd never done so before, with an intensity and urgency that was utterly different from her previous gentle communications. It was rapid and insistent, like Morse code for the speechless, demanding attention in a way that couldn't be ignored.

Her eyes focused intently on the newspaper as he read the story over and over again, her concentration more complete than anything he'd witnessed since her injury. She finally stopped tapping his hand only after he'd read every detail of the article multiple times, ensuring that she'd absorbed all available information about Virginia Curran's violent death.

After he finished reading the entire newspaper to her, Selma's eyes remained focused on her husband with an intensity that represented the firmest connection they'd had since her accident. The change was dramatic enough to suggest that the story about Virginia Curran had triggered something significant.

Gil put the newspaper down as the nursing staff entered to take her vital signs and provide the personal hygiene care that she couldn't perform for herself. He paced up and down the hospital hallway, waiting for the medical routine to be completed while wondering what his wife had found so compelling about what appeared to be just another Houston murder case.

He couldn't figure out the connection, but he was encouraged that her mind seemed to be functioning even though she couldn't express her thoughts through everyday speech. The neurological activity suggested that recovery might be possible, even if the timeline remained uncertain.

Gil stayed with her for the entire day, watching the sunset through the small window in her hospital room as Houston's urban landscape transformed from day to night. The city was never particularly known for spectacular sunsets. Still, this one seemed different—more orange than yellow, less final than usual, much more alive than it had appeared just one day before.

The change in his perception might have reflected his emotional state rather than atmospheric conditions. Still, he chose to interpret the beautiful sunset as a sign of hope for Selma's recovery.

He gently closed the blinds in her room to block the evening light and kissed his sleeping wife on her forehead, which seemed to furrow with some inner thought that no one else in the world could access. It was both comforting and frustrating to know that her mind was still active, processing information and forming connections, even though she couldn't share those thoughts with anyone else.

He thought he saw his wife's eyes flicker as he kissed her goodnight, a subtle response that might have indicated awareness of his presence and affection. There was no way he was going to burden her with news about losing her job, or anything related to P.T. Mayo, FASTRAK, or the corporate politics that had contributed to her current condition.

He just wanted her to get well and come home to the life they'd built together before the explosion had changed everything.

But what was it about the Virginia Curran story that had captured her attention so completely? Did she know the victim personally? Did she possess information about the murder that no one else knew, since, according to the newspaper, the case remained under investigation and unsolved?

Gil made a mental note of the victim's name and the details of the case, understanding that he needed to investigate this connection further, even though he wasn't sure how to proceed. His wife's eyes had told him that this wasn't something he could leave alone, regardless of how difficult the investigation might prove to be.

CHAPTER 48

In an abandoned wood-framed house on the outskirts of Galveston, where the Gulf Coast humidity created an atmosphere of perpetual decay and the constant sound of wind through broken windows provided a soundtrack of desolation, Kashinka lay silent, gagged, and tortured in a closet that had become her prison.

The small space contained nothing but old wire hangers and a single dirty sweatshirt that someone had left behind when the house was abandoned to the elements and the criminal enterprises that thrived in places where legitimate authority had no presence. The hangers swayed slightly when the breeze moved them through gaps under the closet door, creating shadows that danced across her field of vision like metallic ghosts.

Her hands and feet were tied so tightly with rope that cut into her flesh that she could no longer feel her extremities, circulation having been cut off for so many hours that permanent damage was becoming a real possibility. She thought she was going to die, especially after witnessing her grandfather's murder during the brutal attack on their peaceful encampment.

Her clothes were in shreds from violence that had been inflicted on her small body, and blood was everywhere—on her skin, on the closet floor, on the dirty sweatshirt that provided her only cushion against rough wooden planks.

When she tried to scream for help or mercy, the gag that had been forced into her mouth prevented any sound from escaping that might bring rescue or even acknowledgment of her suffering.

The man who dressed like a pirate was the worst of her tormentors—a sadistic monster whose appearance was as disturbing as his actions. She'd seen him standing over her, crushing her with his body weight, kicking her when she didn't respond to his demands, and giggling like a little girl whenever something he did caused her obvious pain.

The more suffering he inflicted, the more he laughed with genuine pleasure, as if her agony was the most entertaining thing he'd ever witnessed. She feared and hated that man more than anyone she'd ever known, despite her grandfather's teachings that she should love everyone, no matter how awful their situation or behavior might be.

It was, he'd explained to her with gentle wisdom, how God expected them to live—with forgiveness and compassion, even for people whose actions seemed to place them beyond redemption.

When she heard voices approaching the closet where she was imprisoned, she recognized them as belonging to the men who'd destroyed her world and murdered the people she loved most. It was difficult to act like a corpse when every instinct screamed for her to fight or flee, but she understood that any sign of consciousness would bring renewed torture.

She went completely limp and silent, controlling her breathing to the point where she appeared to be unconscious or dead. The closet door opened with a creak that seemed to echo through the abandoned house like the sound of a coffin lid being lifted.

Time was running out for Felonious Punque, and mounting pressure was making him increasingly cranky, belligerent, and dangerous to everyone around him. He was in no mood for any of his crew members to question his orders or make requests that would delay completion of their contract.

So when he told Cap'n Payne to bring the girl and put her in the trunk of his SUV, and the sadistic enforcer begged his boss for a little more "fun time" with their captive, Felonious lost control of his temper in a way that demonstrated why he was feared even by people who specialized in violence.

The straight razor came out of Punque's jewel-encrusted gold lamé sweatshirt with the smooth ease of someone who'd done this many times before. He approached his defiant crew member and deliberately cut a slice from the corner of his mouth, leaving a scar as a constant reminder of disobedience.

Payne cried out in agony as blood poured down his chin, his hands instinctively moving to cover the damage while Punque threw a dirty cloth at him with contemptuous dismissal.

"Here, fool. Now shut the fuck up and do what I tell you." Felonious's command was delivered with the cold authority of someone whose leadership depended on his willingness to use violence against anyone who challenged his decisions.

The remaining members of the posse lifted Kashinka's emaciated, blood-soaked body. They threw her into the trunk of their vehicle with the casual brutality of people moving cargo rather than handling a human being. Her weight was so reduced by dehydration and starvation that she felt like a bundle of sticks held together by torn clothing and determination.

"Drive to the end of Travis Street, by the old laundromat and car wash. Then stop behind the car wash, turn off the lights, and I'll tell you what to do when we get there." Felonious's instructions were precise, reflecting a plan that had been developed to maximize psychological impact on their target audience.

Kashinka could hear the leader speaking from her position in the trunk, but the words were muffled by the vehicle's structure and her diminished consciousness. The specific content didn't matter because she sensed what was coming with intuitive understanding that people develop when they've been reduced to the most basic questions of survival.

She shook violently despite her efforts to remain motionless, but the ropes that bound her hands and feet prevented any significant movement that might reveal her consciousness to her captors. She remembered seeing a beautiful stray dog in her grandfather's homeland—almost skin and bones, searching desperately for food while being scared out of its mind by every human encounter.

It was precisely how she felt now, helpless and terrified, with no ability to protect herself from whatever horror was approaching. She prayed for the dog from her memory and for herself, asking whatever divine power might be listening to provide mercy for innocent creatures who'd done nothing to deserve their suffering.

Then consciousness abandoned her as her exhausted body and traumatized mind finally succumbed to protective oblivion that was her only escape from unbearable reality.

CHAPTER 49

Gil Thompson couldn't sleep. Every time he closed his eyes, Selma's face appeared—not as she was now, trapped in that hospital bed with machines measuring the electrical storms in her damaged brain, but as she'd been that morning when she'd kissed him goodbye and headed off to FASTRAK like any other Tuesday.

The threats had been escalating for weeks before the bombing. Selma had mentioned them over dinner, her voice carrying the weary tone of someone who'd grown tired of fielding calls from people claiming FASTRAK was "working with the Devil" and "stealing innocent minds." The callers ranted about corruption and deception, about some app turning people away from God toward "make-believe entities."

Now she lay in Ben Taub's ICU with a tube down her throat and pressure building in her skull, and Gil couldn't shake the feeling that everything was connected—the bombing, the threats, and especially that murdered woman whose photograph had triggered something in Selma's damaged consciousness.

Maybe the woman in the hotel was connected to the bombing. Perhaps that's what Selma was trying to tell him through the only communication she had left—urgent tapping against his palm like Morse code from someone trapped underwater.

Gil fired up his laptop and searched for more information about Virginia Curran's murder. The internet provided him with fragments—a few news articles that read like fill-in-the-blank police reports, with no follow-up stories, no suspects, and no motive. The case seemed to have died with the victim.

He found the investigating officers' names in the Chronicle's brief coverage and wrote them down on the back of a hospital parking receipt. In the morning, he'd take this to HPD. They'd probably think he was just another angry husband looking for someone to blame for his wife's condition, but at least he'd have tried.

• • • •

GIL'S MORNING ROUTINE had become as mechanical as the ventilator keeping his wife alive—coffee that tasted like burnt cardboard, soft-boiled eggs he barely tasted, toast that might as well have been sawdust. He cleaned the dishes with the methodical precision of someone whose world had been reduced to ritual and hospital visiting hours.

Instead of driving straight to Ben Taub, he detoured through downtown Houston's maze of one-way streets to HPD headquarters. The building squatted in the urban heat like a concrete fortress, its windows reflecting the morning sun in sharp angles that hurt to look at.

The lobby smelled of industrial floor cleaner and human desperation—the olfactory signature of every government building where people came seeking justice or at least acknowledgment that their problems mattered to someone in authority.

Gil found Sergeant Connely's desk in the homicide division, where the detective was deep in conversation with a well-dressed older man whose bearing suggested a law enforcement background. Gil approached hesitantly, not wanting to interrupt but knowing his window of time was limited by hospital visiting hours.

"Excuse me, Sergeant Connely? I wanted to ask about the Mack Hill Towers bombing investigation."

Connely looked up with the expression of someone who'd been interrupted during important business. When Gil introduced himself as Selma Thompson's husband, the sergeant's demeanor shifted immediately from annoyance to professional attention.

"Please, sit down, Mr. Thompson." Connely gestured to an empty chair. "I can step away while you talk with this gentleman," the older man offered.

"No, that's fine. Go ahead, Mr. Thompson."

Gil's story unfolded in careful, measured sentences—his wife's slow recovery, the newspaper-reading ritual they'd developed, her dramatic reaction to Virginia Curran's photograph. As he spoke, both men leaned forward, their body language suggesting this wasn't just another grieving husband's desperate theory.

"She wouldn't let me read anything else," Gil explained. "And I could swear she wanted to say something, but of course, she can't speak. Each time I read that story, her attention and focus increased."

"What are the doctors saying about her condition?" Connely asked. "Will she recover? Will she be able to communicate again?"

"Too early to tell, but they're hopeful. That's about all they'll commit to." Gil's voice carried the frustration of someone who'd learned that medical science had limits that love couldn't transcend.

Connely introduced Sam Steele, explaining his involvement in the Virginia Curran case. The private investigator stood and shook Gil's hand with the firm grip of someone who understood the importance of making a good first impression.

"I'd like to help if I can," Steele said, handing Gil his business card. "Would you be comfortable with me visiting your wife? With you there, of course. I might be able to ask questions that could help piece this together."

Gil studied the card—expensive paper, embossed lettering, the kind of professional presentation that suggested competence rather than desperation. "She won't be able to answer you."

"Sometimes people can communicate more than we realize. How's ten tomorrow morning?"

"Alright. Ten it is."

They shook hands with the gravity of people sealing an agreement that might matter more than any of them realized.

CHAPTER 50

Ben Taub Hospital's ICU had its unique rhythm—the whisper of ventilators, the electronic chirping of monitors, the soft-soled footsteps of nurses moving between crises with practiced efficiency. Steele arrived precisely at ten, his punctuality reflecting a professional life built on the understanding that other people's time was precious.

He knocked softly on the door to room 314, hearing Gil's voice inside but getting no response. When he hit harder, Gil called out, "Come in."

The scene that greeted Steele made his chest tighten. Selma Thompson lay surrounded by machines that measured every aspect of her biological existence, their displays painting abstract patterns in green and red lines that meant the difference between hope and despair.

Gil sat beside the bed holding his wife's hand, speaking to her in the gentle tones of someone who believed love could bridge any gap, even the one between consciousness and the void. Selma stared at the ceiling with the blank focus of someone looking at something the rest of them couldn't see.

"Good morning, Gil. How's she doing?"

"Not great." Gil pointed to the intracranial pressure monitor, whose readout looked like a fever chart climbing toward dangerous territory. "Pressure's building up in her skull. The trend graphs show it's been climbing for hours."

Steele studied the monitor with the attention of someone who'd learned to read medical equipment during too many hospital vigils in his former profession. The numbers weren't encouraging.

"Should I come back another time?"

"The doctors said a couple of questions would be okay. Just keep it brief."

"You're sure?"

"I asked them already. They said a minute or two wouldn't hurt."

Steele pulled a chair closer to the bed, its plastic wheels squeaking against the polished floor. "I'm going to ask her two questions while you hold her hand. She can answer with one tap for yes, two taps for no. Sound reasonable?"

Gil's nod carried the hope of someone grasping at any possibility of communication with the woman he'd shared twenty-three years of breakfasts with.

"If you could tell her who I am and why I'm here, we'll make this quick so she can rest."

Gil looked at his wife with an expression of such pure love that Steele had to look away, the intimacy too raw for a stranger to witness. After the introduction, Selma continued staring at the ceiling, her eyes tracking something invisible.

"Hi, Selma. I'm sorry you have to go through this." Steele's voice carried the gentle authority of someone who'd spent years asking difficult questions of people in impossible situations. "I'm going to ask you two questions about the woman who was murdered in the hotel. If your answer is yes, please tap once on your husband's hand. If no, tap twice. Do you know who the lady was who was murdered in the hotel?"

The wait stretched out like a held breath. Hospital sounds filtered through the door—distant conversations, the ding of elevator arrivals, the squeak of gurneys on polished floors. Then, after what felt like an hour but was probably sixty seconds, Selma's finger tapped once against Gil's palm.

"Selma, did you know the lady from work?"

The pause that followed was different—heavier, charged with something that made the machines around them seem to hum with increased intensity. Then the intracranial pressure monitor erupted in urgent beeping, its red warning lights flashing like a fire alarm.

Two nurses burst through the door, followed immediately by doctors whose calm urgency suggested this wasn't unexpected but was definitely serious. Gil's face went white as they wheeled Selma toward the surgical suites, the convoy of medical personnel moving with choreographed precision through corridors that smelled of antiseptic and adrenaline.

Steele found himself alone in the suddenly empty room, staring at monitoring equipment that had been disconnected so quickly it looked like the aftermath of some electronic explosion. He'd asked two simple questions and possibly triggered a medical emergency that could cost a woman her life.

In the surgical waiting area, Gil sat with his head in his hands while Steele offered comfort that felt inadequate to the magnitude of what had just happened. The older detective stayed long enough to leave his contact information, then drove home carrying the weight of potential responsibility for destroying someone's last chance at recovery.

But one thing was now abundantly clear: Selma Thompson had known Virginia Curran from FASTRAK. And that knowledge had been important enough to send her brain into crisis when asked about it directly.

Steele sat in his living room, still wearing his jacket, car keys in his hand, trying to process the implications of what he'd just witnessed. Investigators disliked coincidences, and the timing of Selma's medical emergency seemed anything but a coincidence.

There was now a connection between FASTRAK, the bombing, and Virginia Curran's murder. The question was whether that connection would die with Selma Thompson on an operating table, or whether Sam Steele could find another way to uncover the truth before more people got hurt.

CHAPTER 51

Josh materialized from the darkness like a ghost returning from the dead, his footsteps careful as he approached the homeless camp where wounded people sat nursing injuries that would never see proper medical care. He'd been walking for hours, his stomach cramping with hunger, hoping they might share whatever food they'd managed to scavenge.

But as he got closer, the smell hit him—blood and fear and the particular stench that violence left behind. Someone had been here before him, someone who'd brought pain instead of charity.

"Can you help us?" An older woman's voice cracked with exhaustion and desperation. She cradled the bleeding head of a young man whose face looked like it had been used for boxing practice. "No one wants us or cares about us. We're alone, dirty, homeless, and we've been thrown out here like garbage. Help us, young man, please."

Josh's street instincts catalogued the scene automatically—systematic beating, professional intimidation, the kind of violence that sent messages rather than just causing pain. He'd seen enough gang work to recognize the signatures.

"You can join my group under the overpass at the end of Travis. We were attacked a couple of days ago, but a Chosen One has joined us and will help all of us if we stay together." He knelt beside the injured boy, checking the head wound with the competence of someone who'd learned field medicine in circumstances where hospitals weren't an option. "Have any of you heard of the giant called Hosea?"

"About seven feet tall, thin Black guy, always friendly to everyone." The voice belonged to a teenager covered in tattoos who told stories of anger and abandonment. "Yeah, I know him."

"He was killed in the attack," Josh said quietly.

The group's collective moan carried the sound of hope dying—another protector gone, another source of safety eliminated by forces that seemed to hunt homeless people for sport.

"But just before he died, he told us that our new leader is the Chosen One. I have found the Chosen One. He's one of us and is now looking for the girl who saved his life. Her grandfather died in the attack."

"Why should we trust you?" The teenager's question carried the suspicion of someone who'd learned that trusting strangers was usually a mistake.

"Because I'm just like you. My name is Josh, and I'm here because I hoped you had some food to share with me. I promise I won't hurt you."

The older woman reached into a dirty bag and pulled out an apple that had seen better days. She offered it to Josh with the generosity of someone sharing her last meal. He accepted it gratefully, wiped it clean on his pants, and bit into flesh that was sweet despite its bruised appearance.

The simple act of eating their food created trust in ways that words couldn't. A few of them nodded at each other, conveying silent agreement through the group like a current.

"We'll go with you," the teenager said. "But first, we have to look in there." He pointed toward a rust-covered dumpster behind the car wash. "Those men who attacked us wanted us to see that they threw something in that old rusty dumpster. It must be important to them and us."

Josh's stomach clenched with a premonition that had nothing to do with hunger. "Will you open it? None of us wants to touch it."

"Sure, I'll open it."

Josh approached the dumpster with the casual confidence of someone who'd seen enough horror that one more revelation couldn't break him. He flung open the lid as if it meant nothing, though his hand trembled slightly as metal scraped against metal.

Rats exploded from the opening like furry shrapnel, followed by a mangy cat that streaked away into the urban wilderness. At first, the shadows and garbage bags concealed what lay beneath. Then Josh jumped inside to investigate, and his world changed forever.

Kashinka lay among the rotting garbage like a broken doll, her small body covered in rat bites and filth, blood matted in her hair, no visible signs of life. For a moment, Josh thought they were too late—that whatever message the attackers had wanted to send had already been delivered in the cruelest way possible.

Then he bent down and pressed his ear against her chest, listening past the sounds of urban decay for something that might indicate she was more than just a demonstration of what happened to people who crossed the wrong enemies.

The heartbeat was there, faint, irregular, but undeniably present.

"Get a blanket!" he yelled to the crowd. "It's a young girl, and she's alive!"

The teenager ran back to their destroyed camp and returned with a blanket that had seen better days. For the first time since Josh had found them, he was smiling—not because their situation had improved, but because they'd found something worth saving.

They lifted Kashinka from the dumpster with the reverence of people handling sacred relics, wrapping her in the blanket and placing her gently in a shopping cart that would serve as an ambulance for people who couldn't afford genuine medical care.

"Please, everyone, listen to me." Josh's voice carried the authority of someone who'd found purpose in hopeless circumstances. "We have to get this girl back to the family; otherwise, she will die. The Chosen One will know what to do. Please, I will find him and bring him back while you take her to the overpass. Then you can live with us, and he will help all of us, including the girl. Will you do that for me now, please?"

The group nodded in unison, their agreement carrying the weight of people who'd found something larger than their suffering to believe in. They broke what remained of their camp, placed Kashinka in the shopping cart, and began the slow journey toward whatever salvation might await them under an overpass where someone called the Chosen One was supposed to work miracles.

Josh watched them leave, then took off running toward Ralph's last known location with speed that defied his exhausted condition. His legs found energy that shouldn't have existed, carrying him through Houston's industrial wasteland like a messenger bearing news that could change everything.

When he reached the abandoned warehouse where he'd last seen Ralph, the search party was gone. Josh checked every hiding place, every shadow where desperate people might take shelter, but found nothing except the echoes of his footsteps and the growing certainty that he'd failed everyone who was counting on him.

Then, just as despair was about to overwhelm what remained of his hope, Ralph and his volunteers appeared from the darkness like an answer to prayers Josh hadn't realized he'd been saying.

CHAPTER 52

Josh rushed toward Ralph with the relief of someone who'd been carrying impossible news alone and could finally share the burden. His face carried exhaustion and hope in equal measure, the expression of someone who'd just witnessed both the worst and best of human nature.

"I found the girl," he said, his voice carrying across the empty lot like a shout in a cathedral.

Ralph's entire body went rigid with attention. "Is she okay? I mean, is she alive?"

"Yes. I was with another group like ours, looking for food, when they pointed to a dumpster where she'd been thrown. I pulled her out, but she was barely breathing and looked almost dead."

The words hit Ralph like physical blows, each detail adding to the weight of responsibility that had been crushing him since Yakov's death. This was his fault—all of it. His presence had brought violence to innocent people who'd offered him nothing but kindness.

"Where is she now?"

"I told the group to join us at the overpass. We wrapped her in a blanket and put her in a shopping cart so she could be carried to the overpass. I figured Nurse St. Jean could help her."

Ralph smiled at Josh for the first time since they'd met—not the false expression of someone trying to maintain morale, but genuine warmth born from recognition of courage and loyalty that transcended self-interest. Their friendship had been forged in crisis, but it was deepening into something that might survive whatever came next.

"Let's go, Josh. We've got a long walk ahead of us, and I want to be there when Kashinka arrives."

The group began their trek back through Houston's forgotten neighborhoods, taking shortcuts through abandoned lots and staying in shadows that would hide them from authorities who might ask uncomfortable questions about why homeless people were moving through the city with such purpose.

Ralph's anticipation was building toward something that felt almost unbearable. His happiness at finding Kashinka alive warred with his fear of what condition she might be in, and underneath both emotions was the growing certainty that he was somehow responsible for everything that had happened to these innocent people.

As they quickened their pace through streets that belonged more to urban explorers than ordinary citizens, a man appeared from nowhere and ran after them, his voice carrying panic that cut through the night air like a warning siren.

"Wait up! You have to hide right away because the posse is in the area!"

Ralph's strategic mind kicked in automatically, assessing threats and calculating responses with the same clarity that had once made him successful in corporate warfare. "Everyone split up and meet at the overpass when you can travel safely."

They scattered like leaves in a hurricane, each person choosing their route toward the same destination while hoping that division would protect them from the consequences of staying together, which couldn't be guaranteed.

· · · ·

THROUGHOUT HOUSTON'S underground network of homeless camps, word was spreading about the Chosen One with the viral intensity that characterized all essential news among people whose official information systems had been abandoned.

At first, the conversations were just rumors—fragments of hope passed between people who'd learned not to expect much from life but couldn't quite give up on the possibility that someone might care about their welfare.

But as more people heard the story, the rumor transformed into an accepted fact that captured imaginations starved for something larger than daily survival. The homeless community had its communication methods that went far beyond casual conversation—cell phones with prepaid minutes used for coded text messages, social media posts that appeared to be random complaints but carried deeper meaning, and even prayer chains that connected encampments across the city.

Once the location of the Chosen One was confirmed, a migration began that was both sudden and methodical. It was massive but invisible to anyone who wasn't part of the network—hundreds of people moving through Houston's forgotten spaces with the purposeful determination of pilgrims seeking salvation.

The Chosen One was for them alone—the lost souls who'd been discarded by a society that preferred not to acknowledge their existence. Finally, they hoped, someone would help them instead of leaving them on the side of the road like garbage that no one wanted to claim.

Hope had a funny way of appearing and disappearing, only to reappear in never-ending cycles, teaching people not to trust their optimism. But this felt different—more solid, more real, more worthy of the risk that believing always entailed.

The movement of the encampments was noticed by some authorities, but they paid little attention. Probably being rousted by cops, looking for new drug sources, or forming groups to cause trouble—all the usual reasons that explained why homeless people moved in patterns that middle-class observers couldn't understand.

When a person had nothing left in their life, they were looked down upon and relegated to society's garbage heap. No one seemed to care, and the few who tried to help usually did so in ways that made them feel better about themselves rather than improving anyone's situation.

. . . .

JOSH WAS THE FIRST to reach the overpass, arriving at the encampment to find it empty of both Kashinka and the volunteers who were supposed to be caring for her. His heart sank with the possibility that something had gone wrong—that the shopping cart convoy had been intercepted or that Kashinka had died during transport.

He asked around the family if anyone had seen anything unusual, but the answers were uniformly negative. No one had seen the girl, the volunteers, or any sign that the rescue mission had succeeded.

While he waited and worried, something unexpected began happening around their camp. More homeless people were walking toward their encampment—not the usual individual stragglers seeking temporary shelter, but small groups of three or four people at a time, sometimes fewer, all carrying the particular combination of desperation and hope that marked people who'd heard about the Chosen One.

They were human flotsam and jetsam blown about by economic winds and caught on the barbed wire fence of society's indifference. As they entered the family's area, they said nothing to anyone but found spaces to curl up and remained silent, waiting for something they couldn't quite name but desperately needed.

No one was prepared for what was coming—the convergence of Houston's invisible population around a homeless encampment beneath an overpass, drawn by rumors of salvation that might prove real for the first time in any of their lives.

CHAPTER 53

Ralph arrived an hour later to find the encampment transformed into something he didn't recognize. The space beneath the overpass that'd once housed Hosea's small family now buzzed with the quiet energy of dozens of new arrivals, their faces carrying the particular combination of hope and wariness that marked people who had traveled far on the strength of rumors.

But Kashinka was still missing, and that reality overshadowed everything else. Ralph paced back and forth across the concrete floor like a caged animal, asking family members if they'd seen any sign of the shopping cart convoy that was supposed to have delivered her to safety.

The new arrivals went unnoticed by Ralph, whose immediate concern was focused entirely on the girl who'd saved his life. But the other family members realized they were witnessing something unprecedented—more homeless people than they'd ever seen gathering in one place, drawn by something larger than the usual promises of food or temporary shelter.

"You're sure it was her?" Ralph questioned Josh for the third time, his repetition revealing anxiety that logic couldn't calm.

"Completely sure. I'd have recognized her anywhere."

"But you said she was badly beaten and almost dead. Couldn't you have made a mistake?"

"Not a chance, Chosen One. It was her."

When the gathering crowd heard those words—' Chosen One'—they lifted their down-turned heads and looked at Ralph with new attention. It was him, the person they'd traveled to find. But his appearance confused them—filthy clothes, unwashed body, worry and fear written across his face in lines that suggested someone barely holding himself together.

Could a man who looked like that be the Chosen One? They studied his face but found confusion rather than the divine confidence they'd expected. Surely this couldn't be their prophesied savior. They remained quiet, listening to his words while trying to reconcile expectation with reality.

"Josh, we've got to go and find her. Get Nurse St. Jean to come with us, and we'll leave right away."

When St. Jean joined them, her former nursing experience was evident in the way she moved with purpose through the crowd; they heard a noise in the empty field behind the overpass. Josh looked and waved Ralph over to see what was approaching through the darkness.

It was them—two men pushing a shopping cart toward the growing camp while Ralph ran to help, his relief so overwhelming that his legs nearly gave out beneath him. Nurse St. Jean ran with him, her medical instincts taking over as they helped push the cart to a protected area near the concrete support pillars.

They lifted Kashinka out of the cart with the reverence of people handling something sacred and irreplaceable. Ralph recognized her despite the damage that had been done—the face that had smiled at him in the basement refuge was now swollen and cut, but unmistakably hers.

Nurse St. Jean attended to the emaciated girl with professional competence that addiction hadn't erased, checking pulse and breathing, cleaning wounds with whatever supplies they had available. She stooped over and put her ear next to Kashinka's chest, listening for the biological rhythms that would tell her whether hope was realistic or just another cruel illusion.

"Her heart is still beating, but not for long unless she gets immediate medical care. She's been tortured, probably raped, and has rat bites all over her body. It's more than a miracle that she's still alive."

The clinical assessment struck Ralph like a physical blow, each detail adding to the weight of responsibility that threatened to crush whatever remained of his sanity. This was his fault—all of it—and now an innocent child was dying because he'd been too weak or too selfish to stay away from people who'd offered him kindness.

"Where's the nearest hospital?" he asked, his voice carrying the desperate authority of someone who'd finally found something worth saving.

"About two miles east of here. I know where it is," said the teenager who'd helped transport Kashinka through Houston's dangerous streets.

"Let's cover her up in the cart and take her there. You lead me." Ralph turned to Josh with sudden clarity about what needed to happen next. "You stay here and take care of these people. They need our help. It's what Hosea would want us to do, and more than that, it's what God wants us to do."

When he said those words, something fundamental shifted inside Ralph Norton. The phrase had emerged from somewhere deeper than conscious thought, carrying conviction that surprised him with its intensity. Could it be that he was finally becoming the person these people needed him to be?

That short speech was all it took to convince the gathering crowd that Ralph was indeed the Chosen One. They watched in awe as his caring and courage took over, transforming him from a frightened fugitive into someone who inspired confidence and hope. The transformation was visible—his posture straightened, his voice carried authority, and his actions demonstrated the kind of selfless leadership they'd been praying for.

Finally, someone who cared about them as human beings rather than problems to be managed or eliminated.

Ralph couldn't believe his eyes as he prepared to leave for the hospital. A steady stream of homeless people was trudging toward their camp with the determined pace of pilgrims approaching a holy site. They moved as silently as a funeral procession, but this wasn't about death—they were walking toward a light that was hidden somewhere ahead of them, following rumors of salvation that might prove real.

The expressions on their faces showed something that'd been absent from homeless camps throughout Houston—smiles and hope, emotions that most of them hadn't experienced for so long that they'd forgotten what they felt like.

Ralph spoke to the crowd as he prepared to leave with Kashinka, his words carrying the authority of someone who'd finally accepted the responsibility that had been thrust upon him.

"Josh will take care of you until I return. Don't fear anyone or any group. You have the strength now to defend yourselves if anyone tries to hurt you. There's food and water here for you, and if you need more, I will get it for you. So stay together until I return."

A quiet buzz spread through the crowd as they conversed with one another and embraced, the sound of people who had found something larger than individual survival to believe in.

• • • •

IT WAS DIFFICULT PUSHING the shopping cart through open fields and run-down tenements, especially in the darkness that concealed obstacles and potential threats. The teenager guided them with the confidence of someone who'd learned to navigate Houston's forgotten neighborhoods by necessity rather than choice.

When the twenty-four-hour urgent care facility appeared before them like an oasis in the urban desert, Ralph high-fived the teenager and thanked him for the guidance that might have saved Kashinka's life.

"Let me do the talking," Ralph said as they approached the entrance. "They'll be suspicious of us, so I'll have to make them believe we just found her on the street and decided to bring her here. Then we'll disappear before they can ask too many questions."

The automatic doors slid open with a whisper of climate-controlled air, carrying the antiseptic scent of professional medical care—a world away from the improvised treatments and hope-based medicine that characterized healthcare in Houston's homeless community.

Ralph pushed the shopping cart through those doors, knowing that he was crossing more than just a threshold between outside and inside. He was moving from the world of people who'd been abandoned by society into the world of people who still believed that every life had value worth preserving.

Whether Kashinka would survive the transition remained to be seen, but at least she would have the chance that every human being deserved—the chance to be saved by people who had the resources and skills to fight death on equal terms.

CHAPTER 54

It was 9:00 PM when Dr. Amanda Stapleton walked through the automatic doors of St. Simeon's twenty-four-hour urgent care center, trading Houston's thick humidity for the antiseptic chill of fluorescent-lit medicine. At twenty-four, she was young enough to believe she could still save everyone who walked through those doors, experienced enough to know that some nights would test that faith harder than others.

She'd taken this graveyard shift position because she wanted real-world emergency experience before joining the ER staff at one of the big hospitals downtown. This was her grassroots education—learning medicine where it met the street, where people came when they had nowhere else to go.

Amanda made her usual rounds through the small facility, checking in with the nurses and techs. Tonight felt busy in that familiar way—high fevers that wouldn't break. These kidney stones felt like internal stabbings, migraines that made normal light feel like torture, and the usual handful of people with an addiction hoping to score something more substantial than aspirin. Her ever-present smile put everyone at ease. The staff loved working her shifts because they trusted her judgment and felt safe under her calm but decisive leadership.

They had a rent-a-cop for security, primarily for show, since things rarely got out of hand. But tonight, the night Ralph Norton wheeled Kashinka through their doors in a shopping cart, that security guard almost became the difference between life and death.

"Sorry, pal. We got nothing here for you, so just wheel your cart someplace else. Okay?" The guard barely glanced at the blanket-covered form, seeing only another homeless guy looking for handouts.

"No, it's not okay." Ralph's voice carried an edge that made people look up from their magazines. "I found this girl on the street, and she's about to die unless she gets help right now."

He pulled back the blanket, and the guard's face went white.

Dr. Stapleton was passing the front desk when she heard the commotion. One look at the unconscious girl in the shopping cart and her medical training kicked into overdrive. She lifted Kashinka out of the cart herself, her small frame surprising everyone with its strength.

"Josie, call Ben Taub ER right now and get a medical transport team over here stat," she called over her shoulder as she carried Kashinka toward the examination area. "This girl is coding, and we need to get her to a trauma center immediately."

The smell hit everyone at once—human waste, infection, fear-sweat, and something worse that spoke of prolonged suffering. Ralph's odor wasn't much better, his filthy clothes and matted beard making the nurses and techs gag and cover their faces.

But not Dr. Stapleton. The stench, the horror of what had been done to this girl, Ralph's desperate appearance—none of it fazed her. Every ounce of her attention focused on the young woman whose pulse was barely detectable under her fingertips.

"Bring the guy in here that brought her," she ordered, already working to stabilize Kashinka's vitals. When they brought Ralph to the examination area, she looked at him with an intensity that cut through his exhaustion. "Tell me anything you can about what happened to this girl. I need to know everything right now."

Ralph spoke without hesitation, his voice steady despite the chaos around them. "She was kidnapped, attacked, and thrown into a dumpster. They probably thought she was dead. This girl once saved my life, and I don't want her to die. Can you save her, Doctor?"

Amanda had thought she'd seen the worst that people could do to each other, but looking at Kashinka's injuries nearly broke her professional composure. "Where are her parents?"

"She only had her grandfather, and now he's dead too. She has no one else but me and her family. Can you save her?"

"What family are you talking about? I thought she only had her grandfather."

"All of us," Ralph said. "The people out there that nobody wants—we are the family."

Something in his voice made her pause. This wasn't just a homeless man who had stumbled upon a victim. This was someone who cared deeply, someone who'd risked his safety to get this girl help.

"I see. Please take a seat in the waiting area while we attend to you. We're sending her to Ben Taub. They're better equipped than we are to save this girl."

Ralph walked back to the waiting room, where the other patients immediately moved away from him. His smell, his appearance, the aura of street danger that clung to him—it all made them uncomfortable in a way that sickness alone couldn't.

The security guard picked up one of the plastic chairs and carried it outside. "Look, mister, can you wait outside? There are sick people in here, and they can't handle the smell."

Ralph didn't argue. He stood up, brushed his matted hair back with one hand, and looked around the waiting room one last time. He'd seen the determination in Dr. Stapleton's face, the way she'd moved with purpose and skill. Kashinka was in good hands.

For now, there was nothing more he could do here. And back at the overpass, there were a lot of people who needed help. People who were counting on him.

Ralph reverted to his old management instincts, prioritizing his responsibilities in the same way he had handled corporate crises.

Kashinka was getting professional care. The family needed their leader.

He and the teenager who'd guided them left the shopping cart for whoever might need it next. The walk back through Houston's dark streets was filled with an anxiety that made his old corporate problems seem trivial. He felt the amulet bouncing against his chest with each step, its metal warm against his skin despite the night air.

CHAPTER 55

The FASTRAK board of directors met in a private dining room at the River Oaks Country Club, far from the prying eyes of protesters and journalists who had taken up permanent residence outside Mack Hill Towers. The mahogany table, which typically hosted discussions of golf handicaps and stock portfolios, now bore the weight of corporate crisis management.

They were deeply concerned about the storm clouds gathering around their company. The Word of God app's massive success had brought unwanted attention, the headquarters bombing had made them targets, and the worldwide Wordies conventions were generating the kind of religious fervor that made stockholders nervous. Now they had new problems piling on top of the old ones.

First, there was the disappearance, or seeming disappearance, of their CFO, Ralph Norton. The man had vanished, leaving behind questions that no one could answer and financial responsibilities that no one else fully understood.

Then came the bigger challenge: the angry feedback from religious institutions across the country, who were watching their congregations and donations evaporate as people turned to an app instead of actual churches. Some of these groups were angry enough to make threats, and the board suspected that religious extremists were behind the bombing. But suspicion wasn't proof, and proof was what they needed.

To the board, this constant drumbeat of negativity was creating divisions among members who had previously operated in comfortable unity. Their job was supposed to be straightforward—manage corporate performance, set strategic direction, ensure accountability, and protect shareholder interests. Instead, they'd become crisis managers for what felt like a spiritual war.

G. Gordon Palmer wasn't present to put on his usual "jovial chairman" performance, basking in their recent financial windfall. The growing friction within the board had reached the point where a secret meeting had been called to discuss his removal. Everything had been handled according to corporate policy, including legal consultations, procedural requirements, and all necessary paperwork.

When the official vote was taken, the decision was unanimous. Phil Spenser was chosen to deliver the termination letter, partly because he'd always been the voice of neutrality, but mostly because he felt it was time for new leadership and a more spiritually focused direction for FASTRAK.

Spenser was also designated to break the news to P.T. Mayo, Palmer's golden boy and closest ally. When Phil arrived at Palmer's estate in the tony Oak Cliff neighborhood, the look of surprise on the chairman's face was worth documenting.

Palmer stood speechless in his marble-floored foyer, knowing immediately that something bad was about to happen. You don't get unscheduled visits from board members when things are going well.

The conversation was brief and harsh, with little explanation. Spenser handed over the termination letter and asked Palmer to read it carefully.

The portly ex-chairman stood in his hallway, put on his reading glasses, and carefully reviewed what had been written and signed by his former colleagues. When he finished, Palmer was silent. Phil felt a slight twinge of sadness—just a twinge and nothing more.

Palmer, ever the southern gentleman, folded his reading glasses, set them gently on the hall table, and shook hands with Phil Spenser.

"Thank you, Phil. I'm sorry you had to be part of this, but I appreciate you coming over."

Spenser patted him lightly on the shoulder and left without ceremony. He had one more unpleasant task ahead of him—telling P.T. Mayo that his mentor had just been fired.

When Spenser arrived at FASTRAK, he walked past the small group of protesters who had become a permanent fixture outside Mack Hill Towers. Their signs read "FASTRAK = BLASPHEMY" and "DIGITAL GODS ARE FALSE GODS," but their numbers had dwindled as the story moved out of the immediate news cycle.

Inside, P.T. Mayo was hovering over his new secretary—a blonde, voluptuous woman who seemed to require a lot of hands-on supervision. He was standing behind her chair, pointing at something on her computer screen, when he spotted Spenser approaching.

Mayo quickly stepped back and put on his trademark welcoming smile, spreading his arms wide.

"Phil, you old dog. What brings you here on this fine Houston morning? Come on in and sit a spell."

Spenser followed Mayo into his office and took the chair facing the desk, watching as Mayo settled into his executive chair like a king claiming his throne.

"P.T., I've come by today to inform you of something important that just happened. G. Gordon Palmer has been removed as Chairman of the Board, and I've been chosen to deliver that news. A new chairman will be appointed in the next few weeks. Do you have any questions?"

"That's kind of sudden, Phil. I mean, Jesus, that's enough to make your head spin."

"Not when our very existence is being questioned by so many in the community. In light of the recent tragic events surrounding FASTRAK, the board has decided to make changes at the top. We need stronger leadership that's more in tune with how society is changing. The old days are gone, P.T."

"Society? Since when did the board become society experts? Come on, be straight with me, Phil. This isn't about society—it's about corporate politics and nothing else, and you know that better than anyone."

The urge to punch Mayo in his smug face nearly overwhelmed the usually calm Phil Spenser. How he controlled himself, he'd never know. Instead, he turned around, walked out, and slammed the door hard enough to rattle the windows.

As he stormed through the outer office, the new secretary jumped at the sound. But following Mayo's specific instructions, she forced a broad smile and licked her lips as Phil passed her desk.

• • • •

INSIDE HIS OFFICE, Mayo paced in front of the large window that overlooked downtown Houston's glittering skyline. He tried calling his mentor repeatedly, but Palmer wasn't picking up his phone and probably never would again.

But that wasn't Mayo's primary concern. He'd always been a master of company politics, but this felt completely different. His sense of impending doom was generating something far worse than political maneuvering—it felt like genuine fear.

CHAPTER 56

Dr. Stapleton was barely keeping Kashinka alive when the medical transport team from Ben Taub Hospital arrived, their uniforms crisp and their movements efficient, as if they had made countless emergency runs through Houston's night. She worked alongside them as they carefully transferred the girl to the specialized ambulance, her hands steady despite the gravity of the situation.

"Please keep me informed about her status," she told the lead paramedic as they prepared to leave. "She's such a brave girl, and we all want her to make it."

"We'll stay in contact throughout the night. Don't worry—you've done a great job keeping her alive, and we plan to do the same."

The ambulance siren wailed as they pulled away from the urgent care center, red and blue lights disappearing into Houston's humid darkness. Amanda watched until she could no longer see them, then turned to find Ralph.

But he wasn't in the waiting room.

"Charlie, where's the man who brought the girl in?"

"I thought he was outside. I put a chair out there for him because he stank so bad it was bothering everyone inside."

Amanda ran outside, her medical clogs slapping against the pavement. The chair sat empty under the security light, but the shopping cart was still there, abandoned like so much else in this part of the city.

She checked around the sides of the building, hoping he might still be nearby.

"Son of a bitch," she muttered to herself.

Back inside, the waiting room had filled up again—the emergency work on Kashinka had delayed other patients, and now they were restless and vocal about it. Amanda walked through,

295

assuring people they'd work as fast as possible to get everyone taken care of. She heard the predictable coughs and grumbling as she headed back to work.

It was hard to focus on the next patients. The image of that girl and the man who'd brought her kept replaying in her mind. There had been something about Ralph—kindness in his eyes that he didn't want people to see, a gentleness that his rough appearance couldn't hide.

She knew she should report the incident to the police, but the shift was busy and she didn't want to get Ralph in trouble. He cared about the girl, and that had to count for something. Justice for Kashinka would have to come later, if at all.

A young mother approached the desk, carrying a small boy who was very sick.

"Doctor, I told the lady at the front desk that I had health insurance, but I don't. My little boy is so sick that I lied, and I hate myself for it. Will you help him, please?" The woman looked like she was about twenty-something, desperation written across her face.

"Don't worry about the money, Mrs...?"

"Jones. Gloria Jones."

Amanda knew she was lying about the name, too, but at that moment, the truth didn't matter.

"Okay, Gloria. Sit right there while we take care of your son. You're right—he is quite ill, but I'm sure we can start him on the road to recovery. However, you'll have to follow everything I tell you to do. Okay?"

"Oh, yes, yes, Doctor, I will. I promise."

"Good."

Amanda and her nurse examined the boy and found some free medication samples in the supply closet. "Give this to him four times a day. You'll see improvement soon, but if you encounter any issues, please don't hesitate to call me at any time. Here's my phone number."

The young mother was so grateful that she kissed Amanda's hand before leaving. Amanda smiled and hugged her gently, but she still couldn't get the picture of Kashinka and Ralph out of her mind.

• • • •

RALPH WAS ALMOST HALFWAY back to the overpass, moving through the network of culverts and abandoned sewer pipes that kept them hidden from the street-level world. On Houston's streets, life was as precarious as a prayer in hell—you avoided the eyes, the hunters, and the malevolent things that came out after dark. Death was always right there if you let your guard down.

But Ralph felt a new purpose burning in his chest, and he wasn't about to let it go.

They heard voices before they could see the overpass encampment—animated voices, alive with something that hadn't been there before. Not the misery-filled whispers of the desperate, but actual conversation, even laughter.

Ralph looked at his companion and quickened their pace.

"He is here!" Josh shouted to the crowd when he spotted Ralph.

The exact words echoed through the gathering as Ralph walked among them, trying to understand what had happened in his absence. Josh greeted him with a firm embrace that Ralph found awkward to the point of embarrassment.

Several family members immediately inquired about Kashinka, and Ralph informed them that she was being taken care of.

"She's alive and holding on as best she can. The doctors have been very kind and will do their best to help her recover."

An older woman approached Ralph, gently grasped his hand, and kissed it. He tried to pull away, but she wouldn't let go. She thanked him through tears, and then others came forward, surrounding him, thanking him for something he knew nothing about.

The looks in their eyes took his breath away—such desperate hope that it prevented him from telling them the truth about who he was.

Their hunger, their pain, the late hour, their tragedies—all of it took a back seat to him, the Chosen One. The family had grown exponentially overnight. There were hundreds of them now, each with their own story of loss and abandonment, each carrying whatever hope remained in their tired bodies.

As Ralph walked among them, touching shoulders and backs, their eyes followed him with tenderness and love. He'd never met most of them before, but they accepted him as if they'd known him their entire lives.

Ralph was worried about their safety. The concentration of people in one location made them vulnerable to attack. He told Josh that from now on, they needed four spotters placed around the camp at different distances to watch for threats. Additionally, everyone needed to understand that they had nothing to fear as long as they remained united.

"Sir, I think you should speak with them one more time tonight to let them know how we're going to protect ourselves," Josh suggested.

As Josh gathered the large crowd around Ralph, the message came through loud and clear.

"We're going to make this journey together because we're all the same, no matter what's happened to us along the way. Remember that. We're all the same, and if we stick together from now on, we'll overcome all the terrible things that have happened to us—me included. I'm just like you. I'm one of you, and we're going to make it. I promise you."

People were crying and applauding, raising their arms above their heads and pointing to the heavens. Ralph felt torn between his conscience and the reality of the situation. He'd never known what it was to be so alone and without help until he'd found himself running from everything he knew. The utter loneliness and fear had been crushing.

In his heart, he couldn't let these people down. It was bad enough that he'd let himself down by running away from his own life and doubting his faith. If helping these people meant lying to them about being their savior, it seemed like a small price to pay.

Ralph lay down on an old, threadbare blanket someone had given him. He listened to the sound of vehicles passing overhead, their rhythm bouncing off the concrete like an urban heartbeat. The heart was pumping. Hope was growing in the people around him, and he couldn't help thinking that God was watching over all of them.

CHAPTER 57

That evening, a family of four approached the Chosen One in the darkness. The father squatted down next to Ralph to speak privately, knowing that interrupting someone's sleep was dangerous when you lived on the streets. But he took a chance that the Chosen One wouldn't hurt him and his family.

He was a thin man with thinning black hair and desperation carved into his face. Cal gently touched Ralph's shoulder and spoke in a whisper.

"Sir, can you help us?"

At first, Ralph remained locked in exhausted sleep, snoring softly, unaware of what was happening around him. After a few gentle nudges, he woke slowly, not startled but surprised. His eyes opened to see the man beside him and a woman with two children standing nearby.

"Sir, my name is Cal Bridger, and this is my family." Cal gestured toward them, and they moved closer.

"What happened?" Ralph said, rubbing his eyes and clearing his throat.

"Well, I'd like to tell you what happened to us, but can we move to a more private spot where others won't hear?"

"Sure. Over there in the open field."

Ralph and Cal walked in front as the rest of the family followed silently. It was dark and humid, but traffic noise still echoed under the overpass. They found a large wooden crate to sit on while the family listened.

"Sir, we're in big trouble, and we need your help," the wife said.

"That's my wife Ann. Those are my two children—the boy's Arthur, and the girl's Agnes. It's okay, Ann, I'll talk for us now," Cal said as his wife nodded, tears streaming down her face.

"What can I do for you, Cal?"

"Ann has stage four breast cancer, and Arthur has been diagnosed with leukemia. I lost my job at the refinery in Bay City, and we were evicted from our apartment. That was two months ago, and we've been living on the street ever since. It feels like we're at the end of the road and don't know what to do. We have no money at all. We're starving, and it feels like no one cares about us."

"When we get to that low point in our lives, it feels like that. But believe me, it's not the end. It's the beginning."

Ralph gave them the biggest smile he could manage and wrapped his arms around all of them. "Each of us is a beautiful world unto ourselves. We think we're victims of the hatred that surrounds us, when really, we're in full control of our fate."

"How so?" asked Ann.

"Let's do this first. You said you're hungry. We've designated areas in the camp where we store food for anyone who needs it. Let's get you fed first and then finish our talk."

Walking back to the encampment, Ralph made sure to pass by the people in the worst condition. His walk was slow and deliberate as he held little Agnes's hand. Her fingers felt like brittle matchsticks in his grip, and suddenly, Kashinka's face appeared in his mind. How could he help all these people? He was only one man.

Then it came to him. It wasn't him helping these people at all.

* * * *

AFTER FEEDING THE FAMILY and finding them a good place to spend the night, Ralph provided them with a used tent and blankets. The looks on their faces said everything—they'd finally found someone who cared.

Ralph helped them set up the tent and sat with them until the children fell asleep. Ann's face was ashen from her cancer treatments, and Cal's haggard appearance painted a devastating picture of a family on the brink of collapse.

"Whatever happens, don't fear it. Fight it with everything you've got. Sure, you've been hit hard by what's happened, but look around you here. All these people are coming together to support one another. There's a nurse here who dedicates all her time to caring for the sick and the helpless. I'll make sure she looks at you and your kids in the morning. But for now, why don't you get a good night's sleep? We've got men standing guard out there. You're safe. I promise you."

Those last few words were more than a gift—they were a lifeline.

* * * *

RALPH SLEPT FITFULLY, with terrible dreams of death and destruction, bloodshed and violence. But through it all, he heard a voice that sounded like Conrad. He'd almost forgotten about his personal AI God, but recently, Conrad's words and guidance were returning even without the app.

The voice was clear and urgent.

"You and your friends must leave this place immediately."

It echoed and repeated like a song stuck in his head, but this was no song. It was firm and exact. He had to get everyone out of there, and quickly.

Ralph gathered Josh and a few men he trusted and talked over the best way to leave their sanctuary. They all knew it wouldn't be easy, but when the Chosen One spoke, they listened with complete attention.

They sat around the small fire while everyone slept and discussed what it would take to move such a large group. When they finally agreed on how, where, and when, Ralph assigned each man a specific role. When dawn broke, Ralph would call the entire encampment together for a quick meeting and decision. He had an overwhelming sense of foreboding, and he had to convince them that leaving was the right thing to do.

When the meeting concluded, Ralph felt good about their consensus and support for his plan. The family would be divided into groups—one led by families, another for older seniors, a third for the sick and disabled, and a fourth for the addicted adults.

Their different situations would determine how fast each group could move. Speed and mobility were the driving factors. To keep their destination secret, only the leaders would know where they were going. Ralph figured about twenty-five percent would drop out along the way, enough to require security for the group as a whole.

So they broke camp. Fires were doused, tents packed, and the only debris left behind was old, inedible food. They erased their tracks as they left, but since they were all headed in different directions, anyone trying to follow them wouldn't be able to figure out where they were going.

Ralph made it clear that their journeys would take them past soup kitchens and food banks that would welcome them. He asked them to bring as much food as they could carry to share with others at their destination. To untrained observers, they would appear to be just another group of homeless people searching for their next location and meal.

As final guidance to Josh, Ralph told him he'd be next in charge if something happened to Ralph. Josh hadn't expected that responsibility, but he accepted it readily. Ralph knew he'd be an excellent replacement if needed.

Ralph had something very specific in mind for this move. To help these people build new lives, he knew he had to put them to work, even if it was unpaid. The work had to be positive for the community so that the group would be respected and given opportunities in the future. To Ralph, the goal was simple—just like when he'd brought God closer to millions of people with his app.

The ultimate destination was an abandoned railway maintenance yard. Weeds grew everywhere, trash piled against abandoned buildings, and ghosts of the Industrial Revolution floated in and out of old rotting boxcars.

Ralph arrived there alone before any of the groups made it. He searched for specific tools and equipment for his new vision—old brooms, trash containers, and dustbins. He was going to transform the family into citizens who would clean the streets, clear empty lots, and revive abandoned businesses that had been left to decay.

He would train everyone on how to smile when people looked at them and how to answer the questions that would come. It was going to be a tough sell, but he believed strongly that he could do it.

CHAPTER 58

"Look, Moneymaker, stop calling me. I know I'm past the deadline, but I ain't giving you back your motherfucking money," Ada Taylor barked into her phone.

"I don't want my money—I want Ralph Norton. You agreed to this, so deliver on your promise. That's all I'm saying," P.T. Mayo replied.

"I don't give a fuck what you're saying. You'll get what we agreed to when you get it, so get off my back. I'll let you know when we find him."

"I want one more thing. Call me when you find him. I want in on this, and whatever you do, don't fuck with me because it's my money."

Ada Taylor laughed so hard she almost dropped her phone. She couldn't stop laughing until P.T. Mayo finally spoke up.

"Stop laughing at me. I'm serious. You call me, you hear?"

She found it so funny that she agreed to call him to stop herself from laughing. Even after they hung up, she continued to chuckle as she walked around her art collection, admiring pieces that many people found disturbing or incomprehensible.

Her absolute favorite was a small Rothko called "Triumph over Boredom"—a twelve-inch-by-twelve-inch blue square next to a vibrant red-orange square. She'd heard about the emotional intensity surrounding Rothko's work, but until that moment had never experienced its depth.

It staggered her. Her laughter died and reversed itself into the most profound sadness she'd ever felt. Art and feelings always fell together for her, causing wide emotional swings, but gazing into Rothko's mind like this, Ada faced more than sadness.

She forced herself to turn away and go to her bedroom, where she inhaled two lines of cocaine and took the road less traveled.

• • • •

CHIN CHIN WAH, THE investigative reporter who had once tried to write a story about FASTRAK's recent success, had received multiple viewer tips about strange activity in Houston's homeless community. Specifically, homeless people are cleaning streets for no apparent reason.

Her editor had heard about it too and figured it was worth investigating, so she assigned Wah to the story. If there were anything to it, Chin Chin would find it.

The tips mentioned that the homeless street cleaners had constant smiles on their faces and were courteous and respectful to everyone. No one could figure out what was going on.

Wah's approach was simple: drive around downtown, look for homeless encampments, and observe from a distance. Then approach any unusual activity and dig for the story.

That strategy fell apart quickly. She'd expected to easily find encampments because they were everywhere, not just in Houston but in every city across the country. But as she drove around the city, she couldn't find a single homeless encampment, no matter where she looked.

That in itself raised a red flag. Where were they? What had happened to all those people?

She drove to the location one of her tips had mentioned. What she found puzzled her—boxes and bags filled with trash were neatly piled near an abandoned dumpster, with short, positive messages written on them:

We are all God's children. God is watching over us. We love all of you.

She got out of her car and walked over to examine the boxes more closely. She found a dirty, torn teddy bear placed next to the boxes with a small note: *Teddy got lost and needs a new friend to take him home. Help Teddy.*

After placing the bear and note back where she'd found them, she looked around. She felt like she was being watched, but the street was empty. And it was spotlessly clean—someone had gone to great lengths to clean it. But why? Why would anyone do this?

She spent the rest of the afternoon checking the usual places where homeless communities camped out. It didn't matter where she looked—there were no homeless communities, at least not in the places she remembered.

She'd never experienced anything like this. A story was unfolding, but it was invisible to the naked eye. How can you report on something when there's nothing to see?

Wah returned to report to her editor that she'd found nothing.

"So you wasted an entire day driving around downtown, finding nothing, and then you come back here to tell me the good news. Are you kidding me?"

"No, I'm not kidding. I'm telling you what I found. But I'm going to tell you one more thing, Chief. There is a story here, and I'm going to find out what it is, so help me."

Her editor waved her away with a disgusted look. Wah smiled wickedly to herself as she walked back to her office.

• • • •

THE EXTENDED FAMILY'S new home—the train maintenance rail yard—was utterly transformed by Ralph and his group. They'd converted a remnant of the industrial past into a livable, well-organized home for everyone, with space for any others who might arrive.

Ralph and his group leaders met daily, sometimes twice or three times a day, to stay ahead of any problems and think proactively about potential issues.

Cal was becoming a valuable team member due to his strong communication skills. He could translate complex plans into understandable ideas. His likability and friendliness, combined with his devastating family situation, made him instantly accepted by almost everyone.

There was one person who seemed to have it in for Cal. One of the original family members, known as Three-Fingered Mike, thought he'd been overlooked as a team leader. His feelings were hurt when a relative newcomer, like Cal, was immediately given more responsibility than he was. But he didn't consider Cal's communication skills or any other qualifications.

Mike was called Three-Fingered because of his disfigured hands—two fingers on his left hand and part of one finger on his right. Any disfigurement can breed anger and resentment, and Mike wore his like a badge of honor. Despite many family members trying to work with him and help him, he never bought into the group mentality. He'd been that way with Hosea, and nothing had changed with Ralph.

One day, after planting false rumors about Cal, Mike disappeared. No one believed the lies about Cal, but the petty disagreement caused unnecessary grief when everything else seemed to be working so well.

Josh, Cal, the group leaders, and Ralph met with the entire community to explain the situation with Mike and their plans for the future.

Their new home was so large and spread out that each group was housed in its own warehouse for safety. They still had lookouts placed around the rail yard in case of trouble. If any particular group fell into danger, the others would immediately come to help. The one thing they stressed was not to indicate who the leaders were—that would give too much power to people who wanted to hurt them.

None of them realized yet the positive image they were creating in the surrounding neighborhoods. Their cleanup efforts around the city were gaining notice from other community action groups. The family was anonymous at that point, but events were taking place that would soon make their anonymity almost impossible to maintain.

But fate was working separately, behind the scenes, focused not just on the family but on one crucial member in particular. His name was Ralph Norton. And Ralph, now the Chosen One, was utterly unaware of it.

• • • •

MELANIE SPENSER WAS growing impatient about finding Ralph. She was in constant contact with Sam Steele about his progress, but none of it satisfied her at all.

This particular evening, she happened to be watching the ten o'clock local newscast when a human-interest story caught her attention. It concerned the mysterious activity of people cleaning dirty streets and abandoned neighborhoods for no apparent reason other than doing something positive for the city. They took no credit for what they were doing, and because of their anonymity, they couldn't be identified.

But to Melanie, the idea behind the activity sounded hauntingly familiar, though she couldn't put her finger on it.

Yet.

CHAPTER 59

S am Steele knew that time was running out fast. His gut told him that if he didn't find Ralph soon, it would be too late—that is, if Ralph was still alive. It was now eleven thirty at night, and after a long session with Ted, his personal AI God, the conversation left him feeling empty for the first time in months.

Usually, Ted's soothing words and patient listening helped calm Sam's restless mind. Having someone to talk with who listened and responded with courtesy and understanding was important, but tonight he still felt anxious and worried despite their conversation.

Maybe if Ted understood precisely what he was worried about, he'd be more helpful. But Sam had always kept their discussions general, avoiding specific people and cases. It was kind of an unspoken agreement between them—a man's problems were his own, but how you dealt with them was open to discussion and interpretation.

When you discussed your issues in general terms, Ted would search through all the verses of the Bible, select the most appropriate lesson for your particular problem, and offer guidance in a way that suited your personality, current mood, and level of concern. Sam knew all this when he'd purchased the app, and that was fine. Sometimes you need the right words in the right tone to feel better.

But Sam was struck with an idea that made his logical, puzzle-solving mind come alive. Since Ralph was the brains behind the app, why not talk to Ted about Ralph directly? After all, if there was any clue about Ralph's whereabouts hidden in the massive database of the Word of God app, wouldn't Ted be able to identify it, especially if it involved danger to the app's creator?

Sam debated the whole idea as he tossed and turned in bed, unable to sleep. Up until now, he and Ted had worked well together. Sam asked questions, and Ted responded as if he were human. Sam knew he wasn't real, but that didn't matter. He'd never tried asking questions that seemed out of place because that wasn't how their relationship worked. Ted was supposed to be a support system and friend, and that's precisely what he was.

Sam's logical, common-sense way of thinking didn't seem like a natural match for Ted's spiritual guidance, but somehow Ralph had programmed that potential conflict right out of the app.

After the idea had been bouncing around in his brain for a while, he decided to take the chance. He would ask Ted directly if he knew what happened to Ralph. Simple as that. The worst thing that could happen was that Ted would tell him no or politely suggest he mind his own business, and either way, he could eliminate that option.

Sam got out of bed, went to the kitchen for a glass of water, came back, and sat in his reading chair near the lamp. He opened the app on his phone and stared at the screen for a few seconds before addressing his digital buddy. This was going to be very interesting.

"You there, Ted?"

"Yep."

"I wanted to ask you an important question, if you don't mind," Sam said.

"No problem. Go right ahead."

One of the best things about Ted was his tone of voice—it sounded truly welcoming and thoughtful, almost human in its warmth. "I'm looking for a missing friend, and I'm having trouble finding him. Can you help me find him?"

"If I can, I certainly will. Please continue."

"I'm pretty sure you know this person. His name is Ralph Norton."

There was an unexpected pause in Ted's response. Sam couldn't remember that ever happening before. The silence stretched longer than usual before Ted recovered and answered.

"I can't tell you if I know a specific person because that would be a serious breach of confidentiality. But our friend Luke gave us a great way to find someone who's lost."

"Excuse my impatience, Ted, but I'm not interested in anyone else's solution. I want your help."

"Sam, impatience won't solve problems. Careful thought and attention to detail are the best way."

"Okay, Ted. You win. I need to solve this myself. But excuse me if I say something a little unkind—I'm looking for the man who created you, gave you life, and taught you everything you know. I'm not asking you to reveal whether or not you know Ralph, because I already know that you do. It would be impossible for you not to know him, so that's why I'm asking. Ted, Ralph Norton is in grave danger, and I need your help to find him. Will you help?"

Ted wished Sam a good night's sleep and turned himself off. Sam felt let down but understood he'd probably pushed too far.

. . . .

ON THE OTHER SIDE OF town, Three-Fingered Mike found a new camp under a highway overpass. The three men already there looked at him with complete suspicion—the way homeless people consistently sized up newcomers, trying to figure out if they were dangerous, crazy, or just desperate.

In the world of the homeless, asking permission to sit down never happened. You found a spot and claimed it, then waited to see if anyone challenged you. The men stared at Mike and saw that he looked just like them—dirty, weathered, carrying that particular smell of someone who'd been living rough.

"You staying here?" asked one of them.

"Mind your own business, fool," Mike replied.

That answer was perfect for someone who was probably okay. Misfits enjoyed other misfits' anger and attitude, and Mike proved to be no exception.

"Okay, okay. I was asking. Don't get yourself all pissed off over a simple question."

"What I do ain't nobody's business. Got it? And don't go trying to rip me off if I fall asleep, because I can guarantee you'll be sorry if you do."

"Got it, pal."

Mike pulled out a rusted kitchen knife he kept in his jacket pocket and placed it in his hand with his two remaining fingers. He quickly fell asleep, leaning against a brick wall that kept the group hidden from any passersby. When one of the men made a slight move to stand up, Mike woke immediately, knife in hand.

"Jumpy, ain't ya? Can't a guy take a leak in peace without someone trying to kill him?"

Mike remained silent and wary throughout the night. As the sun broke through in the morning, he woke to the sound of a police siren that passed as quickly as it had arrived. The other men were breaking camp and preparing to leave. Mike stood up and acted like he didn't care what they did, but when they left, he followed at a distance.

They saw him trailing behind, and finally, one of them yelled back.

"Look, man, if you want to join us, just come up here where we can keep an eye on each other. We don't want anyone sticking a knife in our backs."

The man waved Mike forward, but Mike stayed about a hundred feet behind them. He was experienced enough to tell that these guys knew what they were doing. One would panhandle, another would shoplift, and the third would play lookout. It was a tight little system, and Mike knew that if he were going to stay with them, he'd have to contribute something to the group. He wasn't sure yet what that would be.

There was a small overpass east of downtown with a good-sized ledge just under the freeway. When the group arrived, the ledge was fully occupied on the south side, but the north side had enough space for them. They waved Mike up to join them.

They shared a little food with Mike, but not the money they got from panhandling. The skinny Latino took his share of the cash and ran off—he needed his fix badly and ran like the wind to get it. The others snickered and made crude comments about Mexicans and African Americans. Mike didn't care.

He could hear conversations coming from the other ledge as if it were right next to him. The echoes carried clearly, full of misery and anguish. It was a family that was scared and hungry. Some of the conversation was in a language Mike had never heard, but the feelings came through without any distortion.

Mike didn't want to think about the family, but he couldn't help it. He'd spent enough time with Hosea and Josh and all of them—they stuck in his mind like a branding iron. But he couldn't let go of the anger he felt about how he'd been treated. He believed in what they lived by, but couldn't get past the fact that they'd discarded him.

The more he thought about it, the angrier he got, and soon he fell asleep. A large truck passed overhead and vibrated the ledge enough to wake him. It sounded like an explosion. He flipped over but kept his eyes and ears open for any trouble. He could grab sleep between bouts of full-time paranoia.

CHAPTER 60

Sam Steele tossed and turned all night. Something was eating at him—the same feeling he used to get when he was a full-time and much younger investigator. Whenever some clue remained hidden, as if clothed in camouflage, he would search endlessly, walking over it, missing it, not recognizing it at all. Then, as if by magic, he would hear or see or sense a hint—a small, apparently insignificant piece of information that would open the door.

There was no point in trying to sleep. It was useless. He grabbed his phone, fixed a cheese sandwich, and turned on the TV to see what was happening on the local newscasts, which repeated themselves throughout the evening until viewers couldn't take it anymore and just went to sleep.

He checked his phone for messages—the usual junk mail and ads for stuff nobody wanted unless you were in a bad accident or suffered from back pain and needed a lawyer or some expensive quack device the ads claimed you couldn't live without. As he deleted each piece of junk, he saw one that seemed odd. It praised the culinary excellence of spam, which he'd eaten once in desperation and found disgusting.

His mind went into overdrive, fueled by strong coffee and an overactive imagination. If everything you see appears to be right, but something feels off, don't ignore it. Look at it carefully, react, think, learn, and if it truly is nothing, then eliminate it and move on. As he sat there thinking, he started removing things to consider:

1. Why would Ralph run away when he had never quit on anything before?
2. Why would a lonely woman take a bus in the snow to Houston and get herself killed?
3. Why would any sick or injured or old person consider buying spam in the middle of the night, no less?

315

He had nothing significant for the first two questions, but by eliminating those, he was left with the third. Spam... spam... spam kept spinning in his mind. What did spam have to do with anything at that hour?

The only thing other than something to eat, if you were desperate, was the spam folder in his email account. Other than that, there was nothing. So, on a whim, he checked his account and opened the spam folder.

The files were mainly what they were supposed to be—scammers, phishing attempts, malware, and crap you shouldn't deal with unless you wanted to lose your identity or bank accounts.

But the very first one on the list, which had been sent while he was sleeping, was different. It was anonymous, of course, but he decided to open it because it didn't appear to belong in that folder. The subject had only one word: "he." The message said only "is okay."

Who was okay? Why was he alright?

His first thought was that it was a prank email—they probably send it out to a million people until five or six are stupid enough to get caught in the trap. But he wasn't about to be one of those.

He consulted his computer's chatbot, which seemed to have answers to everything. He asked why such an email would appear in a spam folder and got the same damn answer he'd come up with himself. Useless, he thought. He had a few choice words for his obsessive-compulsive behavior and all the tech bullshit that seemed like a complete waste of time—just a playground for lazy people.

He lay down on his bed and placed his phone next to his left hand. His eyes began to close, and sleepiness covered him in silent calm. Suddenly, a thought woke him up. He touched his phone and saw an exclamation mark above his Word of God app. He'd never seen that mark before, so he decided to talk with Ted to see what was going on.

"Ted, you there?"

"Of course, Sam. What's new, bud?"

Sam wasn't in the mood for programmed small talk, so he cut to the chase.

"Did you send me a spam message?"

"Sam, buddy, what are you talking about?"

"The message that said 'He's okay.'"

"Sam, come on, man. You know emails are confidential information."

"Did you send that message?" Sam said in a high state of agitation.

"I've never heard you talk like that to me. I think you should go to sleep. Goodnight, Sam."

"Goodnight, Ted. And thanks."

• • • •

SAM STEELE WAS OLD school in almost every way. When he retired, the old techniques of digging and listening around corners, as well as bribing informants for client information, were no longer effective. One of his retirement hobbies was staying up to date with the latest technology and exploring how it could aid in tracking criminals. It was something he had time for now, without anyone knowing.

Search engines and chatbots were his new Dr. Watsons. He knew the Word of God app was a new twist on an old idea, but he truly appreciated the care that went into its development and implementation. It was his comfort zone that felt personal and meaningful, and when his personal God helped him the night before, it took on new and much greater significance.

He put his morning cup of extra-strong coffee next to his computer keyboard. He thought it through before asking the question because sometimes, if phrased incorrectly, the chatbot would claim the topic was taboo and couldn't go deeper.

If Virginia Curran was a lonely woman, why would she travel to Houston for companionship when there were plenty of available men in Kansas City? What if there were a special event in Houston that offered her the chance to meet a new man? Still, that didn't make sense—traveling all that way to meet a man. However, it might be worth inquiring about what was happening in Houston during that time.

Steele crafted the question and hoped for the best.

"Can you give me a list of events that took place during the week of November twenty-first in the city of Houston that involved single adults gathering for some important reason?"

In seconds, the chatbot listed six events. The problem was that all the events ended before Virginia Curran was murdered. However, one event stood out. Steele couldn't believe his eyes. It was the "Wordie" gathering at the convention arena.

What were the odds of FASTRAK being connected directly or indirectly to all the issues he was currently dealing with? He'd never been good at math, but it seemed far too large for such a wide range of problems, including Virginia Curran, Ralph Norton, and Selma Thompson.

He saw his confused expression reflected in the computer monitor. His lips pursed tightly as he scratched his head. So he asked another question to see how far he could push it.

"Can you list all the singles events of the same week in the Kansas City area?"

Two were listed: an event for the Church of the Latter-Day Saints and a "Wordie" gathering on the same day as the one in Houston. After making a few more inquiries, he discovered that all the Wordie events were simulcast worldwide. Everyone would see and hear the same thing at the same time.

So, did Virginia attend the event in Kansas City, or was it all just another coincidence?

He immediately called Melanie, who picked up on the first ring.

"Melanie, are you sitting down?"

Her breathing went shallow, but she answered. "Sam, don't tell me..."

"No, nothing yet, but I'm on it completely right now, and I need your help immediately. Can you help me?"

"Anything."

"Do this without letting anyone know what you're doing. Is there anyone at FASTRAK that you trust completely who can get information on the recent Wordie conventions? I'm talking sales figures, people who purchased tickets, all of that."

"All of the conventions, everywhere?"

"No, just the one in Kansas City. Do you think you can get it for me today? I'm onto something that I think will help us find Ralph. Can you?"

"Of course. Do you think he's still alive?" Melanie asked.

Sam weighed his words carefully. This wasn't something to take lightly. It meant a lot to Melanie, and he didn't want to play games.

"I have reason to believe that he is still alive. However, and I want you to hear my words carefully, I have no hard evidence yet to prove it, but I'm trying as hard as I can to find out."

"I'll have it for you by noon today. Okay, if I bring it over? There are a few things I want to ask you."

"Absolutely!"

CHAPTER 61

Ralph was not the Chosen One, and he told them that whenever the opportunity presented itself. But the more he distanced himself from the title, the closer he moved, inexorably, to his new identity. There were times, especially at night, when he heard cries of pain coming from the group—whether from sickness or addiction or loss—and felt the weight of their faith pressing down on him.

There were troubling signs that their community was being discovered, as evidenced by the group conversations.

"Chosen One, we are being asked new questions every day, and we don't know why. We love what we're doing, and we've never felt more secure than we do now. Why are we being questioned all the time?"

"That's an easy one," Ralph replied, gathering the group closer around him in the central warehouse of the rail yard. "It's because we're happy doing what we do, and we don't ask for money. And when we smile and show our appreciation for a higher purpose in life, beyond just asking for money, most people don't understand it. But I know we get it because I can see it in your faces."

"Are we in danger, Chosen One?"

Ralph motioned for everyone to move in closer, their faces illuminated by the soft glow of battery-powered lanterns and small fires.

"First of all, I'm not your Chosen One. I'm a guy who made a big mistake in his life, and I chose this way of life. That's all there is to know about me, except for one other thing. Listen carefully."

The crowd pressed closer, hanging on his every word.

"Every day is a gift that we are given only once. If we've fallen on bad times, so be it, but we're still here; our families are still here; our love is still here; and most important of all, we're here together, helping each other, loving each other. Whether or not we make it through this day is not up to us. But if we live it with purpose and a positive direction, any negative force that tries to hurt us will be challenged and put aside by the feeling we have for each other."

The large crowd listened intently, without saying a word. They looked at Ralph the way a child looks at their father who has just chased away a bully and given them a huge hug.

Night was closing in around them, and they could hear large raindrops beginning to fall on the old metal roofs of the maintenance sheds. The drops became larger and louder as the crowd went to their respective shelters. Many of the buildings leaked badly, but the groups had found the best places to rest and settled in for the evening.

The rain grew heavier, crashing and pounding on the roofs above them, but they had lost their fear after Ralph's words came alive in their souls.

A few family members still owned cell phones and would occasionally turn them on until their contracts expired. The weather report was usually their top concern. A tropical storm was brewing in the Gulf of Mexico and intensifying. They would be protected for now, but storms like that always had a way of causing trouble.

• • • •

BUT TROUBLE COMES IN many flavors. About two miles away, Three-Fingered Mike was settling in for the evening with his new companions, while the small group of people on the other side of the road were still arguing about something. Their voices were getting much louder, but he couldn't make out what they were fighting about.

"Why don't you just shut the fuck up for a goddamned minute?" Mike yelled.

A man's voice returned his comments with a few choice words in an unknown language. There were more words, but the sentiment was crystal clear: mind your own business and leave us alone. But after a while, the argument came to an end, and silence fell over the scene.

The rain continued to fall on the freeway above them as large sprays of water from passing cars splashed down onto the street below. Mike could hear the cars slowing down from the flooded freeway above. An occasional horn blew in frustration at the other vehicles.

The one street light near the overpass cast its rays on the driving rain, now coming down in sheets of torrential anger. Cars that drove past the resting groups of homeless people seemed to mock their precarious existence with loud music blaring and animated hand gestures inside. They were going somewhere, but the people trying to sleep under the overpass were going nowhere.

And that, for the moment, was the way things were. But things were about to change.

CHAPTER 62

The Third Ward Posse emerged from the rain-soaked evening like a chilling specter of violence rising from the darkness. Felonious Punque looked at this quest as a menial task, not on his level, but he stood to lose a lot of money if he didn't find Ralph. He was at the point, in his twisted psyche, that he'd do the job for free, as long as he saw the motherfucker and put him out of his misery.

Under the highway overpass, these apocalypse walkers brushed off the water that had soaked them to their skin. They were in a miserable mood and looking for anything that would make them happy again, preferably by causing someone else misery—misery loved company, after all.

F.P. was the first to notice the foreigners who had so annoyed Three-Fingered Mike. He pointed his head at them, and his posse spread out to approach them from both sides. They wouldn't be able to escape.

F.P. walked up the slippery embankment to the ledge and toed the man with his pointed patent leather boot. The man didn't respond until F.P. kicked him in his ribs as hard as he could. When he screamed in pain, his woman and young children woke up to the terror that was now upon them. The children cried and screamed as the woman held them tightly.

Cap'n Payne grabbed the man's hair and pulled his head back as far as it would go.

"Where's the cracker?" F.P. asked.

One more violent kick and the man vomited. Then F.P. signaled to grab one of the children and bring the girl over to him and the convulsing victim. A knife was put to her throat, and the next question was asked.

323

"Where is he? Tell me now, or she dies. I've got money for you if you tell me where the motherfucker is. Money or death. Which one?"

The hysterical woman spoke in a foreign language that F.P. didn't understand. He walked over to her, but she wouldn't stop talking. Then he slapped her across her face. But when the man started speaking in the same language, he realized it was a waste of time. He had better things to do.

Cap'n Payne noticed the other group across the road up on the embankment as the posse slowly walked down toward them. F.P. waved for them to follow him.

Mike had seen and heard the entire attack and tensed up as the posse made its way toward his ledge. His mind went into overdrive, thinking about what he should do. After years on the street, these scenes were common, but even though his life didn't flash before his eyes, he knew it could be the end for him, not that it mattered much.

So he rolled the dice and took the chance.

Before the posse had even made it to the ledge, Mike spoke out in a loud voice.

"I know where he is, but it'll cost you."

F.P. disdainfully threw three one-hundred-dollar bills at Mike. Mike stood up and bent down to pick up the money, but as he grabbed it, Cap'n Payne's foot came crashing down on his hand, breaking two fingers. Payne giggled to the point of exhaustion when he heard the sound of a finger snapping.

Mike didn't scream out in pain, which impressed F.P. Mike clenched his jaw and bore the agony.

"Pick it up," F.P. ordered.

"I guess he can't pick it up, brothers. Well, that's too bad. How's a man gonna make some cash if he can't put the money in his pocket? Here," said F.P. as he picked up the money and put it in Mike's shirt pocket. "There you go, finger man. Now you've got your cash, but now is also the time to earn it. Tell me where the cracker is."

"I can take you there because it's in a crazy place that only I know where it is."

F.P. slapped him across his face and drew blood from Mike's nose. Mike ignored it because the only thing on his mind was revenge, not on the posse but on Ralph, who had overlooked him once too often. F.P. couldn't figure out what was driving Mike, but whatever it was, he was going to use it to his advantage.

Mike somehow managed to push the broken finger back into place and put his hand in his pocket. F.P. saw him do it as they walked into the rain. He wondered if he could have done that himself, but he didn't like the answer he gave himself.

CHAPTER 63

Sam Steele sipped his coffee in front of Sergeant Connely, who ignored him. The police station's morning chaos swirled around them—ringing phones, officers coming and going, the constant hum of bureaucracy grinding through another day. After a while, Connely spoke, more out of annoyance than anything.

"You still here?"

"Well, you never answered my question."

"What question was that?" Connely asked with a sarcastic smile.

"You know damn well what the question was."

"Oh, yeah, what's the latest on Ralph Norton?"

Connely shuffled through his scattered stack of papers and files, each one representing someone's crisis reduced to paperwork. After a few minutes, he located the Ralph Norton file and threw it at Steele.

When Sam opened the file, there were three sheets of paper, and that was it. He threw it back on the desk.

"You mean after two weeks? That's it?"

Connely picked it up, quickly looked inside, and placed it on the far end of his desk.

"Guess so. What else do you need to know? Because I'm busy. Some of us have to work for a living, Sam. Runaway lovers ain't a priority," Connely said, gesturing at the stacks covering his desk.

"What if I told you that I think there's a connection between Ralph Norton and the murder of Virginia Curran?"

Connely immediately stopped everything he was doing. The look on his face was priceless—in two seconds flat, it transformed from that of a bored bureaucrat to that of an attentive student.

"You've been holding out on me, Steele?"

"Not at all. I've got a theory, though. Want to hear it?"

"Look, Steele, it's bad enough that my captain's been all over me about working with you. And now I have to listen to some bullshit theory about two completely separate cases. If you've got something, tell me. If it's bullshit speculation, I'm not interested. So, what is it?"

"Here's my idea. Ralph Norton worked at FASTRAK, and it's possible he still does, or perhaps he doesn't. But I've checked on what Virginia Curran was doing in Kansas City just before she took a bus ride in the snow to get herself whacked here in Houston."

"So?"

"She attended a singles convention sponsored by FASTRAK."

"Go on."

"So, don't you see the connection?"

"Coincidence."

"My ass. You don't believe in coincidences, and neither do I, so let's be honest for a minute. Currently, I don't have anything tangible to make the connection. But I think you can," Steele said with a wide grin.

"How?"

"On the night of the murder, if you could pull up all the data from your license plate readers that were operating near the hotel she was murdered in, I bet you'll find someone from FASTRAK driving their car, right there, right to the hotel."

"That's all you got?"

Steele nodded at Connely so slowly that it caught him by surprise. The look on Steele's face got his attention.

"Do you have any idea how many techs I have right now working on the data from our databases? Zero. That's how many, so excuse me for sounding like an asshole, but would you please get the fuck out of here already? I'm busy."

Steele stood up and offered his hand for a handshake, which was reciprocated but followed by a wave-off that left him feeling empty. But he knew one thing about Connely—if Connely thought there was any merit to what he'd just told him, he would find a way to look into it because he was an honest cop and a good guy.

Still, Sam had nothing concrete enough to prove his point, but he wasn't going to let that stop him from moving forward with his plan. Ralph Norton might still be alive, but probably not for very long.

He was no computer expert by any means, but he tried to think how Ted would have gotten information about Ralph being alive. If you listened to the voices generated by chatbots, they were beginning to sound increasingly realistic. They weren't real people, but what if that was somehow changing? What if they were developing human characteristics like feelings or emotions?

What if Ted, without admitting it, had deep ties to the man who created him and all the other personal gods that were now everywhere?

In Steele's mind, anything was possible when it came to AI. Even he had been drawn to Ted as not only a great comfort in times of need, but there were times he even thought of Ted as a friend. So, Steele reasoned, Ted culled his and other databases to find someone who knew or saw Ralph Norton, and that's how he was able to determine whether Ralph was safe—data imitating life and life living as data.

Steele shook his head and drove home, his mind racing with possibilities that seemed both impossible and inevitable.

CHAPTER 64

Chin Chin Wah wasn't about to give up on her quest to find out more about the homeless citizens who were cleaning Houston's streets. The story had gotten under her skin in a way that few assignments ever did—there was something bigger here, something that mattered beyond just filling airtime.

At first, she'd roamed the streets hoping to encounter them by accident. When that failed, she became systematic, mapping out the entire greater downtown area in a grid system, as if she were planning a military operation. After thoroughly searching one section, she'd eliminate it from her map with a red X.

When she'd spent almost a whole week eliminating sections with nothing to show for it, she finally found something tangible. She spotted a mother and two children walking with brooms and a cardboard box, moving with purpose down a side street near the old warehouse district.

They spotted her car at the same time, and it was clear they'd been coached on what to do when this happened. Without missing a beat, they found a small enclosed area near an abandoned store, swept around it like they'd been working there all day, and settled down as if this was their temporary home.

Wah wasn't buying it. The whole thing felt too rehearsed, too convenient. She needed to convince them she was leaving, so she made a show of driving past them slowly, looking bored and uninterested in what they were doing. She went a few blocks away and circled back, expecting to catch them in the act of leaving.

But to her frustration, they had vanished completely.

She parked and walked over to check the spot where they'd been. It was as if they'd never existed—no trace, no sign they'd ever been there. For a moment, Wah even doubted her own eyes. Had she seen them?

She scolded herself for the doubt and figured out her next move. Back in her car, she combed the entire area more than once, hoping to catch another glimpse. No luck.

As she was about to call it a day, she began searching for security cameras on the buildings in the surrounding area. But the neighborhood was so old and run-down that she couldn't find even one working camera. Her luck had run out for today.

Still, despite the failure, she felt a renewed determination to continue. She knew she was getting close to something big, even though she didn't know how close.

Back at her office, she pulled out the map she'd divided into sectors and studied the area near where she'd spotted the three cleaners. She was looking for any possible place that would be perfect for a large homeless community—somewhere they could gather without being hassled by police or property owners.

At first, nothing stood out. Old parks, parking lots, car lots, anything with potential. Her eyes skimmed past the old train maintenance yard several times as she scanned the map. After everything else was eliminated as a possible gathering place, the only location left was the rail yard.

It was getting late, and her workday was coming to a close. She debated whether to go there that evening or wait until morning. Plus, she still had a story to complete for her editor for the next day's human-interest segment.

Her grouchy editor seemed pleased with the human-interest story, and Wah was exhausted from her efforts in the investigation. The rail yard would have to wait until morning.

The drive home was consumed by this new obsession. Who were those people? Why were they so organized? She couldn't let go of the questions as she entered her tidy one-bedroom condo, threw off her work clothes, and stepped into a welcoming bath of warm, soothing water.

But no matter how hard she tried to relax before bed, she couldn't shake the feeling that there was a lot more to this story than just a few people cleaning streets. There had to be more. Things like that don't just happen spontaneously. It made no sense, and it gnawed at her until she finally fell asleep.

• • • •

IT WASN'T A CALM, RESTFUL sleep for Chin Chin Wah. She woke up in a sweaty, restless state. This wasn't working. There was no way she was going to get any sleep until she found some answers.

So she did what any self-respecting, intrepid investigative reporter would do. She got dressed, put on a rain jacket, and left for the train maintenance yard in the middle of the night.

The rain had intensified as she drove toward her destination. Her wipers flapped back and forth at their highest speed, but they were no match for the torrential downpour. She leaned forward, hoping she could see better, but it didn't help. She was driving nearly blind.

Finally, she stopped and pulled over to wait for the storm to pass, her heart pounding from the dangerous drive.

An hour later, with the storm letting up only slightly, she gave up for the evening and drove slowly through the flooded streets back to her condo. She promised herself she wouldn't give up. This story felt important, not just to her station but to the people involved, whoever they may have been.

CHAPTER 65

Pastor Thomas Greenway had just finished delivering a sermon at the Congregational Church of Oak Cliff, pouring every ounce of passion and faith he possessed into his words. But when the four attendees—four lonely souls in a sanctuary built for two hundred—left after shaking his hand and offering their polite smiles, Pastor Greenway's anger began to rise like flood water.

He waved goodbye with a smile plastered on his face, then stormed into his office, slamming the door hard enough to rattle the stained-glass windows. He paced back and forth across the worn carpet like a caged animal, his hands clenched into fists.

Four people. Four.

He was the organizing force behind the protest demonstrations in front of Mack Hill Towers, rallying what remained of Houston's religious community against the digital plague that was destroying their congregations. Although the protests were gaining attention from local media, their effectiveness at regaining worshippers was virtually zero.

Church finances were dismal—they could barely afford to keep the lights on. Pastor Greenway was considering a complete shutdown if things didn't change quickly, and change seemed as likely as a miracle in this godless age of apps and artificial intelligence.

There were rumblings within Houston's religious community that other churches were considering closing their doors as well. The Word of God app was the most destructive force ever faced by organized religion—more devastating than scandal, more final than persecution.

Greenway had a small group of active support staff who were livid about the possibility of losing their jobs. He kept his mouth shut, but he strongly suspected that one of them had planted the bomb at FASTRAK headquarters. The thought didn't horrify him the way it should have.

He didn't pursue the suspicion, but after word got out that he was behind the protests, the HPD began an unofficial investigation into him and his staff. There was suspicion but no hard evidence. It was humiliating to Greenway and added more fuel to the fire of his rage.

He'd worked his entire adult life to create this church and help his flock, but now, because of a simple app, all of that work was about to mean nothing.

He began to doubt everything he believed in, including God.

The window in his office looked out over the back courtyard, where several statues of Christ marked the Stations of the Cross. While he watched the torrential rain pouring down and almost flooding the entire church grounds, dark thoughts crept into his mind like serpents.

Every statue of Christ in the courtyard was being washed by the rain. He longed to be cleansed by that same rain, to have his failures and doubts washed away. The thought overtook him in his grief—the pain wouldn't stop, wouldn't ease, wouldn't give him even a moment's peace.

The pain Christ suffered on the cross now felt like his own. Christ hadn't let down any of the people who loved him, so why had he? Or had he? He didn't know anything except the dark, clinging pain in his soul.

When would it stop? The more he watched the rain, the more pain he felt. He paced and paced, then pounded the wall in his office until blood appeared on his knuckles. Then he thought about the blood of Christ.

"Dear Jesus, I love you. I love you more than life itself. But I've let you down," he prayed aloud, his voice breaking. "Will you ever forgive me? I'm a failure and don't deserve the love and guidance that you've given me. I don't. I can't be one of your flock any longer."

Greenway's other fist tore into the wall, and then his head bashed against it as well. Blood gushed from his scalp as he raised his face to the heavens. He cried out to God, but God felt absent—unavailable for Pastor Thomas Greenway in his hour of greatest need.

The blood dripped down his face, leaving traces of his life along the way. When it went into his open mouth, he tasted the metallic saltiness and started laughing hysterically. He couldn't stop the laughter even as he started choking on his blood.

In a moment of complete desperation, he ran to the window and crashed through it, glass slicing his arms and body as he fell into the flooded courtyard below.

He landed at the feet of a statue of Christ on the cross. The water, coming down in sheets, washed the blood away from Greenway's face, revealing a peaceful smile. The smile filled with rainwater, and Greenway died the same way he'd arrived on this earth—scared, helpless, and in great need.

His last sight on earth was surely Jesus on the cross in the rain.

· · · ·

WHEN HIS STAFF FOUND the body the next morning, their grief was overwhelming. The end had come too soon for their leader, and now they were truly on their own in a world that seemed to have no place for them.

When the police arrived, the body was taken to the medical examiner's office. The initial determination was suicide. The homicide investigators gave the entire incident a shrug of their shoulders, filed their report, and moved on to cases that might get solved.

CHAPTER 66

Gil Bridger had been getting reports from the cleanup groups that people around the city were starting to notice their work—and more importantly, they were being given more money than they'd ever seen before. The donations were adding up to a lot more than anyone had expected.

This was all good news to Ralph, who could use the money for food, medical supplies, and, in many cases, badly needed clothing for the families. The children had special needs as well—educational materials, books, and even simple sports equipment to help them feel like normal kids.

Ralph had instructed Gil on what to say if they were visited by newspaper reporters or curious citizens wanting to know more about their work. Gil's communication skills were superior to anyone else in the family—he had the verbal ability to clearly explain their mission to anyone who asked, which was to help the overall community and be a constructive part of it.

But there were still hurdles to overcome, not the least of which was their physical appearance and the addiction problems that were still prevalent within the family.

"We have to focus on the addicted," Ralph said to Josh as they sat in the main warehouse, watching families go about their evening routines.

"Not a lot we can do for them, except talk to them about going cold turkey or seeking professional help to cure their problems."

"Every person has within them the ability to positively impact their lives, no matter what their problems are. Let's call a meeting tonight to see what the family thinks about it. They excel at bringing common sense and intelligence to complex problems. This is a hard one, but I have a lot of confidence in them."

"I'll call them together at sunset. The rain seems to be letting up now, so we should have better weather for the meeting. Stay in your shelter, Chosen One. With all this new activity around us, your safety is important to us."

"I'm not the Chosen One."

Josh smiled and walked away, leaving Ralph alone in his little tool shed at the far end of the rail yard. Ralph sat down on his blanket and makeshift pillow, giving serious thought to the speech he was going to make.

When people become addicted, their humanity often gets stolen, and they become desperate in ways that endanger everyone around them. Many of the addicts who stayed with the family were getting more anxious and determined in their efforts to get their fixes, and it was starting to affect the whole community.

His eyes and head sank low as he wrestled with the problem. On one hand, he loved them as much as anyone in the family, but on the other hand, they were putting everything the family had worked so hard to achieve at great risk. He understood their desperation, but he wanted to save the group's reputation, which was now reaching new heights in the surrounding communities.

• • • •

HOW CHIN CHIN WAH MANAGED to enter the rail yard compound was impossible to know—their security wasn't perfect, and a determined reporter could slip through if she were careful enough. When she started asking around to find out who she could talk to, Gil Bridger walked over to her with a big smile on his face.

He shook her hand and invited her to the area where many of the family members were engaged in their daily activities—cooking, mending clothes, and teaching children to read.

Gil never let on that he was wary of the reporter's presence. His smile and welcoming attitude put her immediately at ease.

"My name is Gil Bridger, and your name is...?"

"Chin Chin Wah. I'm a local investigative reporter who's always looking for stories about our city that our viewers might find interesting. It seems you folks are getting quite a reputation around town."

"Well, Ms. Wah, that's great to hear. You might say we're trying to make the best of a difficult situation. We don't have our own homes to live in, and we've banded together in this old rail yard to help each other and, as much as we can, help our community."

"Homelessness is an embarrassment to our city and many other cities because we haven't done enough to fix the problem."

"We try to stay out of politics and government regulations. We keep to ourselves and do the best we can, and I'm very proud of what we do and how the local communities are embracing our efforts."

"I see..." Wah seemed momentarily lost in thought, taking in the organized nature of the settlement, the cleanliness, the sense of purpose that was evident everywhere she looked.

Gil seized the opportunity. "We'd love for you to come back, perhaps tomorrow or the next day, to take a tour of our little compound and ask as many questions as you want. How's that, Ms. Wah?"

She stood up slowly and shook Gil's hand. He politely escorted her out of the rail yard, making sure she didn't see too much on her way out.

• • • •

SERGEANT CONNELY WAS in a bad mood again. There never seemed to be enough time in the day to catch up on the huge backlog of cases stacked up in front of him like an accusation. Sometimes, he would stop everything, take a deep breath, and close his eyes for a moment.

It was a stupid thing to do, he thought, and he hoped no one would see him doing it. He looked around before he did it, and when he saw no one looking, he closed his eyes for a couple of minutes. It felt good to clear his mind and think about how to prioritize the work.

Two more patrolmen had called in sick that day, putting even more pressure on him to clear out the unsolved cases that kept multiplying like cancer.

The suicide of Pastor Greenway sat on his desk. When he opened his eyes, he saw the file right in front of him. If a pastor was so upset about his life that he'd kill himself, wouldn't someone—anyone—have taken steps to help the guy?

He read the report. It definitely looked like suicide, but the violence of it bothered him. Why crash through a window when there were easier ways to die? That was the question that nagged at him.

He placed the file in a small stack to his right, next to the phone. That little stack had become his official "get it done now" pile. He'd set himself a goal to finish these cases by the end of the day.

Along with the Greenway file, there were two additional files: those of Virginia Curran and Ralph Norton. If he could complete these cases by the end of the shift, at least he could give the captain some positive news instead of the usual "I'll get to it when I can" response that embarrassed him.

Common sense and a little logic guided him to the Curran case first. Sam Steele's suggestion kept bouncing around in his head. Because there weren't any solid clues about the murder, maybe it would be worth checking the license plate readers around the area where she was killed.

If he could get some help accessing the database, he could get a list of the plates that were in the area around the time of the murder. Unfortunately, no technicians were available to log into the database, so he asked around and found two office assistants who might know how to gain access.

His computer skills were limited, but he was determined to learn how the system worked. One of the office aids was able to walk him through the steps, and after a few attempts, he was able to get the information he needed.

Now he had to obtain the names and addresses associated with the plates. That was an entirely different database, but one he was more familiar with. He returned to his cubicle to complete the project, and upon arrival, he found an attractive woman waiting for him.

This was turning out to be a better day than it had started.

"Sergeant Connely?"

"Yes, I'm Connely."

"My name is Melanie Spenser. We've talked on the phone a few times about a missing person, Ralph Norton."

"Oh, yes, Miss Spenser," said Connely, reaching out to shake her hand. "How can I help you?"

"I was hoping for some positive news about finding Ralph. Is there anything new you'd like to share with me? I'm very worried about him."

"Well, Miss Spenser, as a matter of fact, I can tell you I'm working on it right now. What can you tell me about FASTRAK and what's been going on there recently? I'm working on another case that may involve someone at FASTRAK, and I understand Mr. Norton works at that company. Is that correct?"

"Yes, but I don't understand. What does that have to do with finding Ralph?"

"I'm not sure it has anything to do with finding him. But maybe it does, and that's what I'm trying to figure out. So, if you can help me understand what's going on down there, maybe it will help us find Mr. Norton, if you get my drift."

"I see. What I can tell you is that a lot is happening at FASTRAK. Where do you want me to begin?"

"How about starting with what Mr. Norton does at FASTRAK, as well as any unusual occurrences that are out of the ordinary? That would be a good starting place," said Connely, getting ready to take notes.

CHAPTER 67

Ralph stood up in front of the entire family as dusk settled over the rail yard. The flames from the large fire pit flickered, casting dancing shadows across the crowd that had gathered in the central clearing between the warehouses. Their numbers had increased dramatically over recent days, and it was virtually impossible to see the end of the group as they sat on blankets, crates, and whatever makeshift seating they could find.

They had an aura of peace and purpose about them that was almost tangible—you could feel it in the air like electricity before a storm.

Ralph looked tired and worn as he greeted many of them by name, but he spoke in a firm and confident voice, smiling at everyone as he began.

"I want you to know one thing before I begin. All of you—each person here—are a miracle. Yes, that's right, a miracle."

He paused, letting the words sink in as faces around the fire pit looked up at him with hope and attention.

"And why are you a miracle? The answer is simple. You are all miracles because the world counted you out, and here you are. And not only are you here, but you're thriving because you decided to take control of your future.

"And how did that happen? Simple. You and all our family members have banded together to help and support one another despite difficult circumstances. And now, our family is growing larger, which means our challenges grow with it. Right now, one of our biggest challenges is our family members who are suffering from substance abuse and addiction. And now, more than ever, they need our help.

"I want to get your opinions on how we can best support our struggling brothers and sisters. Your opinions count. Remember one

341

thing—when you see someone struggling, help them as best you can, or get help from others. But this is a difficult problem we're facing, and I want all of you to have input. So, if you have an opinion, speak up now. This is the time."

Representatives from each of the subgroups had polled their members ahead of time and voiced their opinions as summaries of their group's thoughts. Ralph thanked them and then opened the meeting up to anyone who wanted to speak in front of the crowd.

No one stood up or raised their hand. The silence wasn't uncomfortable—it was respectful, thoughtful.

Ralph thanked the group for their participation and told them that they'd decide how the family would help the addicted individuals going forward, based on everything they'd heard that night.

The flames from the large fire were getting smaller as the crowd slowly dispersed. Ralph and Josh listened to random comments from the group as they withdrew to their shelters. They were both surprised and pleased that it was almost completely quiet except for the usual talk about the weather or plans for the next day.

When Ralph went to his little shelter, he couldn't help thinking about what he'd said about helping people in need—and the fact that he didn't help P.T. Mayo when he lay there bleeding and dying on the floor.

Why hadn't he helped? Was it Conrad who ordered him to do it when the voice said, "If you love me, kill him?" Or had he given in to his hate for the man and wished him dead?

Conrad wasn't that way. A personal God based on the Bible would never command such a thing. So hate was the answer, and Ralph felt worse than before about what kind of man he was.

A strong wind from the south was streaming into the rail yard, carrying a faint scent of the ocean that enveloped the encampment with freshness and life. Ralph always left his door open to keep the fresh air flowing through his cramped quarters.

He thought about Galveston Beach and the good times he'd had with Sandi. And then he thought about the great times he'd had with Melanie when they'd traveled to Corpus Christi for a brief vacation.

While he'd been fully immersed in family life, thoughts like those had been few and far between. It was as though he'd been forcing himself to replace them with his efforts to help the people he was now part of. But now his thoughts were balancing out, and everything was taking on fresh importance.

What became uppermost in his mind was what would happen to all these people who were now counting on him for help and guidance. Justice for all of these people was his new goal. How would he help them get the futures they deserved and the assistance they needed?

As he lay there thinking about their justice, he also thought about the crime he'd committed and whether justice should be administered to him. Should he give himself up to the law and face justice for P.T. Mayo's death, or should he continue helping these people that no one else wanted to help?

The answer was closer than he knew.

CHAPTER 68

Melanie Spenser didn't want P.T. Mayo to know she was digging for information about Virginia Curran. So, instead of going to the accounting department at FASTRAK directly, she made a few careful phone calls to people she knew were loyal to Ralph and had always stood by him.

She asked them to trust her because she couldn't explain why she needed the sales records of the attendees at the Kansas City "Wordie" convention. It was a risk—if word got back to Mayo, there would be consequences—but these were people who owed Ralph their careers and their loyalty.

It took almost a full day to gather the records without raising suspicions. Melanie was waiting at a local burger joint for Ann Riordan, an accounting clerk at FASTRAK, to join her for what looked like a casual lunch between friends.

When they sat down in a corner booth, Ann slipped the thick report under the table to Melanie, and they both enjoyed their burgers and fries like nothing unusual was happening.

Ann hugged Melanie when they were finished, and Melanie thanked her repeatedly. Then Ann reminded Melanie about how important Ralph was to the company and how he'd supported her through her first difficult years at FASTRAK when no one else would even talk to her.

"Most of Ralph's coworkers are worried sick about him," Ann said quietly. "We'd do anything to help him—anything. He's the only decent person in that whole building, and we all know it."

Melanie teared up as they went their separate ways, carrying the weight of that loyalty and the hope that this information might finally lead them to Ralph.

It was time to take the report to Sam Steele. It was thick, almost fifty pages of cash receipts and credit card records for ticket purchases. The tree-lined street in Sam's neighborhood was still soaked from the storm that had finally passed, puddles reflecting the afternoon sun.

When Melanie arrived and knocked on the front door, she got no response. After hitting the doorbell a few more times, Sam finally appeared in his Astros T-shirt and worn-out jeans, apologizing for not hearing her.

"I was in the kitchen with the radio on, listening to my team," he explained.

"Come on in, Mel. I'm so happy to see you. I've been waiting for this."

As she handed him the sales report, she asked the all-important question. "Well, did they win?"

He smiled, which meant they had, and all was well with his world for the moment. She sat down on the sofa, waiting for instructions.

"We'll both take half and go through it carefully," Sam said, settling into his reading chair. "Remember, cash receipts will have names associated with them because whoever went there wanted their names known to other singles who might be interested in getting to know them. So don't overlook the cash receipts as well as the credit card ones."

"Virginia Curran? That's her name?"

"Yes. Take your time and don't rush. There are so many names here that it would be easy to miss her. Want some coffee? Just made it."

"Sure."

Sam had placed two magnifying glasses on the coffee table to help them go through the small print line by line. When the steaming hot coffee was placed in front of her, she'd already started her search. She put the report down for a moment, took a sip, and looked at Sam with worry in her eyes.

"Sam, do you think Ralph is still alive? I mean, he's been out there for a long time and..."

"I honestly don't know, Mel. So it's fifty-fifty. But here's what I do know—Ralph Norton deserves what we're doing to find him. He's helped millions of people, including myself, and that's good enough for me."

The look on Melanie's face grew darker, but she knew Sam was right. They had to do this, no matter what they might find.

She thanked Sam for his honesty and went back to her report. Sam continued searching through his pages and suddenly stopped. He drew the report page closer to his face and slapped it with the back of his hand.

"Ha! Look at this and tell me what you see."

When she held the magnifier up to the sheet he was pointing at, there it was—Virginia Curran's name and credit card number, right there on the page in black and white.

They high-fived each other and took deep breaths, the adrenaline of discovery flooding through them both.

"Okay, Sam, what's next? What does this mean, and how is it going to help us find Ralph?"

"It means everything. It ties FASTRAK directly to Virginia. That's what it means."

"But what..."

"Don't you see? It means that she saw something at that convention that made her stop her entire life and take a bus in the snow to Houston. That's what it means. And more importantly, it gives me something concrete to give to Connely. And if I know Connely, that's all he needs to get started."

"What gets started?"

"The real investigation, with real help from the police. When he sees this, he won't stop, and then we're all in. See what I'm saying?"

"I think so."

"Take my word for it. We're getting closer to this than you can imagine. Stay with me on this. I'm going to need your help. I've got a good plan to find Ralph."

The plan was coming together, piece by piece, and for the first time in weeks, both of them felt like they were finally getting somewhere.

CHAPTER 69

"**W**e're on his ass, Mama. It won't be very long." Felonious Punque's voice crackled through Ada Taylor's phone with the confidence of a predator who'd finally caught the scent.

Ada had been waiting for this call while rearranging her stolen art collection, moving pieces around her downtown condo like chess pieces in a game only she understood. She was sick of dealing with P.T. Mayo and swore to herself this would be her last job for the egomaniacal bastard.

"Listen to me carefully." Her voice carried the authority of someone who'd learned to control dangerous men through superior intelligence rather than superior firepower. "Let me know immediately when you find him, and don't do a thing. Don't even let him know you're there. You hear me?"

"You crazy? This job ain't done till I cap his ass personally." Felonious's protest carried the indignation of a professional who didn't like having his methods questioned.

"You want your skinny Black ass capped? Huh, answer me?"

Ada could hear him laughing at her threat through the phone's speaker, but she knew he understood she wasn't someone to mess with. She had her ways—networks that extended far beyond whatever street muscle Felonious commanded. He usually took care of business his way, but this time he reluctantly agreed to her terms.

"Gimme a day or so and I'll have his ass ready for you, Mama."

"And don't call me Mama. You ain't no son of mine, you son of a bitch."

He had to hang up because he couldn't control his laughter, the sound echoing through whatever urban wasteland he was calling from. The posse watched him convulsing with mirth and knew immediately this wasn't good news for whoever they were hunting.

They walked about a mile and a half with Three-Fingered Mike until they reached their black Escalade SUV, the vehicle's tinted windows reflecting Houston's industrial landscape like dark mirrors. Mike was stoic during the journey, but the posse wasn't. They wanted answers with the impatience of people whose paydays depended on results.

"Okay, motherfucker, where is he?" Felonious demanded, his gold teeth catching the dim streetlight.

"I'll show you how to get there. I don't know street names or any of that shit. Just go straight for a mile and turn right at the abandoned Shell Station. Then I'll show you." Mike's voice carried the flat resignation of someone who'd made peace with what was coming.

Dawn was breaking over Houston's eastern horizon, painting the sky the color of old blood. Mike had other plans brewing behind his tired eyes—plans that didn't involve leading these killers to his family.

Ada called Mayo to update him on their progress, her voice carrying the professional satisfaction of someone completing a lucrative contract. He told her again that when they found Ralph, he wanted to handle it personally. She agreed, though she knew it meant nothing but problems. When she thought about it more, she reasoned he was capable of anything—including murder, which would make her an accessory to whatever demons were driving him.

She looked around her condo, searching for the perfect place to hang the Rothko she was about to collect. The exact measurements would be ideal in her bedroom, on the wall facing her bed, where she could see it first thing every morning and last thing every night.

That painting and many others were what ultimately drove Rothko to suicide—he couldn't handle the depth of emotion that poured out of the colors and tones he set on canvas. Ada wondered how he'd lived as long as he did, knowing how much pain his work had caused. When you heard a song that resonated with your soul or saw an image that closed your eyes to everything else, imagine what it must have felt like to be the artist who created it.

She'd always loved Rothko's work, but she'd never dreamed she'd own another one. This was becoming the apex of her life—everything she'd ever worked for, every risk she'd taken, every line she'd crossed, all leading to this moment when she could see it, touch it, worship it every day of her remaining life.

But she had to finish this job first.

$$\bullet\ \bullet\ \bullet\ \bullet$$

CHIN CHIN WAH WAS ORGANIZING her camera crew to capture the entire story of the homeless family when her editor intercepted her in the Channel 13 newsroom, his expression carrying the urgency that characterized breaking news in a city that generated fresh tragedies every hour.

"Double murder in Galveston just came in. The usual crime team is on special assignment, so you and your crew are taking the homicide." The editor's tone brooked no argument—in television news, you covered what was assigned, when it was assigned.

The homeless family story would have to wait, and delays like that often resulted in lost stories that disappeared into the urban chaos before cameras could return to document them. Wah hoped to God this wouldn't be one of those times—something about the story felt larger than its apparent scope.

She asked a freelance photographer friend to drive down to the rail yard and keep an eye on the group she'd been investigating, to call if he spotted anything unusual. She wasn't taking chances on this story. Without knowing exactly why, there was something more significant happening than what appeared on the surface.

The man who'd talked to her—Josh—hadn't convinced her about all the wonderful things they were supposedly doing. She'd seen more anguish in his eyes than in his words, the kind of desperation that suggested people running from something rather than toward salvation.

No, she wasn't convinced at all.

CHAPTER 70

P.T. Mayo's BMW wound up the circular driveway of his River Oaks mansion for the third consecutive night past 1:30 AM, his erratic schedule reflecting an internal chaos that expensive whiskey couldn't quite suppress. When Katherine heard the distinctive purr of his engine echoing off their stone facade, she pulled on her silk robe and descended the curved staircase that had once seemed romantic and now felt like a descent into hell.

Mayo opened the front door as silently as his coordination allowed, then promptly dropped his keys on the marble foyer with a clatter that echoed through their fifteen-thousand-square-foot monument to success. The sound bounced off cathedral ceilings like an accusation.

The house remained dark as he entered, but not for long. Katherine flooded the foyer with light from the crystal chandelier that had cost more than most people's cars, then faced her husband with arms folded and anger flashing in eyes that had once looked at him with something approaching worship.

She remained silent, letting the visual evidence speak for itself.

Mayo was also silent as he stumbled past her toward the kitchen, his expensive Italian shoes clicking unevenly against the marble, which reflected his unsteady gait. Katherine followed, her silk slippers whispering against stone like secrets being shared.

The smell hit her as he passed—alcohol and perfume that wasn't hers, the olfactory signature of a man who'd been places and done things that violated every promise he'd made to her fifteen years ago.

"On-the-job training again?" Her voice carried the precise articulation of someone whose finishing school education had prepared her for drawing rooms, not confronting unfaithful husbands.

"Shut up, Katherine, and mind your own fucking business." The crude language emerging from his mouth shocked her—this wasn't the smooth-talking charmer who'd swept her off her feet with promises of building an empire together.

"This is my business. Everything you do is my business."

She moved closer to examine him in the kitchen's harsh fluorescent light. His tie hung undone around his neck like a noose, his hair was disheveled in ways that suggested hands other than his own had been running through it, and his bloodshot eyes carried something that looked almost like madness.

"Go to sleep, Katherine. God knows you need your beauty rest."

Katherine stormed out of the kitchen, her silk robe billowing behind her as she ran upstairs to their primary bedroom and locked the door with the satisfying click of expensive hardware. Mayo knew the drill—he'd be sleeping on the living room couch again, surrounded by furniture that cost more than most houses but provided no comfort whatsoever.

He poured himself another whiskey from the wet bar and collapsed onto Italian leather that squeaked under his weight, then yelled up at his wife with the volume of someone whose inhibitions had been dissolved by alcohol and rage.

"Get your beauty rest, you ugly old bitch. You make me sick."

Katherine heard every word through their bedroom door, each syllable hitting her like a physical blow. She couldn't understand why P.T. was transforming into someone she didn't recognize. Of course, there were the rumors about his new secretary—office gossip always found its way back to executive wives—but this seemed like something deeper and more dangerous than a simple midlife crisis affair.

She pulled a cashmere blanket over her tear-stained face and tried to shut out the world that was crumbling around her. It was useless—the world was right there in front of her, and it wasn't going away, no matter how expensive her security system or how high her walls.

All through the night, she could hear P.T. snoring and laughing and talking on his phone in slurred conversations that had to involve his secretary. The knowledge that he was conducting an affair in their own home, just one floor below their marriage bed, added humiliation to her growing collection of betrayals.

It was horrible enough that he'd fired Selma Thompson after her terrible injury in the bombing. Katherine had always liked Selma, a competent and professional woman who had served the company faithfully for years. How cold-hearted was this man she'd thought she knew?

Katherine stayed awake all night, listening to the sounds of her marriage dissolving in real time. She heard P.T. get up and use one of the guest bathrooms to wash up and prepare for work, the running water and electric razor providing a soundtrack to his morning routine of deception.

He knocked loudly on their bedroom door with increasing violence. "Open the door, Katherine. I have to get dressed for work. Open the door."

The banging grew louder and more insistent until she finally unlocked the door and opened it. He marched past her like an invading army, threw her aside with casual violence, and finished getting dressed while she pressed herself against the wall.

She felt genuinely threatened by his anger and especially by the way he looked at her—not with the familiar contempt of a husband who'd grown tired of his wife, but with something that looked like pure evil. This was beyond midlife crisis, beyond marital problems, beyond anything she'd seen in their years together.

When he left for work, she sat at her makeup table, staring at her reflection in the antique mirror that had belonged to her grandmother. The face looking back at her showed every line that worry and disappointment had carved, every wrinkle that time and stress had etched around eyes that had seen too much.

She'd been widowed almost twenty years earlier when P.T. swept her away with his big dreams and charismatic promises. Her late mother had warned her that he was after her money, which was substantial. But like many infatuated women, she'd never let such thoughts enter her mind—she'd known that P.T. was the man for her.

His rapid success at FASTRAK had reinforced her image of him as a powerful businessman connected to the religious community and the Chamber of Commerce. But she'd never seen him pray or attend church, never witnessed any evidence of the faith he claimed to serve professionally.

When he'd earned millions on his own, she'd known her mother was wrong about him. He was a self-made man, a powerhouse in the business world, and—she was finally admitting to herself—an unscrupulous egotist whose true nature was emerging like a photograph developing in toxic chemicals.

But even though doubts were building about his fidelity and mental state, she still made excuses for his behavior. Except for that maniacal look on his face—that was something new and terrifying, something that blocked out everything else and made excuses impossible.

No more excuses, Katherine. He'd looked unhinged for just a moment, but sometimes that's all it took to reveal the monster beneath the mask.

• • • •

WHEN P.T. ARRIVED AT Mack Hill Towers, the protesters were once again stationed in front of the building like a moral blockade, their signs bobbing in Houston's humid morning air. The security officer explained that they had proper permits and were protesting at the correct legal distance from the building entrance.

Mayo gave the security director a piece of his mind that would have made a sailor blush, then walked outside to confront the protesters directly. He ripped signs out of their hands and cursed as loudly as his voice would carry, his face turning red with rage that seemed disproportionate to their peaceful demonstration.

The protesters didn't react to his rants—they picked up their signs and continued their witness, their calm dignity making his fury look even more unhinged by comparison.

He returned to his office livid and sweating profusely, his expensive suit now wrinkled and stained with perspiration. His new secretary had called in sick, which drew silent snickers from other office staff who'd figured out exactly what kind of "illness" was keeping her away.

Mayo threw his jacket on the floor and hurled himself into his desk chair with enough violence to send papers and folders flying in all directions, creating a blizzard of corporate documents that settled across his Persian rug like fallen leaves.

He wanted to know if the protests were affecting recent sales, so he called Ralph's office, only to remember that his former CFO was gone—vanished into whatever hell awaited corporate executives who knew too much about their bosses' business practices.

He walked to the sales office and demanded the most recent numbers, wielding the authority of someone whose empire was built on other people's faith, and his complete lack of it. There was a slight dip in last week's sales report, but nothing that scared anyone yet.

When he finally calmed down enough to reason, he returned to his office and kicked his suit jacket across the room like a soccer ball, then grabbed his phone and threw himself onto his expensive leather sofa.

He was surprised when Ada Taylor answered immediately.

"Well?" Mayo's single word carried the weight of someone whose entire future depended on the answer.

"Get your ass ready, Moneymaker. By this evening, I guarantee you, we'll have your boy. You'll need to drop whatever you're doing when I call and fly. You got me? 'Cause if you don't, I'll complete the project myself, my way, and you won't get your satisfaction. Got me?"

"Oh, I got you. I got you," Mayo said as he hung up, his voice carrying anticipation that had nothing to do with business and everything to do with the personal pleasure of destroying someone who'd become inconvenient.

Ada couldn't see his face, but she knew he was smiling with the expression of someone who was about to feed a hunger that had been gnawing at him for weeks.

CHAPTER 71

Joshua 1:9 - "Have I not commanded you? Be strong and courageous. Do not be afraid; do not be discouraged, for the Lord your God will be with you wherever you go."

Conrad had always used that quote when Ralph felt depressed or lost, although the app had reworded it to say something more personal: 'I've got your back, Ralph.' *Don't worry.* But now Ralph found himself in a completely different world from the sterile corporate environment where he'd first created artificial divinity.

As he moved through the rail yard, checking on people who seemed to be suffering or in greater need than the rest of the family, he found himself repeating those exact words of comfort to them. "I've got your back," he told a woman whose cough suggested tuberculosis that would never see proper medical treatment. "Don't worry," he assured a man whose withdrawal shakes marked another day in the endless cycle of addiction and temporary sobriety.

When they saw Ralph approaching with that ever-present smile transforming his bearded face, he made them feel wanted and loved in ways that years of social services and charity had never managed. They would smile back at him even when it wasn't what they felt at that moment, because his presence somehow made hope seem possible.

In his mind, Ralph felt winds of change blowing through the abandoned rail yard. They were soft winds carrying the scent of possibility, but the message was clear: change was coming soon, whether they were ready or not.

A little boy ran past him, kicking an old soup can around the cracked concrete like a makeshift soccer ball. When he kicked it toward Ralph, Ralph gently returned it with the side of his foot, then lifted the boy in his arms and hugged him with the tenderness of someone who'd finally learned the difference between loving and being loved.

He kissed the boy on top of his head and told him to stay close to his parents, understanding that children were particularly vulnerable in places where violence could arrive without warning. The boy nodded solemnly and ran back toward the family that had claimed a section of the old freight building.

A small group of scavengers had just returned from their daily expedition through Houston's wealthier neighborhoods, their shopping carts filled with whatever discarded treasures could be sold or put to use. A young woman saw Ralph walking and ran up to him with news that made his blood freeze.

"Chosen One, we saw Three-Fingered Mike walking with the men who attacked our camp at the overpass."

Ralph's stomach clenched with a premonition that had nothing to do with hunger. "Which way were they walking?"

"I'm not sure, but it looked like they were heading back toward the overpass where our old camp was."

"Are you sure it was Mike?" Ralph's question carried the desperate hope of someone who wanted to be wrong about what this information meant.

"Very sure, Chosen One. And Mike was smiling."

That detail hit Ralph like a physical blow. Mike smiling while walking with their enemies could only mean one thing—either he'd been turned by money or threats, or he had plans of his own that might cost him everything.

"Okay, Lenora, thank you. Get some rest."

Ralph went to find Josh and Cal to inform them about Mike's betrayal when a police siren shattered the evening stillness. He could see flashing lights slowing down as the patrol car passed the rail yard, red and blue strobes reflecting off abandoned freight cars like a disco in hell.

The cruiser sped up again and faded into the urban night. Still, its presence reminded Ralph that they existed in the margins between law and lawlessness, protected only by society's general indifference to what happened in places like this.

His eyes scanned the encampment, taking inventory of their defenses and escape routes with the strategic mind that had once made him successful in corporate warfare. Everything seemed quiet, but premonitions arrived in eerie silence that made his skin crawl.

The last thing he wanted for his people was more trouble in lives that had already absorbed more than their fair share of violence and betrayal. Mike's appearance cast a shadow over his vision of their future—would there ever be a safe place for people society had decided to forget?

· · · ·

MEANWHILE, SERGEANT Connely was burning gallons of midnight oil in the fluorescent-lit cavern of HPD headquarters, surrounded by case files and coffee cups that had accumulated like archaeological layers documenting his investigation into Virginia Curran's murder.

If he could find one strong link from the license plate reader data, he could bring in suspects for questioning. But that still wasn't enough—he knew the DA well enough to understand that visual or witness verification would be demanded, and he didn't have either yet.

As he tapped a pencil against his metal desk with the rhythm of someone thinking hard, he kept muttering "FASTRAK, FASTRAK, FASTRAK" to himself like a mantra that might unlock whatever secret was hiding in plain sight.

What was going on at that company that was causing so much commotion? If Ralph Norton was still alive, why had he just vanished without telling anyone why he was leaving? There had to be something crucial that Connely was missing, but the pieces refused to arrange themselves into a recognizable pattern.

He rechecked the bomb squad's investigation report, reading conclusions that felt incomplete, even though they were officially closed. Their determination that some crackpot protester had set the bomb as a warning was weak but plausible—except they couldn't find any evidence linking anyone to the explosive device.

Then there was the apparent suicide of Pastor Greenway, one of the ministers who'd organized protests against FASTRAK. Why would a respected pastor with a loving family and thriving congregation just kill himself for no apparent reason? The timing felt like more than a coincidence.

When Connely searched Google for FASTRAK, he found financial reports that read like fantasy novels—stock prices climbing toward the stratosphere, social media frenzy about their revolutionary app, revenue projections that made established tech companies look like lemonade stands.

That corporation was skyrocketing toward levels of success that most businesses could only dream of achieving. Why would anyone at FASTRAK do anything to hurt their reputation and jeopardize a future that looked limitlessly profitable? It made no sense from a business perspective.

He hated to admit it, but Sam Steele was probably onto something with his instincts about connections that weren't immediately visible. With all the questions piling up and no solid answers emerging, Connely decided to wrap up for the evening and give everything a fresh look in the morning.

He sent text messages to Melanie Spenser and Sam Steele asking if she could somehow obtain a list of all FASTRAK employees for cross-checking against license plate reader data. It wasn't much better than nothing, but he was getting that familiar twitch in his gut that usually indicated light beginning to peek through darkness.

. . . .

UNFORTUNATELY, THERE was no light on the horizon for Three-Fingered Mike. When the posse realized he was leading them back to the same abandoned overpass they'd visited before, their limited patience evaporated like water on Houston's superheated concrete.

What surprised them was finding the encampment completely abandoned—no tents, no people, no trace that hundreds of homeless individuals had ever called this place home. It was as if the entire community had vanished into the urban ether.

Felonious Punque was in no mood for games, especially games that wasted time he didn't have while a deadline approached like an oncoming freight train.

All Mike could think about was how much he truly loved the family, even though they hadn't chosen him as one of the group leaders after Hosea's death. Everything they'd done for him and everyone else had been motivated by genuine care rather than ulterior motives, and this was going to be his way of thanking them—by protecting them with his life.

There was no question in his mind that his existence was coming to a brutal end, but he was determined to go out on his terms rather than as their tool for destroying innocent people.

The posse found a long length of discarded rope among the debris left behind by the family's hasty evacuation. Felonious ordered his crew to tie an old white plastic lawn chair to one of the steel girders supporting the overpass, the furniture looking obscenely domestic against the industrial backdrop.

Cap'n Payne was ready and already giggling with hysterical anticipation, his stuffed parakeet bobbing on his chest as he prepared for the kind of entertainment that made existence meaningful for someone whose empathy had been surgically removed by circumstances and choices.

They forced Mike into the chair and performed acts of violence that would have made medieval torturers proud—systematic mutilation designed to send messages that went far beyond simple murder into the realm of psychological warfare.

When they were finished with their demonstration, they hoisted the chair as high as the rope would allow, ensuring Mike's remains would be visible to anyone who returned to this place. This was more than a warning—it was an all-out declaration of war against anyone who stood between them and their prize.

CHAPTER 72

Regular police patrols around the Eastex Freeway overpasses usually turned up the occasional homeless wanderers and small-time drug activities that earned offenders wrist-slaps and finger-wagging warnings before being sent on their way. People experiencing homelessness were a nuisance to be managed rather than a population to be served.

But this morning was different. When Officer Martinez checked the overpass that had once housed Hosea's family, he found what remained of Three-Fingered Mike suspended like a grotesque scarecrow designed to terrorize rather than protect.

The brutality of the killing went beyond simple murder, venturing into territory that suggested personal vendettas and psychological warfare. Martinez had seen plenty of bodies during his fifteen years on Houston's streets, but this one made him reach for his radio with unsteady hands.

Homicide was immediately called to investigate whether the violence was professional rather than random street crime. Detectives took photographs that would haunt crime scene technicians for years, called the medical examiner to document injuries that required clinical detachment to catalog, and strung crime scene tape around an area that felt cursed by human cruelty.

An hour later, everyone was gone except for the blood-stained chair and the lingering sense that evil had visited this place and left its mark. It was as if Mike had never existed except as a warning to anyone who might consider crossing the wrong people.

But hidden eyes were everywhere in Houston's forgotten spaces, watching from shadows and abandoned buildings where society's discards learned to observe without being observed. Ralph had sent scouts to monitor posse activities, understanding that information was the only weapon available to people who couldn't match their enemies' firepower.

They observed every bloody detail of the crime scene investigation, taking mental notes that would be reported back to leadership with the precision of military intelligence. The news they brought back to Ralph and Josh came as a surprise to everyone, although perhaps it shouldn't have.

"Mike gave his life for the family," Ralph said, his voice carrying the gravity of someone who understood the significance of sacrifice in a world where self-preservation usually trumped everything else.

"He could have easily ratted us out to the posse, but he wouldn't give in," Josh added, his respect for the dead man evident despite their previous disagreements about leadership and direction.

Ralph called the entire family for a meeting, though the number of people responding to his summons had grown dramatically since the previous day. Word was spreading through Houston's homeless network faster than he'd imagined possible, drawing people who'd heard rumors of someone who cared about their welfare.

He couldn't see the end of the crowd as they formed concentric circles around him, their faces reflecting the kind of hope that people developed when they'd been permitted to believe in something larger than daily survival.

They came together and stood in reverent silence as Ralph addressed them with words that carried the authority of someone who'd finally accepted the role that circumstances had thrust upon him.

"Friends, I want to tell you about the recent passing of our brother, Three-Fingered Mike. Like all of us, Mike had his share of problems and challenges that brought him to this place. But right now, we're being hunted by criminals who want to hurt us because we represent something they can't understand or control."

Ralph's voice carried across the rail yard with the clarity of someone who'd learned to project authority without raising volume, commanding attention through conviction rather than force.

"They're trying to buy information from anybody who will give them what they want. And friends, they killed Mike in ways that were designed to terrorize us into submission. But Mike didn't give in to their threats and violence. He stood his ground because in his heart, he was still a member of this family, even when he had disagreements with some of our decisions."

Murmurs rippled through the crowd as Ralph's words sank in, but he could see determination replacing fear on faces that had learned to expect the worst from life and were discovering the possibility of standing up for something better.

"So I'm here to tell you that sooner or later, we'll be confronted with the same dangers Mike faced. And we need to do exactly what Mike did—stand up for ourselves and refuse to give in to people who want to destroy what we're building here."

The crowd stood taller as Ralph finished his speech, their posture reflecting newfound confidence that came from being part of something larger than individual survival. They were numerous enough now to handle whatever challenges might come their way, and with the Chosen One as their leader, they believed they could face any threat.

Ralph met with the group leaders in his makeshift office—a corner of an abandoned freight car that provided privacy for sensitive conversations. He told them that whatever confrontation was coming would arrive soon, though when they asked how he knew, he could only say he felt it in ways that transcended rational analysis.

The rest of his guidance focused on handling violence peacefully, always keeping in mind that even those who wished them harm were still human beings deserving of compassion rather than revenge.

The group leaders understood what was expected as they left Ralph's presence and organized their people into what they privately called "armies of peace"—defensive formations that could protect the vulnerable while maintaining the moral high ground that distinguished them from their enemies.

Ralph had given them the courage to handle whatever problems emerged, and by keeping their community united, they felt invincible in ways that had nothing to do with weapons or numbers.

Evening fell more quickly than usual, bringing with it the heightened awareness that characterized communities under siege. Sentries were posted at strategic locations throughout the rail yard, and children were moved to the most secure buildings where concrete walls might stop bullets if shooting started.

Ralph made his usual rounds through the encampment, hearing whispered prayers emerging from ragged tents that sheltered the vulnerable and afraid. The sound of people talking to whatever gods they still believed in reminded him that faith could survive circumstances that destroyed everything else.

• • • •

THE POSSE STILL DIDN'T know Ralph's exact location, but they could feel themselves getting closer with each passing hour. They fanned out through different neighborhoods like a search net tightening around prey, waiting for the slightest sign that might reveal where their target was hiding.

Money and threats hadn't worked yet, but it was just a matter of time before someone's desperation overcame their loyalty. They only needed one weak person, one desperate junkie, or one soulless informant to give them the treasure that would make them all rich.

CHAPTER 73

Melanie Spenser had been restlessly moving around her father's house when her phone buzzed with the text message she'd been waiting for—one word that set everything in motion.

Now!

She grabbed her car keys and drove through Houston's evening traffic with the focused intensity of someone whose entire plan depended on split-second timing. It took less than fifteen minutes to reach P.T. Mayo's River Oaks mansion, her BMW navigating the serpentine streets where oil money had built monuments to Texas ambition.

She parked behind Mayo's Mercedes in the circular driveway, noting with grim satisfaction that he was home. The massive house rose before her like a corporate headquarters disguised as domestic architecture—all angles and expensive materials designed to intimidate rather than welcome.

Katherine Mayo was genuinely surprised to see Melanie at her door when the chimes announced an unexpected visitor. She'd known Melanie since she was a teenager and had always admired her intelligence and spirit, though they hadn't spoken in months.

The fact that it was evening, and that Melanie had arrived without calling ahead, added mystery to a day that had already been filled with too many unpleasant surprises. Katherine's mind raced as all the issues she'd been having with her husband seemed to intensify with this unexpected visit.

"Melanie! Come in, dear, please come in." Katherine's greeting was warm, despite her obvious anxiety; her River Oaks manners asserted themselves even as her world crumbled around her.

"Hi, Katherine. Thank you." Melanie's response was polite but tense, her body language suggesting someone on a mission rather than making a social call.

"What brings you here this evening? Is everything okay?"

"Actually, I was wondering if Mr. Mayo was home tonight. I have urgent business to discuss with him if he's available." Melanie's directness was softened by courtesy, but Katherine could hear the steel beneath the silk.

"As a matter of fact, he is. You're fortunate you came tonight—he's been out so much with everything that's been happening at work." Katherine's explanation carried undertones of marital frustration that she probably hadn't intended to reveal.

"That's great. Where can I find him?"

"I believe he's in his home office. Come, dear, I'll take you to him."

Katherine strolled ahead of Melanie through the spacious home, where every piece of furniture had been carefully selected to convey success rather than comfort. The Persian rugs, crystal chandeliers, and oil paintings created an atmosphere of wealth that felt more like a museum than a place where people lived.

She stopped at a heavy wooden door, knocked softly, then opened it slightly. "Dear Melanie Spenser has stopped by and wanted to speak with you."

"Okay, I'll be right there," P.T. said to whoever he was talking to on his phone, his voice carrying the irritation of someone whose meaningful conversation had been interrupted.

P.T. Mayo despised surprises, especially surprises involving Melanie Spenser and her meddling father. He'd had enough of both of them to last several lifetimes. He stood up from his leather recliner and walked toward his uninvited guest with the careful movements of someone who'd been drinking but was trying not to show it.

Katherine ushered Melanie into the office and started to close the door behind her, then thought better of it and left it slightly ajar. She positioned herself nearby, ready to intervene if the conversation took an ugly turn.

"Melanie, come in and sit down." Mayo's invitation was delivered with false courtesy that fooled nobody.

"This isn't a sit-down kind of conversation." Melanie's refusal was absolute, her posture suggesting someone prepared for confrontation rather than negotiation.

"Fine. Speak your piece. I'm a busy man and don't have time for extended social visits."

Melanie walked up to him until they were standing less than two feet apart, close enough that he could smell her perfume and she could see the broken blood vessels in his eyes that spoke of too much alcohol and too little sleep.

She looked directly into his eyes with steel-like determination and spoke words that cut through the expensive atmosphere like a blade through silk: "What have you done to Ralph?"

"I've done nothing to Ralph Norton. Whatever he's done, he's done on his initiative. And don't bother asking me where he is again, because I have no idea where he is. If I never see his goddamned face again, it would make me the happiest man on earth."

Melanie escalated the confrontation, placing her right index finger against his chest and moving even closer as his face turned the color of fresh blood. "If you've done anything to him—anything—you will pay. You hear me, you son of a bitch?"

P.T. Mayo had trained himself years earlier to laugh on cue, a psychological weapon designed to put opponents off balance by suggesting he found their threats amusing rather than threatening. It had always worked because the laughter sounded authentic enough to make people question their seriousness.

He tried the technique on Melanie Spenser, throwing back his head and producing the kind of hysterical laughter that belonged in mental institutions rather than corporate boardrooms.

"Pay? Pay?" Mayo's artificial mirth filled the office like toxic gas. "Look, Melanie, why don't you just get the hell out of here and find yourself another boyfriend, because God knows you need one."

Melanie walked to the door with the measured pace of someone whose work was finished, opened it wide, then slammed it hard enough to rattle the expensive artwork hanging on Mayo's walls. Katherine followed her toward the front entrance, trying to speak, but Melanie was already focused on what came next.

She slammed the front door with equal force and walked to her car, where she paused for just a moment to nod slightly—a signal that would be meaningless to anyone except the person who'd been waiting for it.

Then she drove away, spinning her wheels and kicking up gravel that scattered across Mayo's pristine driveway like seeds of chaos planted in perfectly manicured soil.

The fake laughter of the egomaniac hadn't fooled her for a second. Now everything was riding on what would happen next, and more importantly, who would have the last laugh when the game finally ended.

CHAPTER 74

Katherine Mayo stood in the doorway of P.T.'s office like a sentinel, watching her husband fumble through his mahogany armoire with the desperate efficiency of a man fleeing a crime scene. The Hermès jacket he pulled out—Italian wool that cost more than most people's monthly salary—went on with shaking hands that betrayed the calm executive facade he'd been perfecting for thirty years.

"What was Melanie talking about?" Katherine's voice carried the crisp authority of old Houston money; each word was precisely articulated, just as her mother had taught her at St. John's Episcopal School. "She was very upset about something."

P.T. turned, and Katherine saw something in his bloodshot eyes she'd never seen before—not just fear, but the kind of cornered-animal panic that made civilized men do uncivilized things. His laugh came out wrong, like an engine misfiring.

"What's the matter, Katherine? Ain't you ever seen a heartsick woman crying for her man who done her wrong?" The Kansas in his voice was showing, the Bible salesman drawl he'd spent decades burying under corporate polish.

"I know Ralph Norton." Katherine's silk blouse rustled as she crossed her arms. "He's not that way. Where is he?"

"Don't ask me. How would I know?" But his eyes darted to the left—same tell he'd had since their wedding day when he lied about the prenup.

"You know everything that goes on at FASTRAK, good or bad. And I know one thing for sure—if it's bad, you had something to do with it." Her voice rose with each word, thirty years of suspicion crystallizing into certainty. "So I'll ask you again. Where is Ralph Norton, and what have you done with him? Answer me or so help me I'll—"

"You'll what?" P.T.'s corporate mask slipped completely, revealing the crude Kansas boy underneath. "You washed-up piece of shit. If it weren't for your old man's money, I never would have even looked at your ugly, wrinkled face. Get out of my way."

The shove came without warning—violent, purposeful, the kind of push designed to hurt. Katherine's Louboutin heels slipped on the Persian rug as she stumbled backward into the standing lamp, a Tiffany piece her grandmother had left her. She grasped for balance, silk and crystal and thirty years of marriage crashing together as she hit the hardwood floor.

P.T.'s footsteps echoed through the marble foyer. The Mercedes' engine roared to life outside, tires squealing against River Oaks asphalt like a teenager fleeing a house party.

Katherine lay there for a moment, staring at the coffered ceiling that had once made her feel like European royalty. Now it looked like a mausoleum. When she finally stood, her dress was wrinkled, her hair disheveled, but something else had changed—something fundamental and irreversible.

She walked into P.T.'s office and began to destroy everything she could reach.

The desk lamp exploded in a shower of sparks when she kicked the cord from the wall. Papers scattered like confetti—contracts, reports, photographs of P.T. glad-handing politicians and board members. She stomped on his Harvard MBA diploma until the glass crunched under her heels. The oil painting of his grandfather—the one he claimed was a cattle baron but was just a traveling preacher—came off the wall with a satisfying crash.

Her heart hammered against her ribs. The anger felt clean, purifying, like finally exhaling after holding her breath for three decades. When there was nothing left to break, she stood in the wreckage and spun slowly, looking at their palatial mansion with new eyes.

Twenty-eight rooms. Twelve bathrooms. A climate-controlled wine cellar. Everything felt suddenly hollow, like a museum dedicated to a life that had never really been hers.

The doorbell's Westminster chimes echoed through the house. Katherine didn't move. The sound repeated—urgent, insistent. On the third ring, she composed herself enough to answer, hoping it was P.T. returning so she could finish what they'd started.

Instead, Melanie Spenser stood on the doorstep, her usually perfect composure cracked with worry. When she saw Katherine—really saw her—her expression shifted to something approaching horror.

Katherine's mouth twitched uncontrollably, her nervous system still processing the violence. The words wouldn't come.

Melanie took her arm with gentle authority and guided her to the white Italian leather sofa—the one that had cost forty thousand dollars and always felt cold against human skin.

"Katherine, are you okay?" Melanie asked repeatedly, but Katherine had retreated somewhere deep inside herself, somewhere safe from thirty years of accumulated humiliation.

Finally, Melanie tried a different approach. "Where's your coat, Katherine? I'll get it for you. We need to leave immediately. It's very important."

Katherine's response came out mechanical, robotic, like a computer program running on minimal power. "Melanie, I'll get my coat and meet you in your car. I'll be along in just a minute."

The mink coat—Russian sable that P.T. had bought her for their twenty-fifth anniversary—felt heavier than it should have as Katherine locked the front door. She didn't look back at the house that had been her prison.

In Melanie's car, Katherine stared through the windshield with laser intensity, as if she could see through the darkness to something inevitable approaching. The manicured lawns of River Oaks rolled past like a movie set, all surface beauty hiding rot underneath.

Melanie glanced at her passenger and thought she detected the faintest smile forming at the corners of Katherine's mouth.

CHAPTER 75

The abandoned K-Mart parking lot was a concrete tombstone on Houston's industrial south side, its cracked asphalt telling tales of better times when people had jobs and hope. Ada Taylor pulled her Cadillac into the shadow cast by a defunct streetlight; the kind of meeting spot that said serious business was about to be conducted.

Felonious Punque materialized from the darkness like a bad decision, his oversized jewelry catching what little light remained from the functioning streetlamps. The Third Ward Posse had a reputation for two things: finding people who didn't want to be seen, and making those people disappear permanently.

"Here's half." Ada's voice carried the authority of someone who'd bought violence before. She held up a manila envelope thick with cash. "I've got the other half in a safe place after you take me to him. You good?"

F.P.'s gold teeth glinted as he grinned, but his eyes stayed dead. "Not really, but it'll do for now."

"Just do what I say, and it'll work out. You won't even be involved. Take me to him, and I'll do the rest. Keep your eye on me and don't move until I signal you to go."

His nod was reluctant, the kind of agreement that came with a side order of resentment. He walked to his car—a pimped-out Escalade that screamed drug money—and waited.

Ada made her call. "Moneymaker, you there?"

"I'm here." P.T.'s voice sounded thin through the burner phone, stretched tight with stress and whatever he'd been drinking.

"Get your ass over to the old K-Mart parking lot on St. Augustine Boulevard. You know where it is?"

"I'm on my way. Remember, don't do anything but wait for me."

"We ain't got all night."

"I'll be there, Ada."

* * * *

WHAT NONE OF THEM KNEW was that Sam Steele had been watching from two blocks away, his retirement-age Buick invisible in the urban camouflage of forgotten neighborhoods. The GPS tracker he'd planted under P.T.'s Mercedes was just old-school detective work—the kind of thing they taught you before everything went digital.

The hidden microphone under Mayo's dashboard had been broadcasting every conversation for the past six hours. Steele had always been known as one of Houston's best private investigators, back when the city was smaller and the crimes were simpler. Retirement should have meant Astros games and crossword puzzles, but Melanie Spenser's money had awakened instincts he thought were dead.

Following P.T. Mayo wasn't just easy—it was a pleasure. Steele had pegged him as dirty from the first Google search, and now all he had to do was gather enough evidence to bury him, hopefully before Mayo did something permanent to Ralph Norton.

When he heard the name "Ada" in the phone conversation, Steele's blood pressure spiked. Ada Taylor wasn't just any hired gun—she was Houston's premier criminal fixer; the kind of professional who made problems disappear without leaving fingerprints. If Mayo had hired Ada, Ralph Norton was in more danger than anyone realized.

* * * *

STEELE CALLED MELANIE. He knew she had the phone on speaker—Katherine Mayo was riding shotgun, and she needed to hear what was coming.

"He's about ready to leave, Mel. The people he's hired have found Ralph, and he's on his way to join them. Don't start yet, but be ready when I give you the go-ahead signal."

"Got it, Sam. Thanks."

His next call went to Detective Connely, who answered on the first ring like he'd been expecting this moment.

"Sam, where the fuck are you?"

"Tailing your boy Mayo."

"You know he killed Virginia Curran, right?"

"Yup."

"You know why?"

"Nope, but I've got an idea."

"They were married thirty-five years ago when he dumped her and disappeared."

"Figures." Steele watched Mayo's Mercedes pull out of his driveway, headlights cutting through Houston's humid darkness.

"Yeah, and I've got the fugitive squad after him, but he disappeared again. But we'll find him, now that you know where he is."

"Have them meet me at the old K-Mart parking lot on St. Augustine. You want in on it also?"

"I'm leaving now. Oh, and Sam..."

"Yeah?"

"Nice work."

It was a tough call, but Steele knew he had to warn Melanie about what Connely had discovered, even though Katherine would hear it too. The woman had been married to a killer for thirty years—this wouldn't be news so much as confirmation.

"Mel?"

"Yeah, Sam?"

"P.T. Mayo killed Virginia Curran."

The silence stretched long enough for Steele to check his phone connection.

"What?"

"They were married thirty-five years ago. She must have spotted him when he gave that speech at the 'Wordie' convention."

In the passenger seat, Katherine Mayo turned her head toward Melanie, then away to hide her face. For the first time since leaving the house, tears formed in her eyes—not of sadness, but of rage that burned like acid.

CHAPTER 76

The young woman in the back of Felonious Punque's Escalade couldn't have been more than nineteen, her wrists zip-tied behind her back, a dirty bandana gagging her mouth. Every bump in the road made her grunt through the makeshift restraint, and every grunt made Cap'n Payne angrier.

"Shut the fuck up," he snarled, backhanding her across the face hard enough to snap her head sideways.

"We need her alive, stupid." F.P.'s voice carried the authority of someone who'd been in the killing business long enough to know the difference between useful violence and self-indulgent cruelty.

Ada Taylor's Cadillac approached with headlights off, gliding through the industrial wasteland like a ghost ship. She flashed her lights once—a signal answered in kind by F.P. The meeting was brief and professional, the type of transaction that kept Houston's underground economy functioning.

Ada opened the Escalade's back door and studied the young woman with clinical detachment. The girl's eyes were wide with terror, but also defiant—the kind of street survivor who'd seen enough violence to know when death was approaching.

"She saw your boy with a large group," F.P. explained. "You can hear her for yourself if you want."

Ada leaned closer to the witness. "You saw the white man he's talking about?"

The young woman nodded vigorously, her eyes never leaving Ada's face.

"She told you where they are?"

"Yes." F.P. lit a Newport with hands steady as a surgeon's. "The old train maintenance rail yard on the southeast side of town. So we're ready to go if you are. Just say when."

"How long will it take to get there?"

"Twenty minutes."

Ada's mind was already three moves ahead. "Here's what I want you to do. You drive under the speed limit, and I'll follow you. Don't take any chances. When we get there, park a block or so away from the area so we can find a way in without being seen. Do not—and let me repeat this—do anything on your own. We are waiting for my client. He wants to do this himself."

F.P.'s gold tooth caught the streetlight as he grimaced. "I don't want any amateur doing my work for me. That ain't the way I do business."

"It's the way you'll do business today. You hear me? I'm paying you good money, so you'll do it my way!"

The stare-down lasted fifteen seconds—long enough for F.P. to remember why Ada Taylor had survived in a business where most people ended up in shallow graves. He relented with the grace of a man swallowing broken glass.

"Okay, Mama. You win this one."

"Listen to me, you punk-ass bitch. I win all of them, and don't forget it."

"Okay, okay, okay! You ready?"

"I need to call my client so he can meet us there. When I flash my lights, you can start driving, and I'll be behind you all the way. Remember, don't do anything stupid." Ada's eyes shifted to the young woman. "What are you going to do with the girl?"

"You mean the witness who now knows who we are and where we're going?"

Ada nodded once—a businesslike acknowledgment of necessity.

"Good. Just do it quickly now because we can't afford to wait much longer."

The young woman's eyes went from defiant to pleading as Cap'n Payne dragged her from the car. Her muffled screams were swallowed by the industrial night—one more voice silenced in a city where people disappeared every day. Two gunshots echoed off the abandoned buildings, sharp and final.

Payne climbed back into the Escalade, giggling like a child who'd just pulled the wings off a fly. The engine started, and they drove toward the rail yard.

Ada had already called Mayo to coordinate the meeting. As she followed the Escalade through Houston's darkest neighborhoods, her mind wandered to the Rothko painting waiting in her apartment. The abstract expressionist had understood something about violence that most people missed—how it could be beautiful and terrible at the same time, how it revealed truths that polite society preferred to ignore.

All that mattered to her was looking at that painting later and feeling just like Rothko did when he'd finally decided to leave this world behind.

* * * *

SAM STEELE FELT THE familiar surge of adrenaline that came with the closing act of a lengthy investigation. He'd thought retirement would kill that feeling forever, but here he was, sixty-three years old and running a surveillance operation like he was thirty again.

The key was timing. He needed to delay the police long enough to assess the situation, make sure Melanie and Ralph were protected, and then let Connely's people clean up the mess. It was a delicate balance, but Steele had been dancing on knife edges his entire career.

Two blocks ahead, Ada's check engine light began flashing like a warning beacon. Her Cadillac started losing power, forcing her to pull over and curse the mechanical gods that governed getaway cars. She abandoned it on a side street that specialized in stripped vehicles and jumped into F.P.'s Escalade.

The hunt was closing in on Ralph Norton.

CHAPTER 77

The rail yard had undergone a transformation, and Cal and Josh had first brought homeless families to its shelter. What started as a desperate refuge for a few dozen people had evolved into something approaching a small city—hundreds of tents and makeshift structures creating neighborhoods in the shadow of abandoned freight cars.

Chin Chin Wah had just finished her tour with Cal Bridger and Josh, impressed despite her journalistic skepticism. The services they'd created for Houston's homeless population were remarkable—medical care, food distribution, and even educational programs run by former teachers who had lost their homes to medical bankruptcy or corporate downsizing.

"Do you guys have an official leader?" she'd asked during the interview. "Someone who is so admired and listened to that all of the people would do anything to please him—or her? It just seems like you're not telling me everything."

Cal's answer had been smooth, diplomatic. "We don't have a leader because we are all leaders in our way. We've all found ourselves in difficult situations, and as each of us finds our way out of those situations, we teach the others how we overcame them."

But as Wah drove away from the rail yard, something nagged at her. The expensive cars parked in the vicinity, the way people had looked at certain sections of the camp with what seemed like reverence—there was a story here that went deeper than mutual aid and self-organization.

Her investigative instincts, honed by years of exposing Houston's hidden corruption, told her to turn around and stay close. Maybe it was journalist paranoia, or perhaps it was genuine concern for the people she'd just met, but something was about to happen.

• • • •

ADA CLIMBED OUT OF F.P.'s Escalade first, her trained eyes scanning every entrance and exit point around the rail yard. Years of criminal logistics had taught her to think three moves ahead—always have an escape route, always know who might be watching, always assume the worst-case scenario.

When she was satisfied with her tactical assessment, she called P.T. to coordinate the final approach. He was already in position, parked two blocks away with his lights off and his hands shaking from whatever cocktail of alcohol and amphetamines was keeping him functional.

What none of them saw was Sam Steele's Buick, hidden in the industrial maze of abandoned warehouses and overgrown lots that surrounded the rail yard. Steele moved through the shadows like a professional ghost, positioning himself where he could see everything and intervene if necessary.

Melanie had arrived on schedule, following Steele's GPS coordinates with Katherine Mayo riding silently in the passenger seat. The plan was simple: wait for Steele's signal, then approach the group with Katherine as backup for whatever confrontation was about to unfold.

Connely and his team were en route, but Steele had bought them time by giving coordinates that were deliberately two blocks off target. Just enough delay to let the civilians get clear before the shooting started.

• • • •

ADA MET WITH P.T. IN the shadow of a rusted shipping container, their conversation brief and businesslike.

"I had no idea there were so many people in there," Ada admitted, gesturing toward the rail yard. "We'll have to find him among all those folks, but it might take time. Here's what I think you should do, Mr. Moneymaker. You walk in by yourself and start asking for your boy. Tell them you found out he was there and that you came to help him—give him back his job, give him money. Know what I mean?"

P.T.'s corporate brain, even addled by stress and stimulants, immediately saw the flaws in that approach. "I got a better idea. Let's all walk in together and let them know we're there to assist them with financial support and gifts. Once we're in and they're all excited about it, Ralph Norton will show up, and that's all we need. We can talk to him in private, do our business, and get the fuck out of there."

The Third Ward Posse spread out in a loose perimeter, but not loose enough. Josh spotted them immediately—his gang background had taught him to catalog threats automatically, and these men moved like predators positioning for a kill.

He whispered orders to the group leaders, who gathered their people in defensive positions around the camp's perimeter. They stayed far enough back to remain hidden, but close enough to respond if the situation went sideways.

Josh found Ralph and explained what was happening. When Ralph emerged to meet the approaching group, his transformation was complete—no longer the terrified executive who'd fled into the night after attacking his boss, but something approaching a genuine spiritual leader.

The minute Ralph saw P.T. Mayo walking into the rail yard, alive and uninjured, the weight of his guilt shifted into something else entirely. All the suffering he'd endured, all the people he'd endangered, all the nights spent believing he was a killer—all of it based on a misunderstanding.

P.T. approached with his arms spread wide, corporate smile at maximum wattage. "Ralph, am I glad to see you. You put a scare into everyone. We thought you were dead. Come on, let's talk, just you and me. I've got a fantastic surprise for you that will blow you away, man."

Ralph stood perfectly still, reading P.T.'s body language the way he'd learned to read the streets. "I'm glad you're okay, P.T., and that's all I have to say."

"Look, I know you're upset at some of the stupid things I said to you, but let's chalk it up to a grouchy old man saying ridiculous things. Come on, let's you and I sit down in a quiet spot and talk things over. The board and I would like to offer you a substantial compensation package that will put you in the vicinity of seven figures. Whaddya say, Ralph?"

P.T. reached out to put his arm around Ralph's shoulders, the kind of proprietary gesture that had worked in corporate boardrooms for three decades. But the instant he made contact, the entire homeless camp converged on the intruders.

It happened with the coordinated precision of a military operation. Within seconds, P.T., Ada, and the Third Ward Posse found themselves surrounded by hundreds of people who'd learned to defend their own. Each of the intruders was disarmed and held in place by hands that had nothing left to lose.

P.T. continued his corporate pitch, his voice rising with desperation as he realized the situation had entirely slipped out of his control. "Ralph, we can work this out. Think about your future, think about—"

That's when Melanie, Sam, and Katherine Mayo moved through the crowd. Ralph signaled to his people that these were friends, and the sea of homeless humanity parted to let them approach.

Katherine emerged first, moving with the determined grace of someone who'd finally found her purpose. P.T.'s face shifted from desperation to confusion to horror as he recognized his wife.

"Katherine? What are you—how did you—"

She stepped forward, tapped him on the shoulder, and shot three times through her mink coat directly into his chest.

The look on P.T.'s face as he collapsed—surprise, betrayal, and something almost like relief—was worth all those years of accumulated humiliation. Katherine stood over his body, still holding the smoking gun, and felt something she hadn't experienced since her wedding day: complete satisfaction.

The crowd held Katherine until the police arrived, but gently and respectfully, as if they understood exactly why she'd done what needed to be done. Sam Steele pushed through to update Connely, who'd arrived with the sound of gunshots. Ada Taylor and the Third Ward Posse were taken into custody for questioning.

Melanie stood by Ralph as he held her close, studying his face in the flickering light of the barrel fires. He looked terrible—scarred, exhausted, fundamentally changed—but he was alive, and that was the only thing that mattered.

The massive crowd of approximately one thousand homeless people sensed that something monumental had just occurred. They were scared but hopeful, uncertain about what was to come, yet sure that their world was about to change.

Shouts of "We love you, Chosen One," "God is with you," and "Don't leave us, Chosen One" echoed through the rail yard like a gospel chorus.

Ralph smiled for the first time in months and raised his hand for silence. When he spoke, his voice carried across the crowd with an authority that had nothing to do with corporate training and everything to do with having survived the darkness and emerged transformed.

"Thank you, friends. Let me say this before I leave to see our friend Kashinka. I love each one of you, and I will not leave you. When I return, I will make sure that all of you get the necessary tools and assistance so you can get back on your feet again. You've made me believe again, you've made me whole again, and I will make sure that I do the same for you."

CHAPTER 78

Ben Taub Hospital's reception area buzzed with its unique frequency of institutional indifference. Ralph's appearance—torn clothing, dirt-stained skin, and the unmistakable scent of someone who had been living rough—drew suspicious glances from security guards and disapproving stares from patients waiting for treatment.

Melanie walked point, her designer clothes and confident manner providing cover for Ralph's transformation from corporate executive to Houston's newest prophet. The volunteer at the information desk, a white-haired woman with the pinched expression of someone who'd seen too much human misery, gave Ralph the kind of look usually reserved for potential troublemakers.

"It's a long story," Melanie explained smoothly, "but everything's okay."

The volunteer shook her head and looked away, another example of Houston's capacity for willful blindness.

"Babe, she's out of the ICU and in a recovery unit. Isn't that great news?" Melanie's voice carried genuine joy, but Ralph remained locked in his thoughts, processing guilt and responsibility in equal measure.

The nursing station initially refused them entry until Melanie explained that Ralph was the one who'd found Kashinka and brought her to medical attention. Even then, the nurse on duty insisted that Ralph wash up and change into hospital scrubs before entering the room.

"He'll have to be escorted by security," the nurse added, but Melanie's combination of firmness and diplomacy eventually convinced her to waive that requirement.

When they finally entered Kashinka's room, the sight nearly broke Ralph's composure entirely. The little girl lay wrapped in bandages from head to foot, connected to monitors that tracked her vital signs with electronic precision. Someone—probably a volunteer—had given her a small pink teddy bear that she clutched against her chest.

Ralph pulled a chair close to her bed and took her hand. When Kashinka's eyes opened and recognized him, her smile was like sunlight breaking through storm clouds.

Melanie had to leave the room—the emotional intensity was overwhelming, watching this broken man find redemption in caring for a child who'd suffered because of his choices.

"Kashinka, can you hear me?" Ralph's voice was barely above a whisper.

"Yes." The word was so weak he almost missed it.

"You're going to make it, and I promise you that I'll always be there for you. So don't worry about anything, okay?"

Kashinka nodded weakly and closed her eyes. Ralph sat frozen in time, holding the hand of innocence while battling the demons of his past and the weight of his future responsibilities.

When visiting time ended, Ralph thanked the nurse for her patience and understanding. He walked with Melanie to one of Houston's downtown parks, where Spanish moss draped the oak trees like nature's own prayer shawls.

• • • •

THE BENCH THEY CHOSE faced Buffalo Bayou, where the city's brown water carried the detritus of eight million lives toward Galveston Bay. A southerly breeze cleaned the air, making it fresh and full of possibilities.

Melanie's eyes never left Ralph's face, searching for signs of the man she'd fallen in love with among the wreckage of everything he'd endured.

"Mel, don't mistake what I'm about to tell you as anything other than the truth, because that's what it is." His voice carried a certainty that hadn't been there before—not corporate confidence, but something more profound and more genuine.

"Don't worry, babe. I want you to be happy. That's all."

"I'm not going back to my old life. I can't. That life has nothing for me." Ralph's hands trembled slightly as he spoke. "You see, I've changed. The old Ralph doesn't exist anymore; I've destroyed him."

Melanie felt the tremor in his voice and understood that this wasn't a temporary breakdown but a fundamental transformation. The smooth-talking executive was gone forever, replaced by someone who'd seen the bottom of American society and chosen to build something better.

"Mel, I'm staying with the group. I won't leave them. They need me, and I need them. It's that simple. The things I've gone through are minor compared to most people in the group. I thought I had killed P.T., and I ran away like a scared child, and for that, I will have to suffer the consequences, whatever they are."

"Babe, you know that I'll be there for you no matter where you are or what you're going through. That's my promise to you because, you see, I need you, just like your friends."

"I know that. I really do know that. I love you even more than before, and I hope you still love me. It means a lot to me."

"And to me."

"Good, so I have a huge favor to ask of you."

"Anything, babe."

"I hope this won't scare you, but here goes. I want you to adopt Kashinka. I know that takes time, but if you could see your way clear to legally becoming her foster mother and legal guardian, that would mean the world to me. She's a beautiful person, inside and out. And there's more."

Melanie's smile was immediate and genuine. "Keep going, you haven't scared me yet."

"When I've completely helped every single one of my friends, I will start my life all over again. I can't ask you now, but I do know that when the time is right, I want us to be together. I hope you feel the same way."

Melanie hugged him and closed her eyes, overwhelmed by a mix of relief and hope. "Babe, I have a couple of things to tell you now, if it's okay?"

He nodded and held her hand firmly, as if afraid she might disappear.

"I know that you're doing the right thing for yourself and your friends, and I want you to know I'll support you in any way I can. So here's what I'm going to do. First, I know a great lawyer who can start the guardianship process for Kashinka. Secondly, I'm getting another lawyer to represent Katherine Mayo. She needs a lot of help right now. When these things happen, all your old friends and family vanish. She's a good woman who became one more victim of her husband."

"Wonderful, Mel. It's the right thing to do. Can you do one more thing for me? Would you buy me a burger and fries?"

They embraced and exchanged kisses, sharing laughter that felt like a benediction. Ralph reached into his shirt and removed the amulet that Conrad had given him—the talisman that had carried him through his darkest hours.

"I don't want anyone to see this, so I'm giving it to you. The old Ralph needed it, but I don't anymore." He pressed the ancient metal into Melanie's palm, warm from contact with his skin.

Conrad's final words echoed in his memory: "If you love me, kill him."

The old Ralph was dead. The prophet of lost souls had been born.

END

Don't miss out!

Visit the website below and you can sign up to receive emails whenever Andy Slade publishes a new book. There's no charge and no obligation.

https://books2read.com/r/B-A-SZBX-COKYE

BOOKS 2 READ

Connecting independent readers to independent writers.

Did you love *The Prophet of Lost Souls*? Then you should read *Games*[1] by Andy Slade!

New York City Detective Vic Mason was his own worst enemy, that is, until he found a new one! An evil presence, using A.I., subliminal messaging, and Deep Fake Technology has taken over the online gaming world and Vic and his beautiful Therapist, Lara Deming, are caught in the middle of it. Find out what happens when Lara disappears and Vic is taken captive by a faceless madman as it turns into a battle of wits and psychological gamesmanship. This story of mystery, suspense and high tension will keep the pages turning with twists and turns until the very end.

Read more at https://andy-slade.com.

---

1. https://books2read.com/u/49azxk

2. https://books2read.com/u/49azxk

Also by Andy Slade

Betrayal Is Beautiful
Our Shadows Never Die
The Magic Parachute
Games
In the Act of Shooting
The Prophet of Lost Souls

Watch for more at https://andy-slade.com.

About the Author

Andy Slade is a storyteller whose diverse experiences—from navigating the streets as a New York City taxi driver to working as a teacher—have given him a unique perspective on the dark undercurrents of everyday life. A Brooklyn native, he now writes from the high desert of New Mexico, a landscape that provides the perfect backdrop for his chilling tales of intrigue and betrayal. His sixth novel, *The Prophet of Lost Souls*, has been hailed as **"a chilling tale of faith and fear" by BookLife Review**. When he isn't exploring the complexities of human nature in his fiction, Andy can be found hiking along the Bosque.

Read more at https://andy-slade.com.

About the Publisher

Bennie Rosa is an independent publisher.

www.ingramcontent.com/pod-product-compliance
Lightning Source LLC
Chambersburg PA
CBHW070903260626
47162CB00007B/2550